How to
Fake
It in
Hollywood

How to
Fake
It in
Hollywood

A Novel

AVA WILDER

DELL
New York

A Dell Trade Paperback Original

Copyright © 2022 by Ava Wilder, LLC

Published in the United States by Dell, an imprint of
Random House, a division of Penguin Random House LLC, New York.

DELL and the HOUSE colophon are registered trademarks
of Penguin Random House LLC.

ISBN 978-0-593-35895-5
Ebook ISBN 978-0-593-35896-2

Printed in the United States of America on acid-free paper

randomhousebooks.com

9 8 7 6 5 4 3 2 1

Designed by Debbie Glasserman

How to
Fake
It in
Hollywood

1

"LUCY?"

Grey Brooks almost didn't hear the timid voice behind her. She had slipped into a trancelike state while staring at the coffee shop menu, weighing the wisdom of a medium versus large cold brew: did she merely want to spend the next few hours uncomfortably jittery, or was she in the market for a full-blown caffeine-induced panic attack?

She shifted in her clogs and didn't react. They probably weren't talking to her. Lucy was a fairly common name. She'd finally broken the embarrassing habit of whirling around expectantly every time she heard it, and she wasn't about to relapse now.

Grey's eyes flicked over the other inhabitants of the coffee shop. It was sparsely populated, with only a few tables occupied. Still, it was possible that Lucy was the stylish woman sipping an Americano and flipping through *Variety* over by the ficus.

The voice spoke again, louder and closer this time.

"Lucy LaVey?"

Well, that settled that. Grey pushed her sunglasses to her forehead and plastered on a toothy smile as she turned to face the voice: a bespectacled teenage girl clutching a blended iced mocha (extra whip). The girl's mouth dropped open when their eyes met.

"Hey! How's it going?" Grey made her tone as warm as possible. The girl covered her mouth with her free hand and squealed. A few heads turned at her outburst.

"Ohmigod, it *is* you! I'm sooo sorry to bother you, I know you're just, like, trying to live your life or whatever. I just—I'm literally obsessed with *Poison Paradise*. I'm *such* a big fan."

The first time Grey had been called by her character's name, it thrilled her. The next few times, it had bruised her ego a little. Now, six seasons and 132 episodes of *Poison Paradise* later, she took it in stride. It was better than not being recognized at all.

"Thank you, that's so sweet! Do you want a selfie?"

The fan's eyes looked like they were going to pop out of her head as she nodded, fumbling through her purse for her phone and swiping the camera open. Grey looped an arm over the girl's shoulder as they grinned at the screen. She snapped a couple of pictures, then scrolled back through them to make sure they were satisfactory.

"Should we do a fun one?" Grey suggested. The girl nodded again and stuck her tongue out as Grey crossed her eyes.

"Thank you soooo much," the fan breathed, overwhelmed, as she slid her phone back into her bag.

"My pleasure. What's your name?"

"Kelly."

"Nice to meet you, Kelly. I'm Grey."

Kelly blushed.

"Grey. Ohmigod. Of course! Sorry!"

Grey laughed. "Don't worry about it."

"It's just, like, I feel like I grew up with Lucy, you know? Like,

I started watching the show when I was in, like, elementary school. You were, like . . . my big sister." Kelly turned her face up at Grey with a look of such naked vulnerability that Grey's heart ached a little. She felt guilty for being annoyed at the interruption.

"Thank you. That really means a lot. She kind of felt like my sister, too."

"So what are you doing now that it's over?"

Over. It had been eight months since the last episode of *Poison Paradise* aired, but the reminder still sent a jolt of anxiety through Grey's body. The teen soap had its share of devoted fans, and pulled in solid enough ratings on its small cable network to keep getting renewed, but had never achieved the mainstream crossover success that Grey had naïvely hoped for back when she shot the pilot. Sure, she'd worked a little in between seasons—a bad studio slasher here, a Hallmark Christmas movie there—but her last few auditions had gone nowhere. In her most self-pitying moments, sweating in her bed in the middle of the night, she worried her career was in the same place it had been before she booked the show—only now she was seven years older. Seven years she could not afford to lose.

Grey forced a breezy smile.

"Oh, you know, I'm just taking some time for myself right now." She saw the disappointment creeping over Kelly's face and hastily added, "But I do have a few things coming up that I can't really talk about yet. Too early." She winked, then immediately felt embarrassed. Who *winks*? Lying made her corny.

It worked, though. Kelly beamed.

"That's so awesome! I literally can't wait. You're *so* talented."

Grey suddenly felt very tired. She still hadn't ordered her coffee. "Thanks. It was really nice to meet you, Kelly." She flashed her another smile and turned back toward the menu. Kelly squeaked out a few more words of gratitude before scurrying back to her friends, who were doing a terrible job of pretending not to watch intently from a corner table. They broke out in excited giggles and whispers as soon as she joined them. Every now and then one turned to steal a look at Grey before quickly ducking her head back down to confer with the group. They reminded her of a pack of oversized gophers.

Before Grey had a chance to approach the barista, another stranger sidled up and blocked her path. This time it was a scrawny guy in his late thirties, who had been watching her interaction with Kelly from a nearby table.

"Hey! Can I get a picture, too? Big fan."

"Um . . . sure, no problem." Grey had long ago learned not to be surprised at the variety of people outside the target teen demographic who watched *Poison Paradise*—and were champing at the bit for the opportunity to tell her, in detail, how ashamed they were for enjoying it. Still, the odds were against her running into two of its fans in such quick succession. Maybe he knew her from that stupid horror movie where she'd been in a bikini the whole time, but those guys usually directed their whole conversation at her (not especially substantial) tits.

She smiled and leaned in as he snapped the picture. Grey steeled herself for more small talk, but he just thanked her and quickly crossed to his friend waiting by the door.

They spoke in hushed voices, but Grey heard their conversation clearly as they left the shop.

"Who was that?"

"Dude, I have no idea."

Grey flushed. She felt her chest tighten in humiliation. She gave herself exactly three seconds to be upset: *Three. Two. One.* She took a deep breath, squared her shoulders, and strode up to the barista.

"Large cold brew, please. Black."

———

COFFEE IN HAND, GREY SETTLED INTO ONE OF THE TURQUOISE upholstered chairs and pulled out her laptop. Kamilah had sent back the next draft of their script in the middle of the night and Grey hadn't had a chance to look at her revisions. She opened the screenplay to the title page:

THE EMPTY CHAIR
Written by Kamilah Ross & Grey Brooks
Based on the novel by P. L. Morrison

Before Grey could get any further, her phone buzzed. Her agent, Renata. She quickly swiped to answer the call, careful to keep her voice hushed in the quiet coffee shop.

"Hello?"

Renata's voice came blaring through the phone as loudly as if she'd been on speaker.

"Where are you, honey? Are you alone? Can you talk?" Grey had signed with Renata within a few months of moving out to L.A. Her previous agent in New York had been old as the hills, bald as a newborn, and delivered every piece of news, good or bad, with the hangdog inflection of someone informing her of the death of her entire immediate family.

Renata, on the other hand, was loud and glamorous in an eighties Business Bitch sort of way, with a cloud of teased red hair surrounded by an even larger cloud of Marlboro Light smoke. She'd assigned Grey more pet names over the course of their first meeting than Grey had heard from her own mother in her entire life. Grey had adored her instantly, and the feeling was mutual. Over the years Grey had known her, Renata had kicked the Lights, but still had problems with volume control.

So much for getting some work done. "Yeah, I can be. Give me two minutes." Grey closed her laptop and slid it back into her bag. The coffee shop was still empty enough that she could probably reclaim her table when she returned.

Grey walked around the side of the building toward the parking lot and found a secluded tree to stand under. She lifted the phone to her ear again.

"Okay, I'm ready. What's up?"

"I just got off the phone with the *Golden City* casting director. They loved you."

Grey's stomach flip-flopped. It had been almost two months since her third round of auditions for the adaptation of the latest dystopian franchise dominating the bestseller list. Despite Renata's assurance that this kind of big-budget studio tentpole moved at a snail's pace, and that no news was good news, she had practically given up hope. Her *Poison Paradise* schedule had prevented her from ever being considered for something like this before: three huge sci-fi epics, shot back-to-back-to-back.

Renata continued, oblivious to Grey's pounding heart.

"They want you to meet with the director and do a chemistry read with Owen for the studio heads. Bad news is, they won't both be back in town at the same time for another six weeks at the earliest."

Grey exhaled. More waiting. "All that for the girlfriend role?" She knew she sounded bratty, but Renata was basically her mother at this point. She and Kamilah were the only people in Grey's life who didn't make her feel like she had to second-guess every word before she spoke.

"You know it's not about the part, sweetie. It's about where it can take you."

Grey closed her eyes and leaned back against the tree. "I know. You're right. That's great news." The initial disappointment at yet another obstacle had dissipated and she felt excitement brewing inside her. It wasn't over. She was still in the running. The role she was up for, Catalin, was relatively small, but still the biggest female role in the book. Sci-fi wasn't normally Grey's thing, but she'd devoured the first book practically overnight in preparation for her audition. The second installment, *Golden Kingdom,* might as well have been a brick in the bottom of her bag for the past month. She hadn't been able to bring herself to start it once she thought she'd lost the part. Grey reached inside her bag and stroked the book's embossed cover, as if to apologize for scorning it prematurely.

"That's my girl. I'll send you the new sides as soon as I get them, but knowing this type of project, it might not be until the night before."

"Got it. Thanks, Renata. That's really exciting." Grey expected Renata to say her goodbyes and hang up, but instead she heard her inhale and hesitate. "What is it? Is there something else?"

Renata was silent for another beat. "I also had an interesting call with Audrey Aoki this morning." Grey's new publicist. Most of Audrey's client list was out of Grey's league, but she had taken a liking to Grey after Grey had been in the right place at the right time (the ladies' room at the MTV Video Music Awards) to provide the right assistance (a well-hidden safety pin to repair Audrey's broken dress strap).

Grey and Renata had both been surprised when Audrey had agreed to work with her, but Audrey had waved them away: "You've got the chops, you work hard, you stay out of trouble. You deserve to be huge and I can get you there."

Of course, it wasn't a purely magnanimous offer—her fee was exorbitant. So far, she'd snagged Grey a few modest Instagram brand deals and an *Us Weekly* "What's in My Bag?" feature, but from the sound of Renata's voice she had something bigger brewing.

"What did she say?"

Another pause. "You're not dating anyone right now, are you? I haven't heard you talk about anyone since Callum."

The name made her wince. She'd fallen for Callum Hendrix, who'd played Lucy LaVey's on-again, off-again bad boy love interest, from the first time he'd raised an impeccably sculpted eyebrow at her during the first *Poison Paradise* table read. He was her first love, and for four years, they'd practically been attached at the hip. That is, until the three-month break before they'd started shooting the fifth season, when he'd urged her to turn down a juicy indie role to fly out to visit him on the set of his current gig: a midbudget thriller shooting on a picturesque Greek island.

She'd stepped off the plane, visions of a *Mamma Mia!* summer dancing in her head, only to discover the whole set snickering and gossiping behind her back about how he was secretly fucking his costar. It hadn't stayed a secret for long. *Mamma mia,* indeed. Over the years, her devastation had dulled to vague irritation—it helped that Callum and the costar had flamed out spectacularly before their movie was even out of postproduction—but even now, hearing his name unexpectedly sometimes felt like accidentally bumping a bruise she had forgotten was there.

To add to her misery, the movie she'd passed on had ended up doing fairly well in the festival circuit and picked up a few smaller awards, including one for the actress who'd replaced her. Since then, every time she opened Raya to swipe through the endless hordes of shirtless EDM DJs and smirking agency execs, all she could see was her replacement accepting that damn Independent Spirit Award. Grey wasn't about to make that same mistake again. Dating was a distraction.

"Um, no. No. There's no one."

"Good." Renata heaved a sigh. "You know, I told her you

probably wouldn't go for it, but she thought I should be the one to bring it up, since she knows we're close."

"What? Go for what?"

"How would you feel about being set up?"

That was not what Grey expected. "Set up? Like a blind date?"

"Sort of. Audrey has another client whose profile could also use a boost. She pitched the idea of the two of you possibly entering into some sort of . . . mutually beneficial personal arrangement."

Grey ran her fingers through her hair. "So you're pimping me out now. Awesome. I guess my career is even more dead than I thought." The bitterness in her voice was undercut by a quaver she couldn't hide, tears welling behind her eyes. She willed them to retreat. Being an easy crier was an asset on set, but not so much at literally any other time.

Renata sounded hurt. "Of course not. There wouldn't need to be . . . intimacy. Just the illusion. We would work out the terms and make sure everyone's happy."

Grey was silent. She kicked a clod of dirt at the base of the tree and watched it explode in a satisfying puff. Renata sighed again.

"Grey. Listen to me. Don't be dramatic." Grey knew Renata was serious if she was calling her by her real name. That is, her fake real name. "You've been in this business a long time. You know how it works. I don't blame you for being insulted by the idea. I'm not crazy about it myself. But you're paying out the ass for Audrey's help, and if this is what she thinks it'll take to give you that extra edge with *Golden City,* or to help you and Kamilah get in the right rooms with your script, I think it's worth exploring."

Renata had a point. Grey hated that her desire to keep a low profile outside of work—especially after the humiliation of what she had gone through with Callum—could be counted as a mark against hiring her. But that was what she got for choosing a profession where her skill, her experience, and her drive would always be secondary to how many people knew her name. Even if it was just her character's name.

Now that the initial shock had worn off, she felt herself softening to the idea, but said nothing, sipping her coffee through the soggy paper straw as she turned Renata's words over in her head. A relationship couldn't hurt her career if it was *for* her career, right?

"Will you at least meet him? You two can have a private lunch at Audrey's and get to know each other a little before you decide either way. What do you say, sugar?"

Grey realized that Renata had been withholding the most important piece of information: the identity of the other client. Maybe there was a reason for that. Her blood chilled at the possibility that Audrey would ask her to be an accomplice in rehabilitating the image of some creep who'd been caught banging the nanny, sending skeezy DMs to underage fans, groping his costars—or worse. There were more than enough potential candidates in an industry crawling with men who knew that their wealth, fame, and power would shield them from ever facing consequences for their actions. No career boost was worth selling her soul like that.

Grey steeled herself for the worst, a rejection on the tip of her tongue. "Who is 'him'?"

She was so startled by Renata's reply that she almost dropped her phone in the dirt.

2

ETHAN ATKINS FELT GOOD. OR AT LEAST HE DIDN'T FEEL BAD, which at this point was almost the same thing. The lift in his mood probably couldn't be attributed to the atmosphere. Neon beer signs hummed and flickered, pool balls clacked, competing games blared from multiple televisions, and both the bar top and the floor were sticky with decades of spilled beer.

Maybe it was just the novelty of being around people. Aside from the one weekend a month he spent with Elle and Sydney, limited by his custody agreement with his ex-wife, Ethan frequently went days at a time without seeing another living soul. But then, that was by choice. And even now, he wasn't exactly mingling.

It was still relatively early, but he'd never seen this bar with more than a handful of people inside. There were one or two small groups of men in the booths, intermittently cheering and swearing at the TV; a few guys flirting their way through a game of pool with the only woman in the place south of sixty; and a couple of sad, tired-looking loners sprinkled along the barstools. Ethan supposed he should probably include himself in that last category.

He closed his hand around his third bourbon of the evening and took a long swallow. Warmth spread through him, sending pleasant tingles down through his body all the way to his fingertips. On days when Ethan let himself go out to drink in public, he abstained for a day or two leading up to it. He wanted his head clear, his nerves raw, so he could fully savor the descent into oblivion. The first drink dulled the edges, the second one added a dreamy, hazy filter to his surroundings. Now Ethan felt himself drift outside his body, floating up near the water-stained foam tile ceiling, looking down at himself. Maybe the source of his good mood wasn't so mysterious after all. He picked up a greasy, over-salted french fry from the plate in front of him and dipped it in ketchup. The fries didn't hurt, either.

Once or twice a month, he had his driver escort him from his home in Pacific Palisades to Johnny's, a shitty dive bar hidden deep in the Valley, and leave him there for a few hours. The long ride down the 405 was worth it to camp out on the fringes of the bar, where he could be as alone as possible while still surrounded by people. Nobody recognized him. Nobody bothered him. Nobody wanted anything from him. Nobody pitied him. Which was good, because he pretty much had the market on self-pity cornered.

Maybe it was a stretch to say *nobody* recognized him. Ethan would probably have to travel to the moon to find a place completely free of double takes, that telltale squint as they racked their brains to figure out where they had seen him before, that wide-eyed gasp of recognition when it dawned on them at last.

Slouched in a secluded corner, Mets cap pulled low over his eyes and a heavy shadow of graying stubble covering his jaw, Ethan was as close as he ever got to invisible. Context was on his side. Nobody expected to see him here, so they didn't.

Even so, the group at the pool table had started stealing more and more looks at him, their formerly raucous conversation dropping to whispers. Ethan took another long draw from his glass, draining it in anticipation of the inevitable next step.

Sure enough, he saw someone approaching him out of the corner of his eye. The man had clearly had a few drinks of his own, as indicated by his swaying walk and unfocused eyes. He leaned over Ethan, his concept of personal boundaries obviously as impaired as his motor skills.

"Hey. *Hey,*" he whispered theatrically, spraying hops-scented spittle on Ethan's shirt. "I knew you were you this whole time . . . but don't worry. Your secret's safe with me."

Ethan shoved a few more fries into his mouth, his eyes glued to the television above him.

"I think you have the wrong guy. Sorry."

The man shook his head, crowding Ethan even further.

"It *is* you. You're Ethan Atkins. What are you doing in a shithole like this, dude?" His voice got louder. A few more heads turned.

Ethan finally tilted his head to look at the man, a grim smile slowly creeping across his face.

"Nah, I'm nobody. Just trying to have a quiet drink like everyone else." He lifted his empty glass to punctuate the sentence, catching the eye of the bartender, who grabbed the bottle of Maker's and headed over to top him off. The bartender glanced at Ethan's new friend, eyebrows raised. Ethan shook his head, a small, almost imperceptible movement. *It's okay.*

Ethan lifted his newly full glass toward the man, who blinked at him a few times.

"Cheers. Have a good night, man. Next round's on me." He knocked back half of it in one swallow, then pointedly turned back to his fries.

The man looked like he wanted to say something else, but the bartender cut in, asking what he and his friends were drinking, and assuring him he'd have another round coming right up. Ethan closed his eyes as the murmured conversation between the bartender and the man faded into the vague, rippling ether that enveloped him. Everything was going to be okay. He could almost feel the vibrations of the universe pulsating through his body.

Wait, maybe those were the vibrations of his phone. He dug into the pocket of his jeans and squinted at the caller name. Audrey Aoki. Normally he would let it go to voicemail since he was in public, but after that last round, he was feeling downright chatty.

"Audrey. Babyyy."

Audrey snorted, her clipped British accent oozing over the line. "Why do I feel like I could set your breath on fire right now?"

"That's what you get for calling this late."

"It's eight-thirty."

Ethan could feel renewed attention focusing on him from the pool table. He downed the other half of his drink and reluctantly slid off the barstool, taking a moment to regain his equilibrium before shuffling out the front door.

It was January, so the Valley was about as chilly as it ever got. Not cold enough to wish he'd brought a jacket, but a welcome relief from the stifling heat of the bar. Everything was still and silent. Even the solitary car going through the Jack in the Box drive-through across the street seemed to be moving in slow motion. Beneath his feet, a few blades of grass had optimistically sprung up between the cracks in the concrete, the only green thing he could see in any direction.

Ethan leaned on a low cement wall and pulled a crumpled pack of American Spirits from his back pocket. As he fished around for his lighter, he made sure to over-enunciate every word.

"To what do I owe the pleasure?"

"Can you come into the office for lunch on Friday? There's someone I want you to meet."

Lighter acquired, Ethan pulled a cigarette out of the pack with his mouth. He responded with a muffled "Mmm?" as he lit it.

It had been years since he'd been to Audrey's office. They'd come up together, almost twenty years ago now; he and his best friend, Sam, had been two of her first clients. Their meteoric rise had helped propel her to the elite ranks of L.A.'s publicists, and she, in turn, had helped them stay on top. He had, thus far, resisted her regular attempts to drag him back to something resembling his old career, but for some reason he kept taking her calls. He hated to admit it, but she was the closest thing he had to a friend these days. A friend he paid to check up on him.

Which, now that he thought about it, pretty much described most of his relationships since Sam's death.

Audrey's voice snapped him out of his reverie.

"Well? What do you say?"

Ethan dragged on his cigarette, relishing the rush of the nicotine colliding with his booze-soaked brain.

"What do you mean, meet someone?"

"Does the name Grey Brooks mean anything to you?"

Ethan's brow creased. "Is that the brand that makes those shoes I like?"

"Very funny. She's an actress. A sweetheart. You're gonna love her."

Ethan closed his eyes. The wheels in his head were turning, slowly but surely. A memory was forming of a conversation they'd had last week, the blurry edges coalescing into something tangible. He groaned.

"Is this that fake girlfriend bullshit? I thought that was a joke."

"It's not bullshit. It's the first step to getting you back on track. People want to see you stable. They want to see you happy."

"I *am*." Even as he said it, he knew he wasn't fooling her.

"If you say so. But if you're going to make a comeback, you have to be on the offensive."

"Maybe I don't want to come back yet."

Audrey sighed. "When, Ethan? It's been five years." Her voice softened, dropping the hard-as-nails ball-busting publicist tone. "Don't you want to work again? Don't you want to see your girls more?" She paused, and Ethan could tell she was debating pushing it further. He was surprised to hear what sounded like genuine pain in her voice. "Aren't you sick of wallowing yet?"

Ethan's stomach turned. He *did* feel sick. Those fries weren't sitting as well as he'd like them to. He pictured them in his stomach, tiny golden life rafts bobbing up and down in the ocean of bourbon he'd drowned them in. He crouched next to the wall, willing everything to stay down for the duration of the endless drive back home.

Audrey's voice startled him. He had forgotten he was still on the phone with her. She spoke in that same soft tone, like she was trying to soothe an injured animal into submission before taking it out back and putting it out of its misery.

"It's just one lunch. That's all. You don't have to agree to anything else."

Ethan felt his mouth fill with saliva. He stared at his shoes, trying to fight off the building nausea.

"Fine. Friday. I'll be there."

Then he promptly threw up all over them.

3

GREY PULLED HER PRIUS UP TO THE INTIMIDATING CENTURY City high-rise that housed Greenfield & Aoki Public Relations and took a deep breath. She resisted the urge to flip down the visor and check her reflection yet again before sliding out of the driver's seat and handing the keys to the valet.

She'd tried not to let herself overthink things while getting ready that morning, attempting, as always, to walk the razor-thin edge between trying too hard and not trying hard enough. She'd braided her hair and pinned them in a crown around her face, leaving a few stray curls tucked behind her ears. At first, she'd planned on wearing her favorite floral peasant sundress, but once she checked herself out in the mirror, the overall effect was a little too Von Trapp Family Singers. She swapped it out for a crisp white Oxford shirt, unbuttoned to her sternum, sleeves rolled up, and tied at her waist, with high-rise vintage jeans.

As soon as she pushed her way through the revolving doors and felt the blast of air-conditioning hit her, Grey was grateful she'd changed into pants. Somehow she always forgot that the fancier the office, the more fridge-like the environment. Within seconds her nipples were hard enough to cut glass. She stepped up to the security desk and handed the guard her ID. As he double-checked it against the list on his computer, Grey surreptitiously glanced down to make sure they weren't visible. Thankfully, they were camouflaged by the loose folds of her shirt.

The guard handed back her ID and pressed the button to release the electronic gate. Grey thanked him and walked over to the elevator bank, ten sleek elevators facing one another: one side for floors one through fifteen, the other side for sixteen to thirty. The employees and clients of the firms housed in the high-rise were far too important to be inconvenienced by waiting more than five seconds for an elevator. She pushed the "up" button on the sixteen-to-thirty side and a set of doors on the far end pinged instantly.

The mirrored walls in the elevator gave Grey one last chance to give herself a once-over. She preferred to go without makeup when she wasn't on set in order to give her skin a break, but she also didn't care to be consistently greeted with "Are you okay? You look . . . tired." At least she wasn't famous enough to have ever had an unflattering candid shot of her buying Diet Coke at the gas station published in a tabloid under a headline like Stars without Makeup: They're Hideous—Just Like You!

She usually compromised with a few swipes of mascara and the holy trinity of tinted moisturizer, tinted lip balm, and cheek tint. Examining herself in the unforgiving fluorescent light of the elevator, she was satisfied that she'd achieved the desired look of "woman who is definitely alive and definitely not suffering from a wasting disease," while still appearing charmingly low maintenance and makeup-free to the untrained eye. Grey batted her eyes at her reflection. *Who, me? I woke up like this.*

The elevator pinged again as it opened on the thirtieth floor. Grey felt her stomach drop like a cable had snapped and the car had plunged to the basement instead. For the first time, the full weight of what was about to happen settled on her (still uncomfortably nipped-out) chest. Focusing all her attention on her appearance in the hours leading up to the meeting had allowed her to forget momentarily about what she was trying to look good for. Or more accurately, *who* she was trying to look good for.

Or was it *whom*? Whatever.

Ignoring her racing heart, Grey approached the bored-looking receptionist and gave her name. Barely looking up, he directed her to sit in one of the ultramodern waiting room chairs. She shifted, trying and failing to find a comfortable position on the flat, angular seat that seemed to have been designed by someone with only a passing familiarity with human anatomy. Thankfully, Audrey Aoki quickly materialized, looking elegant as always in her trademark red lipstick and sky-high stilettos. Her glossy black hair was pulled back into a flawless twist— if any strand dared to fall out of place, Grey had no doubt it would have been fired on the spot. Something about Audrey's immaculate appearance combined with her posh British accent always had a calming effect on Grey, as if nothing short of an alien invasion could faze her. And even in that case, Audrey would probably just walk up to the ship and hand them a business card.

She beamed at Grey.

"Grey! Thank you so much for coming in. Come on back with me."

Grey dutifully followed, walking alongside Audrey as she led her through the tastefully minimalist open-plan office. To Grey's surprise, they passed by Audrey's office, encased in glass with floor-to-ceiling windows, in favor of a room with unfashionably opaque walls. As if reading her mind, Audrey whispered in a faux-conspiratorial tone, "I thought you two might want some privacy."

Grey's heart practically leapt out of her throat. She wanted to run as fast as her ankle boots would take her, past the junior publicists, past the bored receptionist, back down the sleek elevator and out the front door. Or maybe just skip the middleman and jump straight out the window. She wasn't ready for this. She needed more time. Despite the aggressive air-conditioning, she felt a bead of sweat trickle down her lower back. *Ethan Atkins was on the other side of that door.*

As a tween, Grey had pulled a page out of *Seventeen,* taking painstaking care not to accidentally rip it more than necessary, and taped it on the wall next to her pillow. For two years, Ethan Atkins had smiled bashfully down at her, hair flopping over one eye, thumb innocently hooked into the pocket of his jeans. The other hand casually lifted his T-shirt over a stretch of lean stomach, revealing the hint of a golden ab or two, along with the tantalizingly defined V of his hip bone dipping below his waistband.

She had taken it down once she entered high school and the possibility of real-life boys one day being in her room had crossed her mind. But by then, she'd reread the neon-pink text so many times it was almost imprinted on the back of her eyelids.

CRUSH OF THE MONTH: Ethan Atkins, 22
Birthday: September 3rd
Hometown: Queens, NY
Turn-ons: Confidence.
Turnoffs: Being fake.

As of right now, she was zero for two.

Time seemed to slow down as Audrey turned the handle. Grey

couldn't hear anything but the pounding of blood in her ears as Audrey pushed the door open to reveal . . . an empty room.

Grey exhaled audibly. Audrey looked back at her and Grey thought she saw a look of sympathy flash across her face. Grey blushed.

"Ethan's running a little late, but I thought you might be more comfortable waiting in here. We have your lunch ready and waiting—we'll bring it in as soon as he gets here."

Grey forced herself to smile, swaying in place a little as the adrenaline drained out of her body. She nodded absently and took a seat in one of the plush leather office chairs. "Thanks, Audrey."

"No problem. Can I bring you anything? Water? Coffee?"

Grey shook her head and pulled her stainless steel water bottle out of her bag.

"I'm all set. But thanks."

"Of course. Shouldn't be too much longer."

Audrey shut the door with a snap and Grey could hear her stilettos clicking a retreat along the hallway. Good. She'd have some warning when she came back.

Grey leaned back in the chair and spun it to face the floor-to-ceiling windows overlooking the city. She'd gotten her wish for more time, but now it was starting to feel like a curse. There was no way she would be able to focus on anything until the moment Ethan walked through the door. Grey took out her phone but didn't unlock it. She stared out the window, watching the traffic patterns undulate far below her. The minutes crawled by.

Unprompted, a vision popped into her head of him entering the room while she was still facing the window. She would slowly and dramatically turn the chair around, eyebrows arched, fingers tented in her best Bond villain impersonation.

Well, well, well. The infamous Mr. Atkins. I've been expecting you. Please, have a seat. I believe we have some business to discuss.

The image was enough to ease her nerves somewhat. This was no big deal. She'd met plenty of big celebrities before. She'd *definitely* eaten lunch before. She'd eaten it yesterday! This would be exactly like yesterday's lunch, except instead of eating reheated pad thai alone in her underwear in front of an old episode of MTV's *True Life,* she'd be eating trendy vegan takeout with her former preteen crush turned acclaimed A-lister turned mysterious tortured recluse turned future fake boyfriend.

Grey swallowed. Okay, now she was nervous again. She pulled *Golden Kingdom* out of her bag and flipped it open to her bookmark. She'd made decent progress since her call with Renata, and it seemed like Catalin already had a much meatier role in this installment than in the first. Grey reread the same sentence at least ten times before she was finally able to process its meaning. When it became clear that Ethan wasn't about to burst through the door at any moment, she felt herself relax a little bit and sink into the narrative.

About fifteen minutes later, she heard the door creak open and slammed the book shut. Audrey poked her head in.

"Just me again. Sorry for the wait, shouldn't be too much longer. He's on his way."

"Oh. Um, that's okay. Thanks for letting me know." She returned to her book. Another thirty minutes passed, with an increasingly perturbed-looking Audrey stopping by twice more to assure her that Ethan would be arriving *any* minute and thank her *so* much for being patient. Grey's stomach growled, her mood beginning to sour.

Grey heard footsteps approaching again. She slid her book back into her bag and stood up. This was ridiculous. She was just going to tell Audrey thanks but no thanks, there was no way she was giving up her time and her dignity for a relationship that was

not only fake, but as of now had only one (barely) willing participant. The door swung open and Grey opened her mouth. Then
she saw who was behind Audrey and forgot how to shut it.

The first thing she noticed was how tall he was. Everything
looked bigger on-screen, and Grey had met enough movie stars to
know that most of them inflated their official heights by at least an
inch or two. Not Ethan. He was a full head taller than Audrey,
even with the assistance of her stilettos.

The second thing she noticed was that boyish half smile that
was so familiar she almost got dizzy, her mind automatically super-
imposing him over that long-lost magazine page. Maybe "boyish"
was the wrong word: his dark hair was streaked with gray, and so
was his stubble, and his eyes, pale green as sea glass, looked lined
and tired behind horn-rimmed glasses. Somehow, these signs of
aging only added to his appeal, transforming him from clean-cut
pretty boy into something more hard-edged and interesting. *Damn
it*. It was so unfair that men were allowed to get hotter as they aged,
while Grey often felt like she had a ticking clock over her head
counting down the years before she would have to choose between
being passed over for jobs for aging naturally, or being passed over
for pumping her face full of fillers.

He exuded an aura she had only come across in person a handful of times, the aura of the Very Famous. More ephemeral than
physical beauty, more powerful and precise than charisma. His
posture was slouched, unassuming, as if he were trying to apologize in advance for how larger than life he was. It didn't help. All
Grey knew was that her mouth went instantly dry and her legs felt
like they were about to give out beneath her. She leaned discreetly
against the table to stabilize herself.

Grey realized that Audrey had been talking the whole time.
She tore her eyes off Ethan's face to focus back on her. His gaze had

been locked on Grey with an unreadable expression, his brow slightly creased.

". . . just go and check on your food," Audrey said, darting back out the door and leaving them alone.

Alone.

Grey looked back at him. She swallowed. She was supposed to say something. She stuck out her hand.

"Hi, I'm Grey."

Ethan smiled that half smile again and took it. Grey's brain short-circuited. The jump from *Ethan Atkins is in front of me* to *Ethan Atkins is touching me* was too much for her to process in such a short time.

"Really? You look pretty blond from here," he said drily.

Grey blinked up at him dumbly. Was that a joke about her name? The sensation of his hand around hers was frying her synapses.

"What?"

He shook his head.

"Sorry. I don't know why I said that." He pulled his hand back abruptly and stuck it into his pocket, clearing his throat and looking away. "Stupid," he muttered to himself under his breath. To her, he said, "It's . . . it's good. It's a good name."

"Um. Thanks."

A realization dawned on her: *he was nervous, too.* Grey felt like laughing. Her annoyance at his lateness started to ebb.

Ethan ran his hands through his hair. "I'm Ethan."

"Yeah, I know," she said, not knowing how else to respond. She crossed her arms and looked down at her boots, suddenly unable to bear looking at him. Just then, Audrey and an assistant burst through the door, carrying a tray with their plates and assorted mealtime accoutrements. They busied themselves setting up the food, which surprisingly still looked appetizing despite sitting around for the better part of an hour, and had hustled back out the door before Grey knew it.

The two of them eased into chairs opposite each other. Neither met the other one's eyes. Grey picked up her fork, feeling like it was the first time she had ever operated one, and appraised her salad. Across from her, Ethan lifted the top bun off his veggie burger, doing his own inspection.

The silence stretched between them. Grey poured her cup of green goddess dressing over her salad and focused all her attention on coating each individual topping equally. He may have been rich and famous and, okay, still super fucking handsome, but he had kept her waiting for forty-five minutes. She wasn't going to do what she always did, chatter to fill the silence, to ease the awkwardness.

After what felt like an eternity, he cleared his throat. She looked up at him, waiting.

"What did you get?"

Grey looked down at her salad. " 'I'm Trying My Best.' "

Ethan's brow furrowed. "What?"

" 'I'm Trying My Best,' " she repeated. He looked at her like she was speaking in code. "You know. Thankfulness Cafe? It's their whole thing. All their dishes have names like that. Like 'I'm a Gift to the World,' or 'I'm Perfect the Way I Am," or 'I'm Praying the Earth Opens Up and Swallows Me Because Placing This Order Is So Humiliating.' "

Ethan laughed, a real laugh, and Grey's nerves eased a little. "I see. I usually just tell Lucas to get me the veggie burger; I didn't realize I was making him debase himself like that."

"Isn't that what assistants are for? To shield you from the petty embarrassments of everyday life?"

Her tone was light, but something dark flickered across Ethan's face.

"I guess so."

He picked up a sweet potato fry, examined it, then put it back down. Grey fidgeted. She took a bite of her salad. In the silence, it felt like the crunch was loud enough to make the room shake. The butter lettuce alone registered 6.1 on the Richter scale.

Ethan sighed. "This is ridiculous," he muttered.

"Excuse me?"

"Sorry. No offense. It's not . . . it's not you. This whole idea. It's weird, right?"

Grey chased a pickled carrot across her plate. "Kinda. I mean, I guess it happens all the time. I just . . . I've never . . ." She trailed off awkwardly. Ethan pursed his lips.

"I don't get it, honestly. How will parading around with some young blonde make people root for me? Isn't that the kind of thing everyone hates? Shouldn't I be 'dating' someone my own age?" He made lazy finger quotation marks around the word "dating."

Grey smirked to herself and said nothing.

"What? What's funny?"

"Nothing. It's just . . . I can't remember the last time someone called me young. Last week I auditioned to play the wife of a guy my dad's age. I'll probably be playing your mother next year."

Ethan laughed again, surprised this time. "How old *are* you?" Grey opened her mouth to protest. He held his hands up defensively. "I know that's a touchy question in this business. But if you're going to be my girlfriend, I should probably know something besides your name."

Grey's blood rushed in her ears. *She was going to be his girlfriend.* Fake girlfriend. Fake girlfriend.

"Twenty-seven. Twenty-eight in a couple of months."

"At least we can use your senior discount."

Grey laughed, despite herself. "Your next wife probably hasn't even been born yet. Ten years is nothing."

Ethan held his hands up. "Excuse me. Eleven. Don't undermine my seniority."

She laughed again, feeling herself loosen up. "I don't get why you even need me," she admitted. "Can't you just make a comeback on your own if you want to? I thought once you get to a certain tier of rich white guy you're basically uncancelable. I mean, even Mel Gibson still gets hired."

Ethan's face fell. He didn't look at her. Grey's stomach clenched. Had she gone too far?

Ethan picked up his veggie burger and took a giant bite. He chewed thoughtfully, then swallowed.

"If I want to play nice with the studio and star in a big dumb Christmas blockbuster that's fun for the whole family, sure. Or pour my own money into some vanity project that no one will ever see. But according to our good friend Audrey, if I want to do anything real again, I need to prove I'm . . . what's the word?" He sipped his sparkling water. "Stable? Dependable? Sane?"

Grey was silent. The unspoken subtext hung heavy between them.

It was unthinkable that the Ethan of a decade ago would've ended up in this position. By the time he'd turned thirty, he was untouchable, both personally and professionally. She shouldn't have worried about skeletons in the closet: for most of his career, his reputation had been pristine. He'd liked to party in his early days, sure, but he'd exchanged that image for Devoted Husband and Father by the time he became a household name.

He'd risen to fame alongside Sam Tanner—childhood best friends made good. The two of them cowrote and starred in four movies together, each better received than the last. Ethan's solo career had blossomed, too, seamlessly transitioning back and forth from being in front of the camera to behind it. He'd had his share of flops and missteps, like anyone, but nothing that couldn't be written off in the face of the next smashing success.

But then, five years ago, Sam was killed in a car accident and Ethan fell apart.

He'd been in the middle of shooting a gritty, big-budget reboot of the *Lone Sentinel* superhero franchise when it happened. Rumors swirled that he'd tried to drop out, but the studio had him locked in an ironclad contract. He began showing up to the set late, wasted, and then not at all, until they had no choice but to fire him. The tabloids ate it up, publishing picture after picture of him stumbling out of clubs at 4 A.M., bleary-eyed and greasy.

Then he'd wound up in court: first when the photographer he'd knocked out at Sam's funeral had decided to press charges, then again for the prolonged custody battle with his (now ex-) wife during their very ugly and very public divorce. Once both cases were settled and out of the news, Ethan had barely been seen since.

Until now.

The man who had, for the last few years, only been glimpsed in blurry long-lens paparazzi shots like the goddamn Loch Ness Monster was sitting right in front of her, clear as day, eating a veggie burger.

She looked him dead in the eye. "Are you?"

He stared right back.

"I'm not sure. I think I'm ready to find out, though."

Grey didn't know how to respond to that. She gave a noncommittal shrug and returned to her salad. They ate in silence for a few moments. She was surprised when he spoke again, unprompted.

"This is a pretty sweet deal for you, though, right?"

"What do you mean?"

"I mean, all you have to do is be photographed with me a few times and your star is on the rise. You get to just skip the line, you don't have to do any work at all. That's pretty exciting, right?" His tone dripped with condescension.

Grey dropped her fork to her plate with a clatter and her face flushed.

She knew she shouldn't take it personally. She shouldn't have been surprised he would have misogynistic preconceptions about the type of woman who would agree to this. He clearly despised himself for having to resort to it; why would she be excluded from that judgment?

But of course, she *was* hurt. She couldn't *not* take it personally. Grey was forced to admit to herself that, as much as she had tried to avoid thinking about how this meeting would go in the days leading up to it, a tiny part of her had held on to a stupid childish fantasy that he would see her and *see* her. See her talent, see her work ethic, see her as an equal. Acknowledge that they were both at strange junctures in their respective careers and laugh about it, agreeing to move forward together in this charade based on a foundation of mutual respect (and also maybe they kissed sometimes). Well, that was out the window.

She willed herself to keep her voice low and controlled. If she could hold in her tears for this monologue, she deserved every acting award under the sun, plus a few new ones made up especially for her.

"Actually, I've been a working actress since I was eight years old. I don't think there's anything exciting about the fact that *apparently* the only thing that will get anyone to take me seriously is my association with a man whose only 'work' the last few years has been working as hard as he can to destroy his career. I think it's pretty fucked up, honestly."

Ethan stared at her, slack-jawed. Grey blushed even deeper. She backtracked, stammering. "I'm sorry. That was— I didn't mean it. I'm sorry. I shouldn't have— I know you've been through— Sorry."

He rubbed his hand across his stubble like he was assessing the damage after a punch to the jaw. "It's fine. Fair, even. I shouldn't have said that. I think . . ." He fixed her with another piercing, impenetrable stare. "I guess I thought you'd be different."

Grey wasn't sure what to make of that. "Sorry to disappoint."

Ethan shook his head. "No. It's . . . it's good." He directed the comment to his sweet potato fries. Grey abandoned the pretense of even trying to eat her salad. Her appetite was gone. When she spoke again, her tone was flat and sarcastic, though inside she was boiling.

"So what were you expecting? Some clout-chasing airhead who'll nod and drool at whatever you say? I'm honored you deigned to grace me with your presence at all, then. Because my time couldn't possibly be worth anything, right? I have nothing better to do than sit around and wait for you until my ass fuses to this seat?"

Her blood sugar must have plunged dangerously low while she was waiting for him, low enough to disable every filter between her brain and her mouth. That was the only explanation for why she was talking to him like this. One word from him and Audrey would drop her like a hot potato. She'd trained herself to be an expert at biting her tongue, but he'd apparently struck a nerve. Or several.

Ethan's jaw tightened. He opened his mouth to retort, but he hesitated. The annoyance seemed to drain out of his expression as quickly as it had appeared. He rubbed both his hands over his face and gave a frustrated groan.

"No! I mean—yes. Yes, you're right. This is coming out all wrong. I don't . . . I can't . . ." He put his hands down flat on the table and stared at her. His next words were sincere, almost pleading. "I don't meet a lot of new people these days. I'm not really good at this anymore. I'm sorry . . . I'm sorry I was late. I'm an asshole." He laughed humorlessly. "I probably needed to hear all that. I guess Audrey knows me better than I thought," he muttered. He rubbed his hands against his eyes again like he was fighting a headache.

Then, to her surprise, he dropped his hands and chuckled softly.

"Seems like she doesn't know *you,* though."

"What do you mean?" Grey asked before she could stop herself.

"She told me you were a sweetheart." He glanced up at her with an expression that bordered on amusement.

Grey felt her chest expand with relief. She hadn't upset him. Still, she kept her mouth shut. She didn't trust what would come out if she opened it again. Ethan seemed lost in his own thoughts. They sat motionless, the world's most boring diorama. They might have sat there for hours, even days, if Audrey hadn't swanned in the door with a bright smile.

"Hi there you two, how's it going in here?"

Grey couldn't meet Ethan's eyes. She looked at her plate, then at Audrey. Ethan cleared his throat.

"Just getting to know each other a little better."

Audrey's eyes swept over their barely touched food. Her brow creased in concern—as much as it could through the tasteful Botox—but her tone revealed nothing. She was a pro.

"That's great! That's what we're here for. So . . . what do we think? Do we have something here?" Audrey waggled her index finger back and forth between the two of them. Grey forced herself to look back at Ethan.

He inclined his head toward her, not breaking eye contact.

"If she'll have me."

A shiver went up her spine. He was leaving it up to her. She could shake his hand, tell him it was nice to meet him, and go back to her life like this surreal encounter had never happened. Audrey probably had an army of ambitious twenty-something blondes exactly like her lined up right outside the door, more than happy to take her place.

But if she was being honest with herself, the option to walk away had disappeared the moment he materialized in the doorway.

She opened and closed her mouth a few times like a goldfish, the words that she couldn't stop fast enough now deserting her.

Finally she choked out, voice cracking:

"Yeah. Sure. Let's do it."

4

ETHAN OPENED HIS LAPTOP. TOOK A SIP OF BEER. CLOSED IT.

Took another sip. Opened it. Got up from his chair and paced around his office. Sat back down. Took another sip. Closed it.

He'd been repeating this particular pattern long enough that he was now halfway through his fourth beer. By now he was almost buzzed enough to do what he had set out to do when he cracked open the first one. He took a long swig and opened his laptop. Again.

He opened the browser and hesitated over the keyboard. This wasn't creepy. She was a public figure. She definitely already knew *way* more about him. This was just leveling the playing field.

Before he could talk himself out of it again, Ethan pulled up a search engine and tapped out a name with his right index finger: Grey Brooks.

Instantly, a menu dropped down with autofilled suggestions of the words most frequently searched with her name. Ethan sighed and drained the bottle. He stood up again and grabbed another beer out of the minifridge next to his desk and popped the cap off. He settled back into his chair, for good this time, and started to work his way down the list, beginning at the top.

Grey Brooks Instagram

@greybrooksofficial, 650k followers. The screen filled with rows of well-curated image cubes: Grey smirking on the red carpet, Grey pouting at a photoshoot, Grey laughing with a friend on a hike. In person, she'd been pretty, even striking. Wide-set blue eyes, dark brows, strong nose, full lips. She'd clearly been nervous when they first met, but the arch of her eyebrows and the naturally downturned corners of her mouth made her resting face look haughty, almost petulant. As their conversation had gone on, she'd softened, her expression becoming open, friendly.

That is, until he'd insulted her.

He'd miscalculated her appeal at first, casually dressed and makeup-free, but when she'd been flushed with emotion while dressing him down, he couldn't take his eyes off her. How fucked in the head was he that he was most attracted to her when she was calling him out for being a patronizing asshole?

Her gutsiness was certainly part of it; she had everything to gain by just smiling and nodding as he disparaged her. But most of all, what he'd seen written on her face when she was glaring daggers at him, what had completely disarmed him, was the confirmation that she could see right through his superficial shields of fame and money and charm, straight down to the rotten core of him.

She was right: he'd expected her to be desperate and vulgar and dying to please. By the time he realized he had underestimated the wry, sharp, guarded woman in front of him, it was too late. He'd already spent the days leading up to their meeting letting his disgust with himself build until he was powerless to do anything but vomit it all over her, trying to purge his self-loathing from his body as quickly as possible. It hadn't worked, but then, nothing did.

In any case, scrolling through the pictures confirmed what Ethan had suspected: she was incredibly photogenic. He clicked on the thumbnail of a picture of her at some awards show, hair cascading down her pale back in shining honey waves, all red lips and glowing cheekbones with mischief in her heavy-lidded eyes, but he was hit with a prompt to create an account to see more.

Damn. On to the next one.

Grey Brooks Poison Paradise

Ethan scrolled through promotional photos of a group of seven or eight attractive twentysomethings, toned limbs draped over one another, smoldering dramatically at the camera. Based on the photos, the cast had rotated somewhat over the years, but Grey was one of the few who appeared in every incarnation. There was something uncanny about her styling combined with the heavy airbrushing of the photos; she looked too perfect to be human. They all did.

He clicked through production stills of her character dressed in a cheerleading uniform, laughing in a convertible, playing guitar in front of a screaming crowd, lying in the hospital recovering from some sort of serious-but-not-permanently-deforming injury, burying a body, and, if he wasn't mistaken, running for president of the United States. He frowned. What the hell was this show about?

Grey Brooks boyfriend

Ethan felt his stomach drop at the suggestion, but he felt obligated to click. The search brought up a few dozen pictures of Grey at press events entangled with a skinny white kid he recognized from the *Poison Paradise* cast photos: young, pretty, pale as a corpse, with long shaggy hair and a smug expression. Ethan disliked him instantly.

A headline caught his eye, accompanied by a paparazzi picture of a distraught Grey sobbing on the phone. "Paradise" Lost: Pretty "Poison" Pair Rocked by Ugly Cheating Rumors! His stomach lurched again. He clicked to the next search suggestion rather than interrogate the queasy feeling he got from looking at the picture of her crying.

Grey Brooks child

Ethan's brow creased. Did she have a kid? He didn't think Audrey had mentioned that, but then again, who could be sure. He was relieved when the search brought up nothing but fuzzy screenshots of projects that Grey had appeared in when she was younger. He remembered now: at lunch she'd mentioned being a child actor.

Ethan clicked over to YouTube and watched a low-res upload of a commercial where a brunette Grey, who couldn't have been more than ten, gushed over a doll that came with matching full-size accessories. The lines were stupid and the doll was pretty creepy looking, but she sold it.

Grey Brooks Kamilah Ross

Ethan smiled to himself as he looked through photos of Grey laughing and embracing Kamilah, a stunning young Black woman he recognized from Grey's Instagram. It seemed like their friendship stretched back years. Grey looked happier in the photos with Kamilah than he'd seen her so far.

A few more clicks and he found himself on the IMDb page for *Beauty Queens,* a microbudget indie the two of them had made a few years back. They had cowritten and costarred, with Kamilah directing. Ethan pulled up a trailer. The plot was ambiguous at best, and, okay, the whole thing seemed a little pretentious, but he had to admit it had a strong visual aesthetic. And Grey, compelling in person and intriguing in photographs, was downright beguiling on-screen.

He watched it three times in a row.

Grey Brooks Don't Forget to Scream bikini

Ethan shifted in his chair. *Do* not *click on that, you pervert. You dirty old man.*

Grey Brooks feet

Ethan slammed his laptop shut and chugged the rest of his beer. That was more than enough for one night.

He stretched his legs and went over to the minifridge, killing the last of the six-pack. He pulled out his phone and texted his assistant, Lucas, knowing that if he waited even another five minutes the thought would fly out of his head: *more Stella for office fridge.*

Lucas was Ethan's nephew, his sister Mary's oldest son. When Lucas had moved out to L.A. a year ago for grad school, she'd begged Ethan to help him find a job. Ethan's last assistant had just put in her two weeks, so Ethan reluctantly took him on. They rarely saw each other in person or even spoke on the phone, but Ethan's fridge was always stocked, his bills paid, and his household managed without him having to think about it. Thinking as little as possible was always the goal.

Ethan walked aimlessly to the kitchen. He never knew what to do with himself these days. He'd rented this house for a few years now, ever since he'd moved out of the home he shared with Nora and the girls a few miles down the same street, but it had never felt quite like home. It had been professionally decorated, cold and modern, before Ethan moved in, but he couldn't bring himself to care enough to change it. Changing it would mean admitting that this was where he lived now. He spent the majority of his time in his office or his bedroom, anyway. Occasionally he swam in the mornings if he wasn't too hungover.

As he padded over to the fridge, he was startled by a sharp rap on the front door. He sighed and pulled the fridge open, inspecting a foil-wrapped lump that, if he remembered correctly, contained the second half of an excellent carne asada burrito. Ethan's fingers worked clumsily to unwrap the foil as he made his way toward the front door. He was drunker than he thought.

At this time of night, there was really only one possibility for who could be on the other side of the door.

"Nora."

His ex-wife stood on his doorstep, arms crossed.

"You weren't answering your phone, thought I'd drop by. This a bad time?"

Ethan moved out of the doorway and gestured her inside with the partially unwrapped burrito.

"Good as any. The girls okay?"

Nora walked ahead of him, striding to the kitchen with purpose. She was dressed in expensive-looking running leggings and a loose sweater, her cropped black hair pulled back in a tiny ponytail. She looked effortlessly chic, but then, he'd never seen her look anything less.

Half Thai and half Swedish, Nora possessed an imposing stature and a willowy frame that had caught the eye of a modeling scout before she'd finished her freshman year of high school. Her varsity basketball team lost their star power forward for good as she quickly became a runway fixture in every international fashion capital before she could legally drink in most of them. Once she'd hit her twenties and become a fossil in the eyes of the fashion industry, she'd considered returning to her native Chicago to attend law school but instead had been coaxed by her reps into moving to L.A. to try her hand at acting first.

The first time Ethan had seen her, he'd thought she had to be the most beautiful woman ever to walk the earth, but in a way where he wasn't sure if he wanted to put her on a pedestal and admire her from afar or take her home and ravish her. He'd split the difference by marrying her.

Though their divorce had seemed to drag on endlessly and he'd been devastated by the result of the custody battle, over the past few years their relationship had evolved into something resembling friendship. Being married with kids for ten years had a way of bonding you to a person for life, whether they liked it or not. At first, she would only come to his house to drop off the girls, but lately, every now and then she came by just to talk. Ethan knew it was more for his benefit than for hers, but he still appreciated the gesture. If he was in the right mood, that is. If he was in a self-loathing spiral he found her kindness unbearable.

Nora had remarried a year ago, to a kind, reliable man named Jeff who worked as a camera operator on her prime-time medical drama. Now she was back to the serene, self-possessed woman he'd married, rather than the melancholy shadow flitting around corners to avoid him during their final months together. She was better off without him.

Nora perched on one of the stools next to the kitchen island.

"Yeah, they're fine. They're asleep. Jeff is with them."

Ethan leaned against the island, finally claiming victory in his battle with the foil.

"Did you decide yet? About maybe letting me have them for the week next time?"

Her pert nose crinkled. "I don't think that's a good idea. You know it's not really supposed to work that way."

His heart sank. Audrey's voice echoed in his mind: *Don't you want to see your girls more?* Maybe she was on to something. If Nora believed that he'd gotten his act together, he might have an opening to renegotiate the custody agreement. Go fifty-fifty, like he'd wanted. Even though their relationship had improved by leaps and bounds since their divorce, she still brushed off all attempts to discuss it. The subtext was clear, fair or not: *how can you take care of them when you can't even take care of yourself?*

In retrospect, he understood her caution back when they'd first separated, in those hazy, dark days after Sam's death. But he was on his best behavior these days. Around the girls, at least. She just refused to see it, understandably skeptical after so many years of his worst.

"Right. Well. What brings you over here, then?" he asked through a mouthful of carne asada. Before Nora could answer, he was back in the fridge, rummaging around for some hot sauce.

"Oh, you know, your standard wellness check," she deadpanned. They both knew she was only half kidding.

Ethan dumped the Valentina on his burrito and took another enormous bite, closing his eyes with pleasure. How long had it been since he'd eaten? He couldn't quite remember. He gestured with the burrito, doing a few exaggerated strongman poses, feeling fortified.

"How do I look?"

Nora's face twisted in a pained smile. He saw she was looking past him at the beer bottle he'd abandoned on the counter.

"What number is that?"

He shrugged. "You come over to count my beers, Nor?"

"Not exclusively." She fidgeted, toying with the sleeve of her sweater. "Has Paul talked to you about the Lincoln Center thing? Have they contacted him?"

"Lincoln Center?"

Nora avoided his eyes. "They want to do a fifteenth-anniversary screening of *Dirtbags* this summer. Part of one of their festivals. Press, red carpet, Q and A, the whole thing." She let herself look at him, gauging his reaction. "I think we should fly out and do it. I think . . . I think it might be good."

Ethan looked down at his burrito.

He didn't like to think about *Dirtbags*. Just hearing the title was like a deep-sea fishing net trawling his subconscious, dredging up all those freaky, gasping, malformed memories that were better left to wallow on the ocean floor where they belonged. It was the first movie he and Sam made that had hit it big. The movie where he and Nora had fallen in love. Their first trip to the Academy Awards, Ethan's win shocking them all. The three of them on the whirlwind media tour, barely believing their good fortune, their whole lives ahead of them.

If it hurt this much just to think about, how could he possibly consider watching it, let alone watch it in a crowd? He shut his eyes. *Uhh, this next question is for Ethan? Yeah, hi, big fan. How does it feel to watch yourself and the two people you loved most in the world as bright-eyed optimistic twentysomethings, knowing that you would go on to ruin all three of your lives and you will never, ever come close to being that happy again?*

He was trembling now. He wasn't sure how long he'd been silent. Ethan realized his hand holding the burrito was now squeezing it so tightly that the filling was oozing out of it and falling onto the pristine white tile. Damn. His housekeeper had just been there that morning.

Nora was already in mom mode, hurrying to the counter and

ripping a paper towel off the roll. She knelt down to pick up the fallen filling.

"You don't have to do that," Ethan said helplessly, not moving.

"Already done," she said, straightening. She crumpled the paper towel and pressed the pedal on the trash can, dropping it in before turning back to him. "You don't have to decide right now. I know . . . I know it's hard."

She bit her lip, as if contemplating whether or not to say more. Her normally placid voice cracked with emotion.

"It's hard for me, too, Ethan. I miss him, too. Every day." Her eyes flicked back to the bottle on the counter, and she hesitated. "But this . . . this isn't what he'd want for you. Shutting yourself away forever. I hope you know that."

Ethan couldn't bring himself to look at her. To give her the validation he knew she needed.

"I'm pretty beat. I think it's time for me to hang it up for the night. Would you mind letting yourself out?"

Nora's brow furrowed with concern, but he knew that she knew better than to express it. He was a lost cause tonight.

"Of course. I should get home, too. Take care of yourself." The final platitude was delivered with a little more emphasis than was traditional.

Ethan heard the door shut. He was alone again.

He slowly moved toward his bedroom, as if in a trance. The burrito lay forgotten on the counter. On the way to his room, he grabbed a bottle of Macallan from the bar cart without missing a beat. No glass.

He shut the bedroom door behind him.

5

GREY HAD TO PEE ALREADY. SHE'D CHANNELED HER NERVE INTO chugging the lemon-mint-infused sparkling water Audrey's office manager had placed in front of her, but the plan seemed to have backfired now that she was almost done with her second glass and the meeting hadn't even started yet. She had dressed intentionally for the climate: jeans again, and a cropped black sweater with her thickest bra underneath. She wasn't taking any chances today.

Ethan had been early, surprisingly, and had already been sitting at the table when she'd arrived. He was dressed, like their last meeting, in jeans and a faded T-shirt, the kind of celebrity outfit that looked deceptively simple but likely cost four figures. Even so, his clothes were distressed in a way that didn't seem prefab. Grey had a feeling if she touched his shirt it would be soft and threadbare from years of washing. She curled her fingers in on themselves to stop herself from reaching out to find out for certain.

He sat across from her at the long, shiny conference table, tracing a finger along the condensation on his own water glass. Next to him was his agent, Paul Blackwell, who intimidated Grey so much she was afraid to look him in the eye. They'd never met before, but his reputation preceded him. He hadn't bothered to introduce himself to her when he'd arrived, simply greeted Ethan and buried his nose in his phone.

She felt a rush of gratitude for Renata, sitting next to her with her rhinestone-encrusted glasses perched at the end of her nose, her phone extended as far away from her face as her arms could stretch. Grey watched Paul smirk as he looked up from his phone and observed Renata's efforts. He glanced over at Ethan, who, to his credit, stared straight ahead, ignoring him. Grey was surprised that she felt grateful for him, too. She'd been Renata's client long enough to know that this display was part of her strategy: lull everyone into thinking she was harmless, and strike when they least expected it. Grey focused on Paul's spray-tanned forehead, trying to figure out exactly where his natural hairline ended and his hair plugs began.

They were in another of the private Greenfield & Aoki conference rooms, this one roomy and spacious, with a table large enough to seat thirty people. At the moment, though, it was just the four of them. Paul leaned over to Ethan and muttered something in his ear. Ethan turned his head to listen, but his eyes were fixed on Grey. She quickly looked away and took another sip of water.

Audrey entered the room, trailed by a middle-aged man in a suit. She smiled at them as they both took seats at the head of the table.

"Thanks again for coming in, everyone. For those of you who don't know, this is Kevin Singh, chief counsel for the firm."

Kevin nodded in greeting as Grey and Renata said hello. Ethan grunted, and Paul ignored him entirely, still scrolling through his phone.

Audrey continued. "Now, I think this goes without saying,

but what we discuss here today never leaves this room. Kevin has drawn up a *very* thorough nondisclosure agreement to that effect that I would appreciate everyone signing before we go any further."

Kevin passed out the contracts. Grey scanned hers. It all looked pretty standard. Her eyes caught on one line in particular: *Each Party acknowledges and agrees that upon a material breach of the Agreement, reimbursement of $1,000,000 (one million dollars) in damages will be owed by the disclosing party.* She swallowed and flicked her eyes up at Ethan, who was signing it without hesitation. Of course. That was probably couch cushion change for him. Grey had spent her *Poison Paradise* money prudently, saving most of it, but a million dollars still represented a huge chunk of her net worth. Not to mention that she wasn't exactly rolling in it after almost a year without work.

She glanced at Renata, who was looking it over herself, lips moving silently as she read. Renata looked back at her and gave her a reassuring nod. Grey picked up her pen, initialed, signed, and dated, and passed back the contract.

Kevin flipped through them and made sure everything was in order. "Looks good."

"Wonderful. Let's proceed." Audrey smiled at the four of them. "I don't think this has to get ugly, do you? I'm quite fond of both of you, and I think you'll enjoy getting to know each other." Grey thought she saw a playful glint in Audrey's eye. "So, before we begin, let's remember that we're all friends here, and this arrangement is meant to benefit everyone. If anyone finds the terms unfair or . . . uncomfortable, for any reason, please, speak up. Don't be shy."

Grey snuck a look at Paul, who was leaning as far back as his chair would allow, tapping his Montblanc against his ivory tie pin impatiently. *No need to worry about that on their end.*

Audrey shuffled her notes. "Let's start with duration. I thought six months was a good starting place, with the opportunity to re-negotiate once we get to that point and see where we are. Thoughts?"

Renata looked at Grey, who gave a little shrug. "Works for us," said Renata.

"Isn't six months a little long?" asked Paul, tapping the pen against the table now.

"We want to give the impression that it's somewhat serious, don't we? If people think it's just a fling we might be worse off than when we started. I think six months is the absolute minimum, don't you agree?"

"Six months is fine," mumbled Ethan.

Paul rolled his eyes. "Six months it is, then."

Kevin recorded it on his laptop. Audrey continued.

"Next item: frequency." She flipped to the next page in her notes. "The two of you need to be photographed together a mini-mum of two times per week. One public outing and one overnight."

Grey blushed and quickly poured herself another glass of water from the pitcher on the table. Renata sensed her discomfort and jumped in to her rescue.

"Define 'overnight.'"

"One of you will be photographed entering the other's resi-dence, and exiting the next morning. Whatever happens in be-tween is none of our business." Audrey smirked. Her words conjured up images that Grey had been fighting to suppress since Ethan's hand had wrapped around hers at their lunch last week: Ethan's hands on her body. Ethan's hot breath on her neck. Ethan's limbs entangled with hers, the solid weight of his body pinning her down.

Grey flushed even redder and stared at the table. Her embarrassment only made her more embarrassed. An ouroboros of embarrassment.

"Audrey." Ethan's tone was soft but chastising.

"Sorry, sorry. Couldn't help myself. Where were we?"

"These public outings," Paul commented, scribbling furiously on his legal pad. "What qualifies as 'public'? My client has purposely cultivated a private image. If he starts showing up at the opening of every bottle in town, it'll attract the wrong kind of attention. People won't buy it."

"Naturally," Audrey responded. "We need to ease into it. Public means grocery store, coffee shop, maybe dinner at a restaurant once in a while." She turned to look at Grey and Renata. "Ladies? Thoughts?"

Renata scrawled a few words on her legal pad and slid it over to Grey. Grey looked at it and nodded. Renata adjusted her glasses.

"My client is also a private person. However, I think we can all agree a certain amount of networking is necessary in this business, no? This may be a change from what your client is used to, but isn't that the point of this whole exercise?" She didn't wait for any of them to respond before barreling ahead. "At least one of those public outings per month needs to be a formal press event. Premieres, galas, launches, anything with a step and repeat. We want it to be clear that *nobody* is *anybody's* dirty little secret."

Renata cleared her throat before casually delivering the final blow. "We would also like to propose one exclusive interview and/or profile with a major news outlet."

At the words "formal press events," Ethan sank down in his chair a little and ran both hands through his hair; he appeared even more perturbed with "major news outlet." Paul glanced over at him, ready to object on his behalf, but Ethan nodded without looking at him, his hand sliding down over his eyes.

Paul sighed. This negotiation was clearly not going the way he wanted it to. "Fine."

"Lovely. Now, how do I put this delicately?" Audrey paused. "We don't need to spell this out in the contract, but I think we need to all be on the same page regarding . . . displays of affection. I'm not suggesting you show up on the red carpet with your tongues down each other's throats, but it wouldn't do to have the two of you out and about with enough space between you to drive a truck through, you gather my meaning? There are people out there with nothing better to do than analyze celebrity couples' body language. We don't want to give *anyone* *any* reason to believe that you two were brought together by *any*thing but the goddamn hand of fate. Otherwise this will all be for naught."

Nobody spoke for a long moment. At the mention of tongues, Grey was once again plagued by intrusive images of Ethan's taking a leisurely tour of her body. She tried not to squirm. Ethan finally broke the silence.

"Of course. We're actors, right? I think we can convincingly pretend to like each other for a few hours a week." He looked straight at Grey, and it was as if he could see right into the heart of her filthiest, most depraved fantasies. She didn't trust herself to do anything but nod.

"Wonderful. Let's move on to the don'ts. I know we didn't give you much time to read the terms of the NDA, so I'll give you the cheat sheet. No one outside this room is to know the details of this arrangement." Audrey pointed at Ethan. "Not Nora." She pointed at Grey. "Not Kamilah. *Nobody*." She slammed her palm down on the desk to punctuate the last word. "If they ask, you were set up by a mutual friend. Which is the truth, in a manner of speaking. Beyond revealing the true nature of the relationship, the only incidents that would qualify as breach of contract are being linked romantically with another party, or causing material damage to the other person's reputation." Audrey ticked them off on her fingers. "Any questions on those points?"

Both Grey and Ethan shook their heads.

"I love it when you make my job easy. Now, is there anything I haven't addressed that either of you would like to bring up?"

Paul turned to Ethan as if to confer with him privately, but Ethan spoke first, his voice gruff. "I don't want my kids involved. I don't want them . . ." He swallowed. "I don't want to get their hopes up. It isn't fair to them."

Audrey nodded. "Absolutely. We can work around your schedule with the girls. I know Nora does an excellent job shielding them from what the press says about you two." She turned to Grey. "Grey?"

Grey took another sip of water. She considered the question. All the eyes in the room turned expectantly to her. She put the glass down. She really, really, really needed to pee now.

"No smoking," she replied.

Audrey looked down at her papers to camouflage her snicker.

Ethan raised his eyebrows in surprise. "I don't—"

Grey cut him off before he could finish. "Yes you do, I can smell it."

He closed his mouth, indignant. She realized those were the first words she'd spoken directly to him the entire meeting.

Grey turned her attention to the rest of the room. "I can't cuddle up with a smoker. Even fake-cuddle. Sorry." She shrugged.

Her imagination said otherwise, but none of them needed to know that.

Renata leaned across the table. "I can lend you the tapes I used if you want."

Grey almost laughed aloud at Ethan's bemused expression.

"Um, I'm okay, thank you," he muttered. Renata shrugged and leaned back again.

"Suit yourself. The patches are a lifesaver, though. You should try the patches."

Paul cleared his throat impatiently. "Are we done here?"

Audrey smiled serenely at him. "It does seem like we are, doesn't it? I'll have the contracts finalized and sent out by end of day tomorrow. Thank you for your cooperation, everybody. I think this is the beginning of a beautiful . . . something."

Paul bolted out the door as soon as the last words left her mouth, his phone already pressed to his ear. Audrey followed, with Renata hurrying to catch her at the door to confer with her about something or other. Kevin closed his laptop and swiftly exited, leaving Grey and Ethan as the lone stragglers.

She fell into step with him as she came around to the other side of the table. They looked at each other. She felt like she should say something, but words failed her. It seemed like around him she could only vacillate between saying the wrong thing, or losing the power of speech entirely.

Ethan held the door open for her. As she walked by him, he leaned over her. She froze. All of a sudden, she had the irrational thought that he was going to kiss her. He did smell faintly of cigarettes, it was true, but it wasn't the sour, overpowering stench of a chain-smoker. Somehow it just enhanced his natural musk, which was clean and spicy and masculine.

He didn't kiss her, of course. He just brushed his lips against her ear and murmured, "You're cute when you blush."

Grey blinked, still frozen to the spot. Before her brain was able to process what happened, he had already swept out of the room without looking back. It was probably for the best: as all the blood in her body rushed to her face, she didn't feel especially cute. She would just have to take his word for it.

6

GREY WAS STUMPED. HER TEENAGE *COSMO* SUBSCRIPTION, which she'd trusted to prepare her to navigate every tricky situation she could ever possibly encounter as an adult, hadn't quite covered this one.

What does the modern, sophisticated, sexually liberated woman pack for her very first overnight stay at her fake boyfriend's house?

She walked over to her dresser and opened the top drawer, rifling through it, and throwing five or six more shirts on top of the already enormous pile of clothes on her bed. She looked at it and groaned, falling face-first into it. She missed Kamilah. Of course, even if Kamilah were here, she couldn't be honest with her about what was going on, so maybe it was better that she was off gallivanting around the world with L.A.'s hottest up-and-coming genderqueer art-pop star, leaving Grey to have her meltdown in peace.

After Grey had returned home from Greece, she'd moved all of her belongings out of Callum's luxury condo and put a down payment on a secluded 1920s Silver Lake bungalow. In a moment of serendipity, Kamilah's housing collective had imploded in a flurry of fermentation-related drama around the same time, and Grey had practically begged her to take the spare room.

It was the shot in the arm their friendship had needed. They'd drifted apart after Grey had booked the *Poison Paradise* pilot and dropped out of USC their senior year. She'd let herself get so wrapped up in the chaos of her shooting schedule, followed by the all-consuming infatuation of her first adult relationship, that she'd let every other relationship in her life fall by the wayside. They'd first reconnected when the *Poison Paradise* producers were looking for new directors to keep on call, and Grey had immediately thrown Kamilah's name into the mix.

Kamilah had grown up in a small western Massachusetts college town, the daughter of two professors. She'd eschewed the free liberal arts tuition to follow her acting-slash-filmmaking dreams out West, her hunger amplified by working part-time at her tiny local video store during its final years of existence. They'd initially bonded over being East Coast refugees, though their upbringings couldn't have been more different. Grey found Kamilah's tales of DIY home piercings and boxed wine in cow fields as fascinating as Kamilah found Grey's stories of growing up on set and backstage.

While Grey's lifetime of industry experience made it easy for her to charm people on a superficial level, she was also most comfortable keeping them at arm's length. Being regularly pulled out of school and bouncing from set to set had shaped her into something of a loner. Kamilah, on the other hand, had an uncanny ability to disarm almost anyone, her quiet magnetism and genuine curiosity drawing people to her like a beacon. By their sophomore year, they'd become inseparable, hosting elaborate dinner parties, working their way through Kamilah's Criterion Collection DVDs, and making grandiose plans about what their careers would look like once they left school. When Kamilah had moved into her house, which they'd filled with flea market and estate sale finds, it was like no time had passed at all.

That is, until Kamilah had been hired to direct Andromeda X's high-concept new music video. Kamilah had left for the shoot early one morning three months ago, and Grey hadn't seen her since. She'd woken up to a dozen drunk, giggly voice memos of Kamilah gushing about how she had found her soulmate, and how within an hour of arriving on set, Andromeda had immediately invited her to tour with them for the next several months.

Grey was thrilled for her, of course, and had been following their exploits on Instagram with only the slightest twinge of envy. She'd scrolled through pictures of them clubbing in Berlin, smoking intimidatingly large blunts in Amsterdam, trying on outrageous streetwear in Tokyo. The video content Kamilah was creating for them on the fly, editing on the plane and in hotel rooms, was stunning, some of her best work ever. Meanwhile, Grey was stuck at home, tragically unemployed, trying unsuccessfully to keep Kamilah's plants alive, and wondering whether she should bother packing anything cuter than her tattered middle school graduation T-shirt to sleep in for her first thrilling night of no-mance with Ethan.

She checked the time on her phone. 6:40. Shit. She needed to get on the road soon. She shoved the tower of clothes onto the floor to reveal her empty overnight bag buried under it, and threw a few random items in without looking. The only thing she really needed was her toothbrush.

Nearly an hour later, she followed her GPS up the winding Santa Monica Mountains road to the gate of Ethan's house. Down the street, she saw a few cars idling. This must be the paparazzi Audrey had called in advance. She tapped out a text to her just to be sure:

I'm here.

A little thrill went through her. There was no going back now. Her phone buzzed immediately with Audrey's response:

Good to go.

The car doors opened and several middle-aged men carrying enormous cameras started toward her. Even though this was all part of the plan, she couldn't help feeling a little freaked out. She rolled down her window and leaned her torso out of the car, pushing her hair behind her ear to give the cameras a clear view of her face as she slowly tapped Ethan's security code into the keypad.

Click-click-click-click. The high-speed shutters snapped in sharp flurries, the flashes sending dark spots dancing in front of her eyes. Once they had their money shots, the photographers politely thanked her and scattered back to their cars before the gate had opened fully. Grey stared apprehensively down the long expanse of driveway, engulfed in shadow.

Honey, I'm home.

SHE WAS HERE. IN HIS HOUSE.

For the first time, Grey existed outside the walls of Greenfield & Aoki or the screen of his computer (and, okay, the screen of his phone, too). She was fidgeting in his hallway, leather overnight bag slung over her shoulder, having trouble meeting his eyes. Not that he was trying, either.

He led her through the house.

"Kitchen—help yourself to anything in the fridge; if you want something else, you can text Lucas and he'll postmates it for you." He turned to face the living room and gestured at the enormous, plush, U-shaped sectional parked in front of a projector screen. "He can also probably help you figure out the remotes if you want to watch something. I think you can stream . . . whatever you want. I pretty much only use it when the girls are here, they're better at that stuff. I can't really make heads or tails of it."

She was silent, taking it all in. He brought her down the hall-way and opened the door to one of the spare bedrooms.

"Normally I would put you in the guesthouse, but there's some kind of pipe thing going on. Lucas says the guy keeps giving him the runaround. The pipe guy, I mean. Sorry about that."

"Um, no, it's fine. I'll just knock a star off your rating."

He jerked his head back to look at her. She looked back at him innocently. He ran his hand through his hair, a little unnerved. There she went again, making jokes, making herself impossible to write off. He wished she wouldn't.

"Right. Well. Make yourself at home." He tried to keep his pace casual as he walked away.

For the next hour, Ethan holed up in his office, doing whatever he could to ignore the new bumps and shuffles and sighs permeating the house, let alone what—make that *who*—was causing them. He felt a little guilty about abandoning her so unceremoniously, but surely she understood that this was how it had to work. Tonight was about the photo op when she entered and when she left. It had to be. He'd watched her lose any illusions about the kind of guy he was at their first meeting, and he wasn't about to show her firsthand all the fun and unique ways he could disappoint her.

He had a glass of bourbon next to him, but he hadn't touched it much. Something about tonight made him want to stay alert. A book lay open on his lap, but he couldn't concentrate, staring out at the pool instead. His house was ranch-style, wrapping around the pool and enclosing it on three sides, with all the back walls re-placed by floor-to-ceiling glass.

He sighed and put the book down, casting his eyes around the room for something else to do. He would *not* go see what she was doing. He picked up his guitar from the corner and gave it a perfunctory tuning before settling back in his chair, strumming absently, lost in thought.

Ethan was so zoned out that he didn't hear the office door, already open a crack, creak open farther.

"Know any Hole?"

Grey was standing in the doorway, hand on her hip like she owned the place. Her confident expression wavered when he met her eyes, but only for a split second.

"Excuse me?"

"That's Nirvana, right?" Her brow furrowed melodramatically. "You're not one of those 'Courtney killed Kurt' guys, are you? Because if that's the case, I'm writing Audrey that milliondollar check right now."

Ethan chuckled. "Oh yeah? That's your dealbreaker? 'Must love Courtney Love'?"

"Is that so much to ask?"

"Not at all. Unfortunately, I can only play about three and a half songs and Courtney didn't make the short list."

"Was that one of the three, or the half?"

He offered the neck of the guitar to her, in mock offense.

"Can you do better?"

She accepted his challenge and slung the strap over her shoulder, still braced on the doorframe. She leaned her head over the fretboard in concentration, a few blond curls slipping over her eyes as she organized her fingers over the strings. She closed her eyes and tilted her head back dramatically, bringing her other arm down in an aggressive strum of the ugliest, most dissonant chord Ethan had ever heard.

Ethan threw back his head and laughed.

"Guess not." Grey shrugged, handing it back to him. "I did have a couple lessons a few years ago, I had to fake it for the show I was on. Seems like they didn't stick."

Ethan let the guitar lie flat on his lap, resting his hands on the strings. He considered her.

For the first time, he tried to put himself in her shoes. She was in an unfamiliar place, in a bizarre situation. He had all the power. And yet she'd sought him out, even though he had tried to shut her away and ignore her. He toyed with the idea of actually getting to know her, letting her get to know him. Just because their relationship wasn't real didn't mean they had to stay strangers. She seemed, so far, to be down-to-earth and easygoing—that is, when she didn't want to bite his head off. Maybe she wouldn't try to claw her way inside his heart, demand things of him that he could never provide.

And, yes, seeing her standing there in her leggings and bare feet and a cloud of wavy blond hair with a smile still lingering at the corners of her lips stirred something inside him that he hadn't felt in years. Like he had a glimpse of something that could be his, something so painfully perfect that his chest ached, something he had done nothing to deserve. All he had to do was reach out and take it. It would be so easy to put the guitar down and pull her into his lap right then, burying his face in her hair.

The fact that he wanted to terrified him.

Grey had been staring at him with an unreadable expression, waiting for him to respond. He needed to say something. He couldn't.

Ethan finally cleared his throat. "Um. I think I'm gonna head to bed. You all right? Got everything you need?"

Disappointment briefly flickered across her face, but she camouflaged it like the professional she was. She smiled tightly.

"Yeah. I'm good. Night."

She disappeared from the doorway. He listened to her steps padding down the hallway, the bedroom door shutting behind her.

GREY WOKE UP THE NEXT MORNING SWEATING AND FRUSTRATED. Though the high-tech thermostat in her room read a cool sixty-eight degrees, she'd been tormented by a night of sexually charged anxiety dreams where she, unbearably aroused, had thrown herself repeatedly at a faceless man who was always just out of reach. She stretched out in the absurdly large California king bed and buried her face in the soft pillows, groaning, unsatisfied.

She rolled over and looked at her phone, which was so full of notifications that she had to scroll and scroll just to reach the end. Grey swiped open an Instagram DM from Kamilah, sent at 4 A.M. thanks to the time difference, which accosted her with caps and an army of exclamation points:

UM!!!!!!! EXPLAIN!!!!! NOW!!!!!

Kamilah had attached a post from a celebrity gossip account. Grey's own face stared back at her, leaning out of her car window in front of Ethan's gate.

SPOTTED: Poison Paradise*'s Grey Brooks entering the elusive Ethan Atkins's Pacific Palisades residence.*

Grey sent back a shocked blushing face emoji, resisting the urge to click through and read the comments. Nothing good ever came from reading the comments.

Her phone buzzed immediately with Kamilah's response.

omg don't even. i leave for 5 minutes and you're running around
getting that a-list d.
without telling me!!!!
i'm sending you to friend jail.

Grey wrote back:

lmao
it's not like that! we're taking it slow.
i don't want to jinx it. i'll tell you everything soon. i promise!!!

She topped it off with an angel emoji and then threw her
phone facedown on the bed. She didn't feel right outright lying to
Kamilah. Everything she said was technically true, but typing it
out still gave her a curdled feeling in her stomach. Suddenly, she
felt very, very alone.

She stilled and listened for signs that Ethan was up and about.
No noise. She had been so focused on the night itself she hadn't
really thought about what would happen in the morning. Based on
how unenthused he had seemed to spend time with her last night,
she wasn't holding out hope for sharing the crossword puzzle over
eggs and mimosas. He probably wouldn't care if she slipped out
without saying goodbye.

He'd probably forgotten she was even here.

Grey rummaged through her overnight bag and was relieved
to find she was able to assemble something resembling a normal
outfit. She splashed water on her face, brushed her teeth, and
finger-combed the knots out of her hair, smoothing it back into a
messy bun.

After giving up the battle with Ethan's complicated (and seemingly never-touched) espresso machine, Grey grabbed an apple out

of his fridge and headed toward the front door. She paused. She hadn't felt comfortable exploring the house the night before, but this might be the time to give herself a more thorough tour.

She left her bag in the kitchen and made her way down the hallway. First door on the right was Ethan's office. Then a bathroom. Then her ("her") room. Then, presumably, the master bedroom, door firmly closed. The next room was another bedroom: two twin beds, two desks. This must be where his kids stayed when they were with him. The room was immaculate, sparse, impersonal. It didn't look like they were here very often.

By now she was on the opposite side of the house, around the other side of the pool. She slid open the glass door to reveal a huge state-of-the-art gym. What must have been tens of thousands of dollars of equipment stared back at her: treadmills, rowing machines, battle ropes, kettlebells, medicine balls, and enough free weights to train an army. Grey paused in front of a punching bag. If she got the role in *Golden City,* she would have to undergo months of stunt training. The idea was kind of exciting. She'd always wanted to learn how to fight, but aside from a handful of drop-in classes at Kamilah's kickboxing gym over the years, she'd never pursued it seriously.

She gave the bag an experimental push. It swung back toward her and she stilled it, before putting her fists up hesitantly. She shuffled around the bag a few times, ducking and dodging, then swinging a fist. Pain shot through her knuckles and wrist.

"*Ow!* Fuck!" She shook out her arm. She heard laughter behind her and whirled around.

Ethan had slid open the door leading out to the pool, towel wrapped around his waist. Tiny droplets of water skated along his bare torso, mingling with the dusting of dark hair that covered his chest, and trailed invitingly down the center of his stomach. His hand moved to unwrap the towel and Grey's eyes widened. He pulled it off to reveal . . . swim trunks. Of course. He wasn't going to just whip it out. That would be insane.

He brought the towel up to his head and rubbed it vigorously over his dripping hair.

"You know you're supposed to wear gloves with that, right?"

"I know, I just . . . I was just trying it out." She tried to change the subject. "This place is amazing. I didn't really peg you for such a gym rat."

"Wow. Thanks," he deadpanned, looking down at his naked torso almost self-consciously.

"No! I mean . . . you're . . . you have . . ." she stammered.

When he'd landed *The Lone Sentinel,* the tabloids had obsessively documented his journey to pack thirty pounds of muscle onto the lean physique of his twenties. These days, he was obviously several years removed from the lifestyle of twice-daily workouts and optimized macronutrient meal plans, but his body still seemed to carry the memory of it. He looked solid and strong, with an added layer of softness to him that Grey found more appealing than overripe, bulging vascularity—not to mention the vanity that usually accompanied it. Though his six-pack from her *Seventeen* pinup was nowhere to be found, his arms and chest were broad and well defined. She'd been thinking about his arms a lot, actually, and seeing them bare and glistening with water droplets wasn't helping.

After what felt like an eternity, he came to her rescue. "The studio sent it all over. When I was training for . . . well. You know." He cleared his throat. "I wanted to just leave everything at my . . . at Nora's, but she made me take it when I moved out. She only likes to use her scary Pilates machines anyway." His eyes scanned over the room. "Honestly, I'm still expecting them to come take it all back any day now."

He had a faraway, glazed expression. Grey tried to steer the conversation in a new direction.

"I'm up for this movie right now where I would have to do the whole boot camp thing, learn to fight, everything. At this point, I don't think I'll ever be able do a pull-up unless I'm getting paid for it."

Ethan's mouth twitched.

"Let's see what you got, then. Put 'em up."

"I thought I needed gloves."

"We need to fix your form first. Bag comes later."

You can fix my form anytime. Grey almost physically shook her head to knock that thought right out of it. She stepped her right leg back and put her fists up. Ethan leaned forward and, with a brush of his fingertips, guided her back elbow up until her fist was nearly touching her jaw.

"Hands protect your face. Always."

He walked behind her.

"Keep your hips square."

His featherlight touch on her hips nearly made her jump out of her skin. She shivered. Fuck. There was no way he hadn't seen that. He stilled, but didn't move his hands away. She might have been imagining it, but it felt like his pressure increased, gripping her tighter for a split second, before his hands disappeared.

When he spoke, his voice was thick.

"Good. Good start."

She turned to face him, dropping her hands, but he'd already started to back away.

"Text Lucas about dinner tomorrow. Can't waste any time getting you out in public if you want to land your big action movie, right?" His voice was light, but laced with bitterness. He picked up his towel and started toward the door.

Irritation rippled through her. Why was it so easy for him to get under her skin?

"So I'm just going to be communicating with Lucas this whole time?"

He stopped. Turned. Shrugged.

"I'm bad with logistics. It's easier this way."

Grey raised her eyebrows.

"Gotcha. Sorry to inconvenience you."

"It's his job."

"Maybe I should be dating him, then."

"As long as you keep it out of the tabloids. You'd make a cute couple."

Grey crossed her arms and set her jaw.

"Will I be getting *your* phone number at any point in this process?"

Ethan looked down, half shaking his head. "I don't see why that's necessary."

Grey scoffed.

"We're supposed to be madly in love and you won't even give me your phone number? Do you resent this whole idea that much? Resent *me* that much? We already signed the damn contract, it's a little late for cold feet."

He said nothing, just raised his eyes to her with an inscrutable expression. She exhaled in frustration. "I don't get you. You ignore me. You flirt with me. You push me away. This doesn't have to be that complicated. Can't we just acknowledge the weirdness of the situation and move on? Be friends, maybe? Or at least friend*ly*? Otherwise the next six months are going to be a fucking nightmare. I don't want that. Do you?"

He stared at her for a long moment, then slowly started back toward her. Grey had to plant herself in place to not instinctively back away.

"You're right. I'm sorry. I've been having . . . conflicting feelings about this whole thing."

Grey snorted. "Yeah, I kinda picked up on that."

He smiled that half smile, and she felt an involuntary flutter. "I shouldn't take it out on you. You haven't done anything wrong. I'd like . . . friends. Friends would be good." He held out his hand, palm up. Grey looked at it, confused. Did he want to shake on it? She started to place her hand on his, but he shook his head.

"Your phone."

Her heart leapt. She pulled her phone out of her back pocket, unlocking it and opening her contacts. He tapped in his number and handed it back to her. She looked down and burst out in surprised laughter. Next to his name, he'd added a heart-eyes emoji.

"Nice touch."

"It's all in the details." He turned back toward the door and walked out of the room. A moment later, he poked his head back in the doorway, grinning wickedly.

"See you tomorrow, *darling*."

7

Are u a vegetarian

?

Or vegan

no, i'll eat anything! not picky.

Cool

We'll go to Carlo's

Pick u up @ 7

Ethan's reticence to text made sense: he wasn't great at it. They had exchanged exactly three messages total, planning their next outing, and he was prone to replacing "you" with "u" in the manner that Gen X–adjacent men were inexplicably fond of. For some reason, the less tech-savvy a guy was, the more likely he was to text like a mid-2000s "Is Your Child Secretly Sexting?" propaganda pamphlet meant to frighten parents.

As was becoming a disturbingly frequent habit, Grey agonized over her outfit. Thankfully, Kamilah was in an accessible enough time zone with reliable enough Wi-Fi for an emergency Face-Time. Grey had filled her in as much as she could, dodging her more probing questions. She could tell Kamilah wasn't mollified by her answers, but she took advantage of the physical distance between them to keep the conversation vague ("What? Sorry, you froze, I didn't get that."). As much as possible, she volleyed questions back at Kamilah, who, as always, was chock-full of adventures to update her on.

They ultimately agreed that it was best to keep it simple: slinky black minidress, delicate gold jewelry, heeled ankle boots, her hair loose and wild. She took her time applying her makeup, using a slightly heavier hand than normal. Her usual policy was to avoid lipstick in situations where there would be even the slightest chance of canoodling. *Guess I don't have to worry about that,* she thought ruefully, painting her lips a vampy shade of crimson.

Their call ended abruptly when Kamilah got pulled away to deal with a malfunctioning projector emergency. As soon as she shut her laptop, her phone buzzed. She couldn't stop her stomach from jumping a little when she saw Ethan's name, with that damn heart eyes emoji next to it. She swiped it open, revealing a single word, no punctuation:

Here

At least he got straight to the point. She grabbed her clutch and headed out the door.

Outside, a black Bentley idled in front of her house. Grey pulled open the passenger door and started to climb in next to . . . a complete stranger. She froze.

"Um, sorry, I think—"

She heard Ethan chuckle from the back seat. The driver smiled.

"You must be Grey. I'm Ozzy. Not that I wouldn't appreciate the company, but you might be more comfortable in the back seat."

Grey tried to hide how flustered she was. "Right. Thanks. Nice to meet you. I'll just . . ."

She closed the door and opened the door to the back seat, thankful that the darkness camouflaged her glowing cheeks. As she slid in beside Ethan, she caught him staring at her, his mouth slightly open. She felt self-conscious all of a sudden. Was her lipstick smudged?

"What?"

He closed his mouth and swallowed. "Nothing. You look . . . you look nice."

"Thanks. I feel like a rube."

He laughed. "I guess the chivalrous thing to do would have been to get out and open the door for you. Avoid any confusion."

She pretended to reach for the door handle again, even though the car had already started moving.

"Should we do another take? Back to one?"

He grinned. "We can just fix it in post."

"A true professional."

Grey looked out the window as Ozzy merged them onto the 101 toward West Hollywood. A slightly awkward silence settled between them. They weren't in public yet, but they still had an audience. They needed to watch what they said.

Which, for now, wasn't a problem, since they said nothing.

OZZY PULLED THE CAR UP OUTSIDE CARLO'S, AN OLD-SCHOOL red sauce joint and noted celebrity haunt. The restaurant was constantly swarmed with paparazzi; Audrey probably hadn't even needed to call anyone in advance.

Ethan snuck a look at Grey, who was staring out the tinted window at the huddle of photographers with trepidation. He felt uneasy, too. What had seemed abstract last week, staring down at the contracts at Audrey's office, was now starting to take real shape. He was about to formally reappear in public for the first time in years. He'd briefed the manager, an old friend, that they'd be there, and reserved the private dining room. All they needed to do was run the gauntlet of paps as they walked into the restaurant and then they would be home free.

He leaned over and took her hand. She looked back at him, eyes wide.

"You ready?"

She nodded.

"Okay. Wait here."

He released her hand and got out of the car, walking around the back to open her door for her. The photographers spotted him instantly and started yelling his name, flashes popping like fireworks.

"Ethan! Ethan! Over here! How's it going, man?" The voices of the paparazzi overlapped in an incoherent roar. As he pulled Grey's door open, the noise faded into the background as she turned those wide blue eyes on him. God, she really was beautiful. Her hesitant expression he had seen just moments ago had vanished. She looked calm, even regal. He held out his hand to her and she took it, her soft fingers clasping his as he guided her out of the car.

"How chivalrous," she murmured with a sly smile. She let him lead her past the photographers into the restaurant. The hostess greeted them and whisked them through a well-hidden doorway to the private dining room. The noise of the restaurant dampened to a hush when the door closed behind them. As the hostess seated them and handed them menus, Ethan exhaled. He had made it. Now all he had to do was make it through an intimate, one-on-one dinner with a beautiful and charming woman he was undeniably, disturbingly attracted to. Piece of cake.

Grey was studying the menu.

"Have you been here before?"

She looked up.

"Yeah, a few years ago. With, um. With my ex." Her mouth twisted and she looked away. He flashed back to the pictures of her crying and felt a twinge of anger.

He needed a drink. Now.

"Should we get a bottle of wine?"

"Sure. I guess. I'm kind of a lightweight, though," she admitted. He nodded, pursing his lips in mock seriousness.

"Oh yeah. Me, too."

He thought that would make her laugh, but instead her eyes flickered with a look that almost seemed like concern. Before he could parse it, she went back to the menu.

The waitress came by to take their drink orders and he ordered them a Cabernet.

"There's something I've been wanting to ask you," Ethan said once the waitress had left.

She looked up at him, eyes wide.

"What?"

"Is Grey your real name?"

The trepidation on her face dissolved as she laughed.

"No. Well, sort of. It's my middle name. My mom's maiden name. My first name is Emily."

"What's wrong with Emily?"

She shrugged. "Nothing. Renata suggested I change it, thought it might be more marketable. I booked my show right after, so I guess she was right."

"Does anyone still call you Emily?"

She looked at him closely, as if trying to figure out his angle. "Um, my mom and my brother. My friend Kamilah, sometimes. I think that's it."

"What should I call you?"

She took a moment to consider it. "It's up to you, I guess. I was never that attached to Emily, though. I don't mind it when people who knew me before use it, but . . . I think I feel more Grey these days." She rolled her eyes, but she was smiling. "Even though I look like a blonde."

"I'm never gonna live that one down, am I?"

"I'm kind of shocked I don't hear it more, honestly."

The waitress came back with the bottle of wine, pouring a little in Ethan's glass. He swirled it, took a sip, and nodded. She poured them both generous glasses.

"Are you ready to order? Need a little more time?"

"I'll have the wedge salad and the rib eye, medium rare. What about you, baby?" He tenderly placed his hand over Grey's. She didn't miss a beat, meeting his eyes with unmasked adoration. The waitress smiled down at them.

"I'll have the beet and burrata salad and the scallops, please." Grey returned the waitress's smile, then interlaced her fingers with Ethan's, turning her gooey gaze back to him.

"Great choices. I'll be right back with your salads."

As the door shut, Ethan leaned in and stage-whispered, "Bet she's on the phone with TMZ already."

"You think? I'm sure everyone here is very discreet."

"Knowing Audrey, she has every waiter in this place on the payroll."

Seemingly at the same time, they realized they were still holding hands. They froze, staring at their intertwined fingers. Ethan didn't want to be the first to pull his hand away. He didn't want to insult her. At last, Grey eased her hand out and picked up her wineglass in one smooth movement. She made a little noise of approval as she tasted it. When she set the glass down, her lipstick left two perfect, crimson half-moons on the rim. He stared at them, hypnotized, imagining the marks she might leave elsewhere.

He forced himself to snap out of it. "Speaking of Renata, is she for real? She's kind of a character. Have you ever thought about switching agents? That might be part of your problem. I could get you a meeting with Paul, if you want."

Grey's face dropped. "No," she said flatly. "Not interested."

Ethan was surprised at the vehemence of her reaction. "Sorry. Didn't mean to offend."

Grey took another leisurely sip from her wineglass. Ethan was transfixed by the long line of her neck as she tilted her head up to drink. Fuck. He was in big trouble.

She seemed like she was internally debating something. Finally, she spoke.

"When I went to my first wardrobe fitting for *Poison Paradise,* the costume designer told me I needed to lose fifteen pounds. Immediately. He kept . . . he wouldn't stop *pinching* me. Everywhere I was . . . bulging." She toyed with the stem of her wineglass. "Renata called me to check in about how my first day went and I couldn't stop crying. I didn't want to tell her, I was so scared I would get fired. She told me she would take care of it. The next day, the producers called me in. I thought that was it. I was out. I'd never work again. I don't know what she said to them but . . . they had fired the designer. They *apologized* to me." She closed her eyes. "I'll never forget it."

Ethan was stunned. "I'm sorry. That's awful."

She shrugged, clearly uncomfortable with his sympathy. "It's fine. It was a long time ago. I mean, at the end of the day I'm still a youngish, skinnyish, white, blond girl. I generally have it pretty easy in this business. And the world in general."

Ethan sipped his own wine. "I guess the only one who has it easier is me."

She met his eyes, her expression placid and unwavering. "I guess so."

The waitress came back in with their salads.

"What about you?" Grey asked after the waitress had disappeared again.

"What do you mean, what about me?"

"I don't know. Anything." She pressed the side of her fork into the burrata and watched it ooze over the rest of her plate. "I feel like I know everything about you and nothing about you at the same time."

He cocked an eyebrow. "Everything?"

She flushed and drained her glass. If she was as much of a lightweight as she claimed, she was going to be on the floor by the time this meal was over. "I mean. A normal amount. I don't know if you're aware of this, but you're *very* famous. It's hard not to know."

"Tell me."

She speared a beet on the end of her fork and nibbled at it, careful to avoid smearing her lipstick.

"Well. You're from Queens. You got started in bad teen movies. You wrote and starred in a movie with your friend Sam Tanner that made you both super famous. You won an Oscar. You married your costar, Nora Lind, and you had two daughters. The three of you did some more movies together, and some apart. You got cast in the *Lone Sentinel* reboot. You . . ." She trailed off. The air in the room seemed to thicken. Grey stilled. Ethan ate a loud, crunchy bite of his salad.

"Don't stop now," he said, his voice light. "It was just starting to get interesting."

Grey's eyes darted from side to side. She poured herself another glass of wine to stall. She sighed and met his eyes again.

"You . . . Sam had . . . an accident. You and Nora got divorced. You . . . you didn't make the movie."

"Why didn't I make the movie?"

"You got fired. You got fired from the movie."

"And then?" His eyes drove into her. She was silent for a moment.

"And then . . . you got set up with me?" She batted her eyes and tossed her hair. The tension evaporated instantly.

He laughed, shaking his head a little, as if trying to clear out the last dregs of gloom that had threatened to overpower the evening. "So what you're saying is, you're the best thing that's happened to me in the last five years?"

She shrugged, taking another sip of wine, seemingly relieved that her attempt had worked. "Unless I missed something."

He shook his head slowly, his eyes never leaving her face.

"No. No, you didn't miss anything."

THERE WAS NO WAY AROUND IT: GREY WAS DRUNK. SHE LEANED her cheek on the cool window of the Bentley, shutting her eyes against the dizzying glare of the passing streetlights. She normally had to cap her wine consumption at two glasses before things started to turn on her. The two of them had polished off the first bottle before their entrées had arrived, and finished the second by the time she'd demolished four-fifths of their "shared" flourless chocolate cake.

Ethan was quiet next to her, his fingers lightly covering hers. They felt like they were the only thing anchoring her, like if he lifted his hand she would float out through the window into the smog. The second half of their dinner had passed in a warm haze. Grey remembered laughing a lot, but she already couldn't recall what was so funny.

Ethan. Ethan was what was so funny. And charismatic. And endearing. And handsome. So fucking handsome. For the first time since she'd met him, she felt like she'd gotten a glimpse of the real Ethan. The sweet, sensitive man hidden beneath the condescension, the iciness, the self-involvement. Over the course of the evening, he'd almost seemed to glow, especially when he looked at her. Then again, maybe that was just the wine talking.

The car slowed and Grey opened her eyes again. They were in front of her house. Ethan gave her fingers a light squeeze before leaning forward to place a hand on Ozzy's shoulder.

"Be right back."

He opened the door and got out. Grey opened hers, too, carefully unfolding her legs onto the ground one at a time. Ethan appeared in front of her and offered his hand.

"You steady, cowgirl?"

She gripped his hand with both of hers and he helped her pull herself to her feet. For a moment, she was tempted to just let the momentum bring her fully against his chest, but the last soggy remnants of her pride forced her to stand up straight. She kept hold of his hand, though.

"I'm good. Great. Never better." They walked to her front door, hidden from street view by a few well-placed trees. She rummaged around in her clutch for her house keys, stumbling a little as her focus shifted. He reached out an arm to steady her.

"I had a really nice time tonight. You're . . . you're really nice," she babbled, her vocabulary apparently having taken the rest of the evening off.

Ethan laughed. "Thanks. You're really nice, too."

She dug out her key and looked back up at him. He looked down at her, his face streaked with shadows from the porch light. His gaze drifted down to her mouth.

"You have something . . ." He cupped his knuckles under her chin and tilted her face toward the light, bringing his thumb to trace the edge of her bottom lip. She shivered. "Lipstick," he murmured. He didn't move his hand away, resting his thumb at the corner of her mouth.

He was going to kiss her. She was going to kiss him. They were going to kiss, lipstick be damned. Her heart started to race. She leaned into him, pressing against the length of his body and sighing a little. She closed her eyes and waited.

And waited.

He dropped his hand and cleared his throat.

"Grey."

She opened her eyes. He was looking at her with a troubled expression. She stepped back and covered her face with her hands, too mortified to even look at him.

"Sorry. I just thought—sorry."

"No, it's okay, I mean, you're very—you're—I wish . . ." He paused, gathering his thoughts. "You were right. Before. We . . . we shouldn't make this complicated."

Grey had already turned toward her front door, trying to maneuver her trembling hands to insert the key in the lock with the focus of a veteran safecracker. She still couldn't look at him.

"Of course. You're right. *So* right. Forget it. I sure will!" Mercifully, she got the door unlocked. She scampered inside, plastering a bright smile on her face. "Thanks for dinner! Get home safe!"

She slammed the door on him before he had a chance to respond. She pressed her back against the door, sinking down onto her heels, burying her head in her hands and half groaning, half screaming in frustration.

Somehow she knew that no matter what they promised each other, things were only going to get more complicated.

8

ETHAN KNEW HE'D FUCKED UP. HE REALIZED IT AS SOON AS HE saw the hurt and embarrassment in Grey's eyes when he'd pulled away from her. Never mind that it had taken every last drop of self-control he had left. When she'd pressed her warm, soft body against his and sighed, smelling faintly of wine and tropical flowers, his brain had come dangerously close to short-circuiting. He didn't know which was worse: the certainty that he'd hurt her with his rejection, or the uncertainty of what would have happened if he'd given in to temptation, pulled her into his arms, and drunk her down.

It was that uncertainty that haunted him over the next several days. In the moment it had seemed like shutting her down was the only option, but as soon as he did, he regretted it. It wasn't just her disappointment that left him rattled—it was his surprise at the intensity of his own need.

He'd seen her once since then. The two of them had gone out to get coffee, Audrey calling ahead to make sure the shop wasn't too busy. They'd spent less than twenty minutes together from start to finish.

She'd been friendly and cordial, acting every inch the devoted girlfriend, but the vulnerability was gone, her eyes frosted and distant. In a way, it was a relief: she'd gotten the message. He was someone who needed to be kept at arm's length. He would only hurt her and let her down. He was thankful that it had just taken something as minimal as a rebuffed kiss for her to figure it out.

The coffee shop was another baby step in his journey back into public-facing life. When they'd entered, holding hands, every head in the place had whipped toward them. After years of brushing off and demurring every time someone had recognized him, he was a little rusty at actually interacting with fans. Grey had taken the lead with grace, steering them through each encounter, providing the delicate illusion of genuine connection, knowing exactly when to cut things off without seeming rude. He was grateful for her. He didn't deserve her, even in the limited capacity he had her.

When he'd gotten home, he finally forced himself to pull out the last script he and Sam had been working on: *Bitter Pill,* a remake of an arthouse Korean film from two decades earlier that the two of them had been fascinated by. They'd acquired the rights shortly before Sam's death, but their option on it was expiring soon.

Looking at the title page filled him with shame. He'd failed Sam by letting it languish for so long. Though he had acted in plenty of movies without Sam, this would be his first time writing and producing without Sam by his side. The prospect made Sam's absence feel as acute as if Ethan had lost one of his own limbs, maybe even his head.

For them, the finished product had been secondary to the galvanizing delight of the creative process. The two of them up all night brainstorming in Sam's office, running on pure adrenaline (and the occasional bump), tossing ideas back and forth until the sun came up.

The process on this one had been slower, though. More laborious. It hadn't helped that Sam had been preoccupied with the dissolution of his three-year marriage to Beth Jordan, a socialite whose father had directed Sam and Ethan's favorite action-comedy film series from their childhood. Neither Ethan nor Nora had been that fond of Beth—she had that glazed nepotism sheen of someone who'd never experienced the world beyond Beverly Hills and didn't care to—but she'd made Sam happy, until she hadn't. Ethan and Nora's relationship was starting to show signs of strain by that point, too, and their work sessions had more often than not devolved into self-pitying, booze-fueled meditations on their floundering personal lives.

They'd barely even finished the first draft before Sam's accident, and Ethan knew there was still a lot of work to be done. He had to finish it, though. It was the only piece of Sam he had left. Forcing himself back out in the world, on the arm of a woman who wanted nothing to do with him, was the first roundabout step to making that happen.

But for now, he put thoughts of *Bitter Pill* and the hurt in Grey's eyes out of his head. He had his kids this weekend, so it would be a few days before he saw her again.

He pulled his car into the driveway of the house he and Nora had shared. While his own house definitely didn't feel like home, neither did this, not anymore. As he walked up the immaculately landscaped pathway, flashes of memories accosted him: bringing Elle home from the hospital. Sydney learning to ride her bike. Waking up to Nora standing over him after he had passed out on the lawn. Time had dulled them enough so the twinges he felt were neither bitter nor sweet. They just were.

Nora opened the door before he even had a chance to knock.

"Girls ready?"

"They need a few more minutes. Come on in."

He followed Nora into the kitchen, declining her offer of a bottle of water.

"You and Jeff got big plans this weekend?"

"Not really. Do *you*?" she asked, arms crossed.

"Uh . . . yeah . . . I have the girls," he deadpanned.

She sighed, drumming her fingers on the countertop. "And will anyone else be joining you?"

"Wasn't planning on it."

He could do this all day. She sighed again, defeated.

"You don't owe me anything. But I think I deserve more than finding out you're dating someone from goddamn Instagram."

He avoided her gaze. "I'm sorry. It's . . . it's still new. I should have told you. I'm just . . . we're figuring things out."

She softened a little. "It's okay. I just want to see you happy." Unbeknownst to her, she had almost exactly parroted Audrey's words to him less than two weeks ago: *people want to see you stable. They want to see you happy.* She'd been talking about strangers, of course, but even his ex-wife, the woman who in theory knew him better than anyone, was so desperate to believe it that she was willing to overlook the battalion of red flags indicating that there was something suspicious about the situation.

Nora continued. "I approve, by the way. I used to watch her show, you know; have you seen it? It's pretty stupid, but I got hooked. Total guilty pleasure. She seems like a sweet girl. Talented, too. Those writers threw some wild stuff at her."

He cleared his throat. "Yeah, she's very . . ." He racked his brain for the right word. "Symmetrical," he finished lamely.

Nora frowned. He blustered ahead before she could say anything.

"Anyway, I'm not ready for her to meet the kids yet. Still too early. I want to make sure it's for real. I'd appreciate you not mentioning it to them, either."

Nora nodded. "Of course. You know I can only protect them from so much, though. Kids talk." She leaned forward on the counter, propping her chin on her hand. "So. How'd you meet her?"

As if coming to his rescue, Sydney and Elle barreled into the kitchen, oversized backpacks bouncing up and down on their shoulders.

"Daddy!" Elle yelled, throwing herself onto him. Ethan picked up the seven-year-old and nestled her onto his hip. "Wanna see my drawing? It's in my backpack. It's a dragon who's a princess." Sydney, just barely too old to be carried at nine but still buzzing for his attention, hovered next to them.

"Dad! Have you seen *Beetlejuice*? It's my favorite movie of all time. Can we watch it tonight?"

"I thought *Minions* was your favorite," Ethan commented, dropping Elle to the floor and ruffling her hair. Sydney rolled her eyes behind her violet frames.

"*Daad. Minions* is for babies."

"I like *Minions,*" Elle protested.

"Well, you're a *baby.*"

Elle stamped her foot. "Am *not.*"

"Are so."

Nora raised her eyebrows at him over the tops of their heads. "Enjoy them."

"Always do." He crouched down to their level. "I think we have time to watch *Beetlejuice and Minions*. How does that sound?"

Elle pouted. "*Beetlejuice* is too scary. It gave me bad dreams."

"Yeah, because you're a baby."

"Okay, that's enough," said Ethan, standing back up. "No more name-calling, Syd. Let's get in the car and we can work it out on the way home. How do you guys feel about pizza tonight?"

They both squealed and nodded vigorously in approval. He began to herd them toward the car. Nora followed them to the door. She leaned in to him, murmuring so the girls wouldn't hear.

"I'd love to meet her. When you're ready, of course."

Ethan jerked his head in something resembling a nod.

"You got it."

GREY PUSHED HER SHOPPING CART THROUGH GELSON'S, PAUSING to eye the antipasti bar. Heaping mounds of stuffed olives, marinated feta, and balsamic-glazed cipollini onions glistened back at her. Her stomach growled. She'd made the rookie mistake of going grocery shopping without eating beforehand. However, since the purpose of this trip was to stock up on snacks for a weekend on her couch with the complete Nora Ephron filmography, maybe it was better to let her whims guide her. She grabbed a plastic tub and started loading it with dolmas.

She was relieved to have a few days without Ethan while he was busy with his kids. Of course, not physically being in his presence didn't mean she was free of him completely. The day after their dinner date, curled up in bed with a debilitating hangover, she hadn't been able to think of anything else. Between napping, chugging coconut water, running to the bathroom, and brooding over every single thing she'd said and done the night before, she'd huddled under her comforter with her phone. Even though she was totally alone in the house, she felt like someone was about to burst in at any moment, rip off the covers, and expose her watching Ethan's Oscar acceptance speech over and over. Maybe that was what fame did to you: made you paranoid that none of your private moments would ever be private again.

Of course, she couldn't really call herself "famous" yet. Sure, her Instagram followers had already almost doubled, and their trip to the coffee shop would have quickly turned into a mob scene if there had been more than five people there at the time. Renata had even sent over a few scripts to look at over the weekend; not a mountain, but still more than the scraps she had been getting. But she didn't delude herself that this was the result of anything more than the proximity to Ethan's fame. He was the sun and she merely orbited around him, reflecting his incandescence.

It was all working out exactly according to plan. The queasy feeling she had watching twenty-four-year-old Ethan, shaggy hair falling over eyes wide with disbelief, embracing Sam, then Nora, before leaping onstage at the Kodak Theatre, was nothing to worry about. Probably just the hangover. He'd made it pretty clear that while he found her pleasant enough to pass the time with, any feelings she had for him stronger than polite indifference were decidedly unwelcome. Fine by her.

Grey circled around the bar, her eyes moving back and forth between the garlic and blue cheese–stuffed olives. She caught a movement out of the corner of her eye: a middle-aged mother pushing a baby in her cart, who immediately turned to inspect the frozen sausages to hide the fact that she'd been gaping at Grey. Grey gave her a warm half smile, which emboldened her to abandon the sausages and make her approach.

"Sorry, I didn't mean to stare. I just . . . you're Ethan Atkins's new girlfriend, aren't you?"

Grey nodded, still smiling, though her heart rate picked up. "That's me! I'm Grey. How's it going?"

Instead of returning her smile, the woman's eyes narrowed

and her face darkened. "I hope you treat him right. He's been through so much . . . he doesn't deserve another heartbreak."

Grey was stunned. She thought she must have misheard. "Um . . . I'm sorry? Do you . . . are you a friend of his?"

The woman got close enough that Grey instinctively clutched her olives tighter. She brandished her finger in Grey's face. "Don't you get cute with me. The last thing he needs is some gold-digging fame whore latching on to him and sucking him dry. You better watch yourself."

Grey's mind raced. Obviously the woman was totally out of line—but also, disturbingly close to the truth. She itched to tell the woman to mind her own business and return to the barn she was clearly raised in, but she had to play nice. Audrey would kill her if she made a scene. But below her indignation was a thrum of fear: *everybody knows. You're screwed.*

Grey turned to the antipasti bar, scooping a heaping spoonful of blue cheese olives into her plastic carton and grabbing a lid. She glanced back at the woman.

"I appreciate that you care so much about Ethan. I do, too. He's . . . a very special person. I'll let him know you send your regards, I'm sure it'll mean a lot to him that everyone is so invested in his well-being." To her relief, she managed to keep her voice from shaking.

Grey placed the olives in her shopping cart and pushed it authoritatively away from the woman before she had a chance to respond, thankfully making it to a deserted aisle before bursting into angry tears.

Ten minutes later, safely back in her Prius after hurriedly checking out, her phone rang. Pulling out of the parking lot, she hit the console button to answer the call. Renata's voice filled the car.

"Hey, pumpkin. This a good time?"

"Sure. What's up?" Grey realized too late that she still had cry voice.

"What's going on? Is everything okay? Do I need to send someone to kill that son of a bitch? I'll make it discreet, no one will ever trace it back to you." Renata's already loud voice amplified itself by several decibels. Grey raced to turn down the volume on the call.

"No, it's not Ethan. Well, not really." She recounted what had happened in the grocery store. Renata's response was instantaneous.

"*Fuck* her. You know that has nothing to do with you, right? She's probably been dating him in her twisted little head since his divorce. I'm sure she'd question the intentions of the goddamn Pope if they started dating."

Grey laughed despite herself. "I mean, I'd be a little suspicious of that couple, too."

"Regardless. I don't think you should worry too much that she speaks for the public about you two. Audrey told me they've been very pleased so far about how everything's going. Speaking of which, I'm on a *very* annoying email thread with her and that asshole Paul about next week. He's been making a stink, but we should be good to go."

They'd decided that Grey and Ethan's first red carpet appearance would be at the premiere of *Clutch,* a highly anticipated action/comedy that would serve as the big-budget debut of a well-regarded cult director. One of Grey's former *Poison Paradise* costars, Mia Pereira, had landed the female lead. Grey had read for the part, too, but hadn't held her breath. She'd never had any luck booking femme fatale sex bomb roles, though she sympathized with Mia (who'd played a similar type on the show) frequently lamenting that she was never sent anything else. She and Mia had never been that close, but Grey didn't begrudge her snagging a big break. If

Clutch was successful, it would propel her out of typecasting purgatory—unless it was *too* successful, and stuck her there for good.

The event would be high profile, but not high pressure, and Grey's connection to Mia was the perfect excuse for them to show up.

"What's Paul's problem?"

"He thinks it's still too early for you two to be stepping out in such a big way yet. Says it'll look fishy."

"I guess he kind of has a point. But Audrey doesn't think so?"

"No, they've been monitoring the public response closely. She says it's the perfect time."

"Great, looking forward to it." Grey overshot the perkiness in her voice, but Renata didn't call her on it. Instead, her voice lowered slightly.

"How are you doing with all of this? Is he treating you okay? How's his drinking?"

"Um, fine, I guess. So far mine has been worse, actually."

Renata made a disapproving noise. "Mmm. You should be rubbing off on him, not the other way around."

Actually, nobody's rubbing off on anybody.

"I'll do my best."

9

GREY AND ETHAN RODE TO THE PREMIERE IN SILENCE. THOUGH being in such close proximity to Ethan normally made Grey's head spin, tonight it was crystal clear. Being in public with him was easy. She was playing a part: the up-and-coming ingenue infatuated with her older, A-list paramour. Not the most original role, sure, but she'd had worse. He was just her costar, and she was a consummate professional. The boundaries of what was required of her were clear. It was when they were alone that things started to get muddled.

She knew the prospect of the red carpet was less appealing for Ethan. He was looking out the window, lips pressed into a thin line, the bags under his eyes more pronounced than usual. Other than that, however, she had to admit that for the first time since she'd met him, he looked every inch the matinee idol of yesteryear. He wore a flawlessly tailored dark gray suit, no tie, and had shaved his omnipresent stubble, revealing the contours of his cheekbones and the hard angles of his jaw. His long legs were spread wide on the seat, one of his ankles loosely balanced on his other knee, bouncing with barely concealed nervous energy.

She'd accepted Audrey's offer of professional styling, and had spent the preceding five hours being primped, prodded, buffed, and smoothed. The final product was worth it, though. After clashing with the hairstylist over whether they should heat-style her waves, which had finally started to recover after years of being fried daily on *Poison Paradise,* Grey had relented, allowing her hair to be straightened and slicked back into a low, glossy ponytail. The stylist had brought in two racks of clothing that probably cost more than Grey's car. They'd settled on a silky midnight-blue jumpsuit, whose modest long sleeves were counteracted by the fact that it was practically cut down to her navel. The color of the jumpsuit, combined with whatever witchcraft the makeup artist had worked on her face, made her eyes seem preternaturally blue.

She couldn't help but preen in front of the mirror once they'd finished. It had been months since she'd been professionally styled. She'd forgotten she could look this good. She had all but strutted out to the Bentley when Ethan had arrived to pick her up, and refused to be deflated when he barely flicked his eyes over at her. It didn't matter what he thought. She was already in character.

As Ozzy pulled into the long line of luxury cars waiting to eject their famous contents onto the red carpet, Ethan turned to look at her for the first time. His eyes swept over her, taking her in from head to toe. She met his eyes, chin tilted up, refusing to let herself be flustered by the intensity of his gaze. They stared at each other for what felt like minutes. Though she felt a little childish having an impromptu staring contest with an almost forty-year-old man, Grey refused to look away first.

Finally, Ethan smirked, raised his eyebrows, and looked back out the window. Grey did the same. A question rose in her throat and she considered swallowing it down, but her propriety won out over her pride.

"Do we need a game plan?" she murmured, low enough that Ozzy wouldn't hear. Ethan's eyes flicked back over to her. Lazily, he uncrossed his legs and slowly leaned over her, his lips brushing her ear. She froze, her skin buzzing with the knowledge that if she turned her face a millimeter to the left, his newly smooth cheek would be pressed against hers. The rule about his proximity not disconcerting her anymore apparently only applied when there was enough room between them for the Holy Spirit. Once he got close enough, however, it was clear that the only spirit he'd been acquainted with lately was decidedly earthly.

"I was thinking," he drawled, his breath hot on her neck and unmistakably oozing with bourbon. "We get out of the car . . . walk into that building . . . watch the movie . . . and go home. How does that sound, *baby*?" The term of endearment dripped with sarcasm, making her stomach roil.

She reared back against the door, trying to communicate the extent of her disapproval through her expression alone as she mouthed silently: *Are you* drunk?

He cast his eyes down and slumped back into his corner of the back seat. Grey rolled her eyes. Fucking perfect.

At that moment, a clipboard-carrying production assistant flung open the door, and Grey was lost in a field of flashes. The next thing she knew, her body was flush against Ethan's with his arm snug around her waist, and the two were smiling and posing in front of a gaping, faceless abyss that howled their names. Well, mostly his name. Grey smiled and leaned into him, rising up on her toes as if to whisper sweet nothings in his ear.

"You've been smoking again."

He laughed and looked at her with what could easily pass as

genuine adoration. Through a gritted smile, he replied, "What are you gonna do? Tell on me to Audrey?"

Grey tilted back her head and laughed as if that was the funniest joke she'd ever heard, making sure to angle her face so the cameras caught her good side. Ethan stepped aside to give Grey a moment to pose solo, showing off her glam squad's handiwork. He then grabbed her hand and whisked her down the carpet toward the huddle of TV correspondents, who practically started trampling one another to get to him. Sadie Boyd, the tenacious host of *Hollywood Tonight,* pushed her way to the front of the throng, all sharp elbows and sparkling veneers.

"Ethan! Long time! Do you have a minute?"

Ethan grinned at her. "For you, Sadie? I have two."

Sadie cackled even louder than Grey had pretended to a moment ago. Her cameraman had finally caught up to her and she contorted her body to face all three of them at once. "So, Ethan! You've been a hard man to pin down over the last few years. I think I speak for everyone when I say I'm *thrilled* to see you back on the red carpet."

Ethan turned to the camera, practically glowing. He looked ten years younger than he had in the car. Grey couldn't believe what she was seeing. She hadn't needed to worry. "Thank you, Sadie. Very happy to be here."

"Tell me, I think we're all *dying* to know: to what do we owe your miraculous reappearance?"

Ethan turned to Grey and wrapped his arm around her shoulders, and she instinctively snaked hers around his waist in return. "This girl right here. *Woman.* Sorry. This . . . amazing woman." His eyes sparkled as he looked at her, crinkling at the corners. Damn. He really was a good actor.

He turned back to Sadie. "You know Grey, right?"

Sadie focused her attention on Grey without missing a beat.

"Grey Brooks, of course! *Poison Paradise*! Huge fan. And your former costar, Mia Pereira, is having her big night tonight. But what about you? Do you have anything exciting on the horizon?"

Grey smiled coyly. "Nothing I can talk about yet. Right now, I'm just . . . enjoying myself." She reached up and stroked Ethan's cheek. He turned his face into her hand and planted a soft kiss on her palm, his eyes never leaving hers. The brush of his lips sent a delicious jolt of electricity through her.

"Well, the two of you are just *too* cute," Sadie gushed. "I can't wait to see what you get up to in the future. Maybe working together is in the cards?"

"I'd love to," Ethan replied instantly. "She's incredibly talented."

Grey lowered her eyes bashfully. "Oh, stop it," she said, giving him a playful push.

Ethan laughed. "We'd better go before I embarrass her too much. Great talking to you, Sadie."

He took Grey's hand again and ushered her past the rest of the reporters, through the VIP entrance into the roped-off lobby of the theater. Dozens of people milled around, sipping complimentary champagne, but miraculously, nobody tried to approach them. They retreated into a corner.

"Laying it on a little thick, don't you think?" Grey muttered.

Ethan craned his neck, as if looking for someone. "I have no idea what you mean."

"How do you know if I'm talented? Have you even seen anything I've done?" The words slipped out more brattily than she'd intended, revealing a glimmer of bruised ego underneath.

"Sure I have. Just now. You were perfect."

Ethan zeroed in on his target, flagging down a waiter and plucking two glasses of champagne from his tray. He offered one to Grey, who shook her head. He shrugged and poured the contents of one into the other, discarding the empty glass on a nearby ledge. Before he could take a drink, Grey snatched the flute out of his hand.

"This isn't fucking cute," she hissed, brandishing it at him, a few drops splashing out of the precariously full rim. "You can't be a mess tonight. I'm not cleaning it up."

He stared at her from under hooded eyes. She expected him to retort, but his gaze slid sideways, focusing on something behind her. She whirled around to see what he was looking at, and her stomach sank.

Callum Hendrix appeared through the throng, his arm slung possessively around the mononymous Peyton, a wide-eyed and excruciatingly wholesome pop star infamous for revealing her exes' dirty laundry in her thinly veiled lyrics. Thankfully, it seemed like neither of them had clocked Grey and Ethan lurking in the corner. Grey briefly considered finding a way to warn Peyton what she was getting into, but thought better of it. There was no way Peyton wasn't aware of his reputation. She must be in it for the material. If there was anyone who deserved to be the subject of a scathing album or two, it was Callum.

She quickly turned to Ethan, her back blocking both of them from view.

"Fuck," she muttered. Of course he would be here; practically the whole cast was here. She took a long swig of the champagne and closed her eyes, concentrating on the feeling of the chilled fizz sliding down her throat, the bubbles working their way up to soothe her frazzled brain.

She'd been prepared to return to *Poison Paradise*'s fifth season with her head held high and her lips sealed about how unenthused she was to be working with Callum every day for the next nine months, only to discover after receiving the script for the premiere that his character would be suffering a tragic (and fatal) accident

involving his motorcycle and a not-quite-frozen lake in the opening scene. She felt a little guilty about letting her personal life spill
over into her work—but not guilty enough to stop her from sending an *extremely* expensive gift basket to the writers' room the next
day.

Callum had made it clear that he blamed her for getting him
written off the show, and his fans had harassed her online for
months. Never mind that his increasingly difficult behavior over
the previous two seasons had already made him unpopular with
the producers. In a fitting bookend to their first meeting, the last
time she'd seen him was at the table read for his final episode, pretending not to notice him glaring daggers at her over their scripts.

Grey opened her eyes again and saw Ethan was watching her.
He extended a hand to her.

"Should we go to our seats?"

She took it gratefully.

"Yes, please."

ETHAN COULDN'T SIT STILL. HE'D SPENT APPROXIMATELY HALF
of the 110-minute runtime fidgeting, squirming, and sighing in his
seat. His internal battle over whether to slip out to the bar for another drink, or respect Grey's wishes and sober up a little, was
spilling out through his tapping fingers and restless feet. He could
tell Grey was ready to murder him. By the time the movie was
nearing its end, she'd clamped her hand firmly over his and an-
chored it to the armrest between them. Surprisingly, it worked.
Something stilled inside him at the pressure of her forearm covering his, her attention never straying from the screen.

He snuck a look over at her, the flickering light of the screen
casting shadows across her elegant profile, her long neck bared by
her ponytail. He couldn't remember the last time he had found

something as innocent as a woman's neck so profoundly erotic. But it wasn't just any woman's neck: it was Grey's neck. He imagined leaning over and touching his lips to the tender spot just below where her jaw met her ear. Ethan already knew how she would react; her eyes would widen, her breath would hitch. He would part his lips to taste her racing pulse and maybe she would moan a little in the back of her throat, the same noise she'd made when she'd tasted the wine at dinner. He shifted again in his seat, for a different reason this time.

As if she could feel the heat of his gaze burning into her, she turned to look at him, her eyes narrowing. He quickly turned back to look at the screen. The movie wasn't half bad, actually, when he was able to focus on it. However, his renewed attention was too little, too late, as the credits began to roll and the audience applauded.

Ethan let out a sigh of relief. He made it. Now all he had to do was deposit Grey and her provocative neck safely back at her house, go home, jerk off, and drink himself to sleep without disappointing anyone. Another successful evening.

His well-laid plans were immediately disrupted when Grey turned to him and said with steely determination, "We're going to the after-party."

"No fucking way," he murmured as they stood up and started to make their way through the slow-moving mass of people trying to exit the theater.

"We need to *network*," she whispered through a smile, low enough that only he could hear it. "We can shut ourselves in your little depression cave the rest of the month if you want. Tonight we need to *talk* to people."

"You go, then. I'm going home."

"Fine. I hope you're working on what you're going to say to Audrey tomorrow when she sees the pictures of me there alone."

They were back in the lobby now. He grabbed her arm and pulled her into another secluded corner so they could talk more freely.

"It's not a breach of contract."

"No, it just makes you look like a dick."

"I *am* a dick; you haven't figured that out yet?"

She looked up at him, her eyes impossibly blue. "I don't think you're a dick. I think you're afraid."

He flinched. As usual, she was right. Was she that observant, or was he just completely transparent? He wasn't sure which one unnerved him more.

"Thirty minutes. Forty-five, max. Then I'm leaving."

Grey seemed to realize that their body language at the moment didn't exactly scream "true love," so she reached out and took both his hands in hers, drawing him closer.

"Thank you," she murmured, leaning up and brushing her lips to his cheek. She smelled fresh and sweet, like a garden after a summer storm. He tightened his grip on her hands, willing them to behave and not break free to traverse her body, her hair, her face. He had to touch her, it was part of the deal. But he couldn't touch her the way he wanted to. It was fucking torture. She looked up at him with a questioning glance, and he released her hands before he broke her fingers. He shoved one traitorous hand into his pocket and dug out his phone with the other, turning his body away from her.

"I'll have Ozzy bring the car around."

THE AFTER-PARTY WAS AROUND THE CORNER AT A TRENDY ART deco cocktail bar, decorated with plush pink velvet booths and gold hardware. The party was already in full swing when the two of them arrived. After posing for photographs at the entrance,

Ethan peeled off from Grey and made a beeline for the bar. Grey grabbed a skewer of something colorful and complicated off a waiter's tray and surveyed the room. She spotted Mia in a corner booth, surrounded by fawning admirers.

As soon as Mia saw her approach, her face lit up, and she shooed the people next to her out of the booth so she could get out and greet Grey. Mia successfully extracted herself and flung herself into Grey's arms. Grey could tell by the enthusiasm of the greeting that Mia was already hammered, but she appreciated it anyway.

"Congratulations! It was so *good*! *You* were so good! You killed it!" Grey gushed, rocking back and forth in Mia's arms. She pulled back to admire her. "And you look fucking *hot,* god*damn*." Mia's bronze curves had been poured into a second-skin pink latex minidress, perfectly complementing the décor of the restaurant.

"Thank yooou," Mia cooed. "But what about *you,* rolling up with motherfucking *Ethan Atkins*? If I didn't know better, I'd say you were trying to upstage me at my own damn premiere."

Grey laughed, putting her hand on her chest in mock offense. "What? Never!"

"That's so *you,* though. You never come out, but when you come out you come *out*."

Grey was about to protest, but realized Mia was right. After she and Callum had broken up, she'd stopped going out to party with the cast, or at all. At first, she'd just wanted to lie low and lick her wounds in private, but soon she became accustomed to the quiet nights at home. After a while, going out seemed irresponsible, another opportunity to be photographed doing something stupid. Another day wasted nursing a hangover. Sometimes she tagged along with Kamilah's other friends, but even back in college, the two of them had been more staying-in friends than going-out friends. Since she'd been gone, Grey had spent most nights home alone. She felt a twinge of guilt at accusing Ethan of hiding away and avoiding the world: to a lesser extent, she'd been doing the same thing.

A few men in suits came up to congratulate Mia, who introduced them to Grey as the *Clutch* producers. Grey fell into easy conversation with them as Mia turned away to greet another well-wisher. An elaborate pink cocktail found its way into her hand, then another, as the group around her ebbed and flowed. Grey was surprised by how much she was enjoying herself. She let herself flirt with one of the producers, lightly resting her hand on his chest, laughing a little too loudly. As much as she hated to admit it, this *was* part of her career, a part she'd been neglecting.

Throughout it all, Ethan remained absent. Grey was kind of relieved. Though he'd been on his best behavior (so far) while they were on display, everything else he'd done tonight had seemed designed to push her buttons, rile her up, force her to chastise him and keep him in line. When she'd caught him staring at her during the movie, his expression was pained and—resentful? Hostile? Whatever it was, it wasn't her problem.

She was midconversation with Mia and one of their other former *Poison Paradise* castmates when she heard an all-too-familiar voice behind her.

"Having a reunion without me?"

Grey stiffened. She didn't bother turning to look at him, but Callum edged his way into the group anyway. God, he was so sleazy. She couldn't believe she'd ever been attracted to him, let alone loved him. His greasy, slicked-back hair and shit-eating grin made her stomach turn.

"Where's your boyfriend, Grey? Didn't I see him over by the bar?" Callum drawled.

"Sounds like you just answered your own question," she replied, keeping her voice impassive.

"Aww, don't be like that. I thought we were cool now." He tried to put his arm around her shoulders, but she instantly shrugged it off, still refusing to look at him.

"So, Mia, did you do all of your own stunts? That fight on top of the semi was insane." Grey's voice was too loud, begging Mia to rescue her.

"Yeah, actually, I—" Mia started. Callum cut in again, interrupting her. He was obviously drunk, too, his breath hot and rancid.

"You look really good tonight. Did he buy this for you?" He stretched out a finger toward her chest to brush the gaping expanse of skin exposed by her jumpsuit, as if he was trying to slip it inside her neckline. Grey jumped back like his touch had singed her. She looked past him into the crowd.

"Isn't that Peyton? Why aren't you over there bothering her?"

"I told her I needed a minute to catch up with some old friends."

"Well, don't let us keep you. Hope you find them!" Grey gave him a sickly sweet smile and tried to turn her back to him as much as possible.

Mia snorted. Callum leaned in too close, trying to speak with her out of earshot of the others. She recoiled. He twisted his face into what he probably thought looked like earnestness, but actually looked like constipation.

"Listen. Grey. I never told you . . . I was a fucking idiot."

"You didn't need to tell me, I figured that one out on my own."

"No, I mean . . . I should never have treated you like that. It was a huge mistake."

"Cool. Thanks." Grey tried to turn away from him again, but

he grabbed her arm and twisted it back. She broke his grip with force this time, anger flaring. "I swear, if you *fucking* touch me again, Callum—"

He held his hands up in surrender, backing away as if she had exploded. "Whoa. Calm down. I was just trying to apologize."

"Oh, really? Because I didn't hear 'I'm sorry' anywhere in there. Save it for your Notes app."

Callum opened his mouth to respond, but words seemed to fail him, leaving him gaping at something behind her.

Grey felt Ethan before she saw him. A solid wall at her shoulder, one hand warming the silk at her hip. Before she had time to process what was happening, the fingers of his other hand were beneath her chin, tilting her face up and back to press her lips against his.

It wasn't a passionate kiss, and from an outside perspective, probably looked downright mundane. It was the kind of kiss that suggested easy intimacy, no different from the hundred that had preceded it and the hundred that would follow. To Grey, however, it was a cosmic event, sending liquid fire rippling through her belly. She was grateful for his sturdy presence behind her as she leaned into him to stop her knees from buckling, more from surprise than from anything else. Instinctively, she reached her hand up to his face, lightly grazing his jaw with her fingertips.

It only lasted a moment: a firm brush of his soft lips. However, in the split second before he pulled away, he gently pulled her lower lip between his teeth in a small but unmistakable bite, sending another bolt of pleasure directly between her legs.

Grey looked up at him, dazed, her face hot. He pressed his forehead to hers and murmured: "Let's get out of here."

She couldn't do anything but nod. He moved his hand away from her hip and she felt regret at the sudden rush of cold air that took its place. She expected him to take her hand in his, but instead he settled it at the small of her back. He started to guide her away before turning back to offer a curt "congratulations" to Mia.

As they swept out of the bar, the pressure of his hand sending tingles up her spine, a thought emerged in Grey's mind with alarming clarity. She felt like an idiot for not realizing it sooner.

He wasn't being difficult because he disliked her.

He was being difficult because he liked her a little too much.

10

OVER THE NEXT MONTH, THEY SETTLED INTO SOMETHING RE-sembling a routine. Once a week, they made a brief, cordial public appearance: hiking in the canyon, laughing over cold-pressed juices, browsing through the farmers market, sitting courtside at the Lakers. They showed up everywhere you'd expect the hottest Hollywood it-couple to be seen, taking pictures, signing autographs, gazing lovingly into each other's eyes.

On the other contractually obligated nights, Grey would let herself into Ethan's house. Most of the time, he would already be shut up in his office. Sometimes she'd leave the next morning without seeing him at all. Against all odds, however, she'd started feeling more at home there. She passed the time reading, working on her screenplay, watching movies on his extremely complicated television whose operation she had *almost* mastered, or creating her own *Chopped* challenges out of the bizarre combinations of ingredients she dug out of his fridge and pantry.

They rarely spoke when not in public, their initial overtures toward friendship mutually abandoned; and when they did, it was bland small talk. They never brought up the kiss. After they'd left the premiere party and gotten back into the car, Ethan had immediately slouched against the window in the back seat, eyes closed, refusing to acknowledge her. Now, however, his evasion didn't rankle her the way it had at the beginning. Instead, it sent a smug little thrill through her every time she heard his footsteps in the hallway, the doors to his office and his bedroom opening and shutting, like she was being haunted by the Ghost of Sexual Frustration Past.

He was avoiding her because he wanted her.

Sure, he wasn't handling it in the most mature way, but he was a celebrity. Everyone knew celebrities' development permanently arrested at the age they became famous. Given the degree and longevity of his fame, she was just grateful he wasn't pulling her hair and pushing her down in the sandbox.

Actually, minus the sandbox, that didn't sound so bad.

But what, really, was the alternative? Their arrangement would be over in a few months. The thought of this turning into a real relationship was laughable. As much as she hated to admit it to the starry-eyed thirteen-year-old who still dwelled somewhere inside her, she couldn't ignore the mounting evidence that Ethan Atkins was a self-centered, self-loathing, emotionally stunted alcoholic. Nothing good could come of acting on their attraction. Besides, the majority of the allure was surely wrapped up in the tension, in the heated, forbidden glances, in the knowledge that nothing could—or should—ever happen between them. As long as he was steering clear of her because he was afraid of the temptation she offered, and not because he found her completely revolting, she didn't care if he never spoke a word to her in private again. Really, she didn't. It was easier this way.

That didn't stop her from replaying the kiss over and over in her mind, though. It had quickly replaced her Oscar acceptance speech as her fantasy of choice as she drifted off to sleep. In her version, instead of quickly releasing her, he would pull her into his arms, deepening the kiss, fulfilling the promise of those hungry looks he gave her when he thought she wasn't looking. He would cup her ass and lift her onto one of the tables like she weighed nothing, and she would wrap her legs around him, grinding into the hard heat of his arousal. The neckline of her jumpsuit had been cut low enough that she'd had to go braless that night. It would have been so easy for him to slip his hand inside and free her breast, dipping his mouth down to cover the nipple already hard and aching for his touch.

"We shouldn't . . . everyone's watching . . ." she'd gasp.

He'd bring his face back up to meet hers, grasping her jaw with both hands, plunging his bourbon-soaked tongue back into her mouth with such force that she would feel it in her toes.

"I don't fucking care," he'd growl. "Let them watch. I need you. Now."

She had already burned through two sets of batteries in her vibrator in the last two weeks. What she really needed was to get laid, preferably by someone who wasn't terrified of what would happen if he spent more than five minutes alone with her. Other than a mediocre one-night stand nearly two years ago in a drunken attempt at a rebound, there'd been no one since Callum. Unfortunately, that desire carried a million-dollar price tag. Replacing the batteries was cheaper—for now.

ONE MORNING, ABOUT A MONTH AND A HALF INTO THEIR AR-rangement, Grey was scrounging through Ethan's barer-than-usual fridge trying to decide if she'd have better luck attempting an omelet or a smoothie for breakfast. Ethan's front door slammed open, surprising Grey so much that she almost dropped the jar of expired cocktail onions she was holding.

The intruder—a tall, gangly man who appeared to be in his early twenties—looked startled, too, but quickly regained his composure. "Oh. Hi. Sorry, I didn't think—you must be Grey."

He walked into the kitchen, placing the two overflowing reusable grocery bags on the island. He extended his hand to her. "I'm Lucas."

Grey raised her eyebrows, reaching her hand out to shake his. "Lucas! Nice to finally meet you outside of my phone."

Lucas grinned, beginning to unpack the bags. Grey went to help him, pulling out a loaf of crusty sourdough and a tub of fancy herbed goat cheese. Her mouth started to water.

"Ethan prefers that I keep myself scarce. You know how he is."

"Oh, I know. This place would fall apart without you, though."

Lucas gave a deep curtsy, arms spread wide. Grey laughed and applauded obligingly. "Nice to be appreciated. Hold on, gotta make one more trip."

He darted back out the front door and quickly returned, balancing several cases of beer in his arms.

"Guess it's party time," Grey muttered under her breath. Lucas shot her a quick look. She toyed with the idea of saying something to him, seeing how much he knew, what he thought. Her courage failed, and instead she asked: "So, how did you land this dream job?"

Lucas went back to unloading the rest of the groceries. "Good old-fashioned nepotism, actually. Ethan's my uncle."

Grey couldn't hide her shock. "Oh! Oh. I had no idea. He never mentioned it. He, um, doesn't talk about his family much."

Or about anything at all. Now that she knew to look for it, though, there was an undeniable resemblance between the two of them.

He shrugged. "I don't really take it personally. I might be the only member of our family he talks to regularly. I kinda think my mom made him hire me just so I can keep an eye on him."

"I knew it," Ethan's voice proclaimed drily behind them. Grey turned around to see him padding over, barefoot, hair still wet from the shower, T-shirt clinging to his damp torso. "Once an older sister, always an older sister. What's in the report this week?"

He was in a good mood today. Grey never knew which Ethan she would get: surly, flirty, charming, distant. Sometimes she got them all in the same night. She didn't take it personally anymore. His issues predated her, and they would still be there once she was out of his life. Still, as he cupped her face with his hands and planted a soft kiss on her forehead—obviously for Lucas's benefit—she wished that this Ethan would show up more often.

"She'll be thrilled to hear I finally met your new girlfriend. She's been on my ass about it for weeks."

Ethan released Grey and moved around the island, opening a plastic clamshell of cherry tomatoes and popping one into his mouth. "And?"

"Way too good for you."

Ethan shrugged. "He's right."

Grey rolled an apple from one hand to another, feeling fidgety. "As long as we're all on the same page."

Lucas unloaded the last few items from the bags and folded them under his arm. "If you don't need anything else, I'll get out of your hair."

"All good," Ethan said curtly, going to the fridge without giving him a second look.

Lucas nodded. "Nice to meet you, Grey."

"You, too. Thank you so much for everything. Really," she replied pointedly.

"Anytime," he called as he headed out the door, leaving the two of them alone.

There was a long moment of silence. Ethan had his head in the fridge for so long that Grey wondered if he was counting every individual egg. She stared at the apple in her hand, contemplating the best way to make her exit.

When Ethan finally spoke, he spoke to the fridge. "Seems like my manners need some work." His tone was even, awaiting her censure. She refused to rise to the bait.

"He's very sweet."

"Guess it skipped a generation."

Grey was glad his back was still toward her so he couldn't see her roll her eyes. She wasn't getting out of this interaction without fluffing his ego a little. She internally swore she would never let herself reach this level of insecure celebrity.

"You can be sweet. When you want to be."

He shut the fridge door without removing anything, turning to face her.

"What are you up to today?" His tone was casual but his eyes searched her face.

"Um, nothing much. I was just about to head out." She kept her answer purposely vague, unsure where he was going.

"Want to stick around for breakfast? I'm full of ingredients. I could cook you something."

Grey felt her stomach twist. Of course she wanted him to cook her breakfast. She wanted to ogle his forearms while he chopped vegetables and tease him about his egg-flipping technique and brush his knee with hers as they ate, like they were a real couple. But she knew that doing that would only make his inevitable sullen withdrawal start to sting again.

"I don't . . . I appreciate the offer. But I really should get going."

Ethan's brow creased. In that moment, he looked like a forlorn little boy. She felt a pang in her chest at turning him down.

"Are you sure?" he asked, almost pitiful.

She slid off the stool next to the island and picked up her overnight bag.

"I . . . yeah. Sorry. Thanks, though. I'll see you in a couple of days."

She slung the bag over her shoulder.

"Do you regret it?"

He wasn't looking at her, instead focusing intently on a small crack in the countertop.

"Regret what?" she replied, confused.

"This. Me." He met her eyes. "I can buy you out of the contract if you want. No hard feelings. I'll take the heat from Audrey."

They held eye contact for a fraught moment before she burst out laughing. She dropped her bag on the floor and strode back to the kitchen island.

"Jesus Christ, fine, I'll have breakfast with you, you big drama queen."

Ethan let out an indignant exhalation. "I'm not—you don't have to—" he stammered. Grey held up her hand to stop him and sat authoritatively back down on the stool.

"Nope. I'm here. I'm hungry. What are you making me?" She propped her elbows on the table and set her chin in her hands, blinking innocently. Ethan opened his mouth again, then closed it and turned back to the fridge.

"Sweet or savory?"

A smile played at the corners of Grey's mouth. "I guess I know better than to ask for sweet."

———

HIS OFFER OF BREAKFAST HAD BEEN KIND OF A BLUFF, ACTU-
ally. He cooked for Elle and Sydney sometimes when they were
there, but it wasn't anything special. He wasn't sure what had compelled him to blurt it out. Grey had something of a stupefying effect on him. So far, avoiding her as much as possible had been the
most surefire way to prevent him from doing anything rash—like
barely stopping short of dropping to his knees and begging her not
to walk out his front door. At least it was better than throwing her
over his shoulder and carrying her to his bedroom like a caveman.

When he heard voices in the kitchen that morning, he'd
thought about hiding in his room until they departed, but that
seemed too childish, even for him. This was his house, after all.
When he walked in to find her lounging in his kitchen, sunlight
glinting off her hair, laughing with Lucas, something had shifted
inside him. He was *happy* to see her there. He would've said anything to make her stay for even ten more minutes.

Ethan at least had the presence of mind to be a little embarrassed that he'd gone so far as to offer to break the contract. What
would he have done if she'd said yes? As disquieting as her presence
was, the prospect of the alternative was much worse. Thankfully,
she had just laughed that smoky, bewitching laugh, gently teased
him at his outburst, and planted herself back where she belonged.

Where she belonged.

Ethan didn't give that thought time to settle before he pushed
it out in favor of the task at hand: breakfast.

"Eggs? I can do scrambled, or . . . scrambled."

Grey laughed again. "Slow down, I'm overwhelmed." She
popped off the stool and came up beside him, his skin prickling at
her proximity. She smelled, like always, of flowers, but there was

something else lingering underneath, warm and earthy and unmistakably Grey. She opened the pantry and pulled out a fresh loaf of sourdough bread. "I don't know about you, but I've been thinking about breakfast sandwiches ever since I saw this."

She tossed it to him and he caught it.

"Sounds good to me."

She went over to the fridge now, and he practically jumped out of her way to avoid grazing her forearm. She began pulling out ingredients and setting them on the counter.

"Hey!" He shooed her back to the other side of the island. "That's my job."

"Fine. Don't forget the avocado."

Twenty minutes later, they headed out to Ethan's patio, overlooking the pool. Ethan carried the plates with the sandwiches, while Grey followed behind with coffee—iced for her, hot for him. They settled across from each other at the slate table, shaded by the jutting roof. Ethan had left the sandwiches open-faced, each one topped with a glistening fried egg. He'd insisted that Grey take the one he hadn't accidentally broken while flipping, and as she pressed the other slice of toasted sourdough on top, the bright yellow yolk oozed over the sides.

"I think you nailed it," she said, wrapping her hands around the sandwich, careful to steer clear of the dripping yolk.

"Taste it first. Looks can be deceiving."

Grey lifted the sandwich to her mouth and bit into it. With the pressure of the bite, more egg yolk spurted out, dripping onto her fingers.

"Oh, fuck," she murmured, dropping the sandwich back onto the plate and bringing her hand to her mouth. Seemingly without thinking, she dipped her slender fingers into her mouth, one at a time, closing her lips around them and sucking them clean.

Ethan gawked at her, his own sandwich untouched, halfway to his mouth. When she realized he was staring, she blushed, dropping her hand to her napkin to finish the job.

"Sorry. That was gross."

Ethan swallowed, his mouth dry, words failing him. "Um. No. It's fine. Not gross." He took an enormous bite of his own sandwich to prevent him from saying anything else.

They ate in comfortable silence for a few minutes. Grey put down her sandwich for a breather and leaned back in her chair, clasping her iced coffee in both hands and staring out at the pool.

"Did you hear anything about your big movie yet?" Ethan asked.

She turned to look back at him. "What? Oh. Not yet. I'm supposed to have a chemistry read in a week or two, Renata said I should hear any day now."

"Do you have the pages?"

"Nah. You know how it is. Top secret. I don't really get it—the book's been out for, like, a year. How secret can it be?" She leaned over her plate to take another bite of her sandwich.

"If you need to run lines or anything, I can do it. When you get them, I mean."

She looked at him with surprise. "Really?"

He shrugged. "Sure. That's what this is all for, right? Your dream role? It's the least I can do."

Grey leaned back again, stretching her legs wide and sipping her iced coffee. She looked contemplative. "It's not my dream role. I mean, getting it would be amazing. The part itself is kind of whatever, though."

He raised his eyebrows. "So . . . what? It's just about being part of the next big thing?" Maybe he'd read her wrong, after all. Maybe she was just in it for the fame for fame's sake.

"Not like that. I'd never want to be you-famous. No offense."

He laughed. "None taken. I wouldn't want to be me-famous, either."

"Yeah, yeah, we're all crying our eyes out for you," she said with a sardonic grin, gesturing vaguely toward the house, the pool, the view. "I just want to get to the point where I have more . . ." She trailed off.

"Money? Cars? Awards? Instagram followers?" he rattled off.

"Control," she said, the corner of her mouth twitching slightly.

Ethan leaned back, too, running his fingers through his hair. "Control is a hard thing to come by in this business. Whenever you think you've gained some, it usually turns out you've just given it up from somewhere else."

She turned and looked him in the eyes. "That's deep," she teased.

He laughed and gave a little half shrug. "Hey, that's just my experience. Take it or leave it."

"No, no, I know you're right. I've just— Kamilah and I have been trying to get our stupid movie made forever. We did what you're supposed to, got some money together and made our own little low-budget thing, did the festivals, won some awards— nothing. No one will produce it. I'd give up some control to have the power to make that happen." She gestured at him. "I mean, I guess I already did."

The reminder that she wasn't sitting there with him by choice sent an odd twinge through him. He ignored it.

"What's your movie?"

She shifted, bashful. "It's based on this book, *The Empty Chair*. Do you know it?" He shook his head and she continued. "It's this weird experimental horror novel from the twenties. Kind of like a Jazz Age *Suspiria*. Kamilah and I were obsessed with it in college."

"You went to college?"

Grey seemed like she wasn't sure if she should be offended. "Yeah, USC. Why, is that surprising?"

"No. Well, yes, sort of. You said you were a child star, so I just assumed. I mean, no judgment either way. *I* didn't go."

"'Star' is pretty generous. And I didn't finish. I booked my show the spring of my junior year. I tried to keep going part-time, but it was too much. I had to drop out."

"Do you ever think about going back?"

She shook her head. "Not really. The degree was never that important to me. I wanted to broaden my horizons a little, see what else was out there for me besides acting. Turns out, not much."

"But not nothing. You found that book. And your friend."

She looked at him, as if appraising him for the first time. "Yeah. That's true." She paused, her gaze drifting away. When she spoke again, it seemed like she was talking to the pool, rather than to him.

"I didn't even plan on majoring in film, I was just doing the gen ed thing at first. I was never really that into school; I missed a lot when I was working. I had no idea what I wanted to study. Intro to Film ended up being the only elective that fit into my schedule my first semester. That's how I met Kamilah, actually. We had to do a group project for our final, and the two of us ended up doing all the work."

Ethan snorted. "God. Group projects. I was always useless at those."

"Color me shocked." She took another sip of coffee. "But it was fascinating. Putting it all into context. Like, I had been on set a ton, obviously, but I'd never really thought about movies as art, as culture, as history. Breaking them down from every angle, how all the different elements add up to the whole, beyond my part in it as an actor. It just reinforced that this was the only thing I wanted

to do. Unfortunately." She laughed sardonically. "And then I immediately booked a series, so that went down the drain. Not that
I'm complaining. But I would love to make something that gets
taught in film schools one day. *Make* it, not just be in it."

She looked down and fidgeted a little in her seat, as if caught
off-guard by her own earnestness. "Do you wish you'd gone? You
still could, it's not too late."

Ethan laughed. "Yeah, I'd blend right in with all the freshmen.
I think that window has closed."

"You could do online classes or something. What else are you
doing with your time?"

Something in the air shifted slightly. Grey seemed to realize
that she had misstepped and quickly tried to recover. "I feel like
I've been talking about myself for, like, an hour. What about you?
What's your big comeback project?"

Ethan suddenly wanted a cigarette. He let out a long exhale,
practically a sigh. She toyed with her napkin, clearly unsure if
she'd said the wrong thing.

He considered deflecting the question, but hesitated. If he was
going to do it, he needed to be able to talk about it.

"Sam and I—" He cleared his throat, the words coming out
more choked than he intended. "Sam and I . . . we'd started working on something." He paused. She stared at him, very still, as if
trying not to spook a wild animal. "We bought the rights to this
Korean movie we both loved. The option expires next year."

"What's the movie? Would I know it?"

"*Bitter Pill*?"

He expected her to give him a blank look in return, but instead her eyes flashed with recognition. "Oh, yeah, the one with
the brothers who murder their dad? I think we watched that in one
of my classes. Kind of a bummer."

Ethan snorted. "Yeah. I guess you could say that."

Grey seemed like she was about to say something, but instead sipped her coffee. "What?" he prodded.

She shrugged. "Nothing. I mean . . . there are some good remakes," she said diplomatically.

"It's not a remake. It's an adaptation," he retorted, more defensively than he intended.

"Right. Of course. Sorry. I'm being such an asshole. You two have an amazing track record, I'm sure it'll be great."

"You mean *had,*" Ethan said softly, almost to himself. "It's just me now."

Grey looked at him with those big limpid eyes, dripping with that familiar expression of sympathy he'd long ago come to loathe. Somehow it seemed less cloying when it came from her. It transformed the pervasive ache inside him into something different, harder to define. She put her hand on the table and hesitated, as if she wanted to touch him but thought better of it.

"I'm so sorry, Ethan. I can't imagine."

He didn't respond, just swallowed hard and stared out at the pool. Despite the best efforts of the coffee and sandwich, his hangover was beginning to creep over him, the sun glinting a little too brightly off the water.

"It's fine. It's been five years. It's time," he said, his voice hollow and mechanical.

"For whatever it's worth, I . . . I think you're really brave to finish it. If something happened to Kamilah . . . I don't know what I would do. I don't think I could even look at our script again. Ever."

Ethan was startled at the tremor in her voice, the cordial distance that had been present since their disastrous dinner date nowhere to be found. He let himself meet her gaze, which was so full of compassion that it was almost physically painful.

"Thank you," he said, his voice hoarse. He didn't trust himself to say anything else.

They held their eye contact for a loaded moment before she looked away. She seemed as unnerved as he felt, and he sensed her walls immediately returning to their rightful place between them. She pushed back her chair and stood up, reaching over the table to gather both their dishes.

"I need to get going, I really should go for a run or something before it gets too late. Thanks for breakfast, see you soon?"

She swept into the house before he had a chance to respond. He sat motionless, listening to the sink running in the kitchen, dishes clinking in the dishwasher, and, eventually, the front door slamming and the sound of her car driving away.

He knew as soon as he got up he would head right to his freshly stocked fridge, tear into a new case of beer, and pop open one of the bottles before it had even had a chance to get cold yet. He craved the peace it would bring, the uncomfortable feelings swirling inside him fizzling and fading into easily ignorable background noise.

Slowly, he pushed his chair back and made his way into the kitchen. He took a glass out of the cabinet and set it on the counter. He opened the fridge and stared at the unopened cases of beer neatly lined up across the bottom. Looking at the cases, all he could see was the revulsion and disappointment on Grey's face the night of the premiere, when he had leaned over her in the car and she had smelled the booze on his breath.

It was barely eleven in the morning.

He hadn't been to Johnny's since the night he'd gotten the call from Audrey. Now that he was out and about again, he was getting more than his fill of contact with the outside world—plus, his anonymity was less of a guarantee than ever. Though he hadn't officially confirmed it, he was pretty sure getting publicly hammered would qualify as damage to Grey's reputation.

But even so, maybe he'd been hitting it a little too hard at home lately. It couldn't hurt to ease off for a day or two.

With a sigh, Ethan reached for his glass and filled it with water. He trudged to his bathroom and dropped two Alka-Seltzers into the glass, watching them disintegrate before chugging it down. It wasn't a beer, but at least it was cold and carbonated. He felt the tension behind his eyes start to release as he opened the door to his office, settling behind his computer. He opened the document containing the last version of the *Bitter Pill* script, still untouched since Sam's death.

He hesitated. Before he could let himself think twice, he was back at the fridge, carrying two cases of beer to unload into his office minifridge. *For later,* he rationalized as he knelt in front of it. He kept one bottle out and took it back to his desk with him. He left it sitting next to his computer, unopened, as he began to read. It would be his reward to himself once he made it through. Just one wouldn't hurt.

Just one.

11

GREY'S LUNGS BURNED AND HER HEART POUNDED. SHE INHALED through her nose and exhaled through her mouth, pumping her arms in time with the sound of her feet slapping the pavement. She spied the sign marking the spot where she had started her jog and willed her feet to keep going. *Almost there*.

She brought the edge of her tank top to her forehead, mopping up the sweat stinging her eyes. Some runs were harder than others, and today it felt like she was trudging through wet sand. It had been hours since breakfast, but the sandwich from that morning still felt like it was sitting like a stone in her stomach. That afternoon, she'd traversed the 2.2-mile loop around the Silver Lake Reservoir in a little over twenty minutes—not her best time, but not terrible. Once she hit her starting point again, she slowed to a walk, allowing herself a minute or two to breathe before she took another lap.

The Missy Elliott blaring through her headphones was abruptly interrupted by the sound of an incoming call. Grey pulled her phone out of her running pouch, snug around her hips, and checked the caller ID.

Mom.

Grey hadn't been avoiding her mother, exactly; it was just a coincidence that they hadn't spoken on the phone since she and Ethan had gone public. It wasn't unusual for them to go a month or so without exchanging more than a sprinkling of texts. She knew her mother was itching for more details; even if Grey had had them, she was reluctant to provide them to her. Still, she couldn't put it off forever.

"Hi, Mom."

"Emily? Are you all right? Why do you sound like that?" Her mother's voice sounded only vaguely concerned.

"I'm fine. I'm out running."

"Is this a bad time?"

"No, it's okay. What's up?"

"Just calling to check in. Do you have any idea if you'll be able to make it back home for Madison's graduation?"

Grey had grown up in Port Chester, a working-class suburb of New York City. Her dad had been out of the picture for as long as she could remember. Her mother had worked as a receptionist in the city, her commute keeping her out of the house from dawn until well after dark. Once Grey started making money from acting, they were finally able to move into an apartment big enough for her mother to stop sleeping on the pull-out couch in the living room.

Shortly after Grey had moved cross-country for college, her mother had remarried: she'd fallen for a C-suite executive at her firm and decamped ten miles west to Scarsdale, into a sprawling house with more than enough bedrooms to spare. Her new husband had a daughter from a previous marriage, Madison, whom Grey had met fewer than five times over the past ten years.

"Um, maybe. My work schedule is really up in the air right now."

"Oh, really? Did you book something?"

Grey winced. "Not yet. But I have some stuff coming up, maybe." She'd repeated the lie so many times over the past few months that it had almost started to feel like the truth. She vowed to herself to text Renata as soon as she got off the phone: she couldn't keep waiting around for *Golden City*. There had to be something else out there for her in the meantime.

"Well, even if you are working, I hope you find the time. You wouldn't have to stay long, you could just fly in and out. Maybe your new *friend* can come with you."

There it was. "Maybe. He's pretty busy, too."

"Look at you, you've finally gone Hollywood," her mother said acidly.

For a brief moment, annoyance flared inside her: *isn't this what you wanted?* But that was unfair. Her mother hadn't asked her for a cent since she'd started dating her now-husband. And even when Grey was young, she had hardly been a nightmare stage mom. Unlike the moms of the other kids she always saw at auditions, whose only job was to cart their precious progeny from dance class to voice class to acting class, Grey's mother had had neither the time nor the energy to take an active role in her career. Her older brother had accompanied her to auditions until she was old enough to take the Metro North into the city by herself.

She knew it was irrational to begrudge her mother for enabling Grey to follow her childhood dreams into an industry that she was still willingly involved in as an adult. Because as much as she wished she didn't, as much as she despised the assorted bullshit that came with it, she really did love acting. From the first moment she'd stepped onstage at her kindergarten holiday pageant, there was no other road her life could have taken. She loved it, she was better at it than anything else, and, at least for now, it was still paying her bills. She was one of the lucky ones.

Still, when her mother tried to talk to her about anything involving her career, something childish and ugly was triggered inside her. Deep down, a part of her still resented being saddled with the responsibility of co-breadwinner before she'd even mastered her multiplication tables.

As a result, a yawning chasm had calcified between them over the years. Grey's role in supporting the family had turned them into something closer to peers than mother and daughter. It would have been bearable if it manifested as polite distance, but it seemed like her mother had some lingering guilt on her side, too. As soon as Grey left the East Coast, every interaction became peppered with passive-aggressive needling about Grey's career, her weight, her finances, or her personal life; as if she were trying to convince herself that she'd taken an active interest in the direction of Grey's life back when it actually mattered.

"Yeah, well, you know how it is," Grey said absently. Her mother took that as an opportunity to launch into a lengthy monologue about the finer points of planning Madison's graduation party. This was the safest conversational zone for them, focusing on a neutral third party. Grey picked up her pace again, now that her input wasn't required beyond the occasional murmur of assent. The second lap came easier, any residual uncertainty lingering from her breakfast with Ethan drowned out by the familiar disquietude that came from talking to her mother. That, at least, she could attempt to outrun.

Later, once she'd finished her second lap and extracted herself from the conversation, Grey found an empty bench to finish her cooldown. As she stretched out one burning quad at a time, she pulled out her phone and scrolled through Instagram. She had a notification that she'd been tagged in a post by a new fan account that had popped up a few weeks ago, @grethan_updates. At first, their couples moniker had made her cringe, but by now she was starting to get used to it.

The account was a painstakingly comprehensive chronicle of her and Ethan's every move, a mixture of paparazzi shots and fan submissions. Grey wasn't sure if she should be flattered or creeped out. Part of her was convinced that one of Audrey's interns was behind it. She had her share of fan accounts, but the majority were focused on her *Poison Paradise* character rather than her personal life, and they had mostly lapsed into inactivity once the show ended. When she had followed this account, their bio had been instantly updated with a breathless *"Grey followed back!!!"* followed by the date.

She shifted to stretch her other leg as she looked at the new tagged picture. Her stomach jolted. This picture was of her, alone, midrun, wearing the same clothes she was currently wearing. The caption read: "@greybrooksofficial jogging around the Silver Lake Reservoir," followed by today's date. Grey whipped her head around, trying in vain to spot the culprit. The path was deserted. She'd been running for forty-five minutes; whoever it was was likely long gone.

She abandoned her stretching and hustled back to her car, her heart beating wildly in her chest. She rested her head on her steering wheel, breathing deeply, willing her hands to stop shaking before she was ready to put the car in drive. Once the initial shock wore off, the adrenaline drained from her body and she was able to think clearly. She wasn't in any real danger. It was probably just an overzealous fan, looking for a way to feel important. She was a public figure in a public place. This was the trade-off for her boost in profile.

Too bad her career still hadn't gotten the memo. So far, this bargain had brought her nothing but trouble.

12

ETHAN NOTICED GREY'S FEET BEFORE ANYTHING ELSE. HE'D never really been a foot guy, but coming around the corner and spying her bare feet dangling off the arm of his sofa, he suddenly understood why so many perverts were trying to google them. He could easily see himself wrapping his hand around her heel, moving up the delicate indent of her ankle, past her smooth calf, up the tantalizing expanse of her thigh barely covered by her cutoff shorts.

She was sprawled on her back across his couch, nose buried in a stapled packet of paper. Based on the way her expression shifted as her eyes darted across the page, she was reading a script, marking her way through her character's emotional arc. He forgot all about her legs as he homed in on her face, captivated by her focus. It must have been several minutes before her eyes shifted to him and she jolted, yelping in surprise.

"How long have you been standing there, you creep?" she asked, her tone playful rather than accusatory.

He evaded the question. "What is that? Your chemistry read?"

She sat up, tucking her legs beneath her and unfolding the stapled pages. "Yep. It's in two days. I kind of can't believe it, it feels like I've been waiting forever." She looked up at him through her lashes, almost shyly. "You still down to run lines?"

Ethan shrugged. "Let's see it."

He moved to the other side of the sectional, grabbing the outstretched pages from Grey's hand on his way. He settled on the sofa, a safe distance away from her. At least, as safe as he could be while still staying in the same zip code. He skimmed the pages.

"So I'm reading for . . . Evander?"

"You got it. Do you want some context, or does it not matter?"

"Sure."

Grey swung her legs around again so she was sitting crosslegged, her hands moving expressively as she talked.

"Okay. So basically there's this big fancy city—the *titular* Golden City, obviously—everyone is rich and beautiful, everything is perfect, blah-blah-blah. There are a few royal families that control everything. I'm part of one, Evander's part of one, he's all set to marry my character and inherit everything. *But,* then he finds out—dun-dun-dun—that there's this secret underclass being tortured and exploited to provide everything they have. *Obviously* he can't just keep living his life like everything's fine, now that the illusion has been shattered. Classic Allegory of the Cave shit, right?

"So then there's this gang of insurgents, the Noxins—don't think I didn't see that eyeroll—who are all former royal kids who have rebelled and live outside the city with the rest of the commoners, trying to bring the city down. This is the scene where Evander is trying to sneak out to join them during the big annual bacchanal or whatever, and I catch him and try to use my feminine wiles to convince him to stay."

She dropped her hands and looked at him expectantly. His amusement must have shown on his face. "What?"

He laughed a little and shook his head. He could've listened to her describe that stupid book for hours. "Nothing. I like the way you tell it."

She ducked her head down, trying to suppress her own smile. "Just let me know when you're ready."

Ethan glanced down at the page. "I think you have the first line."

"Oh. Right." She closed her eyes for a moment, then looked back at him. "Where are you going?" Her tone was neutral. She was holding back, clearly self-conscious about running the scene with him.

He matched her deadpan line reading. "Go back to the party, Caitlin."

"Catalin," she corrected.

He squinted at the paper.

"Sorry. Go back to the party, Catalin."

"Not until you tell me what's going on. It's those men, isn't it? The Noxins?" She spoke quickly, without emotion.

He paused for a long time, slowly flicking through the rest of the pages, lost in thought. Her brow furrowed. "I didn't miss a line, did I?"

He looked back up at her. "I think we should put it on its feet."

Her eyebrows shot up to her hairline. "Really?"

Ethan was already up, pushing the coffee table out of the way to clear some space. "Playing it for real will be more helpful than just making sure you have your lines down."

Grey scooted off the couch. "Whatever you say, Mr. Director."

The two of them squared off, a little awkwardly.

"Um. Do you want me to mark the slap? Or"—she paused—
"or anything?"

He shook his head. "Go full out. All of it."

The corner of her mouth twitched, and what looked like an involuntary shiver rippled through her. The anticipation of what was coming obviously electrified her as much as it did him. He shouldn't be encouraging it. But it was all for the sake of her career. This was a selfless good deed, using his experience to mentor her. Nothing more.

She shook her limbs out a little bit to cover up her reaction. "Yes, sir," she said, a devilish glint in her eye.

Ethan turned his back to her and took a few steps away. He heard her voice behind him, imperious, with a thread of vulnerability laced through it.

"Where are you going?"

He whirled around to face her, a note of warning in his tone. "Go back to the party, Catalin."

She lifted her chin and took a tentative step toward him. "Not until you tell me what's going on." Her eyes widened slightly, and she lowered her voice. "It's those men, isn't it? The Noxins?"

He glanced back down at the script. He was tempted to play his next monologue in the melodramatic manner it deserved, but thought better of it. It would defeat the purpose of the whole exercise to openly belittle the material.

He realized with a jolt that it had been years since he'd actually acted in anything. In the meantime, he'd been demoted from billion-dollar-franchise lead to living-room-audition-scene partner. Surprisingly, the revelation was freeing, rather than humbling. He let himself settle into the character, attacking his lines with gravitas.

"And what if it is? I haven't been able to stop thinking about them. Have you? Thinking about the cost of all of this. The suffering. The thousands we crush under our feet every day for the sake of our own comfort. It's tainted. All of it. I can't live like this for another second."

Grey stared at him for a long beat, frozen, her emotions shifting from confusion to horror. Slowly, realization dawned on her face. Her voice was hollow, resigned.

"You're going with them."

Ethan took another step toward her

"I am. I have to do what's right. I don't have any good reason to stay."

Grey was indignant. "What about your family? Your destiny?" She cast her eyes down, hesitant, then met his gaze again, her voice trembling. "What about me?"

Ethan closed the distance between them and took her hand. "I thought you'd be relieved. You're free now. You don't have to marry me. You can be with Kyran."

Grey tried to laugh but it caught in her throat. She looked up at him in disbelief.

"What makes you think I want to be with Kyran?"

"I saw—I thought—"

She put her hand on his cheek and looked up at him, tears glistening in her eyes. Her next words came out in a throaty whisper.

"You were wrong. It's you. It's always been you."

She placed her other hand on the other side of his face and pulled his lips down to meet hers. He'd expected her to hesitate, at least for a split second, but she dove in without a second thought.

Despite his best efforts, he couldn't *really* remember the kiss from the night of the premiere. He was pretty sure he hadn't done anything horribly inappropriate. He only remembered that he'd liked it, and that it had felt like the only thing to do at the time. Whatever hazy memories he had of their glorified peck were obliterated by the immediacy of this kiss, the passion and the pleading behind it.

She slid her hands into his hair, and the combined sensations of her fingers and lips were so annihilating that he almost forgot where he was, what he was supposed to be doing. The taste of salt mingled with the sweetness of her mouth, and he pulled back a little to see that she was crying. Right. The scene. He inclined his forehead against hers and brushed a tear away with his thumb, stealing a glance at the script pages in his other hand.

"I'm sorry. I have to go," he murmured. She moved her hands down to his shirt, gripping the fabric so hard he thought she might rip it.

"Don't. Please. Stay." The words were practically inaudible, her eyes tightly shut. She leaned up to kiss him again, slowly, with an aching tenderness this time. He savored the fullness of her bottom lip. Without thinking, he slid his tongue over it, past her slightly parted lips. She moaned softly and released her grip on his shirt, sliding her hands up his chest and interlacing them around his neck as she pressed her body flush against his.

Fuck. He was hard as a fucking rock. There was no way she couldn't feel it. He had only a split second to worry about it, however, before she abruptly broke the kiss and slapped him across the face.

Ethan swore he saw literal stars. The whiplash between the pleasure of kissing her and the pain of the slap had him reeling. He almost didn't hear her next line.

"Don't do this to me. Don't you dare." Her tone sliced through him.

He was breathing heavily, which thankfully worked as a character choice.

"Catalin, I—"

She interrupted him, a tremor of fear breaking through her

aloof posturing. "If you leave now, you'll never make it past the front gate."

Ethan took a deep breath, willing his racing heart to return to normal. He spoke slowly, measuring each word.

"If I die, I die. But at least I'll die in pursuit of what's right." He turned away from her.

"Wait!" she cried out. He turned back and had to catch his breath again. Grey's face was flushed from crying, eyes wide and shining with emotion. She was fucking radiant—not to mention nailing every beat of the scene. He'd subconsciously assumed that her inability to book more work was at least partially based on her skill as an actress. He realized now how much he'd underestimated her.

She bit her swollen bottom lip. "If they ask me . . . I never saw you."

He closed the space between them in one stride, gripping her face in his hands again. "That's my girl."

She looked up at him, her face open and unguarded, but clouded with worry. "Good luck," she whispered, bringing her hand up to trace the line of his jaw, as if to memorize it. "I—I love you."

The script called for the scene to end on one last kiss, and Ethan claimed her mouth again without hesitation. She pulled away, eyes glazed, looking as dumbfounded as Ethan felt. They stared at each other for a long, loaded moment. Grey tried to speak first.

"That—"

She barely got the word out before he hooked his arm around her waist and roughly pulled her back into him, covering her mouth with his. If she spoke, the spell would be broken, the scene would be over, and he would have no excuse to kiss her anymore. That prospect was unacceptable. He kissed her hungrily, desperately, and she matched his intensity, twisting her hands in his hair again. He groaned, an involuntary growl deep within his throat, and ran his hands up her back.

He wanted to touch her everywhere, had wanted to for weeks, but now that he finally had the opportunity, he didn't know where to start. He didn't want to push his luck, though judging from the eagerness of her tongue tangling with his, he had a lot of leeway. He slid his hands down the lush curve of her backside and gave a tentative squeeze. She responded by moaning into his mouth and grinding her hips against him.

Well, that answered that. In a flash, he lifted her off the ground and carried her the few steps over to the couch. As soon as he laid her down, she wrapped her bare legs around him, grabbed his shirt, and pulled his face back to hers. He couldn't remember the last time he had been this aroused, driven this crazy with need. In the back of his mind, he knew that he shouldn't defile her right here on the couch, but he couldn't for the life of him remember why not.

He was stone sober, but he felt drunk on Grey. Drunk on her scent, her sighs, her soft skin beneath his hands. He pulled away from her mouth and buried his face in her neck, that exasperating neck, nibbling and sucking on the sensitive skin. She gasped, and the sound went straight to his cock, ensuring that the last remaining higher functions of his brain had shut down for good.

She suddenly tensed and shifted under him, and he lifted his head. His mind cleared enough to register the sound of a phone ringing. His phone, in fact. She met his eyes with a questioning look, breathing heavily. He shook his head and returned his mouth to hers, sliding his hands under her shirt and up her torso.

This time, they both heard it: *her* phone now, buzzing like a cockblocking hornet, on the cushion next to her head. The name on the screen was large enough for both of them to see from their compromised position: Audrey Aoki. They stared at each other, the same unfortunate realization dawning on them both simultaneously. The moment had passed. Back to reality.

"*Fuck,*" he groaned, pushing himself into a seated position as Grey scrambled to do the same, grabbing her phone and swiping to answer the call. She tucked her legs underneath her, face flushed and hair in a tangled cloud, unable to meet his eyes.

Her voice came out in a high, breathy squeak.

"Hello? Hi? Audrey, h-hi!" she stammered. "What? Yeah, no, yeah, I'm fine. I can talk." She paused, listening to Audrey's response. "Um. Yeah. Yeah, he's right here. Hold on." She fumbled with the phone, her hands shaking, trying to put Audrey on speaker. At last she hit the correct button, and Audrey's voice blared out from the phone. Grey shifted a little as if attempting to bring the phone closer to him, though she seemed too nervous to move more than an inch in his direction.

"Grey? Ethan? Are you there?"

"Hey, Aud," Ethan said, trying to keep his tone light as his blood slowly and painfully abandoned his groin and began to recirculate through the rest of his body.

"I hope you two aren't getting into any trouble over there," Audrey cooed. Grey and Ethan exchanged a guilty glance before she quickly looked away.

"We're trying our best," Ethan responded.

"Not to," Grey added quickly. "We're trying our best . . . not to." She winced.

"Good, good. I'm just calling because I have a couple of pieces of *very* exciting news that I wanted to share with you right away." She paused, clearly expecting them to take the bait and ask for more details. Neither of them said a word. "I locked down your big interview: a cover story and an eight-page photo spread in *Vanity Fair,* written by Sugar Clarke."

"Who?" Ethan grunted.

"Didn't you read her Merritt Valentine profile? Merritt's first interview in ten years? It was incredible. *Everyone* was talking about it."

Ethan knew Merritt, sort of, but had no idea what profile Audrey was referring to. Grey seemed to, though. She shut her eyes, her face tense.

"Wow, that's great news, Audrey," Grey said, her tone carrying the enthusiasm that her expression lacked.

"That means that you'll have to be on top of your game. She's very sharp and very observant, that's her job. You'll both be spending a *lot* of time with her, and she'll sniff out any bullshit right away."

Grey swallowed so hard that Ethan almost heard a cartoon *gulp!* sound effect.

"Got it. We'll be . . ." He paused, groping for the right word. "Convincing."

"Perfect. You know I love to hear that. And I have something else on the line that'll help you log some more quality time. The Blue Oasis resort in Palm Springs finished their renovations and are having their soft opening soon. They offered you two a luxury villa next weekend. Ready to take your first couples vacation?"

They looked at each other for a long time. Grey's eyes were remote and unreadable. Finally, she responded, "As ready as we'll ever be."

13

GREY FIDDLED WITH THE AIR CONDITIONER. ETHAN HAD AR-rived to pick her up sans Ozzy and the Bentley, tapping his fingers on the steering wheel of a vintage brick-red Bronco. She was both relieved and chagrined to see him there alone: relieved that they wouldn't have to keep up the doting couple act for the entire two-hour drive to Palm Springs, chagrined at the prospect of the most uninterrupted solo time she'd had with Ethan thus far.

Plus, though this was secondary, she wasn't sure how much she trusted him behind the wheel. When she climbed in next to him, though, he seemed sober and alert, if not especially chatty. What else was new. Though the Bronco set the tone for the occasion better than the Bentley, the air conditioner was spotty, and opening the windows didn't do much to offset the relentless sun beating down on the roof of the car. After thirty silent minutes, Grey was sweating like she was under interrogation. She could feel frizzy little wisps of hair escaping her braid and brushing against her face, taunting her with the knowledge that she was becoming more disheveled by the second.

She wanted to thank him for his help on her audition, but she knew any mention of it would inevitably lead to thoughts of the immediate aftermath. It was clear they were both eager to avoid that particular topic. Easier said than done. Hell, she was thinking about it right now, and they'd barely said ten words to each other.

The audition *had* gone well, though. Owen Chambers, the actor who had already been cast as Evander for months, was sweet and shy, and Grey had felt instantly comfortable with him. Kissing him had been nice, pleasant even, but it had nothing on the finger-in-the-electrical-socket rush from kissing Ethan. Just as well, since the director, casting director, and studio executives would probably have frowned on them ending the audition desperately dry-humping.

She wished she knew what he thought about it. Did he regret it? He certainly seemed upset they'd been interrupted. After they had hung up on Audrey, he had mumbled some excuse and shut himself in his office once again. If only there was some way to find out his true feelings, such as opening her mouth and asking him. No, that was too easy. There had to be a catch. She snuck a look at him, one hand loosely draped over the steering wheel, his eyes impenetrable behind mirrored aviators. Oh, right. The catch was that he was a fucking brick wall.

While attempting to pack for the weekend, she'd hated everything in her closet more than ever. With Kamilah still MIA, she'd crossed her fingers and texted Mia for help. To her surprise, Mia had agreed enthusiastically, dragging her to Venice to spend a lazy afternoon perusing the hip boutiques on Abbot Kinney Boulevard. As Grey swiped her credit card over and over, she ruefully wondered if she could send the receipts to Audrey for reimbursement.

Between Mia's hit movie and Grey's hit relationship, the pair of them had attracted enough attention that their casual day out felt almost like work.

Mia had also talked her into getting her bikini line sugared. Grey was reluctant after a traumatic waxing experience had left her swearing allegiance to home hair removal only, but Mia promised it would be less painful. It was, marginally, but Grey had to admit the results were worth it. It felt like the same kind of naïvely optimistic gesture as when she'd shaved her legs for the very first time before going to see her favorite boy band in sixth grade, as if she needed to be fully prepared for the possibility that they would spy her in the crowd and invite her backstage for some hot below-the-knee action. But then, as now, it never hurt to be overprepared.

After they finished shopping, they'd decamped to a dimly lit wine bar to share tapas and a pitcher of sangria. Grey regretted not getting to know Mia better while they were co-workers; but then, they'd both mostly kept to themselves at the time. Either way, the afternoon had been a delight. Mia had a warm, infectious laugh that was easily triggered, a quality Grey had always envied. She learned that Mia's original goal had been to become a pediatrician, taking modeling and acting gigs to help pay her way through school. She'd dropped out of her pre-med program once her career began to have unexpected legs.

"I still want to go back, eventually. All this isn't going to last forever, you know?"

All day, Mia had prodded her for information about Ethan, but Grey was able to deflect most of the attempts at girl talk by dropping some well-placed "He's a very private person"s. When Mia had brought up their sex life, Grey had blushed so deeply that Mia's laugh could be heard within a three-block radius.

"That look tells me everything I need to know."

Grey wished Mia would share that knowledge with her. Her feelings had settled into a knot in her stomach that felt impossible to untangle. It was unresolved sexual tension, sure, but there was something more than that. Any seedlings of fondness that she'd successfully weeded out over the last few weeks had sprouted back with a vengeance after their stolen moment of frenzied groping. Maybe they just needed to fuck once, get it out of their systems, and move on with their fake relationship like mature adults.

"So, should we get on with it?" Ethan said out of nowhere. Grey jumped, convinced he'd read her mind.

"Get on with what?" she asked, suddenly sweatier than ever.

"You know. Getting to know each other. So that reporter doesn't bust us."

Grey breathed a sigh of relief. "Right. Sure."

They rode in silence for several more minutes.

"Off to a good start," Grey muttered under her breath, and Ethan laughed.

"I don't really know how to do this. Tell me about yourself? I guess?"

"Why don't we review what you already know, and I'll fill in the blanks." Grey turned down the Led Zeppelin playing on the radio. The car was too old for either of them to play their own music, so they'd been listening to the local dad-rock FM station.

Ethan took a big, dramatic breath. "Okay. Name: Emily Grey Brooks."

"Very good."

"Age: twenty . . . seven? Still? Are you twenty-eight yet?"

"Not yet."

"When's your birthday?"

Grey looked at him out of the corner of her eye. "April 22."

"April 22," he repeated to himself. "Coming up soon. Graduated from—sorry, *attended* USC." His brow furrowed. "I don't even know where you're from originally. Did you grow up in L.A.?"

"No, New York. Westchester."

Ethan looked at her, surprised. "I'm from New York, too."

"Yeah, I know," she said automatically.

"How did I not know that?"

She shrugged. "It never came up."

"I don't really know Westchester."

"You're not missing much. I miss the city, though; I was there all the time once I started working." She turned her head the slightest fraction, looking at him as much as she could without actually looking at him. It was easier talking to him this way. "Do you miss it?"

Ethan took his time to consider the question. "I do and I don't. I miss . . . I miss how dense it was. I miss the people. I miss that you can't step out the door without seeing a dozen people from every walk of life. You're never alone."

"Really?"

He glanced at her. "Is that surprising?"

"I mean . . ." She chose her words carefully. "You could be surrounded by people all the time if you wanted."

"It's different here. In New York, they leave me alone. They look, sure, but there's less people coming up to you, less paparazzi. You can just be anonymous. Living there was the last time I *was* anonymous, I guess. I miss that part of it."

"I don't think it's possible for you to ever be anonymous."

Ethan shrugged, his mouth thinning. "Yeah. Maybe not."

Several minutes passed without either of them saying a word. Grey presumed he'd already gotten bored of the "getting-to-know-you" schtick, and looked out the window. She was startled to hear him speak again.

"Do you know *my* birthday?"

Anxiety pooled in her stomach. "Why?"

His smile deepened. "You already know everything about me," he said teasingly.

Grey's mouth dropped open and her face flushed. "What? Do you think I'm, like, some kind of stalker superfan?" Fucking perfect. Guess that answered the question of how he thought of her: a glorified groupie.

"So you don't know it?"

"No!" *September 3.* "Get over yourself, *god.*" She glanced over at him, at the amusement that crinkled the corners of his eyes behind his sunglasses, and felt a surge of courage. She had to know, *now,* or this weekend would be unbearable.

"Thanks for your help on my audition, by the way. It went well, I think. You're a very committed scene partner."

Ethan's face slackened like someone had pulled the power cord on him. He was silent for a long moment, then reached his hand over to her. She flinched, but he was just turning down the radio.

He cleared his throat.

"Listen. Grey."

She was listening all right, but several more seconds passed in loaded silence before he said anything else.

"What happened the other day . . . I think we've all been there, right? We got a little too into the scene, a little carried away. It happens. I didn't mean . . . I mean, we would've stopped before . . ." He paused, then started again. "We just have to keep it professional."

She couldn't help herself. He seemed so flustered she had to tease him a little.

"Professional. Right. Like how both of our last relationships were with our costars?"

"And look how well that worked out for us," he muttered under his breath.

She looked over at him, for real this time, a little surprised at the grimness of his reaction. His mouth was set in a tense line.

Maybe this wasn't the time to bring up the casual sex idea after all.

They pulled up to The Blue Oasis late in the afternoon. The exterior was still the same impeccably preserved original Spanish colonial revival design from when it had been the ultimate getaway for Hollywood stars of the twenties and thirties. However, over the last five years, the interior had been painstakingly renovated to be the pinnacle of modern convenience. Grey and Ethan were ushered into their villa, which was more like a luxury condo than any hotel room Grey had ever stayed in.

There was a full kitchen, a living room area with an enormous couch and a half bath, a master bedroom with a walk-in closet, and a palatial bathroom with a two-headed rain shower and full-sized Jacuzzi. Outside, a tall fence lined with palm trees provided privacy for their small patio and private pool. The perfect lovers' getaway.

When Audrey had said "weekend," Grey had assumed she meant they would be there Friday through Sunday, but apparently her definition had them arriving on Thursday and leaving on Monday. Five days, four nights.

One bed.

"I can take the couch," Ethan said as soon as the bellhop had deposited their bags in their room. "Looks like it's a pull-out. Could be worse."

"Sounds good," Grey said, scolding herself internally for even thinking for a moment that he might consider sharing the bed with her. She brought her bags into the bedroom and ducked into the bathroom to freshen up. When she returned to the living room, Ethan was examining the extravagant gift basket that the resort had laid out for them on the coffee table, which included an expensive bottle of champagne and several chocolate-covered strawberries. He picked one up and inspected it.

"Should we go out to the lobby and feed these to each other?"

Grey laughed. "Bring out the champagne, too, so you can shake it up and spray it all over me."

Ethan looked stricken.

"Um. I meant for the cameras. Never mind." She shifted her weight, desperate to change the subject. "What time is our dinner reservation? Seven? I think I'm going to explore a little. Want to come?"

She was a little relieved when Ethan shook his head.

"I'm just going to hang out here for now. Maybe take a shower. You go do your thing, though." He kicked his shoes off and sprawled out on the couch, flinging an arm over his face dramatically. Grey let herself take one long, languorous look at him; the lift of his arm revealed several tempting inches of skin between the bottom of his T-shirt and the top of his waistband. She wondered how he would react if she crossed the room and straddled him, pushing up his shirt and covering the terrain of his torso with her hands and her mouth. Now that she knew how he felt on top of her with the, well, *firm* evidence of his arousal pressed up against her, the fantasy was more real than it had ever been.

The worst part was, she now knew he wouldn't push her away. It was whatever would happen afterward that was stopping her. If things got awkward between them on this trip, there was no office for him to retreat to, no home of her own to lie low in for a few days.

Ethan shifted his arm a little bit and peeked at her, catching her red-handed. Red-eyed?

"You're still here?"

"I, um . . . I forgot something." Grey dashed into the bedroom and rifled through her bag, pulling out her sunglasses and a baseball cap. She tossed them on as she came out into the living room. "Gotta go incognito, ya know?"

Ethan nodded gravely. "Naturally. I think I have a fake mustache in my dopp kit, if you need it."

Grey laughed. "I'm not sure if I'm at that level yet, but I appreciate the offer."

GREY DIDN'T RETURN UNTIL AN HOUR BEFORE THEIR DINNER reservation, greeting Ethan quickly before shutting herself in the bedroom. Ethan heard the shower running. He had showered shortly after she left, jerking off twice. He wasn't taking any chances.

It was unbelievable. He hadn't slept with anyone since his divorce, and most of the time had little desire to. And yet here he was, unable to think straight around her without coming first, like a horny teenager. He'd come dangerously close to losing control with her the other day on his couch. He didn't want to think about what would have happened if they hadn't been interrupted by Audrey's call. But, of course, he *had* thought about it, hadn't been able to stop thinking about it. It was hard enough trying to keep his mind off of her when he was by himself in his house, let alone when he knew she was, at that moment, a few short steps away, naked and soaking wet.

This weekend was going to be a nightmare.

At first he'd thought it was maybe just the fact that he had barely been in the presence of an attractive woman for the last few years. It had to be the novelty.

But then, he'd had girlfriends before. He'd been married. He'd certainly had more than his share of flings. None of that felt quite like this. Being around her felt like parts of him were being switched on that he'd never known existed. It petrified him.

When she slid open the door to the bedroom forty-five minutes later, he couldn't stop himself from openly gawking. She was wearing a floor-length dress in a gauzy material that clung and draped over her body so alluringly that it almost seemed like magic.

The fabric looked flimsy enough to melt under the heat of his touch. He half expected it to do just that when he rested his hand on the small of her back to guide her out the door. However, he quickly discovered that the dress's halter neck left her entire back exposed, his palm landing flush against the dimples in her lower back.

The unexpected sensation of full skin-to-skin contact almost had him involuntarily pulling his hand away like he'd been scalded. At the same time, he felt as if he couldn't move it if his life depended on it.

They slowly made their way down the path toward the Oasis Lounge. Grey set their pace, carefully placing each step so she wouldn't get her stiletto heels stuck in the cobblestones. Ethan quickly reconfigured his hold on her, sliding his hand all the way around her waist and taking her other hand in his to help steady her.

Though they could hear distant sounds of laughing and splashing from the main pool area, the path was deserted.

"I had an idea," Grey said suddenly, still singularly focused on the path.

"Oh yeah?"

"Should we do the thirty-six questions?"

"The what?"

She leaned her body against him a little more as she navigated a particularly harrowing stretch of terrain. Ethan hoped she couldn't feel his heart start to pound harder.

"You know, the thirty-six questions that make strangers fall in love?" As if regretting what she'd said, she immediately tried to backtrack. "I mean. They just help encourage intimacy or whatever. Some psychologist came up with it. It might be worth a shot."

Ethan tightened his grip on her, considering it. "You're not worried we'll fall in love?" he asked drily.

Grey whipped her head toward him.

"What?" she said, a little too loudly.

At that exact moment, her left heel landed squarely in a crack between the stones, and her ankle gave way. Ethan tried to catch her, but all he could do was watch her fall in slow motion as she slipped out of his arms and toppled to the ground.

"*Fuck* these *fucking* shoes," she groaned, rolling herself into a seated position and clutching her ankle. Ethan instantly crouched down next to her, brushing her skirt aside to examine it. "No, it's okay, you don't have to—I'm fine—" she persisted, though they could both see her ankle was already swelling up like a balloon. "Just help me up, I can walk it off."

Ethan was doubtful, but he still let her wrap her arms around his neck so he could pull her to her feet. She tentatively tried to put pressure on her injured foot, but hissed in pain, digging her nails into his shoulder.

"All right, that's enough of that," Ethan proclaimed, and in one motion swept her legs out from under her and scooped her off the ground. She gasped in protest.

"Wait! But what about our reservation?"

"Fuck our reservation," he said, striding back toward the villa. She was on the taller side and wasn't especially light in his arms, but they'd barely gotten a hundred feet away from the door. He could easily make it. "The only place you're going is bed."

Grey seemed like she was about to resist, but instead nestled her head into the space between his neck and shoulder with a small sigh. He tightened his grasp on her and tried to keep his intentions focused, repeating them over and over again like a mantra: he would bring her home. He would take care of her ankle. And he would leave her alone.

Bring her home. Take care of her. Leave her alone.

14

ETHAN HAD BARELY STOPPED MOVING FROM THE MOMENT HE had dug the villa key out of his pocket, shouldered the door open, and deposited Grey on the couch. He'd immediately propped her leg up on a pile of pillows and unlaced her high-heeled sandal gently, almost tenderly. When she'd flinched in pain as his hand brushed a particularly sore spot, he'd paused and looked up at her with such concern that her heart skipped a beat.

Shortly he'd arranged her on the bed atop her pillow tower, with her phone in one hand and the television remote in the other. Her eyes were on him, though, following his movements as he paced around the room, on the phone with the concierge. He asked them politely but firmly to cancel their dinner reservation and send over the resort medic and as many ice packs as they had on hand. Five minutes after hanging up, he decided that he couldn't wait, and barged out of the room to track down some ice himself.

With him gone, she had a chance to breathe. She tentatively

flexed her foot, groaning when pain shot up her shin. Her ankle was starting to turn a charming shade of purple. Great. Three hours into her extended quality time with Ethan and she had already turned into one of those clumsy rom-com heroines who couldn't get out of bed without falling down and breaking her nose—adorably, of course. This is what she got for trading her usual chunky heels for five-inch stilettos, the type she'd flat out refused to ever wear on the show. She swore to return those traitorous shoes as soon as she got home.

The medic showed up shortly before Ethan returned. He examined Grey and concluded that it was likely just a sprain, but she should probably get an X-ray when she returned to L.A., just to be safe. He bandaged her ankle and loaded her up with supplies: crutches, ice packs, extra bandages, little individual packets of ibuprofen. Only slightly less glamorous than her swag bag from the Emmys gifting suite.

After he left, Ethan hovered in the doorway.

"Are you okay?"

"More than okay. It's nothing. Really. Except . . ." She hesitated. "I'm pretty hungry."

Ethan exhaled, shaking his head. "Of course. Dinner. I totally forgot."

He grabbed the room service menu out of the living room and flopped down on the bed, passing it to her. She flipped through it as he peered at it from his spot next to her, his chin dangerously close to brushing her shoulder. She examined the pages forward, then backward, then forward again.

"Any of that grab you?" Ethan asked finally.

"Honestly, the only thing that's really speaking to me right now is Belgian waffles and bacon, but they only serve breakfast until eleven." She flipped the page one more time. "I guess I'll have the shiitake burger. Please."

Ethan grabbed the menu out of her hand with a dramatic flourish. "You got it."

He disappeared into the living room to make the call. She hoped he would come back, but she heard the television in the living room buzzing softly through the door.

She used this opportunity to hobble to the bathroom, wash her face, and fumble her way out of her dress and into lounge pants and a tank top. She hadn't settled back into her position on the bed for long before she heard a knock on the front door, followed by Ethan's muffled voice. A moment later, he pushed the room service cart into the room and placed one of the trays on the bed next to her.

"That was fast," she commented, lifting up the lid of the tray to reveal—

She gasped. Two golden-brown Belgian waffles, surrounded by tiny dishes containing fresh berries, maple syrup, and butter. She peeked under the lid of the smaller dish to discover four slices of perfectly crisp bacon.

Grey looked up at him, her mouth open. "How did you—"

Ethan shrugged, trying to look nonchalant, but obviously pleased by her reaction. "I don't know if you're aware of this, but I'm *very* famous," he said. She instantly recognized her words to him from their first dinner together.

She laughed, but only because she suspected she was about to cry. "Glad to see you're using your powers for good instead of evil. For once."

"It's important to maintain balance in the universe." He picked up the other tray, and turned toward the living room.

"Wait!" she cried out before she could stop herself. He cocked his head, questioning. She'd already opened her big mouth, might as well follow through. "You're not going to eat with me?"

He froze. Then the side of his mouth crept up slightly.

"Sure. Okay."

He set his tray on the table, then went out to the living room to gather some pillows from the couch, since all the ones on the bed were either behind her back or under her ankle. He opened the minibar, considered the contents, and pulled out a bottle of beer, popping the top off. He set himself up a respectful distance from her and lifted the lid off his own plate. Grey peered over to see what he'd ordered.

"Is that the shiitake burger?"

He grinned. "It sounded good."

Grey balanced her plate on her lap and smothered her waffles with toppings. "Want to trade some fries for a piece of bacon?"

"Deal."

They ate in companionable silence for a few minutes. The waffles were everything Grey had hoped for, and once the edge was taken off her hunger, she began to relax. Maybe it was the cumulative effect of how strange the last two months had been, but something about this felt . . . comfortable. Natural. Words she definitely didn't associate with her relationship with Ethan.

"You wanna watch TV or something?" she asked.

Ethan shrugged. "Whatever you want."

She picked up the remote and started flipping through the channels. An infomercial, a reality show, an old sitcom rerun. She was flipping so fast that she almost missed it: a baby-faced Ethan strutting down a high school hallway in a letterman's jacket. It was his first starring role, the teen dramedy *What's Your Deal?* He'd played the secretly sensitive jock who, despite dating the prom queen, found himself falling for the weird artsy girl (equally as gorgeous as the prom queen, of course, just with brown hair and glasses). Grey recognized it instantly.

"Nooooo," Ethan groaned when he realized what she'd settled on. He leaned over to try to grab the remote out of her hand, but she held it out of reach, laughing.

"You said we could watch whatever I want!"

"Anything but this," he grumbled, taking a long pull from his beer bottle.

"Come on, it's one of my favorites."

He turned to her. "Really?"

She felt her cheeks turn pink. "I mean, it *was*. When I was a kid. It was a big hit at sleepovers."

"As if I didn't feel old enough already," he muttered, but she could tell he was holding back a smile. She thought he'd put up more of a fight, but he fell silent, taking another bite of his burger.

"When's the last time *you've* seen this?" she asked.

He squinted. "The premiere? I think I may have even snuck out early. It was my first time watching myself on the big screen, I was so fucking uncomfortable."

Grey mopped up the syrup on her plate with the last bite of waffle. "We can change it, if you want. I'm not trying to torture you."

"It's okay." He didn't sound very convincing, but it was enough to keep her from turning it off.

They moved their empty plates and trays to the side of the bed. On-screen, Ethan had approached his science teacher after class to ask her to switch his lab partner from Weird Girl to his cheerleader girlfriend. Unfortunately, unbeknownst to him, Weird Girl had been standing right behind him and fled the classroom, crying.

"Harsh," commented Grey. Ethan snorted.

"Come on, she's being a *little* dramatic." They watched him hurry after her to apologize. "Look at that idiot," he commented as a close-up of his face filled the screen. "I'm about to pop a blood vessel from all that emoting."

Grey giggled. "You're being too hard on yourself. You were still figuring it out."

"God, I was so green. I remember the first week of shooting, it took me three takes just to hit my mark. Every single scene. It was humiliating. I thought they were going to fire me."

The scene changed, and now the characters were partying by a lake. Screen-Ethan stripped off his shirt, revealing a gleaming six-pack, and jumped off a rock as his friends cheered.

"With that bod? They'd be crazy to let you go." Grey thought she saw Ethan give her a split-second glance, but she must have been imagining it. He cupped his hand around his mouth and pretended to yell at his younger self.

"Enjoy it, man, it doesn't last."

She thought about telling him that, as much as the fantasy of his twentysomething body had contributed to her pubescent sexual awakening, it was nothing compared to its current incarnation, waxed six-pack or not. Especially now that she'd forever have the sense memory of him gathering her into his arms, his heartbeat racing against her shoulder as she rocked gently against the solid planes of his chest.

But, of course, she bit her tongue.

Ethan stood up to put the trays back on the cart and push it out the front door. When he returned, he had a fresh ice pack in his hand, which he gently exchanged with the one currently melting over her ankle. She swore that he lay back down a little closer to her this time, their hands inches from touching. She wanted to laugh. If only she could go back in time and tell her preteen self that her umpteen viewings of *What's Your Deal?* would culminate in her watching it while lying next to the one and only Ethan Atkins, as he waited on her hand and (literal) foot.

As infuriating as he could be sometimes, she felt a pang of gratitude that, against all odds, she'd been given the opportunity to get to know him beyond the two-dimensional crush object of her youth. Especially now, as he sprawled out next to her, rumpled and relaxed. His leap to action to take care of her had temporarily fractured the barrier between them, as if all they needed was an external obstacle in order to forget why it was even there in the first place.

That familiar feeling washed over her again: not lust, exactly, though there was definitely an element of that. Appreciation? Affection? Whatever it was, it thrilled and frightened her in equal measure. She already knew he was attracted to her, but after tonight, there was no doubt in her mind that he cared about her, too.

They were so fucked.

ETHAN DIDN'T REMEMBER FALLING ASLEEP. HE REMEMBERED helping Grey get under the covers, swapping out her pile of pillows for a single one at the foot of the bed. After the movie ended, he'd intended to retreat to the sofa, drink three or four more beers, and pass out in front of the television. However, Grey had talked him into staying for the movie that had started immediately afterward, an action movie he'd loved as a kid. Okay, maybe she hadn't had to talk him into it, just shot him a mildly pleading glance, and he'd not-so-reluctantly climbed back onto the bed.

He checked his phone blearily, his mouth sour and fuzzy—it was after 2 A.M. The lights and the television were still on, but Grey was fast asleep. He started to get up, gently, so as not to disturb her, but paused. She almost looked like a different person. She was so animated when awake, every fleeting emotion clearly telegraphed on her expressive face. Now, safe from her sharp and searching eyes, he took a long moment to fully savor the artful way her features were assembled: the angular jut of her nose, her over-full bottom lip, the curve of her cheekbone. One honey-blond curl had fallen over her cheek, and he resisted the urge to brush it away.

Slowly, as if it caused him physical pain, he roused himself from the bed. He turned off the television and made his way around the room, switching off the lights. As he flipped the final switch at the doorway, he heard Grey stir. Then her voice, soft, thick with sleep:

"Stay."

He froze. He turned back to look at her, but the room was dark now. Her face was drowned in shadow, her eyes hidden.

He tried to clear his throat, but his response still came out in a rasp.

"What?"

Silence.

He paused for another moment, willing her to repeat herself with every fiber of his being. Nothing. *Of course you fucking imagined it.* She didn't want him to stay. She was still asleep. She'd wanted his company because it would've been awkward for them to try to avoid each other in such close quarters. It didn't mean anything.

He closed the door behind him and slunk back to the couch. He was too groggy to attempt to pull the bed out, so he shed his clothes, dug a pair of sweatpants out of his suitcase, and stretched out across the cushions.

When had he become so pathetic around women? Or more accurately, one specific woman? Unexpectedly coming face-to-face with his twenty-one-year-old self had been jarring, to say the least. He'd forgotten that he'd slept with both his costars in *What's Your Deal?* (and several extras) and somehow managed to keep them from finding out until the wrap party, when all hell broke loose. He didn't miss the callous asshole he'd been in those days, and certainly didn't miss the drama that inevitably ensued. However, *that* Ethan would have had Grey naked and screaming his name at the first hint of an opportunity, so maybe he could learn a thing or two from his younger self.

He could already feel himself getting hard at the thought. This was fucking ridiculous. The more he told himself that he needed to leave her alone, the more his body rebelled. It didn't help that now he knew exactly how soft her skin was, how responsive she was to his touch, how her moans felt in his mouth. He was going to pay for that moment of weakness forever, probably; tormented by the intimate knowledge he had of her, tempted by the prospect of what was still left to discover.

For her sake, he hoped to never find out.

15

"SO, WHAT ABOUT THOSE QUESTIONS?"

Grey peered over her sunglasses, sure she'd misheard. She'd thought Ethan was asleep: he'd been reclined on the lounge chair next to her with a towel covering his head for the past twenty minutes, still as a corpse.

When she'd come out to the pool late that morning, he'd been swimming laps, his form cutting a powerful swath through the water. She'd originally envisioned herself swanning around their villa in her new bikini, flowy cover-up, and giant hat like a sixties Italian film star. Those same items of clothing felt decidedly less glamorous as she hobbled out on her crutches, trying to juggle her coffee and a pile of scripts. She was thankful his head was mostly underwater as she clumsily arranged herself in her seat.

The scripts were mainly just to kill time; Renata had assured her that she would be getting the offer for *Golden City* any day now. She was ten pages into the one in her lap and was already about to give up. How was she being sent both "middle-aged sub-urban mom" *and* "teenage babysitter" roles?

"What?" she asked, flipping the script shut and tossing it back onto the pile. Ethan pulled the towel off his face and rose up on his elbows next to her.

"Those questions. The love questions. Should we try it?" Her stomach flip-flopped. He was wearing sunglasses, too, so his face was impossible to read.

"You're not worried?" She felt so ridiculous asking that she couldn't even fully finish the thought.

He shrugged. "We could come up with a safe word. If we start experiencing any confusing sensations, just say 'shiitake burger' and the whole thing's off."

She grinned, despite herself. "Maybe we can get one of those spray bottles, like when you're trying to keep a cat off the furniture. Just a little spritz to the face."

"Did you pack your electric nipple clamps? That might be a good punishment."

"Yeah, they're right next to your fake mustache."

Ethan laughed and flipped over onto his stomach.

"Is that question thirty-seven? Nipple clamps, yea or nay?" he asked, turning his face toward her and resting his cheek on his folded forearms.

"I think they're supposed to dig a little deeper than that."

"Bring 'em on."

Grey pulled out her phone and searched for the website, a little surprised that he was so into the idea. "We can skip around and do them out of order; maybe the cumulative effect is what leads to love."

"Whatever feels right."

She suspected what felt right would be to sink her teeth into the muscles of his naked back, but that probably wasn't what he meant. She started to scroll, an involuntary chuckle escaping her lips.

"What?" Ethan said.

She shook her head. "I think I already know the answer to this one." She read in a singsong tone: " 'Would you like to be famous?' "

She lowered the phone, expecting him to laugh, too, but he seemed to be taking the question seriously. He propped himself up on his elbows.

"You think I'll say no, I wish I wasn't?"

She shrugged. "You don't?"

"I don't know. I think it's easy to say I'd give it all up, but I was never able to when it came down to it."

"What do you mean?"

"I mean, I thought a million times about selling everything and moving to a ranch in Montana or something. Never could pull the trigger. And now . . ." He trailed off, pushing his sunglasses onto his forehead and piercing her with a thoughtful look. "Now, with you, with everything—I guess I'm asking for it again. I can't stay away. I'm not good for anything else." He tossed the last sentence off almost as an afterthought, but there was an acerbic undertone beneath it.

She bent her good leg and rested her head on her knee. "Do you even *want* to work again?"

He was silent for a long moment. "I want to want to," he said finally.

"You know there are a lot of people who'd kill to be in your shoes." She hadn't meant to chastise him, especially in such a trite way, but it just slipped out. By this point, she could sense when he was on the cusp of sinking into self-pity.

He glanced at her. "Including you?"

"Sorry, but nothing in your wardrobe is worth killing for."

He snickered at that. She leaned back in her chair, stretching both legs straight again. "I already told you, I don't want to be you-famous."

"Right, right, of course. Control. I remember." He rolled onto his side. "Have you been enjoying the perks of being you-famous yet, at least?"

She cast her eyes around their decadent surroundings, then hesitated. "Well . . ." She thought about her encounter with the woman in the grocery store, the invasive Instagram photos. A photo of him carrying her back to their villa had already been posted on @grethan_updates, sourced from god knows where. He seemed to sense the unease lurking behind her expression.

"What? What is it?"

As she filled him in on the details of the last few weeks, his face clouded. He pushed himself to a seated position, facing her, his brow furrowing.

"That's not okay. We need to do something. Did you tell Audrey?"

"Tell her what? What is she going to do?"

Ethan ran his hands through his hair in frustration. Grey forced herself to drag her eyes away from his bare bicep as it flexed with the motion.

"It's so fucked. All this social media bullshit. I'm glad I didn't have to deal with it when I was coming up. Everyone feels entitled to complete access to every part of you, all the time. It's insane."

Grey sighed. "It's not all bad."

He half smiled. "That was your worst read yet."

THEY ATE LUNCH OUT ON THE PATIO; ROOM SERVICE AGAIN. Ethan would've been happy to spend the whole weekend hiding out there, but he knew Audrey would have their heads on a platter. The resort had offered them use of a chauffeured golf cart to transport Grey from place to place; they would be expected to make an appearance at the Oasis Lounge that evening. The clock was rapidly running down on their time-out due to injury.

Grey swallowed a bite of her blackened shrimp salad. "Ready for another question?" She seemed as grateful as he was to have a roster of conversation starters on deck.

"Hit me."

She glanced down at her phone. " 'Name three things you and your partner appear to have in common.' "

"That's not a question."

"You can email them to complain later."

He put down his caprese panini and rubbed his jaw.

"We're both actors," he said, counting off on his fingers, one by one. "We both live in L.A., and . . . we're both in a fake relationship."

"Boooo." Grey cupped her hand around her mouth to heckle him, but she was smiling.

"Top *that*."

Grey popped another piece of shrimp into her mouth and leaned back in her chair, thinking.

"Well, we're both unemployed layabouts," she began. He laughed. She continued. "We both like to run away from our problems . . ."

He wasn't laughing anymore. Her eyes met his, gauging if she was going too far. He inclined his head, indicating that she should keep going. "And . . . we both have a hard time letting new people into our lives. Trusting people."

He looked down at his sandwich. She wasn't wrong.

"We sound fun."

She smiled wryly. "Hey, the whole point of this is to get a little uncomfortable. We can stop anytime you want, just say the word."

"I'm not uncomfortable. Are *you* uncomfortable?"

She shook her head. "Not yet. Should I get the nipple clamps?"

He burst out laughing again.

AS SHE HOPPED AROUND HER ROOM, TRYING TO PREPARE FOR dinner, Grey's phone rang.

"Fuck," she muttered, throwing herself onto the bed and army crawling across it in order to reach her phone in time.

Renata.

"How's it going, honey?"

"So far, so good—I think," she answered truthfully. "Except I fucked up my ankle pretty badly."

"I know, I saw him carrying you over the threshold like goddamn Prince Charming. Nice work."

"I didn't do it on purpose," Grey protested, sitting up on the bed.

"Oh really? You looked pretty pleased with yourself," Renata teased.

"Renata!" Grey laughed, exasperated. "Did you just call me to make fun of me?"

"Only partly. I'm glad I caught you before you went out. I just got off the phone with the *Golden City* execs."

Grey stilled, her blood pounding in her ears. Of course. Why else would she call so late on a Friday?

Renata seemed to pause for a lifetime.

"And?" Grey breathed.

"And . . . you got it. They're sending the contracts over first thing Monday."

Grey shrieked and leapt off the bed, remembering her ankle a moment too late. Her yelp of joy quickly turned into a howl of pain as Ethan burst through the door.

"Are you okay?" he asked, wild-eyed.

She nodded, sitting back down on the bed with a hard *thump*.

"That's incredible, Renata. I can't believe it."

"You deserve it, angel. Really. Congratulations. I'll let you get back to your knight in shining armor."

Grey prayed that for once Renata's voice wouldn't carry.

"Love you."

"Love you, too. Be good."

Grey ended the call. Ethan was still frozen in the doorway. He met her eyes, and a slow smile crept across his face. He didn't have to hear the other half of the call to figure out what was going on.

"You got it."

His exhilarated expression made the news sink in even further. She nodded and covered her face with her hands to shield him from what had to be the dopiest grin of all time.

The next thing she knew, he'd crossed the room in a few long strides and lifted her in his arms, crushing her against his chest. Her legs dangled inches from the ground as he spun her around.

"Congratulations," he murmured into her hair. He suddenly tensed, as if realizing too late that his show of affection was a little extreme.

He slowly released her, careful to give her time to prepare her good foot to take her weight. The slide down his body was agonizing. As soon as she was steady on her feet (or rather, foot), he took a determined step back and cleared his throat.

"I mean. I'm not surprised. You were amazing when—um." He choked, the memories of his "help" with her audition clearly overwhelming him, the same way they did her.

"Thanks, it doesn't feel real," she said quickly, hoping to squash the glazed look of panic growing in his eyes.

"I should—we—are you? I have to . . ." He backed toward the door and dashed out of it before successfully completing a sentence.

Grey knew that she should hurry up and finish getting ready. Instead, she lay back on the bed, allowing herself to bask in her victory for a few glorious seconds.

She had the part.

And secondly, but not insignificantly, she could make Ethan Atkins tongue-tied without even trying.

16

GREY HAD HAD *JUST* ENOUGH TO DRINK AT DINNER THAT SHE didn't even protest when Ethan lifted her out of the seat of the golf cart and carried her to their front door. It was faster and less awkward than fumbling with her crutches, she reasoned, with the added bonus of being able to get a direct hit of the warm, intoxicating smell of his neck.

She now understood why ancient empresses preferred to travel via litter, carried for miles through the desert on the shoulders of burly, handsome men. She felt dainty and all-powerful at the same time. "I could get used to this," she muttered, half forgetting that he could hear her until his throaty laugh vibrated next to her ear.

"Oh yeah?"

"Doesn't fame mean your feet never have to touch the ground again?" she replied quickly, trying to cover her slip. It didn't totally make sense, but it was the best she could manage under the circumstances.

Ethan expertly maneuvered the door open and deposited Grey on the couch.

"Only if you're lucky."

Grey tried to put her foot back up on the coffee table, only to realize that her attempt had been thwarted by an ice bucket holding a bottle of champagne that definitely hadn't been there when they left. She looked up at Ethan, bemused.

"Did you—"

He shook his head, and passed her the card. She turned it over to see it was addressed to her. Inside, there were a few concise but warm sentiments of congratulations from Audrey.

Tears started to fill Grey's eyes. She was already an easy crier when sober, but get a few cocktails in her and she'd start weeping if she saw a bug that was just a little too cute. Ethan took the card back from her, giving her a chance to hurriedly wipe her eyes and compose herself.

"Should we open it, or are you good for tonight? We haven't even opened the one they gave us when we got here; we'll never catch up at this rate."

Grey considered the question. She was buzzed, no doubt about it. She could probably handle *one* more glass. It was her night, after all. She should let herself celebrate.

With a jolt, she realized that under normal circumstances, she'd be celebrating with Kamilah. Her nervousness about accidentally revealing the truth about her relationship with Ethan had led her to straight-up avoid her. Their typical flood of texts, already affected by Kamilah's travels, had slowed to a trickle.

"Let's open it. I need to make a call first, though."

Grey half hobbled, half hopped out to the patio and sat down on one of the lounge chairs. She had no idea what time zone Kamilah was in, and was shocked when she picked up the phone on the second ring.

"Emilyyyyy!" she trilled, shouting over what sounded like a raucous party in the background. "I can't talk long, but gimme one second!"

At the sound of her voice, Grey was a goner. Already primed, she immediately burst into tears. Once Kamilah was somewhere quieter, her voice returned, exhilaration turning to concern as soon as she heard Grey's tears.

"Are you okay? Did something happen?"

Grey choked out a sobbing laugh. "No, it's good," she burbled. "I got it. I got *Golden City*."

Kamilah screamed so loudly that Grey had to hold the phone away from her ear. She started laughing again, uncontrollably this time, the emotions that she kept locked up around Ethan taking over with a strength that almost frightened her.

"I can't really talk, either. But I needed to tell you. And I miss you. And I love you."

"I love you, too. That is so fucking sick. *Please* tell me you're getting your back blown out by your movie star tonight to celebrate."

Grey laughed even harder, tears still streaming down her face.

"We're at a free luxury resort in Palm Springs right now, what do you think?" Again, not exactly a lie.

Behind her, she saw the door to the villa open and Ethan's silhouette carrying the champagne bottle and two glasses. Grey hurriedly said her goodbyes as he approached her.

"Was that your mom?"

"Um, no, it was Kamilah," she called back, trying to camouflage her sniffles.

He sat across from her on the other lounge chair and handed her one of the glasses. She cringed, knowing that she must look like a puffy, snotty mess. When her face caught the light streaming out from the doorway, he looked like he'd seen a ghost. Great.

"Are you okay? Is everything . . . do you need to be alone right now?"

She shook her head, sniffling, wishing she had something to wipe her eyes and nose on besides her arm.

"No, no, it's fine. It's good. I cry at everything. Especially when I'm overwhelmed. Or drunk. Or all of the above."

Ethan laughed. He stood back up and quickly strode into the villa, returning with a box of tissues. She accepted them, trying to pull herself together as gracefully as possible. He picked the champagne bottle back up and tilted it away from them, popping the cork.

"That's not a bad thing, necessarily. Being in touch with your emotions. Good for an actress."

"That's what they tell me. Too bad I look like a sun-dried tomato when I cry."

Ethan chuckled, pouring a generous glass of champagne and passing it to her.

"You don't look like a sun-dried tomato."

"It's okay, you don't have to say that. I wasn't trying to fish."

He poured himself his own glass and set the bottle next to him on the concrete.

"I didn't think you were fishing. But it's true. You look beautiful."

Grey blinked. Normally, hearing that wouldn't faze her. She was confident in her appearance. She had to be, after twenty years of casting directors and wardrobe heads ruthlessly assessing her physical flaws and assets right in front of her, like she was a thoroughbred horse or a luxury car. It was either that, or allow the impossible standards of the industry to chip away at her self-esteem, one nitpick at a time, until she crumbled under the weight of her insecurities. But he said it so easily, without hesitation, as if he'd already told her a million times.

As if tonight weren't surreal enough already.

"What should we toast to?" she asked breezily, changing the subject. They'd already toasted to her victory at dinner; it only seemed right to switch it up.

"How about to Audrey? Wouldn't be here without her." He tilted his glass toward her. She grinned, lifting hers in response.

"To Audrey, through whom all things are possible."

"Amen."

They clinked their glasses and each took a long sip. Grey gave him a sideways glance, taking in the way the light danced across his profile as he drank.

Ethan stretched out on the lounge chair, resting his forearm above his head. He'd changed out of his button-down into a faded Roxy Music T-shirt, and a flash of something shiny glinted from under the sleeve. Without thinking, she wrapped her hand around his bicep and gently angled it toward her.

"What is that?"

His eyes darted to her hand on his arm, with a half smile of amusement.

"Nicotine patch," he said casually, moving so she could get a better look at it.

She jerked her head to look at him, eyes wide. He shrugged.

"What? Renata was right. They do work pretty well."

Grey was speechless. Reluctantly, she released her grip on his arm.

"What are you doing?" she blurted out, the champagne loosening her tongue.

"What do you mean?"

"Why are you being so . . ." She struggled to find the right word. He sipped his champagne, his eyes still on her, waiting for her to finish. He wasn't going to let her out of this one. She tried another approach.

"Since when do you care about . . ." *Me*. ". . . this?"

For a moment, she thought he would try to deflect, to play dumb. Instead, his face turned thoughtful, and he sat up straight. He spoke slowly and earnestly, in short, terse sentences. He'd had several drinks with dinner, too—when did he not?—and she could see how hard he was working to keep his thoughts organized.

"I don't know. It's not easy for me. Any of it. I've been living in this . . . in this . . . *rut* for so long. It's hard to change. Even a little. And . . . and it's scary."

His voice cracked slightly. "I'm sorry if I haven't made it easy for you, either. But I think . . . I like it. Having you around. It's . . . it's nice. It feels good. I'm not used to that. It's been a long time."

He paused, but didn't seem finished yet. She didn't move.

"I think it messes with my head sometimes," he continued, laughing a little. "Everyone in my life right now is in it because they have to be. I pay Audrey and Lucas. Nora, we have the kids. You . . . well, you know. I never thought I'd be that guy." His eyes started to glaze over, off in his own world.

"What guy?" Grey prodded gently.

"Surrounded by yes-men. No one who genuinely cares about me. There's no one left."

Grey shifted in her chair so she was facing him, propping her ankle up on the side of his seat.

"First of all. Do I seem like a yes-man to you?"

Ethan laughed, a genuine laugh that started deep in his chest. "No. No, that's not quite how I'd describe you."

"Thank you. Second of all, *you* are the one who's narrowed your life down so much. You can change it at any time. Lucas is your nephew, I'm sure he would be fucking thrilled if you invited him over for dinner or, like, to watch some sports thing or something. He already knows how to work your stupid TV. Audrey and Nora have known you forever; I bet by this point they're a *little* fond of you, obligations or not. And me . . ." She hesitated. "Yes, I signed a contract. But I had a choice. I wouldn't have done it if I thought I'd hate being around you. I'm not *that* desperate."

She thought about leaving it there, but the frankness of his confession compelled her to match him. "And . . . I do care about you, Ethan. Really. Sure, you make it really fucking hard sometimes, but that's a separate issue."

A slow smile curled at the corners of his mouth. "I care about you, too." The words sent a thrill down her spine. He shook his head a little bit. "Look at us. Becoming friends after all."

"Friends," Grey echoed, trying not to let her involuntary flash of disappointment show as she drained the rest of her glass and set it on the table next to her. She removed her foot from his chair and rearranged herself so they were sitting parallel again, looking out over the pool. She closed her eyes. It seemed like the extra glass of champagne was agreeing with her, her senses pleasantly numbed. The night air was chilly, but she felt warmed from within.

It wasn't until Ethan spoke again that she realized she'd started to doze off.

"I don't want to hurt you," he said suddenly, his words thick, sounding like they were choking him.

Grey opened her eyes, instantly alert.

"What?"

She didn't turn to look at him, but she could see out of the corner of her eye that his hands were trembling.

"It's what I do," he said dully. "Everyone . . ." He swallowed. "Everyone I care about. Eventually."

Ah.

She turned his words over in her mind, petrified of saying the wrong thing, the thing that would break the delicate thread of their intimacy and make him shut down again. "I think . . . I think the only thing you're responsible for is yourself. This moment. Anything else . . . you just have to try to let go. Keep moving forward." She felt stupid as soon as she said it, her fear of upsetting him by getting too specific leading her too far in the other direction, into the realm of banal platitudes.

Her words seemed to affect him, though. He closed his eyes and nodded, just once. Suddenly, she felt like they would both die if she didn't touch him. Without letting herself second-guess the impulse, she leaned over and took his hand in hers. He looked down at their joined hands in surprise, then back up at her. Without breaking eye contact, he brought her hand to his lips, kissing it with devastating tenderness.

"Thank you," he murmured, giving her hand a squeeze before releasing it.

"SHOULD WE DO ANOTHER QUESTION AND CALL IT A NIGHT?"

Grey looked over at him.

"I had no idea you would be so into these questions," she said, her mouth twisting into an expression of sly amusement.

He shrugged. "I like learning more about you."

It was true. The more he found out, the more fascinated he was. He felt like he could have sat there with her for hours, confessing his deepest fears and transgressions to her, discovering hers in return. It had been years since he had let himself open up to someone like this. It was exhilarating.

Maybe he just needed a therapist, he thought ruefully. Though it seemed like it might be some kind of ethical violation for a therapist to trigger exactly the same combination of vulnerability and arousal in him that Grey did.

"I'm not complaining." She picked up her purse and pulled

out a small tin box and a lighter. A whiff of cannabis hit him. She popped open the box to reveal five neat, prerolled joints.

"Should we take this celebration up a notch?"

He shook his head. "I'm good, thanks. But go ahead. I'll stick with this," he said, lifting the champagne bottle and taking a swig.

She brought the joint to her glossy lips and sparked it, inhaling deeply. "Suit yourself," she said, exhaling. The strap of her dress had slipped off her shoulder, leaving it bare. Even though it didn't reveal much of anything, there was something so oddly sensual about the whole picture that he had to force himself to drag his gaze away.

"Do you want to pick this time?" She passed him her phone and took another long, languorous hit. He scrolled down the list, considering his options.

"How about: 'Alternate sharing something you consider a positive characteristic of your partner. Share a total of five items.'"

She giggled, her voice husky from the smoke. "So, when you said you wanted to learn more about me, what you *meant* was, you want me to think of five ways to compliment you."

"It says five total, not five each."

"It's uneven? Why would they do that? I hate that." Her voice had begun to take on a slightly dreamy quality. She stubbed out the joint and slipped it back in the case. "You first."

He considered it.

"I like that you're tough. Scrappy."

She burst out laughing. "Me? I was taken down by a cobblestone."

"Not like that. I mean . . . you've been working since you were, what, ten?"

"Eight."

He shook his head. "How'd you do it?"

"Do what?" She stretched across the lounge chair, languid and relaxed.

"End up so normal. Well adjusted." He'd worked with a handful of child actors over the years, and they'd always kind of freaked him out. Now that he had his own kids to compare them to, they almost seemed like another species, or maybe some type of advanced automaton: dead-eyed, precocious, uncannily poised.

"I wasn't very successful, that's how. I mean, I worked a lot. But nobody knew who the fuck I was, thank god."

"What kind of work were you getting?"

She closed her eyes and half shrugged. "My first job was on Broadway, actually. I was in a revival of *Gypsy*."

"Never heard of it."

"It's an old musical, about this super pushy stage mom. I understudied the girls who played her daughters."

"Is that what your mom is like?"

She opened her eyes again.

"No."

He waited for her to elaborate, but she didn't. She reached her hand out for the bottle. He passed it to her, a little surprised she wanted more, and she tilted her head back to drink deeply.

She wiped her mouth on her arm and passed it back to him.

"My turn. We gotta get through these faster or we'll be out here all night." She flopped her head toward him, her eyes heavy. "I like . . . I like that you go out of your way for people when they need you."

"What makes you say that?"

"Two words: Belgian waffles. Your turn."

"I like how much you speak your mind."

"Only around you. You bring it out of me, for some reason."

He bit back a smile. "Your turn."

"I know, I know, I'm *thinking*."

Her eyes took a long tour up and down his body, leaving a trail of heat in their wake. When they settled back on his, it was impossible to misinterpret: she was giving him fuck-me eyes.

"I like how . . . *talented* you are. I don't think I thanked you enough for your help on my audition." She was practically purring. He shifted in his seat, alarms blaring in his head. This was taking a dangerous turn.

"Thank you. I mean, you're welcome." He cleared his throat. "You're very funny. Okay, that's five."

He stood up abruptly. "I think that's enough for me tonight, I'm exhausted."

She batted her eyes at him. "Aren't you going to carry me?"

Ethan was trapped. He'd be an asshole to refuse her. On the other hand, the last thing he needed was to get up close and personal with her when she suddenly seemed hellbent on seducing him. He forced himself to take an honest inventory of his self-control: if he took her in his arms right now, would he be able to walk away once he laid her down on the bed?

"I'll see you inside," he said gruffly, turning away.

IT HAD BEEN TOO LONG SINCE GREY HAD BEEN STONED. LONG enough to forget a crucial detail: being cross-faded always made her devastatingly, world-destroyingly horny. And that was *without* being primed by weeks of excruciating sexual tension first.

She wasn't deterred by Ethan's initial refusal. She'd known it wouldn't be that easy. She felt like a heat-seeking missile, programmed for a single purpose. Never mind that following that comparison to its natural end would mean mutually assured destruction.

She carefully prepared herself for bed, stripping down to a clingy T-shirt and lacy underwear just cheeky enough to give her plausible deniability. She could hear Ethan watching TV in the living room. She tousled her hair, turned off the lights, and slid open the dividing door.

The lights were out on his side, too, the only illumination the flickering colors of the television. Ethan, beer in hand, looked over at her when he saw the door open. She wished she could have taken a picture of his face when he registered what she was wearing (or, more specifically, what she wasn't wearing).

She leaned against the doorframe. "How'd that couch treat you last night?"

His eyes were heavy-lidded, his voice even and careful.

"Fine. Thinking about actually folding it out this time."

"Plenty of room in here."

The silence crackled between them.

"I don't think that's a good idea."

"I'll behave. I promise." She kept her tone light, teasing. His response was instantaneous.

"But I wouldn't." His voice cracked slightly, the barely restrained force behind it sending a thrill through her lower belly.

"So what?" She began to slink toward him, her bad ankle hardly twinging when she put her weight on it. Every part of her brain, including the pain receptors, apparently, was united by a common goal: Operation Ethan.

"What are you doing, Grey?" His voice was hoarse now, barely above a whisper.

She stopped short of touching him, her bare shins millimeters from grazing his jeans. She looked down at him, taking in the tension vibrating through his body, the way his face was rigid and pained, eyes glued to her face, as if he didn't trust what would happen if his gaze strayed any lower. Slowly, she joined him on the couch, placing one knee, then the other, on either side of his hips, straddling him.

She paused, body suspended over his, waiting to see if he would stop her. He didn't move, didn't speak, his eyes still boring into hers. She slowly lowered herself onto his lap, his eyes closing and breath escaping in a hiss once she was flush against him. The friction of denim against her skin was almost as exquisite as the pressure of the hard length of him between her thighs.

She nuzzled her face into his neck. "I'm not done celebrating."

His breath was ragged, shallow. "This is a bad idea."

She sat back up so they were face-to-face.

"Why? Don't you want me?" She skimmed her fingers over her breasts, her torso, her nipples already straining for attention through the thin fabric.

His eyes followed the path of her fingers, transfixed.

"You have no idea how much I want you," he breathed.

She shivered, both at the words and at the heat behind them, his voice low and raspy with need. His forearms flexed, like he was fighting as hard as he could not to touch her.

"I want you, too. It's all I can think about." She bent her head down again, pressing her open mouth behind his ear as she rocked her hips, grinding against the thick, solid ridge of his erection. The sensation sent sparks across her vision, and she whimpered involuntarily.

"*Fuck,*" he groaned loudly. It was as if she could hear his self-control snap. One hand grabbed a rough handful of her ass as his other arm wrapped tightly around her upper back, hauling her against him.

He kissed her with an intensity that should have scared her, everything he had been holding back pouring into her all at once through his lips, his tongue, his hungry hands roaming her body. She sank into him with a long sigh, her skin buzzing everywhere he touched her.

Then, suddenly, it was over. Before she knew it, he had half pushed, half lifted her off of him, and was somehow standing on the other side of the room.

"We can't do this," he said through gritted teeth.

Grey was incensed. "Why not?" she asked in a tone that would have been dangerously close to whining, if not for the thread of anger pulsing through it. "We both want to. We're not allowed to do it with anyone else. Everyone thinks we're already doing it anyway. It's just sex, it's not a big deal."

"It *would* be for *us!*" he exploded. She was stunned into silence. He rubbed his hands against his face, looking as agitated as she felt. A few long seconds passed, the only sounds their heavy breathing over the murmur of the television. When he spoke again, his voice was calmer, bordering on weary.

"We can talk about this tomorrow. When we're both sober."

Her temper flared. "Oh, so you mean between 8 and 8:02 A.M.? I'll pencil it right in. Unless you'd rather just pretend this never happened. Your specialty," she snarled. He looked like she'd knocked the wind out of him.

She knew it was a low blow, but she didn't care. She was horny, angry, and intoxicated, a combination that had her feeling like one giant exposed nerve. With as much dignity (and as little limping) as possible, she sauntered back into the bedroom, feeling his eyes on her ass as she walked away from him.

Once she was under the covers, the aching pulse between her legs began to throb, alerting her that there was no way she was falling asleep until she dealt with it. She slipped her fingers beneath the waistband of her underwear, her breathing growing deep and heavy as she found the spot that was already slick and wet with anticipation. She let her mind drift back to Ethan: his strong arms around her, his covetous eyes on her body, his unchecked passion when he let himself lose control. An involuntary moan slipped out.

She paused. She'd left the door cracked open, not *not* on purpose. He'd turned the television off as she'd left the room, leaving him sitting in silence. There was no way he hadn't heard her. She willed him to appear in the doorway, ready to help her finish the job.

No such luck.

She heard rustling, then: the unmistakable sound of a zipper opening. Her breath hitched, her fingers circling faster. She could hear his breathing, too, hard and labored. The sound of flesh moving against flesh.

It aroused her so much that her orgasm hit her immediately, almost unexpectedly. She didn't hold back, crying out and gasping as she came. The knowledge that he was listening intently to her every whimper prolonged it, sending one aftershock after another. In the other room, she could hear Ethan's tempo speeding up, trying and failing to suppress his own reactions, his strangled groans. Her fingers began to move again and she felt herself starting to reach another peak already, spurred on by the sounds of his pleasure building. As soon as she heard his breath quicken to a pant, his climactic moan too intense to stifle, she crashed over the edge again, even more strongly than before.

She lay there, blissed out and boneless, listening to the sound of her breathing syncing with and then deviating from his. Eventually, she heard him zip his pants, then the sound of footsteps approaching the door.

Finally. And then—

The door shut the last three inches.

17

ETHAN DIDN'T USUALLY REMEMBER HIS DREAMS. WHEN HE DID, though, they were vivid Technicolor nightmare extravaganzas, usually centered around the morning he found out about Sam. Waking up disoriented, head pounding. Dozens of missed calls on his phone. Nora's ashen face. Bile rising in his throat.

This time, however, there was a new twist. None of the images changed, but somehow he knew this was different. It wasn't Sam who was gone, his world shattering in an instant, his life forever divided into before and after. It was Grey.

He woke up sweaty and shaking. It took a few seconds for the hangover to hit him, and a few more before scenes from last night began trickling back. Grey climbing on top of him. Him pushing her away. Her flouncing into her room and . . . oh. A ripple of arousal went through him, battling his nausea for dominance.

They really needed to talk.

He sat up gingerly, groping around for one of the complimentary bottles of water. When he found one, he drained nearly the whole thing at once. That seemed to help. Something else came back from last night, too: Grey's dig about his drinking. He had to admit the throb of his hangover seemed to back up her point.

But still, she was exaggerating. He'd hurt her feelings, and she lashed out. Sure, he overdid it sometimes—but who didn't? There was nothing wrong with having a few drinks with dinner, a couple of beers at the end of the day. Everyone did. Just because she couldn't hold her alcohol didn't mean that everyone else had to abstain, too.

He heard the shower running; she was awake. Just then, there was a knock on the front door, announcing the arrival of their breakfast they'd preordered the day before. He wheeled it inside, then went into the half bathroom off the living room to brush his teeth and splash his face with water.

By the time she joined him out on the patio, he was halfway through his scrambled eggs. She hopped out, assisted by a single crutch, hair damp and curling down her back. She was wearing her sunglasses, and when she sat down next to him, he could see the sheen of sweat on her forehead. However hungover he felt, she looked ten times worse. She pulled her breakfast dish toward herself—Greek yogurt and fruit—and stared at it for a long moment. She picked up her spoon slowly, like she dreaded the prospect of having to use it. Her lips twitched.

Ethan put down his fork and pushed his plate toward her.

"Here. Eat this."

She turned to him, her face pale, her mirrored lenses reflecting two of him right back.

"You look like you're about to puke all over the table. Don't torture yourself with yogurt."

She nodded slowly and brought the plate in front of her, picking up his fork.

"Coffee?"

She nodded. "Please." Her voice was hoarse.

She avoided the eggs, but was able to finish the toast, sausage, and potatoes. As she drank her coffee, the color returned to her cheeks, and she seemed to perk up slightly. She still left the yogurt untouched, but attacked the fruit cup with alacrity.

"I think I'm going to get a massage today," she said, mouth full of strawberries.

He refilled his own coffee mug. "Sounds good."

"What about you?"

"I'm not really a massage guy."

"No, I mean, what are you going to do today?"

"I don't know yet."

"Mmm."

She sat back, propping her ankle up on the empty chair next to her.

He looked at her. She looked at him.

He couldn't resist.

"Who's pretending nothing happened now?"

She smiled slightly and sipped her coffee. "Mad I'm stealing your move?"

Actually, he kind of was.

"So. Last night."

"Last night," she repeated.

He expected her to go silent again, try to bait him into showing his hand first, but instead she heaved a world-weary sigh and said, matter-of-factly, "I think we just need to fuck and get it over with."

He couldn't help it. He started laughing.

"Glad you think it's so funny," she muttered, but she smiled, too.

"What do you mean, 'get it over with'? Should I be offended?"

"I mean . . ." She idly trailed her fingers over the table, tracing the intricate pattern of the mosaic tiles. "That's the only way to defuse the tension. We both want to, but we think we can't, or we shouldn't, so we *extra* want to. You know?"

"Makes sense."

Maybe it was true. Maybe his preoccupation with her could simply be chalked up to wanting what he couldn't have. It was condescending of him to think he needed to stay away from her in order to protect her; infantilizing, even. She was a grown woman, she could make her own decisions. If she wanted to sleep with him, who was he to say no? He'd had plenty of casual sex before. She was right. He was overthinking it. It didn't have to be a big deal.

She got more animated as she continued, growing more confident in her proposition.

"It'll eliminate the mystery. The taboo. It might even be terrible. That would be great, actually."

"Do you think it'll be terrible?"

The corner of her mouth curled up wickedly. "No. I don't. If you think about it, you've already made me come twice this weekend."

"If we're going by that metric, I think I might have you beat."

She bit her lip and dipped her head a little. "Ethan Atkins, you're going to make me blush."

"So when should we do it?" He kept his voice casual, as if they were discussing the weather, instead of planning out the consummation of the fantasy that he'd been obsessing over for the last two months.

She shrugged. "Whenever. The sooner the better, honestly. Right now?"

He scoffed. "You don't want to do it right *now*."

"Try me. Whip it out and let's see."

He knew she was joking, but that didn't mean he didn't consider it for a split second—and that the thought didn't make him harder.

"I don't have any condoms."

"Well, I guess you just figured out your plans for today." She glanced at him over the top of her glasses. "How long . . . I mean . . . has it been since your divorce, or . . . ?"

He shook his head. "No. And yes. After Nora and I separated, I went a little . . . I had my fun. Or it was supposed to be fun. But it turns out getting divorced takes fucking forever. By the time it was all official, I was over that phase. I stopped going out, stopped seeing anyone. So . . . it's been awhile."

"Me, too."

He turned to her, a little surprised. "Since your . . . the guy from your show?"

She nodded. "Sort of. I had one rebound attempt, but nothing happened . . . successfully. We were both pretty drunk. So, yeah, I guess it's been . . . almost two years? That can't be right."

"Almost three for me." If he was counting from his last sober encounter, it was even longer than that. The revelation sent a thrill of anxiety through him that he hadn't felt since high school. He pushed away the temptation to make a pit stop at the minibar to take the edge off. Drinking beforehand had never done much for his performance. At best, it dulled any morning-after embarrassment about it. But if this was going to be his only chance with her, he wanted to make sure he remembered every goddamn second of it.

She laughed. "God. We're pathetic. No wonder we're so desperate to tear each other's clothes off. So much for those hedonistic Hollywood lifestyles I've heard so much about."

"They're not all they're cracked up to be. Should we lay some ground rules?"

"Like what? No kissing, no eye contact?"

He laughed. "I think we can leave those on the table. But should this be a one-time thing, or . . . ?"

She sat up straighter, her face suddenly focused, thoughtful.

"Do I need to get Paul on the line?" he asked, frowning.

She looked confused. "What?"

"You had that same look on your face when we negotiated the contract."

Her face cleared and she grinned. "We don't need him. You're getting screwed in this deal no matter what."

"Lay it on me."

She popped a blueberry into her mouth. "I think . . . the rest of the time we're here, it's all fair game. We can do it once and then never again, if we want. We can do it nonstop until we die of exhaustion or they kick us out on Monday, whatever comes first. But once we get back to L.A., that's it. Back to normal. I think that's the only way to stop things from getting messy. You'll probably be sick of me by then anyway."

Doubtful. "Deal."

"Should we shake on it? Or would you rather seal it with a kiss?" That wicked smirk again.

"Shaking seems safer. At least until I get the condoms."

ETHAN WENT INSIDE TO SHOWER BEFORE EMBARKING ON HIS mission, so Grey remained on the patio for a little while longer. She took another hit of the joint to help settle her stomach. It eased both sources of her nausea: her hangover, and her nerves.

Despite feeling like warmed-over garbage, she was downright giddy. *She and Ethan were going to have sex.* She realized with a start that, for the first time, she hadn't thought of him as "Ethan Atkins"—just Ethan. Just Ethan, who made her amazing fried-egg sandwiches, wrangled her off-menu Belgian waffles, gave her his toast and potatoes when she was too hungover to eat anything else. She frowned to herself. Why were so many of her fond feelings about him linked to breakfast? Well, no need to unpack that now.

She examined her ankle, which she'd left unwrapped after her shower. Most of the swelling had gone down, and the bruises had started to yellow. She tentatively stood up and put some weight on it. Not great, but not terrible. They wouldn't be able to do anything fancy, but they could definitely get the job done.

As the minutes passed, her excitement ebbed, replaced by a bone-deep exhaustion. As with most nights she drank a little too much, she'd woken up before her body was ready, unable to fall back asleep. Maybe she should try to nap before he came back.

She cleared their breakfast plates and retreated to her room. After her shower, she'd thrown on cutoffs and an old Rye Playland T-shirt she'd turned into a crop top, no bra, and now she quickly slipped out of her shorts. She'd grabbed a random pair of underwear while getting dressed, and she double-checked to make sure it was acceptable. Plain, black, seamless spandex, Brazilian cut. Nothing special, but she didn't want to seem like she was trying too hard. Plus, they made her butt look amazing.

Grey crawled under the spotless white duvet and snuggled into the mountain of plush pillows. She wondered if she should arrange herself to be discovered; one bare leg exposed, hair artfully strewn on the pillow as if placed there by magic birds. That might work if she knew how soon he'd be back; a serenely sleeping princess could turn into a drooling, snoring ogre at the drop of a hat.

She must have drifted off while she was still contemplating her options. The next thing she knew, she was roused by the sound of the bedroom door sliding open. She lifted her head slightly, only opening one eye.

Ethan was at the foot of the bed, holding a plastic grocery bag, looking down at her with an indecipherable expression.

"Success?" she asked, her voice cracking a little. He inclined his head. She flipped the covers back, though not enough to expose her.

"Get in here."

A slow smile crept across his face, heat infusing his gaze. He pulled out the desk chair and sat down, unlacing his boots and removing his socks. As he stood up and tried to get into the bed, she protested.

"No outside clothes in bed, you heathen." Really, she only felt strongly opposed to his jeans, but she thought it was to her benefit to be nonspecific.

He held up his hands in surrender.

"Excuse me."

He reached behind his neck to tug the collar of his shirt over his head. Grey felt her breath start to quicken as his hands moved to the fly of his jeans. When he pushed them down and kicked them to the side, she swallowed. She could see, thanks to the prominent bulge in his boxer briefs, that he was hard already. She did that to him, she realized, without even touching him.

Suddenly, she felt overwhelmed. This was a mistake. There was too much pressure. If this encounter was anything less than mind-blowing for either of them, she would have to leave Los Angeles, change her name (again), and start a new life as a long-distance trucker.

She realized that every story she'd heard from someone who'd had sex with an extremely famous man was mediocre at best, borderline degrading at worst. The years of endless brigades offering them whatever they wanted without any effort on their part inevitably made them bored of sex, turning them lazy, callous, and/or perverse. A model she'd met at a party once told her about the time she'd fucked last year's Sexiest Man Alive, during which he'd refused to kiss her, worn noise-canceling headphones the whole time, and even propped his phone on her back to scroll during doggy-style. She'd heard multiple rumors about an internationally acclaimed musician who would invite women backstage after his shows, instruct them to remove their underwear and bend over, and jerk off without ever touching them. And she wasn't sure if she believed this one, but an old costar had sworn up and down that a certain multi-hyphenate Oscar winner could only get hard if he was disguised in a bedsheet with two eye holes cut out, DIY Halloween ghost—style.

If Ethan turned out to be a pillow princess, or had some bizarre previously undisclosed fetish, at least that would be one way to solve their problem. This could be one and done, and they could move on. She might not be able to look him in the eye again, but thankfully that wasn't a condition of their contract.

As soon as he crawled in beside her, though, all her doubts dissipated. They lay facing each other, eyes locked, not touching. Eventually, she reached out an exploratory foot, sliding it between his ankles and up his shins. He brought his hand to her face, trailing his fingers across her cheek, tracing the line of her ear, her jaw. The look on his face was extraordinary, like he couldn't believe she was real. No one had ever looked at her like that before. She almost wanted to avert her eyes; it felt too intimate.

Grey used the leverage of her foot to draw herself closer, hooking her other leg over his hip until they were flush against each other. They were both more naked than not, and the sensation of that much skin-to-skin contact had every nerve in her body singing. Their lips were inches apart, but still, neither moved to close the gap.

His hand moved from her face to her hip. Slowly, he slid it over her backside, up the curve of her waist, cupping her breast beneath her shirt. He lightly brushed his thumb over her nipple. She gasped, trying to arch deeper into his touch, but it had already moved back to her ribs. Unlike their other encounters, which had been brief, fevered, desperate, this was slow and sensual. He took his time. His hands roamed her body as if he wanted to memorize every inch of her, savoring the opportunity to take leisurely ownership of what had eluded him for so long. It was excruciating. She never wanted him to stop.

At the same time, her hands were moving, too, over the warm, smooth skin of his chest; the swell of his bicep, the dusting of dark hair on his torso. She had no idea how long they lay there, looking into each other's eyes, tracing mystical shapes on each other's bodies. She almost felt like she had been hypnotized. Of course, she was still a little stoned—she had no idea what his excuse was.

Finally, he spoke, his voice hoarse. "You were right," he murmured.

"What?"

"This is better than the couch."

She giggled. "Told you."

His hand returned to her face, running his thumb over her lower lip. She brushed her tongue against it, then shut her lips around it, biting down gently. He closed his eyes and shuddered, and she knew she had broken the trance.

He grasped the back of her head and pulled her mouth to his. But still, the frenzied passion of his other kisses was missing. Maybe she'd been right, after all, that it was the stolen nature of their split-second trysts that had driven their intensity. But there was a different kind of intensity behind the way he explored her mouth now: confident, thorough, claiming. All-consuming. She had to remind herself to keep breathing.

He flipped her onto her back and knelt between her legs, pinning her wrists above her head with one hand. Her stomach jumped at the unchecked desire in his face, the fierce concentration, like if he took his eyes or his hands off her for even a split second she would disappear from beneath him. His gaze rested on her breasts, the position of her arms thrusting them up and out, demanding his attention. With one rough gesture, he pushed her shirt up to her collarbone. Before she knew what was happening, his mouth was on her nipple, licking and nibbling the sensitive peak until she moaned.

She felt him smile against her skin as he moved his head to her other breast. His other hand drifted lower, lower, until it was between her legs. He grazed his finger over the soaking fabric, and she writhed beneath him.

She strained a little under the hand holding her wrists, and he released her immediately. Before she could reach out and touch him again, he pulled her top all the way off and threw it over his shoulder. She grabbed his shoulders and pulled him back down for a long, ravenous kiss. When he pulled away, his fingers were hooked in the edges of her underwear. He paused, his eyes flashing back to hers.

"Is this okay?"

As her answer, she covered his hands with hers and helped guide them down her legs. He dropped the scrap of fabric to the side and sat back on his heels.

"Fuck," he exhaled, his eyes sweeping over her. He looked at her for a long time, his brow knitted in what looked almost like concern.

She propped herself up on her elbows.

"What? Is something wrong?"

He shook his head slowly, his pupils blown out, eyes hungry.

"Not from where I'm sitting."

Her heart skipped a beat.

He wrapped his hands around her calves and slid them up to her knees, gently nudging them apart again. He dipped his head and kissed the inside of her knee, before moving up to nip the crease of her inner thigh. First one side, then the other. She sucked in her breath as he parted her with his fingers, then his tongue.

Goddamn. Why had she gone two years without this? Or more accurately, almost twenty-eight years. Because even though it had been awhile, she didn't remember it ever being quite this good with anyone else. Sure, Callum had been enthusiastic, and over time she'd been able to train him well enough. But she was pretty sure she'd never experienced anything like this, the way Ethan seemed so attuned to her every twitch and gasp, adjusting accordingly, teasing her to the edge and back. After he brought her right to the brink of orgasm for the third time, then paused, she couldn't take it anymore.

"Please," she panted, gripping the bedsheets so hard she was sure her knuckles were white. He glanced up, taking in her desperate squirming. By the way he smirked, she knew she must look as feral as she felt.

When he slipped his index finger inside her, she was already so overstimulated that she thought she was going to rocket off the bed. He dropped his head back down and sucked on her clit as he added a second finger, curling them until he found the spot that made her convulse.

"Oh, *fuck. FUCK.*" She knotted her fingers in his hair as her orgasm ripped through her. He lifted his head to watch her, his fingers still pumping inside her. It felt like she would never stop coming, a new wave of delicious sensations pulsing through her as soon as the last ones subsided.

Her head flopped back onto the bed, her limbs jelly. She felt Ethan remove his fingers, and she turned her head to tell him she needed a minute to recover before they continued. He met her eyes and slowly brought his fingers, the ones that had been inside her, to his lips, and sucked, his gaze heating her from head to toe.

Never mind. She was good to go.

"Condom," she breathed, her voice weak. He rolled off the bed and found the bag on the floor, ripping open the packaging. He disposed of his drawers quickly and began to roll the condom onto his slightly intimidating erection, which was twitching and straining toward his navel.

She watched him, basking in her postorgasmic haze. He was fucking perfect. And he was hers.

Only until Monday, a tiny voice in her head reminded her. However, that voice was easy to push aside as he crawled back on top of her, settling between her thighs. He braced his body over hers on one forearm, jerking a little as she reached down and guided him into place. They both gasped when the blunt head of his cock nudged against her entrance.

He rocked his hips slowly, easing into her an inch, then two. A whimper escaped the back of her throat.

"Wait," he choked, veins bulging in his forehead.

"What?" she cried out, louder than she'd intended.

"Maybe . . . this isn't a good idea," he gulped. "What if we get too . . . what if we want to keep doing this after . . ."

Grey let out an animal groan, digging her nails into his bicep in frustration. Her words tumbled out breathy and fast.

"Ethan, the time to have this conversation is *not* when you're literally *in the process* of entering me. It's gonna be *fine.* I hate you, that was the worst orgasm of my life, whatever you need to hear right now to make you feel okay about—*ohh!*"

The end of her sentence transformed into a moan as Ethan gripped her hip and slammed the rest of the way inside her, accompanied by a sound that seemed torn from deep in his chest.

They were both speechless then. He froze, his breathing shallow. She could feel his heart racing against her. His eyes were closed, jaw tense. She reached up to touch his face, and he flinched.

"Are you okay?" she murmured. He nodded jerkily.

"Just need a second. Before I, um." He exhaled shakily, laughing a little. "I told you, it's been . . . a long time. And . . . you feel *really* fucking good."

She stilled underneath him. She was grateful for a moment to catch her breath, too; the feeling of him inside her, stretching her out, filling her to the hilt, was almost too much to bear.

Eventually, he began to move, agonizingly slowly at first. She couldn't tell if she wanted him to slow down or speed up, every roll of his hips sending seismic waves of pleasure through her, each one building on the last. Her mind emptied, her focus narrowing to the spot where they were joined, to the feeling of his even, powerful strokes.

She wrapped her legs around him and groped around for a pillow, wedging it under her hips to get more leverage, and they both groaned at the change in angle as he sank deeper. He buried his face in her neck, biting and sucking so hard she knew it would leave marks, but she was so obliterated by sensation that she couldn't bring herself to care.

He was moving faster now. He slung one of her legs over his shoulder, leaning over her, driving deeper than she thought possible. She felt her eyes roll back in her head as she dug her fingernails into his back, hanging on for dear life.

She was dimly aware sounds were coming out of her, sounds that ordinarily might have made her self-conscious, but she was mindless with pleasure, taken over by pure instinct. She realized he was talking to her, too; murmuring how beautiful she was, how perfect, how long he'd wanted her, how good she felt, how wet, how tight. She let the words wash over her, enveloping her, filling her up even further than he already was with his body.

She was close, so close, and she could tell he was, too, by the catch in his breath, the slowing of his strokes, the way he felt somehow harder than ever. She reached one hand between her legs and pulled his face to hers with the other, biting his lower lip, crying out into his mouth as she came.

At her first spasm, her muscles clenching tightly around him, he shuddered inside her. She slid her leg off his shoulder so she could wrap her arms around his back, clutching his chest close against hers. He buried his face into her hair, tensing, groaning her name.

Finally, he stilled, breathing heavily, his weight pinning her to the mattress. She ran her palms up and down his sweat-slicked back as she felt his heart rate start to calm, pressing featherlight kisses into the side of his face. She felt a rush of disappointment as he slowly lifted himself onto his forearms, depriving her of his weight.

He looked into her eyes, shifting so one arm was free to stroke her face, her hair. She had never seen him look so young before, so vulnerable and unsure, his eyes moving over her like it was the first time he had ever seen her. She lifted her head up and kissed him slowly, tenderly. He seemed to relish the kiss, but when it was over, he pulled away, carefully sliding out of her and rolling onto his back.

She wasn't sure how long they lay there, silent except for the sounds of their ragged breathing. She couldn't bring herself to look at him. The full weight of what they had just done settled over her, replacing the weight of his body. She felt like she couldn't breathe. If he got weird again now, clammed up, pushed her away for the rest of the weekend, she didn't know what she would do. She couldn't take it. Her chest tightened even further at the thought.

She felt the mattress shift as he got up, heard the snap of rubber as he disposed of the condom. He climbed back into bed beside her, the sheets whispering as he adjusted himself. Turning her head, she saw that he'd rolled over to face her again, so she did the same. He was looking at her with that inscrutable look of his. Back to where they'd started—only now, everything was different.

"Did it work?" he asked, his voice husky.

She creased her brow in confusion.

"I mean . . . are we cured?"

It took her sex-addled brain a few long moments to process what he meant. Once she realized, though, laughter started bubbling up inside her, almost hysterical. Her laughter was infectious, overtaking Ethan, too, and the two of them lay there cackling like hyenas.

"Yes. Yes, we're cured," she wheezed, wiping tears from her eyes. "Get the hell away from me, ugly."

She punctuated the sentence by hooking her leg over his hip, pushing him onto his back, and straddling him.

18

THE NEXT DAY AND A HALF PASSED IN A HAZE. THEY CANCELED all their other obligations Audrey had set up for them in favor of fucking on every surface of the villa, interior and exterior, horizontal and vertical. Privately, Ethan was astonished by his own stamina. Even in his prime, he'd had his limits—unless there was some kind of upper involved. But when Grey looked at him, when she touched him, no matter how innocently, he was ready for her again in an instant. If a pharmaceutical company could figure out how to bottle her, they would drive Viagra out of business. All the benefits, with no side effects.

Well. Maybe one side effect.

Her theory that their attraction would be defused by consummation was wrong, to put it mildly. The more he had her, the more he wanted her. The clear boundaries of their arrangement had freed him from all of his inhibitions surrounding her, and to his surprise, she met him with enthusiasm at every turn. Any past friction between them had been totally self-imposed; once they stopped fighting their temptation, they were so in sync that it almost frightened him.

The fast-approaching deadline of Monday should have put a damper on things, but it only increased their urgency. Ethan tried not to think about it. Even though their physical relationship would soon be over, they were still bound by their contract for nearly four more months. Now that the cold war between them had officially reached an armistice, Ethan found himself grateful for how many more opportunities they had lined up to spend time together—even in non-naked contexts.

Late Sunday evening, after they had made thorough use of the dual-head shower, they sat in bed watching television, her legs across his lap, feeding each other dinner off their room service plates. Three months ago, witnessing this kind of display would have made his stomach turn, the prospect of his own involvement in it downright unthinkable. But now, Ethan happily took the bite of steak Grey proffered from her fork. They were the most clothed they'd been all day; him in his underwear, her swaddled in one of the resort's enormous fluffy robes.

He idly stroked one hand up and down her shin, letting it creep a little higher each time. Over her knee, up her thigh. Once he got high enough, she squirmed a little, laughing.

"Let me at least eat my ice cream before it melts," she demurred, reaching for a covered dish on the other side of the bed. He let his other hand join the exploration this time.

"We can put it in the freezer," he murmured into her ear. She playfully swatted him away.

"I don't know if you know this, but we don't have to compensate for three years of celibacy in thirty-six hours."

"Too late."

She laughed, spooning a bite of chocolate ice cream into her mouth. She closed her eyes and sighed. When she opened them again, she noticed him watching her and smiled shyly. The fact that she could still get bashful over something so small, after a day and a half of him seeing her naked in every position known to man, charmed him so much that his stomach did a little flip.

"I gotta enjoy this while I can. I hope they make me do some crazy muscle-building diet where I'll have to get up in the middle of the night to eat cod, like The Rock."

"Just as long as you don't wake me up when you do."

She paused, her spoon halfway to her mouth. *Fuck*. Why had he said that? The only topic they'd been careful to avoid: the prospect of things continuing past tomorrow. He hadn't meant it. It had just slipped out. He knew that it would be impossible. Their sexual compatibility, as electric as it might be, was not enough to sustain a full-blown relationship. They both knew that.

He cleared his throat and shifted. He needed to change the subject, fast.

"We've really been slacking on those questions."

Her eyes glinted with amusement.

"You're right. How will we ever get to know each other now?"

"Well, I sure hope Sugar Sweetums or whoever won't be grilling me on your blow job skills."

Grey rolled her eyes, but she was laughing. "Sugar *Clarke*. But if she does, you'll say . . . ?"

"Top-notch, obviously."

"Brownnoser." She put the empty ice cream dish on the night-stand and grabbed her phone as he reached for the remote to turn off the TV. "I'll try to find a juicy one."

She snuggled back against his shoulder as she scrolled, and he put his arm around her, planting a soft kiss on the crown of her head without even thinking. Like it was the most natural thing in the world.

"Okay. Here's a two-parter. Part one: 'What is your most treasured memory?'"

He answered immediately. "When my kids were born."

"That is *such* a dad answer. You're so predictable," she teased. He laughed, squeezing her shoulder.

"I'm serious. It's pretty amazing. And terrifying. Just . . . overwhelming. In every sense of the word."

He thought about the first time he'd held Sydney, her tiny fingers grasping his. Unraveled by the thought that he'd played even the tiniest part in creating something so perfect. Vowing to do better than his own father had. He felt a squeeze in his chest. He'd fucked that up, too. He didn't like to think about all the firsts he'd missed since he'd moved out. The way he'd been demoted overnight from active participant in their lives to glorified bystander, perpetually playing catch-up. How he had only himself to blame.

Grey seemed to sense the shift in his mood and nuzzled deeper into his neck. He craned his head to look at her.

"Do *you* want kids?"

She looked up in alarm. "We didn't run out of condoms, did we?"

He laughed. "Just curious. That seems like the type of thing our friend Sugar might ask; we should probably be on the same page."

She pursed her lips and considered it, her hand sliding down to rest on her abdomen almost unconsciously. "I don't know. I like kids, I guess. But I've never felt strongly about growing my own. People keep telling me I will once I turn thirty, which, whatever. Kind of condescending. Maybe they're right. For now, I could take or leave 'em."

"I get that. I hadn't thought much about it, either, until I had them. I ended up with some pretty great ones, though."

She smirked. "I wouldn't know, I'm contractually banned

from ever meeting them." He laughed, and she snuggled back against him. "I feel like the miracle of life should be off the table. That one's kind of a gimme."

"Fine. You tell me yours while I think of something else."

She put her phone down and twirled a strand of hair around her finger, pulling it straight as if to inspect it for split ends.

"So . . . the summer after sixth grade, I got cast in my first big movie."

"What was it?"

"*The Sister Switch?*" It was a question, like she doubted he'd heard of it.

He looked at her in surprise. "You were in that? My kids love that movie—I've probably seen it fifteen times."

"Sort of. Not really. I was Morgan Mitchell's double. So, like, all the scenes that had both twins were shot with both of us, switching off who was playing who, and then they spliced them together in post so they were both her."

He stroked her hair. "And that's your most treasured memory?"

She half shrugged. She toyed with the palm of his other hand, tracing her fingers over it as she spoke. "I guess so. It was my first time on a big movie set. I mean, I'd been on set before, I'd done commercials and procedurals and soaps and everything, but that was nothing compared to this. We shot in Paris, in Vermont, in Big Sur. Morgan and I got really close; it was like actually having a sister. The whole set was like a big family. It was nice. I felt really . . . cared for. I feel like I've been chasing that experience ever since," she finished softly.

He turned her palm over so it was flat against his. "Are you still in touch with Morgan at all?"

She shook her head. "We were for a while. We would see each other once or twice a year, whenever she was in New York. We kind of drifted apart when . . . well. You know. I wrote to her the first time she went to rehab, she sent me a nice note back. We DM sometimes. She was so sweet when I knew her. It's sad. I don't think she's ever had good people around her. You want to talk about scary stage moms, hers was . . . intense."

"I used to see her out all the time. Morgan, I mean. Well, actually, her mom, too, sometimes. We partied together a few times; she must not have even been twenty-one yet. She was pretty wild."

"Yeah." Grey sounded a million miles away. "I think about her a lot, actually. Like if I had been more successful. Maybe that would've been me."

"Maybe. You'd have to be able to handle more than one drink per night, though."

Grey laughed, and the sound made his heart feel like it was about to burst.

"Okay. You've had enough time to think about it. Whattaya got?"

Ethan took a long moment before he answered. He moved his arm from around her shoulders down to her waist, pressing her closer against him. She leaned into him, wrapping her arms around his neck, nuzzling her face deep into the crook of his shoulder. Though the gesture aroused him, naturally, it made him feel something else, too. Brave.

"When I was growing up, things were . . . not great. At home. I spent a lot of time at . . . at Sam's. With his family. There were times when I basically lived at his house. For months."

He hesitated. Grey gave a little murmur of sympathy, her lips brushing his neck. He gave her thigh a firm squeeze before continuing.

"One summer—I think I was twelve? Thirteen? Some cousin let his family use their beach house in Cape May, and I went with them. We were there for two weeks. Sam and I would take our bikes out every morning and be gone all day, out on the beach, on the boardwalk. We'd come back to the house and his dad would be grilling. We'd watch movies, make fires on the beach, look at the stars. It was just . . . peaceful. I knew everything was going to be okay. Everything at home . . . it didn't matter. Nothing else felt real."

He felt Grey smile against his neck.

"How wholesome."

"Did I mention I also got to second base for the first time? Under the boardwalk."

"That's very *Grease* of you. Don't tell me you also stayed out till ten o'clock."

Laughing, Ethan flipped Grey off his lap and onto her back, pinning her underneath him. She giggled and fidgeted a little, but didn't fight him.

"So that's what I get for trusting you with my most intimate, personal memories. I see how it is."

She looked up at him innocently. "What do *I* get?"

He dipped his head down to kiss her, sliding his tongue past her lips, which yielded to him instantly. She sighed a little in the back of her throat, and tangled her hands in his hair, pulling him closer, deeper. That tiny noise was enough to drive him crazy. He slipped his hands inside her robe, running his hands over her satin skin.

Something pulled at the back of his mind, and he lifted his head again. Grey whimpered a little in protest.

"We're not done yet. You said it was a two-part question."

Grey threw her head back and half laughed, half groaned in frustration. She scooted out from under him and propped herself up against the headboard. He rested his head in her lap, her fingers automatically moving to caress his hair, her nails tracing gentle circles on his scalp.

"What's part two?" he prodded, trying not to let himself get distracted by the pleasurable tingles her fingers were sending down his spine.

She looked down at him, her mouth twisted. "What do you think?" she asked softly.

He closed his eyes.

"Worst memory."

She didn't respond for a moment, just kept at him with those hypnotizing circles.

"We don't have to. We can just leave it."

He shook his head.

"No. I want to. But . . . you go first."

She sighed. He kept his eyes closed.

"Probably finding out about my . . . about Callum. It wasn't just the cheating. It was that *everyone* knew before I did. Then the tabloids picked it up . . . the whole thing was so humiliating."

He reached up and squeezed her thigh in sympathy.

"How long were you together?"

"Four years."

"What a fucking asshole. And everything was fine before then? Blissfully in love? Birds appearing every time he was near?" He kept his tone light, trying to mask how curious he was to hear the answer.

She hesitated. When she spoke again, her voice was dreamy and contemplative. "I don't know. I thought so at the time. The betrayal was worse than the heartbreak, honestly. Looking back, I don't think either of us was ever that emotionally invested in it. Working together . . . it was just so convenient. It felt like the kind of relationship I was *supposed* to want to be in, the kind of person I was *supposed* to want to be with. But we never really talked about anything important. Sometimes he would say these things out of nowhere where I'd be like . . . *what?* Who *are* you? Do we even know each other at all? But I always just . . . ignored it. I think we were both happier keeping things surface level."

"Like what kind of things would he say?"

"Oh, I don't know. There were a few offhand comments here and there that made me think that he *might* possibly be . . ." She paused before lowering her voice. He could tell she was trying not to laugh. ". . . a flat earther."

Ethan burst out laughing. "You dated a guy who thought the Earth was flat, for four years?"

"For *four years*. I don't know what the fuck I was thinking. We were even talking about getting engaged for half of it. I should've known it was never going to happen if we needed to spend that much time discussing it."

"You dodged a bullet, though. Nora and I got engaged after a month. We probably could've used a little more talking first."

She laughed, his head vibrating on her lap.

"Would you ever do it again? Get married, I mean." She paused. "You know. Just in case she asks. For the article."

He surprised himself with how easily the answer came to him. "Yeah. I would. I loved being married. Can't say I recommend divorce, though. I'd like to only do that once, if possible."

He'd barely even admitted that to himself before. His thoughts about his romantic future were typically limited to ensuring no one else would be put through the gauntlet of being with him. But now, after the seamless intimacy of these past few days with her—maybe this *was* something he would want again. One day. In theory.

She was silent. She stopped making circles with her fingers and moved on to stroking his hair.

"It's funny," he said. He felt her shift, tense.

"What?"

"Your best memory is about work, and your worst memory is about love. That explains a lot about you."

"Well, I turned down a movie to have the privilege of finding out I was being cheated on, so it's still sort of work related. And also . . ." She hesitated. "*The Sister Switch* wasn't all good, either."

He opened his eyes, looking up at her.

"What happened?"

She shook her head a little. "Never mind. It's stupid."

"Tell me."

She exhaled. "They flew me out to L.A. for the premiere. I was so fucking excited I couldn't sleep the night before. But when the movie started . . . I don't know if I can explain it. I mean, I *knew* I wouldn't actually be in it. But it felt like everything I had worked on, everything I was so proud of, had been erased. Or never even existed in the first place. I don't know. It feels silly saying it out loud. I was just a kid; I couldn't really wrap my head around it. I had to go into the lobby and cry."

Ethan took her hand out of his hair and kissed her palm. His heart broke for tiny Grey—or rather, tiny Emily—for her hard work, for her big dreams that would never come to pass.

"It's not silly. It makes total sense."

"It all ended up being okay. Carol, the director—you know Carol Hayes?—she came out to comfort me. She got it right away. She told me that even though my face wasn't on-screen, I was there in Morgan's performance, in her reactions. Her physicality. Some of her line readings, even. We created those characters together. She told me they could never have done it without me." She bit her lip. "It was exactly what I needed to hear."

He didn't say anything, just kept holding her hand. She shifted, suddenly a little uncomfortable.

"That's enough about me." She looked down at him, her eyes

seeming to bore straight through him. "Do you want to tell me about Sam?"

Her directness shook him, but not as much as the realization that he did, in fact, want to tell her. He'd barely talked about it with anyone, now that he thought about it. Nora had begged him at first; to talk to her, to anyone, but he had stonewalled her. Eventually she'd given up. After that, there had been no one left to beg him.

"Can we get in bed first?"

She nodded, and the two of them set about cleaning up their dishes. When he came back from putting the cart outside, she was already curled up under the comforter, her robe discarded on the floor. He slid in next to her and shut off the bedside lamp, plunging them into darkness.

He wrapped his arms around her, gathering her smooth back into his chest. Even though her body was no longer a mystery to him, he felt like it would take a lifetime before he stopped being amazed by it, before the sight and the touch of it stopped triggering the most primal reactions in him. He considered forgetting all about the stupid questions and just taking her instead. By the way she arched her back and shifted against him, he could tell that she was thinking the same thing. It would be so easy to just slide into her right there, straight into blissful oblivion, where nothing existed except the two of them.

He was tired of oblivion, he realized. He wanted to be here. With her.

He took a deep, calming breath of her hair, making a mental note to check the ingredients in her shampoo to see if there was anything hiding there that would explain the narcotic effect it had on him.

"Nora and I were fighting. I don't even remember why. We

were fighting a lot in those days, even before . . . I think we would have split no matter what, eventually. I was holed up in some bar somewhere and I begged Sam to come meet me. I must have called him a hundred times. I don't remember much after he got there." He burrowed deeper in her hair, trying to muffle his voice as much as possible so she wouldn't hear it crack. "That's the worst part. The last time I ever saw him, and I was in a fucking black-out."

She tightened her grip on his arm, draped across her chest.

"We were there for hours. I think I had some Oxys, too." He felt her tense. "I don't do any of that anymore, though. No drugs. Not since that night."

She relaxed again, her lips gently pressed against his arm.

"I don't know why he tried to drive himself home. I was too fucked up to do anything. There were so many things . . ."

She was silent. He could feel her heart hammering against his chest, her deep breaths helping to keep his own slow and even.

"You know that feeling . . . maybe you don't. The morning after a blackout. You're just waiting to get that call or that text about what horrible thing you did the night before. And even if you do, it's usually nothing. Maybe you accidentally insulted someone, or you broke something expensive."

His words became thick. "And . . . maybe this sounds bad. But when you get to . . . where I am, there's not a lot you can't undo. That you can't fix or get away with. If you call in enough favors, if you spend enough money. But this . . ."

He swallowed hard against his rapidly closing throat, eyelashes fluttering against her hair. He couldn't remember the last time he'd cried. He'd almost forgotten he still could. He realized he was still talking, half-formed sentences tumbling out of his mouth, switching directions midthought like a malfunctioning train signal.

"I should've just . . . no. It wasn't. I couldn't. I'm just so . . . *fuck*."

He shut his eyes, feeling hot, helpless tears stream down his cheeks, into her hair. "He was the wrong one."

She rolled over to face him. Her eyes were wide and earnest. She brushed her thumb against his wet cheekbone, then brought her lips to the same spot. She tilted his head in her hands to do the same on the other side, kissing away the new tears that had sprung up in their place. He trailed off eventually, letting her continue her ministrations without resisting.

He felt the familiar weightlessness he experienced after he'd had a little too much to drink, but it couldn't be that. He'd only had a beer or two with dinner. He wasn't even buzzed. But that all-consuming stillness swept over him, just the same. He couldn't remember the last time he'd felt this calm and peaceful without any outside assistance. Maybe he never had.

Despite everything they'd done over the last two days, this was the first moment he truly felt naked in front of her. And later that night, when their breathing heightened and she undulated on top of him once more, there seemed to be an invisible thread connecting them that hadn't been there before. Like they were fused by more than just their bodies. Ethan had never experienced anything quite like it. The feeling was so potent, so unnerving, that when he came, quaking underneath her as she arched and moaned, he thought he might start crying again.

Though the next morning loomed ominously, in some ways it couldn't arrive fast enough for him. It was less terrifying than what might happen if things were to continue this way between them for even one more day.

———

GREY WASN'T SURE WHAT CAUSED HER TO JOLT AWAKE. AFTER their exertions of the past two days, it certainly wasn't because she was well rested—she felt like she could sleep for another year. She could feel Ethan all around her; his heat, his scent, his slow breathing on the back of her neck, the weight of his arm slung over her chest. The pressure in her abdomen quickly alerted her to the real reason behind her rude awakening: she had to pee. Badly.

Reluctantly, she ducked out from beneath his arm. He groaned in protest, but remained unconscious. On the way to the bathroom, she checked the clock. It wasn't even nine yet. They'd pushed their checkout time from eleven to one, though it was a futile gesture. Reality was still coming for them, one minute at a time.

She ached all over, a throb that began between her legs and extended up through her heart. How were they ever going to return to normal now? In the heat of the moment, it seemed like the only thing to do was surrender, for the sake of their sanity. It was supposed to simplify things. Remove temptation. She'd realized too late that maybe there had been a *tiny* bit of denial involved, at least on her end. She didn't regret it, though. No matter what happened next, she knew she'd be reliving every moment of this perfect, stolen weekend for the rest of her life. For now, that was enough to quell her uncertainty.

She considered crawling back into bed without looking at her phone, but it buzzed in the corner, demanding her attention. When she picked it up, her stomach sank.

Missed calls from both Renata and Audrey. Dozens of texts. As she unlocked her phone and swiped through everything, her heart raced. She started shaking. She threw on one of Ethan's T-shirts and hobbled out to the patio as quickly as she could. Renata picked up on the first ring.

"Grey. Thank god. How soon can you be at Audrey's?"

Grey closed her eyes, trying to calm her racing thoughts long enough to formulate a response. She felt like she was going to vomit.

"I'm leaving now. Give me two hours."

She darted around the villa, trying to pack as quietly as possible. However, her attempt at stealth was thwarted when she tripped over a stray shoe with her bad ankle, howling in pain.

She heard Ethan stir.

"What's going on?" His voice was warm and sleepy. She felt a pang at the sound of it, struck by the sudden urge to crawl back in next to him and pretend none of this was happening. She pushed it aside. Letting herself develop those kinds of fuzzy feelings for him was what had gotten her into this mess in the first place.

"Check your phone" was all she could say, her voice coming out high and pinched. As if on cue, it vibrated on the nightstand. She'd already had to fully silence hers, the constant buzzing only making her more agitated. He groped for it as he sat up, his hair mussed and sticking out in all directions, blinking slowly.

She swept into the bathroom to pack her makeup kit.

"Fuck. What the *fuck*," she heard him exclaim from the bedroom.

She gave one last once-over to make sure she wasn't missing anything and limped back to the bedroom to dump everything into her suitcase. Ethan was scrolling through his phone. He spoke without looking up at her.

"This is bad."

"Uh-huh." She was mostly done packing, but she forced herself to keep moving so she wouldn't have to look at him. Her heart was jackhammering in her chest, waiting for his reaction.

"Are you okay?" he asked quietly, his eyes searching her face.

"I don't know." She closed her suitcase with such force that she almost pulled off the zipper.

He glanced down at her bags. His mouth tightened.

"You were going to leave without me." It wasn't a question.

"I need to deal with this." Better to deal with that than with *this,* she wanted to add. Whatever the fuck *this* was. He was still naked, partially covered by the duvet, but from the way he was looking at her he might as well have been wearing a full suit of armor.

When she saw the look in his eyes, her stomach sank. She realized that her initial gut instinct to bail had been right on the money. Rational Grey had chastised her, encouraging her to talk to him, try to work through it together. But Rational Grey wasn't driving at the moment. And now, with his expression this hard and cold, asking him to come with her after all felt as dangerous and ill-advised as staring into the sun.

"How are you getting back?" This was an Ethan she hadn't seen in weeks, the standoffish stranger punishing her for his own attraction to her.

"I had them call me a car."

He didn't say anything, just locked eyes with her. She met his gaze, refusing to look away. There was a knock at the door; the golf cart had arrived. She was frozen to the spot, waiting for him to say something. Tell her to come back to bed, tell her to wait while he got dressed, offer to carry her bags to the door—anything that would give her some hint that he felt anything besides shock and regret.

"Shouldn't you get that?"

She nodded, perversely grateful that her throat had squeezed shut so she wouldn't be tempted to say anything. She wished she *had* been able to sneak out while he was sleeping, so his parting image of her wouldn't be of her clumsily juggling her luggage as she limped toward the door.

19

"I'M SO SORRY, GREY."

Grey thought she should have cried by now. It would be normal, expected, even. But instead, she felt strangely calm. Numb.

In the back seat of the town car on the way back to L.A., she scrolled through one headline after another, until her phone grew hot in her hand and the battery dipped into single digits.

50 Shades of Grey: Ethan Atkins's Starlet Girlfriend Bares All During Hot 'n' Heavy Palm Springs Getaway!

Then there were the photos, taken from a high angle with a long-range telephoto lens, or maybe by a drone. Slightly blurry, but unmistakable. Her and Ethan, stark naked, fucking like porn stars on the lounge chairs, in the pool, up against the glass door. Most of the publications had been thoughtful enough to censor their genitalia with cute little stars or hearts, as if that made the images any less obscene.

There were other photos, too: her smoking a joint on the patio. Drinking champagne straight from the bottle. Ethan at a gas station, baseball cap and glasses proving useless at camouflaging his identity, buying condoms. *Should've worn the fake mustache after all,* she thought ruefully. She wanted to laugh. How had this become her life? She'd spent twenty years keeping her head down, petrified of scandal, but now that it was at her doorstep wearing nothing but cartoon hearts, she felt nothing.

She had the car take her straight to Audrey's, even though she desperately needed an iced coffee and a shower. The receptionist immediately ushered her back to Audrey's office, where Audrey and Renata were already waiting. Audrey had drawn the curtains over the glass walls of her office, giving the whole endeavor an air of high drama that almost had Grey laughing again before she even sat down. She hoped this would be her new inappropriate response to everything going forward; it certainly beat crying.

However, her urge to laugh quickly died down when Renata confirmed Grey's worst fears: the *Golden City* producers had withdrawn their offer. Though the news made her feel like someone had taken a sledgehammer to her chest, Grey's voice was emotionless.

"So, let me get this straight. I'm being punished for . . . what, exactly? Having my privacy invaded? Having sex with someone everyone thinks I've been dating for months?"

Audrey shook her head.

"I'm on your side here, Grey. I agree, you've done nothing wrong. I've tried to reason with them, but they're being overly cautious about this sort of thing. This is supposed to be a family franchise, and the author of the books is extremely religious. Even if you *had* signed the contract already, they've included a strict morality clause. They're not budging."

"I don't think I've done anything immoral. Can't we sue the photographers or something? How is selling naked photos of me without my consent not a crime?" She felt herself get angrier as she spoke, clutching the arms of her chair.

Audrey pursed her lips. "I'm looking into it. But, I'm afraid . . . I owe you an apology."

The realization hit her, the second sledgehammer coming through to destroy any remnants the first one had missed. She couldn't even bring herself to get angry at Audrey. It was their own fault for being so fucking stupid. Of course Audrey had planted photographers. Of course they were never *really* alone. Of course.

"I'm so sorry, Grey. When I spoke with him last week, he told me there was nothing going on between you two. Those pictures of him carrying you went over so well, I just thought . . . by the time I realized, they had already sold the photos."

Grey had never seen Audrey, calm, competent Audrey, so flustered. It made her feel better and worse at the same time. Better, in that she knew Audrey took the situation seriously. Worse, in that it seemed like they were only scratching the surface of how serious the situation actually was.

Grey shook her head jerkily. "It's nothing. We're not . . . there's nothing. It's over." Her mask of tranquillity cracked for the first time, her voice shaking.

Renata looked at her sympathetically. Grey didn't meet her eyes, staring straight ahead instead. She felt suddenly, mortifyingly aware of how disheveled she was, of the traces of him that still lingered all over her. The marks that hadn't had a chance to fade from her throat. Her clothes brushing against skin scraped tender by his stubble every time she shifted in her seat.

"I want out. Out of the contract. I'm done."

Audrey looked chagrined.

"I know this is all a lot to process, but there's no need to do anything rash. The two of you can recover from this. Public sympathy is on your side."

"There is no 'two of us.' This was supposed to *help* me, help my career, but so far I've just been harassed, stalked, humiliated, violated, and fired. You have to let me out for, what is it? Material damage to my reputation? I'd say my reputation has been pretty goddamn materially damaged, wouldn't you?"

Grey was trembling again, but her voice became stronger as she went on, downright steely. To her surprise, Audrey didn't push back.

"You're absolutely right. We'll see that you're released immediately. And I will do everything in my power to turn this around for you." Audrey began typing furiously on her computer. She paused to look back at Grey.

"I know it doesn't feel that way right now, but I have a feeling this might end up being a good thing. Really."

She was right. It didn't feel that way. Grey walked back to the elevator bank with Renata in silence. It wasn't until the elevator doors closed on them that Grey finally let herself collapse in tears in Renata's arms.

ETHAN WAS VAGUELY AWARE OF DAYS PASSING. DURING HIS brief periods of consciousness, he had no idea whether it was light or dark outside. Not that it mattered, since he'd closed the black-out curtains over every window in his house as soon as he returned from Palm Springs. It had taken him an exasperating amount of time, since his house seemed to be nothing but windows.

By his rough calculations, he'd woken up alone thousands of times over the last five years, maybe tens of thousands over the course of his life. Why then did he now wake up expecting to find Grey in his arms, when it had only happened a handful of times, over the course of less than two days?

When it had dawned on him that Grey was trying to sneak out without waking him, part of him wasn't surprised. That didn't stop him from feeling like all the air had been sucked out of the room. He knew things would have to end between them eventually, but he hadn't expected it to happen quite so soon. Not while he was still naked and half-asleep in their sex-rumpled sheets. So of course he'd panicked. Shut down completely.

He kept replaying his last glimpse of her face before she'd left. Jaw set, eyes distant, ready to hobble alone into the firestorm that awaited her like Joan of fucking Arc. *Alone*. Because he'd been too paralyzed by her rejection to do anything but lie there and watch her leave.

He barely remembered packing his things and making the drive home. Once back in L.A., he'd immediately called Audrey, ready to ream her out for allowing it to happen, for not protecting Grey. Once he'd reached her, though, she'd solemnly let him know that Grey had requested to be released from their contract.

Well. That was that, then.

Ethan woke up to the sound of his phone buzzing obnoxiously. He had passed out in his office chair, his neck stiff and sore. He scrambled to pick up the phone.

"Grey?" he slurred.

Nora's voice, sharp and annoyed.

"Ethan? Where the hell are you? You were supposed to pick up the girls an hour ago."

The words pinballed through his head before falling straight back out again. He struggled unsuccessfully to make sense of them. Game over.

"Nora?" was the best he could manage.

Her tone shifted to one of alarm. "Is everything okay? I saw the pictures. Do you need me to come over there?"

"No. No. No no no."

"Are you alone?"

More alone than ever. He must not have said anything, because he heard her exhale in frustration. Elle and Sydney must have been within earshot, because she lowered her voice to a whisper.

"This isn't supposed to be my job anymore, Ethan. I had plans, you know. The world doesn't stop because you want to get fucked up and feel sorry for yourself."

"Then leave me alone. I'm not your problem."

He hung up.

20

GREY HAD BEEN INSTRUCTED TO LIE LOW FOR A WEEK OR SO, TO give Audrey a chance to figure out their next move. Audrey probably hadn't meant it quite so literally: sprawled facedown on her couch, surrounded by empty takeout containers and Diet Coke cans, Grey felt like it had been days since she had been vertical.

Normally she responded to stress or disappointment by leaping into action, setting her sights on the next goal on her list. However, somewhere between the months of waiting in limbo for *Golden City* and Kamilah's absence pausing the momentum of their work on *The Empty Chair,* her ambition had atrophied. Her arrangement with Ethan hadn't helped matters, either; with him, loafing around had become part of her job. It had happened so slowly, like a frog in a pot of boiling water, that she barely recognized the greasy, lethargic figure that stared back at her in the mirror on the days she remembered to brush her teeth.

To compound her suffering, her weekend of no-holds-barred sex had led to the worst UTI of her life. She'd thought about soliciting, interviewing, and hiring an assistant just so she wouldn't have to risk being photographed picking up her antibiotics at the pharmacy. Thankfully, she'd survived the process unnoticed, a small mercy in what felt like an endless line of kicks to the head.

She wanted to text Ethan, that goddamn heart-eyes emoji taunting her every time she looked at his name. She didn't even know what she would say to him. She wanted to apologize for trying to leave without saying goodbye, for breaking the contract without talking to him first. To tell him how much she already regretted it. How much she missed him. But every time she tried, she just stared blankly at her phone, the blinking cursor more mesmerizing than a hypnotist's watch.

She couldn't stop rereading his last text to her, barely even two words, when he'd been on the way to pick her up. 5 mins. Their text thread told the true story of their relationship: brief, transactional, as few details as possible.

> Tomorrow's no good.
> Wednesday?
> I'll be over by 8.
> Can we reschedule coffee?

She felt ridiculous at the prospect of ejaculating her messy, amorphous feelings all over such a sparse and impersonal exchange. A wall of vulnerable blue text pushing his five terse characters right off the screen. The idea of calling him left her even more overwhelmed. After three days without hearing from him, either, she knew it was time to stop torturing herself about what she should say to him. It was over. She'd been seduced by the fantasy of her and Ethan, Ethan and her, and she'd let it ruin everything. She'd fucked up, and she needed to move on.

Eventually she turned her phone off entirely and put it in the drawer of her nightstand like it was radioactive. There was nothing good on there for her right now. Though Audrey kept telling her that any attention was better than no attention, Grey found that hard to believe. No attention seemed preferable to the endless reposts and tags of the photos of her and Ethan, the supportive texts from friends and acquaintances doing nothing to mitigate the indignity of the nonstop stream of filthy and harassing DMs flooding every inbox.

Audrey had assured her that she was working overtime to get the pictures taken down, but beyond that, Grey's legal options were limited. Apparently, since she and Ethan were public figures, California's revenge porn laws did not extend to them. And now that they were online, trying to get the pictures removed was like fighting a pornographic hydra: take one down, and ten more spring up in its place.

Grey lay listless on the couch, unable to endure anything more stimulating than *Planet Earth*. Suddenly, her front door knob began to shake and rattle. She sat bolt upright. Was this the grand finale of her week from hell? Getting murdered in her own home? Her phone was too far away for her to do anything other than watch as the front door swung open to reveal Kamilah, laden with several enormous suitcases.

Grey took one look at her and burst into tears.

"Is this real? What are you doing here?" she sobbed.

"This leg of the tour is over next week, so I figured I'd head home a little early. Which you would *know* if you'd answered any texts for the last three days." Kamilah's voice was teasing, but her brow knitted in sympathy behind her wire-rimmed glasses. Grey knew she must look like a fucking mess. Kamilah, as always, looked gorgeous, showing little to no signs of her transcontinental journey. Her hair, which had been curly and voluminous when she'd left, was buzzed short, making her razor-sharp cheekbones pop even more than they normally did.

She put down her luggage and crossed over to Grey, embracing her. Grey clutched her tightly, her shoulders shaking. She had never been happier to see anyone in her life.

"You look so beautiful," Grey gulped through her tears. Kamilah laughed.

"I'm going to go wash the plane off me," Kamilah said gently. "Then we'll talk. Then we'll plan. It's all going to be okay." She sniffed. "Maybe the first part of this plan should include *you* showering, too."

An hour later, the dishwasher and washing machine hummed, and the trash that had covered the living room was now confined to a garbage bag by the door. Grey and Kamilah, squeaky clean, lounged on the couch as Grey regaled her with the saga of the last two months.

"I *knew* it! You were being so weird about everything, I knew something had to be up," Kamilah said smugly.

"I know, I know, I'm sorry. I've been the worst friend lately. I was kind of relieved you weren't here, honestly, it would've been impossible to hide it from you. But I'm so fucking glad you're back."

"So where are things now? Have you guys talked?"

Grey shook her head. Kamilah's jaw dropped.

"What? Like not at all? Emil*yyy,* come *on.* Has he been trying to talk to you, at least?"

Grey buried her face in her hands. "I don't know. I don't think so. I haven't looked at my phone in days. I don't even know what I would say to him. I just want to forget everything and move on."

"I bet you do," Kamilah said drily.

Grey bent her knees to her chin and folded her arms on top of them. "I mean, we agreed that things couldn't continue past the weekend. And now that the contract's over, there's really no reason for us to see each other again. It's simple. No need to hash it out and prolong the drama." Maybe saying it out loud would help her actually believe it.

Kamilah looked skeptical. "But whose idea was it for things to stop after the weekend?"

"Mine," Grey admitted.

"And who broke the contract?"

Grey didn't like where this was going. "I did."

Kamilah scoffed.

"You are cold as ice sometimes. You obviously like him, you two were liking each other all over the house. You do this all the time. You're always looking for reasons to cut people out, stop them from getting too close."

Grey opened her mouth to deny it, but realized she'd admitted that exact thing to Ethan.

"This is different," she spluttered. "I lost my first job in a *year* because of him. This whole thing has been nothing but trouble since day one. Plus, he's a fucking mess. I don't need someone I have to take care of. I don't need that shit in my life. I don't." Although she hadn't had to take care of him this weekend. From falling on the cobblestones to falling asleep in his arms, he'd been thoughtful and attentive to her every need.

She closed her eyes, her words catching on the image she couldn't get out of her mind: the winter in his expression as she walked out the door. Fighting ice with ice until they both froze to death. "He's been so hot and cold with me from the beginning. I can't take it anymore. If I hadn't done it, he would have. Eventually."

Kamilah shrugged. "You know better, I guess. But I don't really see how he's the bad guy here."

Grey sighed and rested her cheek on her folded arms. "He's not. Maybe I am. I don't know. This whole thing just makes me feel like I'm gonna puke. All the time."

Kamilah pursed her lips sympathetically, then widened her eyes as if something had just occurred to her. "Wait, are you even allowed to be telling me this? Is the NDA still in effect?"

Grey shook her head. "No, it's all over. I mean, I probably shouldn't be shouting it from the rooftops or anything, but I'm sure nobody's questioning whether it's real now. My image is just fucked. No pun intended." She sat up straight. "Enough about my fucking disaster of a love life. I want to hear about the tour. And Andromeda."

Kamilah's face lit up, her mouth stretching into a dreamy grin. Grey felt the weight in her chest lift a little at the sight of her friend's giddiness. "God. Where do I even start? The last few months have just been . . . unreal. Like, how the fuck is this my life right now?" She clapped her hands under her chin. "Oh! Did I tell you they flew out my mom and sisters for a week to surprise me while we were in Paris? My brain is so jet-lag scrambled, I can't remember what I've already told you. Tell me when I'm repeating myself."

Grey adjusted the pillow at her back and snuggled into the corner of the couch. "Just start at the beginning. And tell me everything."

ETHAN CAME TO, VAGUELY AWARE OF SOMEONE STANDING OVER him.

Grey.

"Not exactly," came a deep voice. Ethan hadn't realized he'd spoken out loud. He opened his eyes with considerable effort to see Lucas looming above him.

"What are you doing in my room?" he asked, his voice dry and cracked.

"This is the living room, Ethan," Lucas said slowly, as if speaking to a child.

He had a point. Ethan slung an arm over the back of the couch and hoisted himself up, groaning. His head spun as Lucas tossed him a bottle of water. Ethan's reflexes failed him as he threw his arm out, in vain, to prevent it from hitting him with a *thud* square in the chest. He fumbled to open it.

"What are you doing *here,* I mean?"

"You texted me, like, ten times, saying you needed help. I almost called 911 first."

Ethan frowned. He looked around the room, trying to gather evidence of what would have compelled him to send an SOS to Lucas. His eyes strayed to the floor, where four or five remotes lay in disarray, along with a handful of loose batteries of indeterminate origin.

"Um. I think I was trying to turn on the TV."

Lucas bent down and picked up the largest remote, handing it to Ethan.

"This is the universal remote, I programmed it last month. You turn it on by pressing 'on.' Anything else?" Ethan expected him to sound irritated, but he realized he'd never seen Lucas look anything less than sunny and affable. Apparently, even being dragged from West Hollywood to the Palisades for such a stupid reason wasn't enough to rattle him.

Ethan cleared his throat, embarrassed. "No. No, you can go."

Lucas inclined his head and turned to leave.

"Wait," Ethan called impulsively. Lucas turned back, eyebrows raised in anticipation. "Do you . . . do you want to watch the game or something?"

The question hung suspended in midair.

"What game? It's one o'clock on a Wednesday."

"The. Um. Texas?"

Lucas looked like he was trying not to laugh, a dimple appearing in his left cheek.

"I have to head to class, but I can come back . . . later?" he said tentatively, as if expecting Ethan to change his mind and reprimand him for even suggesting it.

Ethan nodded, a little chagrined at his outburst.

"I can pick you up some dinner. Burrito okay?" Lucas said.

"Sure. Get yourself something, too. I . . ." Ethan hesitated. "I don't need you to be here as my assistant. You can just . . . you can just be my nephew." He directed that last part at the remote, ashamed at his open admission of how lonely he was. He'd gone out of his way to put Lucas in his place, make sure that he never saw their relationship as anything beyond employer/employee, and now here Ethan was, laid low, desperate for a little familial kindness.

Lucas didn't flinch.

"Sure. Seven?"

Ethan felt a swell of wonder that his sister had managed to raise such a kindhearted and good-natured young man. She certainly hadn't learned it from their parents.

"Seven is great."

Lucas turned toward the door again.

"Lucas?"

"Yeah?"

Ethan met his eyes this time.

"Thank you."

21

GREY DRESSED AS IF SHE WERE GOING INTO BATTLE, SWIPING ON
layer after layer of eyeliner like warpaint. It had been nearly two
weeks since she had seen herself in anything but sweatpants and a
sullen expression, and the sight of her smoldering, black-clad reflection had a fortifying effect on her. When she stepped out of her
bedroom, Kamilah eyed her approvingly.

"You look like an evil Charlie's Angel."

Grey ran her hands down her legs. They squeaked slightly
against her glossy, faux-leather leggings.

"Is it too much? I think I might change."

"Don't. That is *exactly* the energy I need from you tonight.
Can you help me shorten my straps?"

Once Grey obliged, they stood side by side at the mirror.

"*You* look fucking incredible," Grey said admiringly. Kamilah
was a vision in gold, from her silky sheath dress to her septum ring
to the bangles snaking up her arms. The dress's black leather ac-
cents at the shoulders and waist perfectly matched her knee-high

lace-up boots. "Did you get those boots while you were away? I don't recognize them."

"Berlin, *mein Liebchen,*" Kamilah said, batting her eyelashes. "I almost sold my hard drives to make room for them in my bag."

"Worth it. I'm just mad I can't borrow them." The two of them were roughly the same height, and wore the same size in everything except shoes, Kamilah measuring in at a dainty size six next to Grey's eight-and-a-half.

Now that the Europe and Asia legs of their tour were over, Andromeda X was celebrating their return to L.A. by performing a secret, invite-only show at the El Rey. Grey had tried to flake out in the days leading up to it, but Kamilah had reminded her how outrageous it was that Grey still hadn't met Andromeda even though they'd been dating for months.

"To be fair, you didn't really give me a chance," Grey had pointed out.

"Well, here's your chance," Kamilah had retorted. Grey couldn't argue with that. She knew she was being selfish, that it was time to suck it up and get over herself—at least for a night.

For most of the day, Kamilah had been down at the venue, overseeing the technical execution of the video elements of Andromeda's stage show. She'd kept her promise to return to the house in time for them to get ready together, which Grey suspected was also a tactic to keep her from trying to bail at the last second.

Kamilah's phone dinged, indicating their car had arrived. Grey locked the door behind them, her heart in her throat. This would be her first time stepping out in public since she'd returned from Palm Springs. Her first appearance sans Ethan.

She'd finally stopped jumping every time her phone buzzed, waiting for some kind of overture from him that was obviously never coming. Fine. They'd agreed things should end after Palm

Springs, and he was sticking to it. Still, that knowledge did nothing to fix the constant low-level ache in the pit of her stomach.

As they cruised down Beverly Boulevard, Kamilah filled Grey in on the various members of Andromeda's entourage she'd bonded with over the course of the tour, along with the assorted alliances and rivalries that inevitably sprung up in such close quarters. Grey focused on trying to keep it all straight, grateful for something to distract her from her nerves.

"Oh, and remind me to introduce you to Jaya; she's a fucking genius. Best cinematographer I've ever worked with. I lent her the book and she's totally in."

"In?"

Kamilah raised her eyebrows. "The movie. Our movie. You know, the one we've been trying to make for years? Slip your mind for a second?"

Grey felt a wave of gloom overtake her, blurting out the fear that she'd been too scared to voice aloud.

"What if we never get to make it? After . . . after everything? I can always bow out if it comes down to it, and you can take over. I don't want all my drama and bullshit to stand in your way."

Kamilah shrugged. "I mean . . . it's a total nightmare, but at the end of the day, getting your sex pics leaked never killed anyone's career. Everyone will get bored of their cute little *Grey's Anatomy* puns and move on to the next thing soon enough. Fuck *Golden City,* fuck the tabloids. You have to keep living your life. I'm back, you're famous, and we're going to get this shit *made.*"

She sounded so convincing that Grey almost believed it.

"I hope so."

When they reached the venue, they were immediately escorted backstage to the greenroom. A dozen or so painfully cool people were already milling about, eating, drinking, and posturing. A small monitor displayed a view of the stage, where the opening act was making their way through their set.

Grey's eyes found Andromeda right away: petite, ethereal, exquisite, and surrounded by stylists putting the finishing touches on their outfit. Their body was encircled with white spandex straps crisscrossing their glowing brown skin in a serpentine design. Their hair was half shaved, half hanging down to their waist in bleached-white micro braids. As the stylist at their hip untangled and smoothed the last strap, Andromeda lifted their arms, and another stylist guided a loose, translucent dress over their head. The dress shimmered with a different color of the rainbow every time Andromeda moved.

As the stylists stepped away, Kamilah sauntered over and wrapped her arms around Andromeda from behind, giving them a brief, tender kiss on the expanse between their neck and shoulder. Grey hung back, watching the two of them sway slightly in front of the mirror for a moment, whispering to each other as if they were the only two people in the room.

Her chest ached at the sight of them. She was elated to see Kamilah so smitten. Through the years Grey had known her, she'd watched Kamilah break heart after heart—through no fault of her own. She knew what she wanted in a partner and refused to settle for less, but it didn't take much for her openhearted charisma to inspire unrequited infatuation in most people she encountered (including Grey's own brother, in a visit that had quickly become more awkward than any of them had anticipated). But though Grey chastised herself for her self-involvement, seeing Kamilah getting serious with someone who finally seemed worthy of her talent, attention, and love felt bittersweet in the face of her own circumstances. Grey let herself wallow in self-pity for a count of three, before joining them by the mirror.

When Kamilah introduced them, Andromeda clasped Grey's hand with both of theirs and looked into her eyes warmly.

"Thank you so much for coming tonight. I'm so glad to meet you." Their voice was light and slightly raspy. Grey instantly felt guilty that she had ever considered staying home.

"Same here. Kamilah has told me so much about you. It's great seeing her so happy. I *guess* I can forgive you for stealing her away for so long. She deserves it."

Andromeda laughed, sweeping their eyes back to Kamilah with a look of adoration.

"She really does."

Kamilah batted her eyes, basking in the attention. "Don't stop now."

A makeup artist buzzed around Andromeda's shoulders, and they tilted their head up obediently so the artist could fix their lip liner. They gestured to the table in the corner, piled high with refreshments.

"Help yourself to whatever. You're welcome to watch from backstage, but I think the best view is probably from the audience. Especially if you want to see K's genius in action."

Kamilah grinned. "As if anyone even notices my videos when you're up there."

"Well, I can't wait to finally see the show in person after stalking everyone's shaky Instagram stories of it for months," Grey said. "*That*'s the ideal way to watch it, right?"

Andromeda laughed. "Exactly."

At that, Andromeda was whisked away by another member of their entourage to deal with some other pressing preshow issue.

Kamilah leaned over to Grey and muttered, "I didn't want to say anything in front of them because I want you to be able to say no, but—wouldn't Andromeda be amazing as Our Lady of Infinite Sorrows? And I think they might be interested in scoring the whole thing, too."

Grey beamed. "That's fucking *perfect*. You're a genius."

She and Kamilah made their way out of the greenroom and on to the VIP seating area upstairs. They immediately headed to the bar to kick the evening off with tequila shots, a tradition dating back to their college days. Grey's tolerance for shots had only declined since then, but she was usually fine with one—as long as she slowed down after that.

"If you're ready to cleanse your palate, tonight might be a good opportunity," Kamilah said, dropping her lime in the shot glass and pushing it back across the bar.

Grey mulled it over. She turned her back to the bar and rested her bare shoulder blades against it, taking in the array of young, lithe bodies that were slowly crowding the VIP section. Her gaze settled on a guy chatting up his friends in the corner. He was long and lanky, with tanned skin and an unruly head of curly black hair. As if he felt her eyes on him, he glanced up, his full lips curling into an insouciant smile as he kept talking, before looking away again. Grey blushed and looked down. Kamilah subtly turned her head to see what Grey had been looking at, then grinned and rolled her eyes.

"You always did like the tall ones."

The stage lights went down and the crowd roared as Andromeda's band took the stage. Latex-clad dancers undulated under strobe lights as Andromeda descended from the ceiling on wires. They floated around the stage, lifted high on an elegant and ever-changing arrangement of their dancers' raised arms and bent shoulders, as they cooed their way through their first song. Behind them, Kamilah's videos were projected on enormous screens: objects, shapes, faces, perfectly timed with the music, starting as abstractions and cutting away moments before becoming identifiable. The overall effect was mesmerizing.

Grey sipped a vodka soda and leaned against the railing. She was vaguely aware that the guy from earlier was now standing only a few feet away. She tilted her head slightly, looking at him without looking at him. He was younger than he'd seemed from a distance; early twenties at most. Well, that wasn't a dealbreaker, and she had to admit he was even cuter up close—cute, but not seasoned enough to be handsome. She noticed him sneaking glances at her, too.

Did she want to talk to him? She supposed she should enjoy her new freedom, though she wasn't entirely sure how much she was allowed to. As far as the press knew, she and Ethan were still together, just keeping a low profile. But she had no obligations to him anymore, contractual or otherwise. There was nothing wrong with a little flirting. She only hoped that this guy was sizing her up due to how good her ass looked in her leather leggings, and not because he'd already seen, in detail, what it looked like underneath them.

Her weekend with Ethan had reminded her what it felt like to be desired. It had also reminded her what it felt like to be publicly humiliated. But now she felt something else: powerful. She'd had a debauched lost weekend with an A-lister, had her indiscretions smeared on the front page of every tabloid, and lived to tell the tale. What else did she have to lose? She'd already lost everything that mattered.

She scooted a little closer as Andromeda's second song came to a close. He looked over at her and smiled.

"They're amazing, right?"

"Unbelievable," Grey agreed. He turned fully toward her and offered his hand.

"I'm Max."

"Grey."

He leaned forward, frowning, as the crowd cheered louder.

"Grace?"

"*Grey*. Like the color."

Her lips were practically touching his ear as she shouted to be heard over the din. His eyes lit up in comprehension, and he leaned back again.

"*Grey!* Got it. Nice to meet you. So how do you know Andromeda?"

"My friend Kamilah—" Grey looked behind her to point to Kamilah, who had conveniently disappeared. "Well, I'm not sure where she is right now. But she's dating Andromeda, and she does all their video stuff." She gestured at the screen behind Andromeda. Max looked suitably impressed. "What about you?"

"See the guitarist?" He pointed to an angular man to Andromeda's left. "That's my brother."

Grey oohed and aahed, inching slightly closer to him. He nodded at her drink, which was now mostly ice.

"What are you drinking? Can I get you another?"

"Vodka soda, please," she said, flashing her most charming grin.

"You got it."

He headed toward the bar. Grey turned to see Kamilah immersed in conversation with a group of three or four people, but when they made eye contact, she excused herself and made her way back over.

"So?" she asked, eyes flicking over to Max, busy at the bar.

"I don't know, we barely even said anything. He says the guitarist's his brother?"

"Ohhhh, so *that's* Zane's brother. You know he's, like, twenty-two, right? You little cradle robber."

"Relax, I'm not planning on ever seeing his crib."

Kamilah laughed and returned to her conversation. Grey didn't even have to look to know that Max was behind her with their drinks. She accepted hers with gratitude, and they went back to the railing.

"So, what are you into?"

Grey frowned. "What?"

"Like, what do you do?"

"Oh. I'm an actress. Unemployed, right now."

"Oh, nice. Anything I've seen?"

Grey hated that question, even under normal circumstances. She always had to bite her tongue to stop from responding, *How should I know?* Now, with her recent X-rated output, the question was even more loaded. She played it safe, going with her usual (unfortunately accurate) answer, "Probably not."

Max's face fell in disappointment. It seemed genuine, so Grey chose to believe that he was oblivious.

"What about you?" she asked quickly.

"I'm a musician, too," he said, gesturing his head at the stage. Grey cringed internally. She'd gotten over her musician phase in high school, when her boyfriend had dumped her after she'd been cast in an off-Broadway play, rendering her too busy to sit on the couch in his friend's basement every afternoon and make eyes at him during rehearsal like his bandmates' girlfriends.

"What kind of music?"

"Industrial noise, mostly. I dabble a little in glitch, too. Sometimes I rap over it. It's all kind of freeform."

"Oh, cool," Grey said, suddenly very interested in her drink. She had no idea what to say next. Her brain felt like a shaken Etch A Sketch. Her eyes strayed back to the show, and the two of them resumed watching in silence.

After a few more minutes, he nodded at her, and left to go back to his friends. Grey's stomach twisted. So much for being a powerful heartbreaker. She couldn't help but feel like her leather leggings were disappointed in her.

She returned to Kamilah's side after that, spending most of the evening smiling and nodding vacantly as Kamilah and her new friends recounted one outrageous tour anecdote after another. At the bottom of her third drink (fourth, including the tequila shot), her mind was loose enough to wander, against her will, to Ethan. What was he doing right now? Probably shut up in his office, drunker than she was. The thought should have made her feel relief at a bullet dodged, but instead she felt like crying. Did he miss her? Was he thinking about her? Why hadn't he tried to contact her?

She scanned the room for Max, and caught his eye as he talked to his friends. She tilted her head a little, and he came sidling back over immediately. Maybe she wouldn't have to turn in her seductress credentials after all.

"Wanna make out?" she asked, setting her empty glass on the table next to her with a punctuating *clink*. His eyes widened a little in surprise, then a grin crept over his face.

"Yeah. Sure."

She took his hand and led him out to the back stairwell, which was deserted, lit by dim red lights. Her intention was to find somewhere even more private, but as soon as the door shut behind them Max had her up against the wall, his mouth coming down on hers so hard their teeth clicked.

He immediately drove his tongue between her lips, alternating thrusting, sucking, and licking with a level of enthusiasm that left her gasping for air. Meanwhile, his hands found her breasts, squeezing and kneading in a manner that could only be described as dough-adjacent. She imagined this was what it might feel like to go through a car wash.

Grey tried her best to salvage the situation. She gently guided his hands down to her waist, then took his face in her own hands, pulling his head back a little to try to temper the vigorous on-slaught of his tongue. However, this only seemed to encourage him to double down on his efforts. After several minutes of sloppy, ineffective tussling, she broke away, untangling herself from what seemed to be hundreds of groping hands and thrusting tongues.

"I, um—sorry. Thanks. Nice to meet you. Sorry," she stammered, unable to meet his eyes as she stumbled back through the door. Miraculously, Kamilah was alone by the railing, and as she turned and took in Grey's disheveled appearance and stricken expression, opened her arms to her wordlessly.

Grey wrapped her arms around Kamilah's waist and rested her head on her shoulder.

"I missed you so fucking much," she mumbled drunkenly. Kamilah leaned her head on top of Grey's.

"Missed you, too. I assume you're not up for the after-party?"

Grey shook her head. "You should still go, though. I'll get a car. But can you come back for breakfast? Both of you. I want to hang out with Andromeda for more than five seconds."

"As long as you're okay with breakfast happening after 3 P.M."

Grey laughed. "Deal. I'll make vegan pancakes."

"Blueberry banana?"

"Obviously."

Onstage, Andromeda reappeared for their encore, stripped down to the spandex straps, with huge, skeletal angel wings strapped to their back. They sat alone in front of a keyboard, and played a long, eerie chord.

Their voice rang out, cool and clear, sending a dagger straight to Grey's heart.

"*It's been seven hours and fifteen days . . . since you took your love away . . .*"

The tears that had been brewing in her chest all evening bubbled up abruptly in an embarrassingly loud sob. Kamilah squeezed her shoulder as Grey wept openly, cathartically, through the entirety of Andromeda's plaintive rendition of "Nothing Compares 2 U." When the song ended, she was so emotionally exhausted she thought she might fall asleep standing up.

She felt purged. Cleansed. And more fucking confused than ever.

22

"PREVIOUSLY, ON *POISON PARADISE* . . . "

Ethan had only meant to watch one.

Lucas had already left for the evening. To both of their surprise, Ethan's awkward invitation for sports and a burrito had turned into a semiregular hang. When Lucas returned that first night, the two of them had sized each other up, trying to make the other one be the first to admit that he didn't actually want to watch sports.

"How do you feel about Ken Burns?" Lucas finally asked.

So now, twice a week, the two of them ate takeout and watched an episode or two of *The Vietnam War*. They didn't talk much, but Ethan had still learned more about Lucas in the past few weeks than he'd known in the past year Lucas had worked for him—or the twenty-three years that had preceded it.

He learned that Lucas lived with his boyfriend, Cal, and their rescue pug, Squidward (who, naturally, had his own Instagram).

He was working on his MFA in graphic design, with a goal of getting into production design. And eventually Ethan learned more about the family that he'd been avoiding. The nieces and nephews he'd never met, the milestones he'd missed. He tried not to shut it down when his guilt made it too hard to listen. He'd even called his sister for the first time since she'd forced him to hire Lucas. He hadn't said much, but she'd been more than happy to fill the silence.

Though he'd never expected Lucas to assume the role of his main companion, right now it was the only thing forcing him to keep track of what day it was. He'd called Nora to apologize for missing his weekend with the girls, and though she'd been furious at first, she was ultimately sympathetic. He'd asked, with some trepidation, if Elle and Sydney had seen the pictures, but she'd assured him that they were (miraculously) ignorant of the whole situation. He promised to take them for an unscheduled weekend later in the month to make it up to her. Both she and Lucas had tried to pry information about Grey out of him, but he refused. He wasn't ready to talk about her. She was already on his mind enough.

After Lucas left, disposing of their Thai containers on his way out, Ethan took advantage of the television already being up and running to scroll through his streaming options. When he saw Grey's face pouting at him from one of the on-screen squares, he felt like he'd just been defibrillated.

It probably wasn't a good idea to watch it in his current state. But seeing Grey's eyes staring back at him for the first time in weeks—as lifeless and airbrushed as they were—rendered him physically incapable of doing anything but pressing "play." He'd just meant to watch the pilot. But before he knew it, it was 3 A.M. and he had watched six episodes in a row.

There was no way around it: the show was pretty bad. It was

also completely addictive, though he doubted it would have had the same effect on him without Grey's presence. It had been unreasonable to expect himself to go cold turkey, he rationalized. For two months, he had gotten regular infusions of her company, taking for granted how much he had come to depend on it. Watching her show was like methadone: not as good as the real thing, but better than nothing at all.

As he watched, he felt like someone was reaching into his chest and squeezing his heart every time she made an expression he recognized. The chilly hauteur when she felt insulted, the little smile and blush when she received a compliment, her wary eyes when she was sizing up a new situation. His heart ached even more for the expressions he didn't see, the ones that had been for him alone: the way the corners of her mouth twitched after she'd made a joke she knew he'd like. The unvarnished empathy in her eyes when he'd opened up to her. The way her face flushed right before she came.

He'd tried to pace himself, but by the time Lucas showed up with a pizza box for their next date with Ken Burns, Ethan was halfway through the fourth season. He'd been so absorbed with watching Grey perform an emergency tracheotomy on one of her classmates that he hadn't heard the front door open. A subtle throat-clearing noise, combined with the aroma of freshly baked dough, alerted him to Lucas's presence a little too late. Ethan scrambled to pause.

"Lucas! I didn't hear you come in. I was just . . . um . . ."

Lucas raised an eyebrow. Ethan realized there was no way to spin it, and quickly exited out of the episode and navigated to the last place they had left off in *The Vietnam War*. Thankfully, Lucas said nothing, just turned around and set the pizza on the kitchen island. Ethan made a mental note to give him a raise.

"Sorry I'm late. Audrey asked me to stop by and pick this up for you." Lucas tossed a manila folder onto the couch next to him before going back to the island to grab a slice. Ethan flipped it over to read Audrey's inscription on the back, in her neat, precise handwriting:

E—

This won't go to press for a few more weeks, but I thought you might like to see it now.

xxx

Audrey

Intrigued, he bent back the metal prongs, opened the flap, and slid out the heavy stack of paper inside. Even though he'd been bingeing on Grey for the past week, the top page still felt like a punch in the gut.

It was a glossy black-and-white headshot. Bare face, bare shoulders, the harsh lights of the studio narrowing her pupils to pinpricks. She stared directly into the camera, stunning, defiant, hair framing her face in delicate tendrils. He'd been watching her in Lucy LaVey drag for so long that he'd almost forgotten how much of a separation there was between her and the character. This picture, though, was one-hundred-proof Grey.

He was careful not to spend too long staring at it as Lucas made his way over to the couch with a heaping plate of pizza. He flipped to the next page, which was all text. It wasn't until his eyes fell on Sugar Clarke's byline that he realized: this was the profile they were supposed to have done together. Classic Audrey.

Ethan glanced up at Lucas.

"Do you mind?"

Lucas shrugged. "Take your time." He pulled out his phone and started scrolling.

Ethan settled back into the couch and began to read.

You Don't Know Grey Brooks

Then again, maybe you do. Maybe you were one of the million people who tuned in regularly to *Poison Paradise,* the prime-time teen cable drama on which she played bright-eyed good-girl Lucy LaVey for six years. Maybe you saw her running for her life fetchingly in the sleeper horror hit *Don't Forget to Scream* four (or was it five?) summers ago. Maybe you recognize her from her stint as a child actress, back when she was still Emily Brooks, during which she made guest appearances on just about every soap opera and procedural ever to shoot in New York City.

Or maybe, like most of us, you first became aware of her earlier this year, when she began stepping out regularly on the arm of Ethan Atkins.

The first time I meet Brooks, we're sitting on the roof of Lexington House, the luxe West Hollywood members-only club to which neither of us belongs, sipping iced jasmine rose tea. Brooks is twenty-seven; by the time you read this, she'll be twenty-eight. Depending on the way the light hits her face, she looks both younger and older than her age, girlish and world-weary all at once. She's beautiful, of course—the girl next door, but in the most Hollywood sense of the term. Still a fantasy, but with the crucial illusion of attainability.

She's ill at ease but trying to hide it. It could be the unfamiliarity of the atmosphere. It could be (as she tells me) her nerves at being profiled by a major outlet for the first time, despite a career that's already spanned more than two-thirds of her short life. But when I bring up Atkins, she flinches.

It doesn't take a leap of imagination to figure out why. Full disclosure: until two weeks ago, this story was intended to be a joint profile of both Atkins and Brooks. That is, until a racy series of photos of the two of them in flagrante began to circulate, sending the most spotted couple in town back underground, the current status of their relationship a red-letter question.

When I tell her we don't need to talk about Atkins if she doesn't want to, she smiles wryly.

"It's fine. Whether I talk about him or not, you're still going to put his name on the cover anyway, right?"

Still, she declines to respond when I ask for details about how they met, or whether or not they're still together. When I bring up the unconfirmed rumor that her offer of a role in the hotly anticipated adaptation of *Golden City* was rescinded as a result of the pictures, the look on her face says it all.

"It just doesn't make sense to me," she says. Her voice is calm, but her hands betray her agitation by delicately shredding her paper napkin as she speaks. She fixes me with a piercing blue stare. "I don't understand why I'm the one suffering the consequences for being violated by the press, for having my most private moments made public without my consent. For falling in love." When she says the word "love," her voice catches. For all the cynical whispers that the union between her and Atkins has (had?) the distinctive whiff of a publicity stunt, the glimpse of pain in her eyes before she looks away seems agonizingly real.

Ethan read that last paragraph twice. Three times. With trembling hands, he forced himself to skim through the rest of the story. It contained a few new details he hadn't known about her, including that when she was thirteen, she'd been one of the final two actresses in contention to play the titular regular-girl-slash-secret-pop-star on the hit Disney Channel show *Virginia Virginia*—though, of course, she'd lost out in the end. He flipped through the other pages; more photographs of Grey, looking varying degrees of wounded and fearless.

Suddenly, with perfect clarity, Ethan realized what he had to do. He looked up to see Lucas, already down to the crust on his second piece of pizza, watching him intently.

"I need your help with something."

23

THE DAYS LEADING UP TO HER BIRTHDAY FILLED GREY WITH dread. Even under the best circumstances, she'd never really been a fan: in her line of work, she'd been conditioned to see birthdays as one more precious year slipping through her fingers, her goals still just out of reach. This year in particular didn't feel like there was much worth celebrating. Still, she'd agreed to let Kamilah take her out to their favorite dim sum place and stuff her full of veggie dumplings.

They trudged up the stone pathway to their front door, stomachs bursting, giggling about the job Kamilah had booked for the next week—a repeat gig directing a music video for a boy band with notoriously overzealous fans.

"Can you *please* give Thorne my number this time, at least?" Grey teased as Kamilah pulled her keys out of her pocket.

"I should. Last time all he did between takes was sit around eating Swedish Fish and not talking to anybody. You two would probably get along." Kamilah unlocked the door and Grey tilted her head back dreamily.

"Man, I haven't had Swedish Fish in *forever*. Remember in college when we ate that two-pound bag from Costco in one sit—"

As Kamilah pushed the door open, Grey was drowned out by a chorus of shouting voices:

"Surprise!"

Grey blinked, her mouth falling open. Her house was packed with people. As she looked around the room, registering the faces beaming back at her, it seemed like everyone she'd ever known and loved in L.A. was there.

Well. Almost everyone.

She looked at Kamilah, mouth still hanging open. Kamilah grinned.

"I thought you might need a little distraction after all."

Grey barely had time to thank her before Mia pounced, eager to introduce Grey to her new boyfriend. The party swung into gear, people spilling out into the backyard, which had been set up with a booming sound system and strung with twinkle lights.

As soon as Grey stepped into the backyard, someone pressed a can of beer into her hand, cold and slick with condensation. She whirled around to see who it was, accidentally bumping into Renata, who squeezed her shoulder and planted a fat red lipstick mark on her cheek.

"Happy birthday, kiddo," she said fondly. "How you been holding up?"

"Better. Still not great," Grey replied honestly, cracking the beer open and taking a sip.

"Are you ready to get back out there soon? No pressure."

Grey couldn't hide her shock. "You have work for me?"

"Nothing that'll knock your socks off, but it's starting to pile up. You're definitely on people's minds, for better or worse. How's the script coming, though? This might be a good time to strike on that."

"Good. Really good, actually. You think you can get us some meetings? Because of my . . . because of everything?"

Renata nodded. "Absolutely. It'll get you in the room, at least. If they underestimate you, fuck 'em. That's their mistake."

Grey felt a rush of gratitude and wrapped Renata in a hug. "Thank you, Renata."

Renata stroked her hair. "Of course, my love. You know I'm proud of you no matter what, right? You'll fight your way through this. You always do."

Grey blinked back tears, clutching Renata tighter.

Later in the evening, after they'd cut the cake, she stood alone in a corner of the backyard, nursing a seltzer and surveying the scene. The party was mostly made up of Grey's casual acquaintances and Kamilah's close friends, which wasn't surprising. Grey's inner circle could barely fill their kitchen, let alone their backyard. She was grateful Kamilah had ignored her request for a quiet birthday. She'd needed this more than she thought.

And then, as he usually did when her mind was slack and drifting, Ethan snuck in. She closed her eyes, her face flushing, the spring air feeling unseasonably warm. She hated how much she wished he was there. How keenly she felt his absence.

When she opened her eyes again, she saw him.

That part wasn't unusual. She thought she saw him everywhere these days. But that was usually a quick glimpse out of the corner of her eye, disappearing as soon as she turned her head. Now he was still there even when she looked away and looked back, moving steadily through the crowd toward her. Grey was frozen to the spot. Had she actually wished him into existence, trying in vain to keep him out of her thoughts when she'd blown out her candles?

Only when he was close enough for his all-too-familiar scent to hit her did she allow herself to believe he was really there. She was too dumbfounded to do anything but stare at him.

As if his presence weren't enough on its own, she realized with a jolt that he was wearing his navy blue T-shirt with the threadbare chest pocket. The same shirt he'd been wearing that day in Palm Springs, the one he'd pulled over his head in a flash before slipping into bed with her for the first time. Was it on purpose? Were all the details of that day, and the ones that followed, etched in his mind as indelibly as they were in hers?

He seemed overwhelmed by the sight of her, too, shifting his weight, his eyes skittering to her face, then away again. She was dimly aware that people were staring at them, but she was glued to the spot.

Finally, he spoke.

"Hey."

"What are you doing here?" She meant to sound accusatory, but the question came out as pure astonishment.

"I wanted to wish you a happy birthday," he said as if it were obvious.

"How did you . . ."

His head turned toward Kamilah, cuddling with Andromeda on the other side of the backyard. Grey's face must have clouded over, because he quickly interjected, "Don't blame her. I was the one who reached out to her."

Anger flared in her stomach anyway. "You reached out to her, but not to me? Did you lose my number or something?" People around them were beginning to stare.

He shifted his weight. "Can we talk somewhere else?"

Grey made a quick calculation. There were too many people inside the house for the living room to be an option. But her bedroom was obviously out of the question. "Fine. Let's go out front."

———

AS ETHAN FOLLOWED GREY THROUGH THE BACK DOOR INTO THE kitchen, he instantly regretted all the nights they'd spent at his place, that sterile, impersonal prison he'd created for himself. Her house was cozy and charming; not cluttered enough to be maximalist, but still bursting with color and texture on every wall and surface. He wanted to ask her to slow down and give him a chance to take it in, examine every book on her shelves, every print on her walls, every Polaroid on her fridge. Each object another clue to help him unravel her further. But all too soon, they were out the door and in her front yard.

She stopped abruptly and turned to face him, crossing her arms. He stopped, too, the look on her face warning him to keep his distance.

"How's your ankle?"

"It's fine. Why are you here?" she repeated without missing a beat.

"I missed you." At first, that seemed to be the right thing to say, her expression softening, but then she turned her face to the ground. When she spoke again, there was something aching in her tone.

"You could've texted me. You didn't need to go behind my back and, like, *conspire* to show up and blindside me."

"I didn't think you wanted to hear from me. You tried to leave before I woke up. You broke the contract. I was just trying to feel out the situation. I'm sorry if that was the wrong thing to do."

She was silent. The faint sounds of laughter and pulsating bass drifted over from the backyard, sounding like they were coming from a different world.

"It was too much. I couldn't handle it. The pictures . . . the whole weekend . . . everything. I thought it would make things easier if I didn't. If we didn't."

"So you were just ready to go the rest of your life without ever talking to me again?"

She looked back at him.

"I thought that was what you wanted. Not to get too close."

He shook his head in frustration, jamming his hands into his pockets.

"I didn't want you to break the fucking *contract,* Grey. Without even talking to me first. I thought this meant something to you."

"It did. It *does.*" She covered her face with her hands and groaned, her next words coming out muffled. "It means so much that it scares the shit out of me. That's why it's good that we . . . that it ended when it did. It needed to happen before we got in too deep." Her hands fell back to her sides.

His heart leapt, then plummeted. They fell back into silence for a moment.

"I read your profile. The Sugar Clarke piece. Audrey sent it to me."

She looked at him again, her eyes searching, trying to figure out where he was heading. She recrossed her arms.

"And?"

"And . . . I saw what you said. About . . . about how you . . . love me." He wasn't sure he would be able to successfully get the words out. Her eyes widened, quickly, almost imperceptibly, before she looked away again.

"Of course I said that. I had to. That's what everyone thinks, right?" Her voice was dull, unconvincing. He knew she was a better actress than that. She wasn't even trying.

"Right. So you don't, then."

She said nothing.

"Grey. Look at me."

She looked back up at him, the sharpness in her expression

gone, replaced by apprehension. He was seized by a fierce, over-powering need to get to the bottom of her feelings for him, right now, whether or not he made an idiot of himself in the process. He had to know. He wasn't going to waste what might be his last opportunity to do so.

"If you don't love me, tell me now. I'll leave you alone. We can move on with our lives. But if you have any kind of feelings for me . . . it doesn't even have to be love, if that's too much. Because I don't know about you, but it's way too late for me. I'm already in too deep, and it scares the shit out of me, too. I just need to know. I need to know if you . . . if you feel the same."

It was like time stopped. Ethan started to open his mouth again to equivocate, to soften the intensity that had shocked even him. She was staring at him, mouth slightly open, her eyes dark, gleaming pools.

The next thing he knew, she was moving closer, the distance between them going from respectful to intimate in a heartbeat, her hand knotting in his shirt and pulling his face down to meet hers. Then nothing mattered besides the feeling of her tongue sliding between his lips, the warmth of her body against his, his hands tangling in the silk of her hair.

Suddenly, silently, but with as much impact as a gunshot, a camera flashed next to their faces. They froze, and without thinking, Ethan released Grey and took off after it.

ONCE THE SHOCK OF THE FLASH HAD FADED FROM HER VISION, Grey sat numbly on her front stoop, waiting for Ethan to come back. Thankfully, there only seemed to be one photographer at large. Her stomach curdled. He must have followed Ethan to her house. She'd never been bothered here before. She'd let herself believe she was safe here.

Her eyes glazed over and she brought her fingers to her swollen lips. Right now, she had something even bigger to grapple with than her privacy (or lack thereof).

Ethan loved her.

Ethan loved her.

What the fuck was she supposed to do with that?

More important, did she love him?

She'd thought she loved Callum, but the more time passed, the more she questioned it. Their relationship had been like a marble statue: beautiful, cold, immutable. The illusion of indestructibility belying how fragile it was. It had been so easy for her to skim over the tiny cracks in its surface, her mind filling in the flawless expanse it wanted to see.

If Callum was like a statue, Ethan was like a river: powerful and unpredictable. Sometimes she was one with the current, floating peacefully, basking in the sunshine. Sometimes she was drowning. The worst part was, she wasn't sure which one she preferred.

She broke out of her reverie in time to see Ethan walking back up the path. As soon as he got close enough, she started peppering him with questions.

"What happened? Did you catch him? What did you say?"

"I got him to delete the picture," Ethan said, sitting on the stoop next to her.

Grey's eyes widened. "You didn't beat him up, did you?"

Ethan's brow creased in confusion. "What? Of course not. I paid him."

"You did? How much?"

"Twenty."

"Twenty dollars? He did it for that little?"

"Twenty thousand."

"*What?*" Grey thought she was going to fall off the stairs.

He shrugged. "That's how much he said it would sell for."

"There's, like, a hundred photos of us full-on fucking online already. Who *cares* if he sells it?"

Ethan looked nonplussed.

"Sorry, I thought . . . I didn't want to make things worse for you."

Grey drew her knees up to her chest and rested her head in her hands. Exhaustion swept over her.

"No, I'm sorry. Thank you. Thank you for doing that. That's like the nicest fucking thing anyone's ever done for me. What the *fuck,* Ethan." She slid her hands down her face, laughing in disbelief. "This whole thing is fucking crazy. What are you saying to me right now? What do you want from me?"

Ethan ran his hands through his hair.

"I want to be with you. Whatever that means. We can figure it out."

Grey closed her eyes, a *yes* dancing on the tip of her tongue. But when she opened her mouth, everything that came attached to that tiny word felt too huge and heavy to process.

"I . . . I don't know. I need some time. I need to think. Everything . . . it's all a lot." She turned to him. "Is that okay?"

He nodded, his face placid. Controlled.

"Of course."

She leaned over and brushed her lips over his, using every last ounce of self-control to keep it brief and not lean in deeper. He kissed her back, but remained where he was, too. When she pulled away, he stood up.

"One sec. I have something in the car for you."

When he returned, he had a large cardboard tube tucked under his arm. She took it, looking at him quizzically.

"What is this?"

"Happy birthday. Sorry, I should have wrapped it."

"You didn't have to get me anything. I mean, thank you." She felt awkward all of a sudden. She didn't want him to leave, but he had to. She'd rejected him. Sort of.

She stood up, too.

"I, um . . . okay. I'll see you . . . we'll talk later."

"Okay." His tone was unreadable. She wanted to walk with him to his car, but all she could do was stand there, watching him disappear into the darkness.

When Grey let herself back into the house, Kamilah was lurking nervously next to the front door. Her brow knitted in concern when she saw Grey was alone.

"Are you okay? Was he . . . should I not have? I didn't want to meddle. I just thought . . . you seemed like you were struggling."

Grey shook her head. "It's okay. It needed to happen. I couldn't run away forever."

"What did he say?"

"He wants to get back together. Or get together for the first time, I guess."

"And . . . you don't?"

Grey thought back to the camera flashing feet away from her front door. She swallowed. "I have no fucking idea what I want."

Kamilah's eyes flicked down to the cardboard tube in Grey's hands. "What is that?"

"I don't know. He said it was my birthday present."

Grey popped off the white plastic top of the cardboard tube and pulled out the contents.

It was a poster, a big one. With Kamilah at her side, she cleared off her coffee table, anchoring one end with a book as she unrolled it. The living room was still fairly full, and the people on the couch leaned forward to watch her progress with interest. A few more gathered around to peer at it as she flattened it out.

It was the original theatrical poster for *The Sister Switch*: two identical tween girls grinning back-to-back, arms crossed, as their parents leaned in from either edge of the frame, giving them looks of benevolent annoyance. Grey felt a twinge of nostalgia at the sight of it. As she looked closer, however, she felt a twinge of something else, something immense and ineffable. Instead of seeing Morgan Mitchell's face doubled back at her, Grey was staring at her own eleven-year-old visage.

She ran her fingers over the slick paper, stopping once they reached the text at the bottom:

And Introducing EMILY BROOKS as HEATHER and ASHLEY.

There were a few giggles and murmurs of confusion around her. Grey looked up and met Kamilah's eyes. She could tell Kamilah understood immediately. They were both speechless.

Grey rolled the poster back up as quickly as she could without damaging it. It felt wrong to have it laid out in public with everyone staring at it. In a way, she felt more exposed by it than by the photos of her own naked body that had been everywhere for weeks. A hidden piece of her soul laid bare. She slid it back into the tube, her hands shaking.

"I have to— I— Sorry," she muttered, her feet carrying her out of the room before she knew what was happening.

24

IT WAS STILL TOO EARLY FOR ETHAN TO GO TO BED. HE POPPED open a beer to calm his racing mind and navigated, almost unconsciously, to the next episode of *Poison Paradise*. As the now-familiar theme song started playing, his stomach curdled. Maybe this wasn't a good idea. Maybe he'd had enough Grey for the night. But it seemed like there was no such thing as too much. There was something perversely enjoyable about it now, rubbing salt in the wound, reveling in her rejection.

Well. She hadn't rejected him, exactly, but he didn't have his hopes up. Ethan hadn't professed his love many times, but he'd done it enough to know that anything less than an enthusiastic affirmation was a rejection. At least he still had another season to go before he really had to worry about it. He supposed he could always start it over from the beginning, again and again, growing old, alone, as the world's foremost *Poison Paradise* scholar.

He kicked off his shoes and stretched out on the couch. Lucy had just discovered that her boyfriend's accidental death may not have been an accident after all, and there was a cabal of shadowy forces at work in the idyllic town of Paradise Point. Ethan had been glad to see Callum's character make his unceremonious exit, and not just for the obvious reasons. His presence had really dragged Grey down toward the end—although Ethan hadn't yet seen her have a story line that wasn't completely bonkers.

Grey and Mia peered around a corner, eavesdropping on a group of shady-looking men having a private conversation in broad daylight.

"What do you think it all means?" Mia mused loudly.

Grey bit her lip. "I don't know. The more we find out, the less sense everything makes. How does Jackson's secret greenhouse fit into all of this?"

"Turns out Mia was behind it all along. Killed my boyfriend and then had the nerve to act like she didn't know a thing. What a bitch, right?" came a dry voice from behind him. Ethan sat up with a start, tearing his eyes off two-dimensional Grey so abruptly that it took him a moment to readjust to the three-dimensional version standing behind him.

"I— You—" he sputtered.

"Oh. Sorry. Spoilers." The corners of her mouth twitched as he scrambled off the couch, stopping short in front of her. She let her overnight bag slide off her shoulder onto the ground, her eyes flicking from his face to the screen and then back again. "You weren't kidding."

"What?" he asked, taking another step toward her so she had to tilt her head back to meet his eyes.

"You *are* in too deep." Her tone remained sardonic, but the vulnerable quiver at the end of her sentence gave her away.

He was still smiling when he kissed her. She twined her arms around his neck, and he pulled her as close to him as she could possibly get while still remaining a separate entity. That wasn't good enough for him. The thought of being inside her wasn't good enough for him, either. He wanted to devour her. Somehow, if she could become part of him, he would never come close to losing her again.

When they came up for air, he realized at some point he had hoisted her onto the back of the couch, her legs wrapped around his waist.

"It's really not a bad show," he said, pulling her shirt over her head and dropping it on the ground.

"At least you weren't jerking off to it."

"Not this time, anyway."

She laughed and smacked him lightly on the chest. He got his revenge by bending his head down to nip and suck at her throat until she moaned.

"Sometimes I just get too carried away by Lucy LaVey's adventures. That girl sure knows how to get herself into trouble."

Grey unwrapped her legs from around him and hopped off the back of the couch, kneeling in front of him. She looked up at him with an expression that could pass for innocent, if she weren't already halfway done unbuckling his belt. His breath caught in his throat at the sight of her. She smirked.

"Wait till you hear what she's been up to lately."

GREY REALIZED THAT AS MANY TIMES AS SHE'D WOKEN UP IN Ethan's house, this was her first time waking up in his bed. It was her first time in his room at all, actually. The blackout curtains were closed, plunging the room into eerie darkness, where the distinction between day and night ceased to have meaning. She shifted against the solid heat of Ethan at her back, his arm thrown over her chest like a roller coaster safety bar. Being here with him conjured the same feeling she'd had in Palm Springs, like time and the outside world bent to their whims, and not the other way around. They couldn't live in that bubble forever, but being able to catch a glimpse of it every now and then was enough for her. Maybe that was what love was, after all.

Her movements must have woken him up, and she felt him tighten his hold on her with a sharp inhale, brushing meltingly soft kisses over her neck and shoulder.

"What time is it?" she sighed, yawning and arching her back against him.

"Who cares?" he mumbled. He lazily circled her nipple with his fingers, then pinched, laughing into her shoulder as she squirmed.

"Good point." She rolled over so she was facing him and moved her hand to his face, brushing her thumb across his cheekbone.

"What now?" she asked softly. He answered by pulling her into a deep kiss, his hand sliding down her body and settling on her hip, nudging her closer. He was already hard against her stomach, though since it was first thing in the morning she couldn't take all the credit. She pulled her face away, laughing. "After that, I mean."

"I don't know." His eyes searched her face. "You're here."

"I'm here."

She thought he was going to kiss her again, but instead he stretched his head up to kiss her forehead.

"That's all that matters."

An hour later, they were in Ethan's kitchen. Grey thought back to the first time he'd cooked for her, how she'd yearned for an excuse for them to act like a real couple in private. The reality was even better than she'd imagined. It was definitely slowing down their brunch progress, though; she'd barely gotten halfway through chopping the onion before Ethan had her pinned against the kitchen island with his hands up her shirt. That poor onion might have been abandoned forever if not for the sound of the door slamming open, followed by multiple sets of footsteps. The two of them leapt apart instantly. Grey stared at Ethan, wide-eyed, his expression of shock mirroring hers.

"*Daddy!*"

Ethan groaned.

"Fuck. I forgot I told Nora I'd take the kids this weekend," he muttered, seconds before two little girls came careening excitedly around the corner. They stopped dead when they saw Grey. She thanked her lucky stars that she'd ignored Ethan's coaxing and come out to the kitchen fully clothed.

They looked up at her, mouths slightly open, eyes going immediately to Ethan for help. A tall, slender woman rounded the corner after them. When Grey registered her identity, her stomach lurched.

Grey's brief tween crush on Ethan hadn't been a territorial one; she'd been pragmatic enough to accept that Nora Lind was the only woman cool enough to deserve him. Grey had spent hours poring over pictures of them on the red carpet. In the years before everyone was impeccably and impersonally styled, Nora would show up in a buzz cut and a vintage tuxedo and outshine everyone who had been foolish enough to wear a designer gown and diamonds. At the premiere of *Dirtbags,* she'd worn a sheer black maxi dress with nothing underneath but men's briefs and white X's taped over her nipples; Ethan next to her in a T-shirt with one of her old modeling photos printed across the chest, cigarette between his lips, arm around her shoulders, gazing down at her with adoration.

Even dressed down, makeup-free—*actually* makeup-free, not just the illusion of it—she was stunning. Her eyes registered Grey with shock, then her pouty mouth twisted in amusement. She raised an eyebrow at Ethan, who exhaled heavily.

"Elle, Sydney," he said, moving over to stand next to the girls. "This is Grey. My girlfriend."

Grey waved and smiled, as her stomach did another jump. *Girlfriend.* For real this time. "I'm so happy to meet you two. I've heard so much about you."

They looked up at her with saucer-round eyes. The younger one backed up to Nora, taking her hand.

"I think they're feeling a little shy today," Ethan said in a stage whisper.

"That's okay. Sometimes I feel shy, too."

The older girl crept over to Ethan and tugged on the bottom of his shirt.

"Can we go swimming? I want to show you my backflip."

"Sure. Let's go drop your bags off in your room first."

He ushered the two of them down the hall, shooting Grey a brief look of apology for abandoning her with Nora.

Once the two of them were alone, Grey could see Nora sizing her up—but not unkindly.

"Grey. Nice to finally meet you in the flesh." The emphasis she put on the word "flesh" made Grey's cheeks flush scarlet.

"I, um. They don't know, right? About . . ."

Nora shook her head, smiling slightly.

"No, thank god. If they were a few years older it might be another story. They know about you, though. Or they know he's been seeing someone."

Grey shifted her weight, trying to figure out what exactly Nora knew, what Ethan had told her. After all, they'd never "officially" broken up.

"I am sorry, though. That they'll have to . . . eventually. That's shitty."

Nora shrugged. "I'm sure it was worse for you than it'll be for them. Ethan and I have done our share of sex scenes over the years, together and apart. And he's certainly been in the news for worse. They'll have to deal with all that one day, too. Just one more item for the therapist's couch."

Grey laughed, relieved.

"Can I get you some coffee or anything? Latte? Or do you have to get going?"

Nora looked like she was about to decline, then thought better of it.

"Sure. A latte would be great."

Grey turned toward Ethan's espresso machine, grateful to have something to keep her occupied. Nora perched on one of the island stools.

"So, how have things been? With you two. With everything."

"Um . . . things are good. We've had our ups and downs," Grey answered diplomatically, measuring the espresso beans. She turned around to see Nora studying her.

"I know we only just met. I don't want to pry into your relationship. But he missed his last weekend with the girls—which is why we're here now—and when I called him . . . he was a mess."

Grey felt like the temperature of the room dipped ten degrees. She shivered, but said nothing, pulling a mug out of the cabinet. Nora seemed like she was trying to choose her next words carefully.

"I just . . . I just want to make sure. That he's treating you well."

Grey shrugged. Outside, Ethan and the girls had taken over the pool, laughing and splashing.

"So far, so good," she said breezily. She met Nora's eyes, and was startled to see concern creasing her face.

Nora exhaled. "Look. I know what it's like to be with him. When it's good, it feels like the whole world revolves around the two of you. Like nothing could ever go wrong. But when it's bad . . ."

Grey's stomach clenched. She tilted the shot of espresso into the mug and poured the steamed milk over it. "What do you mean?"

"Oh, I'm not trying to scare you," Nora said reassuringly. "He never cheated. He never hurt me. Well, I guess that's not true, he did hurt me. Not physically, I mean. But I hurt him, too. Maybe that all goes without saying. But Ethan . . ." Her gaze strayed out to the pool. "Ethan is tricky. He's one of the sweetest people I've ever known. The most sensitive. The most loving. But he also carries a lot of pain. A lot of guilt. He's never quite figured out how to hold it."

"Yeah. I know," Grey said softly. Nora looked back at her, accepting the coffee mug gratefully.

"I just hope you don't think it's your job to fix him. No matter how much you care about him." She drank a sip of coffee and shook her head. "I'm sorry. I don't know why I'm telling you all this. You're obviously a smart young woman, I'm sure you can take care of yourself. I don't want to assume anything. Please tell me if I'm overstepping."

Grey sipped her own coffee. "No, no, it's fine. It's . . . it's helpful, actually. Thank you."

Nora waved her hand in front of her face, as if she was trying to physically banish the somber mood that had settled over them. "Anyway. Enough about him. What about you? What else are you up to these days? I was a big fan of your show, by the way."

Grey laughed in surprise. "Really?"

"Oh yeah."

"Thanks for not being ashamed to admit it, at least. I know I would be."

Nora laughed. "So do you have anything exciting lined up? I always thought you'd be the one to break out."

Grey thought about brushing off the question the way she normally did, the loss of *Golden City* still stinging, but something about Nora's frankness—not to mention her compliments—had relaxed her.

"Actually . . . my friend and I—she's a director—we've been trying to get our own movie made. We've been working on the script on and off for years. She's been out of the country for the last few months, but we're just about ready to start trying to get some meetings going."

She expected Nora to respond with a bland "That's great," but to her surprise, Nora seemed genuinely interested.

"What's the movie?"

"*The Empty Chair*. It's—"

"P. L. Morrison," Nora finished, her eyes lighting up. "I love that book. You said you have a script ready? What's your friend's name?"

"Kamilah Ross. She mostly does music videos right now, but we wrote an indie together that she directed a couple of years ago, kind of as a warm-up for this. She's super talented."

Nora sipped her coffee, but Grey could tell her mind was whirring.

"So you would play Vivian?"

"That's the idea. And she would play Florence."

"She acts, too?"

"Only in her own stuff, but she's amazing. She's never been interested in doing the whole audition thing, getting sent out for the same one-dimensional supporting characters over and over."

"I don't blame her. I had to fire my first agent because he only ever sent me out for roles that had 'exotic' in the breakdown."

Grey winced. "Ugh. I'm so sorry."

Nora tapped her fingers against the island and stared off into the distance for a moment, lost in thought. "You know, I've been working on getting my own production company off the ground for the past year or so. We're still trying to nail down some of the money stuff, but this is exactly the kind of project we're looking for. Maybe we can set up a meeting."

Grey blinked a few times, stunned into silence. "Wow, Nora . . . I don't know what to say. That would be . . . wow. Thank you," she finally managed to say.

Nora grinned. "I mean, I'm not making any promises beyond a meeting. You two still have to bring your A-game. I'd be interested in seeing the other movie you made, too, if you can send it along beforehand."

"Of course. Thank you. If there's anything I can do for you . . ." Grey trailed off awkwardly, feeling unsure. What could she offer Nora that could compare with the monumental favor she was doing for her? But Nora put her empty coffee cup on the island and fixed her with another thoughtful stare.

"Has he said anything to you about the *Dirtbags* screening?"

Grey frowned and shook her head.

"No, nothing. What is it?"

"They want to do a fifteenth-anniversary screening in a couple of months at Lincoln Center. It's the movie where . . ." She trailed off.

"Yeah, I know. That's . . . hmmm." Grey leaned against the island, propping herself on her forearms. She'd seen *Dirtbags* a couple of times; she'd even written a paper on it in college. Of all the movies Ethan and Sam had made together, it was her favorite: visceral, thrilling, and kinetic.

"I'm not surprised he hasn't said anything. He seemed against it when I brought it up. I bet he doesn't even remember. But I think it would be good for him. It might help him remember that part of his life as more than just . . . regrets. Something to be buried."

Grey nodded. "I can try to talk to him."

"Thank you. I really appreciate it." Nora moved as if to get up from the stool. Something else occurred to Grey.

"Do you know anything about the last movie he was working on with Sam? *Bitter Pill*?"

Nora's brow furrowed. "Sounds familiar. I don't think they'd gotten very far on it, though. Why? Is he still trying to get it made?"

"I don't know," Grey replied truthfully. "He says that's why"—she caught herself seconds before accidentally revealing the original nature of their relationship—"he's been putting himself back out there. But he doesn't really seem that interested in it."

Nora looked at her sympathetically. "Has he talked about Sam much with you?"

Grey shook her head. "A little. I can tell it's hard for him."

Nora's eyes went distant.

"Yeah. Yeah, that was a terrible time. For all of us."

Grey shifted her weight. "I can't imagine."

Nora sighed. "I've made my peace with it. Ethan . . . he still has a lot of stuff he needs to resolve where Sam is concerned. Preferably with a professional." She stood up and stretched. "I should get going. Thank you for the coffee, this was lovely. I'm going to go out and say goodbye to the girls."

"Of course. I'm glad you decided to hang out for a little." Grey returned to the onion and picked up the knife again, suddenly starving.

"Me, too." Nora smiled. "See you soon, I hope."

She slid open the glass door and strolled outside. Grey watched her approach the trio in the pool, crouching down to talk to them. Ethan shook his soaking hair, pushing it out of his eyes. His younger daughter jumped onto his back, and the two of them plunged underwater, faking a struggle.

Grey felt like she was spying on something intimate, something she was never meant to be part of. The four of them made sense together: the picture-perfect family. But something invisible had ruptured, driving them apart. If it hadn't, she wouldn't be there, observing from the kitchen.

Ethan emerged from under the water again, turning to look right at her. He was so beautiful her chest ached. Was he the one to blame? She knew it was never that simple. But still, she turned Nora's words over in her head: *it's not your job to fix him.*

He beckoned to her, beaming, and her doubts evaporated like water droplets on the hot concrete as she went out to the patio to join them.

25

ETHAN SWISHED THE BOURBON AROUND HIS GLASS, ICE CUBES clinking. The television was on, but he wasn't watching. Grey wouldn't be home for hours. After over a month of preparation, she and Kamilah were finally pitching their movie to Nora's company. She'd left him with a kiss late that afternoon, telling him not to wait up—depending on how it went, she and Kamilah would be out late either celebrating or drowning their sorrows. For the first time since they'd gotten back together, he had the whole evening to himself.

They spent most of their time at his place these days, only occasionally venturing into the outside world. Now that their status as a couple had been officially confirmed once again, the scarcity of their public appearances meant that they created nothing short of a frenzy whenever they stepped out together. Photographers were parked outside his gate all the time now, even without Audrey calling them in advance.

He resisted the temptation to text her to check in. She would let him know when she had any news. He drained his glass and unfolded himself to standing in one motion, heading to the bar cart for a refill. He hadn't been drunk since the night of her birthday, the night she came back to him. A beer or two at dinner, a glass of bourbon as a nightcap. And most of the time, he barely even thought about it. When she was around, her presence was loud enough to drown out his doubts, his fears, his most self-sabotaging impulses. But sure enough, like clockwork, as soon as the door had shut behind her and the prospect of several unaccompanied hours stretched in front of him, the bar cart beckoned like a siren.

Ethan poured himself another glass of bourbon, more generous this time. He'd been good. He'd earned this. Once in a while was no big deal. He'd be in bed sleeping it off before she got home, and she'd never have to see this side of him. He loved who he was around her, the version of himself he saw reflected back at him when she opened her eyes in the morning, when he made her laugh, when he was inside her. He wanted to be that man all the time. That was what she deserved.

He heard his phone buzz back on the coffee table, and hurried to answer it. Sure enough, it was Grey.

"Hey! How did it go?" He tried to keep his voice neutral, prepared for either response. To his relief, her excitement was palpable, even over the phone.

"They fucking *loved* it. Couldn't have gone better. I kind of can't believe it, it's basically a done deal," she gushed. Ethan's face split into a grin.

"Congratulations. That's amazing. You two have been working so hard, I'm not surprised." He settled back on the couch. "So are you on your way to celebrate now?"

"Change of plans. We were talking to Nora afterward and we

thought it might be fun if everyone came over for dinner tonight instead."

Ethan sat up with a jolt. "Everyone? Tonight? Here?"

"Yeah. Like, Kamilah, Andromeda, Nora, Jeff. Sorry I didn't check with you first, it all happened kind of fast. But that'll be nice, right? We haven't had everyone over all together yet."

Ethan rubbed his hand over his eyes, trying to process the sudden U-turn his night had taken. "No, um, it's fine. The girls, too?"

"Lucas is watching them."

"Great. Great. That's great," Ethan repeated dumbly. "And we're gonna . . . cook?"

"I was going to pick up from Taj, if I ever get out of this *fucking* traffic. Any requests? I was thinking mostly veggie stuff, since you and Jeff and I are the only meat eaters."

"Oh. Uh . . . no, that sounds good."

"Okay. I should be back in an hour, hopefully less. Everyone else is coming over at eight."

They exchanged their goodbyes and hung up. Ethan leaned back into the couch and took another sip. He'd been so focused on supporting Grey as she prepared for her pitch that he'd barely stopped to consider what would happen if it went well: his girlfriend was going to make a movie with his ex-wife. They'd had dinner with Nora and Jeff and the girls a handful of times over the past month, and everyone had gotten along better than he could've hoped for. Still, anxiety started to pool in the pit of his stomach.

Maybe Nora would start undermining him as soon as his back was turned, whispering secrets about his lowest moments into Grey's ear, poisoning her against him. Maybe Grey was still using him for the career bump, the connections and exposure he could provide—contract or no contract. Or maybe he was just being paranoid, and this had nothing to do with him.

With the formation of this alliance, Grey would become inextricably entrenched in his life, something he craved and feared in equal measure. It was almost too much pressure. He wondered if they would still want to work together if he fucked it all up, if they broke up. His chest tightened at the thought. Then Grey and Nora would have even more in common: the exclusive club of women whose lives he'd ruined.

He ran his hands through his hair and stood up, then sat back down again. Should he shower? Change his clothes? Drink some water?

He drained his glass and felt his stomach slowly begin to unknot. He was getting ahead of himself. It was a good thing that they were so friendly with each other. No need to twist positive news into something ugly, assume the worst in people. He could put his own bullshit anxieties aside for a night and be there for Grey.

GREY HAD BARELY PLACED THE INDIAN FOOD BAGS ON THE counter before Ethan was on her, grabbing her waist from the side and peppering her with machine-gun kisses all over her face.

"Augh! Jesus!" She laughed, twisting around to give him a real kiss. His mouth tasted freshly brushed, the mint on his tongue making her lips tingle. "Someone's friendly tonight."

"I'm just proud of you. And I missed you." He settled behind her as she unpacked the plastic containers, resting his chin on the top of her head.

"I was only gone for, like, five hours." Even as she teased him, she felt her heart flutter a little at his words. "Can you finish this and pull out a couple bottles of wine? I want to change before everyone gets here."

She tried to walk toward the bedroom but he stayed wrapped around her like a barnacle, following in lockstep. "Need help?"

She laughed again and tried to peel herself out of his arms. "Mmm . . . tempting, but I don't want to get all sweaty. My hair already looks weird today."

He pretended to pout as he released her with a farewell kiss on the head and slap on the ass.

"I think your hair looks great."

She practically floated to Ethan's bedroom. As she rummaged around in the space in his closet she'd corralled for herself, she paused for a moment. Six months ago, she was unemployed and directionless. Six weeks ago, she was fired, humiliated, and heartbroken. Now she was shacking up with her former pinup crush, about to make her dream project with her best friend, with the help of one of her idols. The goalposts for her life had shifted so quickly that she had whiplash. She tried to ignore the nagging anxiety whispering to her that these kinds of highs could only precede a desperate drop.

An hour later, the six of them were gathered around Ethan's dining room table, surrounded by empty serving dishes. Grey wiped up the remains of her saag paneer with a piece of garlic naan, chiming in with the occasional detail as Kamilah regaled the rest of the group with the story of the time the two of them had misread a package of edibles, accidentally eating quadruple the recommended dose before going on a hellish trip to Disneyland after finals their sophomore year. Grey scooted her chair closer to Ethan's and snuggled into his side, feeling tipsy and warm and perfectly content.

Once the conversation reached a lull, Nora opened another bottle of wine and topped off all their glasses—with the exception of Ethan, who'd been drinking bourbon all evening. She sat back down and beamed at Kamilah, Grey, and Andromeda, lifting her glass.

"I just wanted to tell you again how thrilled I am to be working with the three of you." She knocked on the wooden table. "I mean, you know how it is. It could all fall through tomorrow, of course. But I'm going to do everything in my power to make it happen."

Grey raised her glass, too. "We're so grateful that we found you. Like, we truly couldn't ask for anyone better."

They all clinked their glasses and took a drink.

Kamilah set her glass down and laced her fingers through Andromeda's on the table. "Our other meetings were a fucking nightmare. You were kind of our last hope. Literally the first one we went to, one of the guys looked at her like this—" She gave a leering, exaggerated once-over. "And then was like, *So I assume you're comfortable with full nudity?*"

Grey fake-gagged as Ethan squeezed her shoulder. "That wasn't even the worst one. Last week we did the whole pitch and then they were, like, we want to do it—with a different director. We bailed the fuck out of there after that."

Kamilah's mouth twisted as she and Grey exchanged glances. She'd been so upset after that meeting that she'd practically vibrated as they walked out, Grey embracing her tightly in the hallway until she'd calmed down enough to drive home.

"Fuck 'em," Jeff grunted. All their eyes locked on him. It was one of the only things he'd said all night.

Grey had quickly learned that Jeff was a man of few words. He was a good match for Nora, though, and he obviously adored her. Their calm, stoic energy mirrored each other. He was handsome, but not ostentatiously so, with a salt-and-pepper beard and warm brown eyes. The tawny skin of both arms was covered in full-sleeve tattoos, and he carried himself with the quiet confidence of someone used to being the tallest person in every room—he was six five at least, even towering over Ethan.

Kamilah lifted her glass at him. "Cheers to that."

They drank again. Next to her, Ethan drained his glass. Grey half rose and began gathering up the empty plates. Andromeda leaned back in their chair.

"So, what's the next step? Is it too early for me to start working on the music?"

"A little, but if you're feeling inspired, that's always a good thing." Nora tore off the corner of a piece of naan and chewed thoughtfully. "Right now I have to start working on the budget projections, figure out the schedule, round up some coproducers. It would be better if we could shoot on location in New York, but that might be too expensive. I have a couple of people I want to talk to when I'm there next month." She nodded at Grey and Ethan pointedly. "If you two *do* end up coming, you're welcome to join me, Grey."

Ethan's arm tensed around her shoulder. She felt his eyes on her, but she didn't look at him. She realized that he'd started the meal cheerful and gregarious, but had grown more withdrawn as the night had gone on, silently nursing his bourbon next to her. When he spoke, his voice was gruff. "I didn't realize that was something you had discussed."

Grey shrugged, keeping her voice casual. "She just brought it up in passing."

Nora didn't say anything, her eyes locked on Ethan's—firmly, but not aggressively. It seemed like something passed between them, some kind of ex-spouse ESP that the rest of them weren't privy to.

"Give it a rest, Nor," he finally grumbled, ducking his head.

The table was silent. Grey saw Andromeda and Kamilah exchange uncomfortable glances.

Nora cleared her throat and stood up, collecting the pile of dishes. "Enough shop talk. We can worry about all of this tomorrow. Tonight is for celebrating."

———

THEY CLEARED THE TABLE AND DECAMPED TO THE POOL WITH another bottle of wine. The LED lights gave the bright blue water an otherworldly glow, wispy clouds of steam rising into the cool night air. Ethan was drunker than he'd been in months—but then, they all were. Grey cuddled against his shoulder on the lounge chair, legs strewn over his lap, playing with a strand of her hair. The weight and warmth of her body against his was nothing short of a miracle, he thought absently. He let himself zone in and out of the conversation without contributing, their voices dulling to a pleasant hum.

Kamilah took a fortifying sip of wine and sighed dramatically. "Ethan."

Ethan looked up. "Hmm?"

"Can I ask you a personal question?"

He felt Grey's breath speed up against him. He rubbed her shoulder reassuringly. "Go for it."

"Where's your Oscar?"

Ethan was so surprised he couldn't stop himself from laughing. "I think it's buried in the closet in my office." He paused. "You want me to get it?"

Kamilah grinned. "If you wouldn't mind."

He untangled himself from Grey and went inside the house, his head spinning slightly as he reoriented himself upright. As expected, it was in his closet behind a pile of old screeners, some old enough to still be on VHS cassettes. His shoe nudged a crumpled pack of cigarettes on the floor, poking out from under his ski gear. They were months old, if not years, but the stale scent of tobacco triggered something in his bombed-out brain like a sleeper agent being activated. He dug a pack of matches from his desk drawer and had one lit and in his mouth while he still had one foot inside the house.

It wasn't until he saw the confused look on Grey's face that he realized what he was doing.

"Oh. Shit. Sorry." He let the cigarette fall from his lips and stubbed it beneath his heel. He shuffled back over to Kamilah and handed her the Oscar before returning to Grey's side, slightly abashed.

Kamilah's arms immediately collapsed into her lap from the unexpected weight of it. She lifted it to her face to examine it, rotating it under the dim light.

"He's kinda hot, right? Like, why is he so *buff*? Was that necessary?"

"Um, *excuse* me, I'm right here." Andromeda placed their hand on their chest in mock outrage as the rest of them laughed.

"What? You know I've always had a thing for bald guys."

"Well, he's not coming home with us tonight."

Kamilah laughed and passed it back to Ethan. "Not tonight, but one day. I'm manifesting here."

He rested it against his bent knees, running his thumb across the gold plate at the bottom, smudging his name with his fingerprints. He glanced up to see Nora watching him, leaning against Jeff's shoulder.

"Do you remember that night?" she asked, softly enough that he almost didn't hear her.

He nodded. "Of course." Grey rested her head against him, tethering him to the present as he felt himself start to drift into his memories. "Nobody thought I would win. I sure as hell didn't."

Nora smiled. "You tried to get us to leave early. You were hungry."

"Yeah, well. We all thought—" He stopped himself short. Sam had seemed like the sure thing that night, his consolation for being pushed into supporting while Ethan was up for lead with an equally sized role. Ethan had barely been paying attention when his category was called; it had taken Nora's and Sam's twin expressions of shock on either side of him for him to realize what had happened.

The exhilaration had carried him through the next weeks on a high. Only in retrospect did he remember Sam's tight smile at the after-party, the way he'd left early without saying goodbye, been slow to return his calls for the next few weeks. They never talked about it, but Ethan always suspected that Sam blamed Ethan's win for the opposite roads their individual careers had taken.

Despite his talent, Sam never had a success on his own that equaled anything he'd done with Ethan. But it wasn't about the award: it was because Sam was a character actor in denial trying (and failing) to have the career of a leading man. Everyone seemed to understand that except Sam. But any time Ethan tried to bring it up tactfully, Sam brushed it off with a joke, like he always did.

He closed his fist around the statuette, his fingers overlapping across the narrow legs.

"It's stupid," he mumbled, almost to himself. Grey stirred next to him.

"What is?"

He rubbed his other hand over his eyes, his words coming out thick and sluggish, matching the slow churn of his thoughts. "That something this small can . . . mean so much. *Do* so much." Open so many doors, cause so much damage. He hadn't deserved it, hadn't even wanted it, but it had created a rift between him and Sam that had never fully healed. Now it never could.

Slowly, he pushed himself to his feet and wandered over to the edge of the water, the award still clutched in his hand. All of a sudden, it disgusted him to look at it.

"Ethan?" Grey's voice sounded far away.

It felt like he was watching himself from outside of his body as his arm reared back and launched the golden statuette into the pool. It landed with a dramatic splash and sank to the bottom immediately.

He turned around to see everyone staring at him, wide-eyed and frozen.

Finally, Jeff spoke. "You good, man?"

Ethan blinked a few times. He suddenly felt everything he'd had to drink that night hit him all at once. "Yeah. I . . . um. Sorry. I don't know . . . that was— I'm sorry." He looked back at the pool. Why the fuck had he done that? He was embarrassing himself, embarrassing Grey. Giving Nora more ammunition against him. He needed to fix it, fast.

In a haze, he stripped off his shirt and kicked off one of his shoes. He took a couple of unsuccessful passes at removing the other one, before giving up and leaping into the pool still wearing it.

The statuette had landed in the shallow end, so it was easy enough to retrieve it. He laid it on its side on the tiled edge of the pool, his sodden jeans weighing him down as he clumsily hoisted himself out. He straightened up and looked back at the group expectantly—but their expressions seemed even more stricken than before.

Grey stood up and walked over to him slowly, like she was approaching a skittish horse. She spoke quietly, so the others couldn't hear.

"Why don't you get those clothes off and get in the shower. I'll see you inside."

He couldn't do anything but nod. As he trudged back toward the house, his jeans and single waterlogged shoe squelching and dripping with every step, he heard Grey's apologetic murmurs to the others. Though the air was chilly, made even chillier by his wet clothes, shame heated him from the inside out. The rest of them would be gone by the time he was out of the shower, that much he was sure of. The only thing he cared about was whether Grey would be gone, too.

26

THE NEXT MORNING, GREY'S HEAD WAS POUNDING BEFORE SHE even opened her eyes. She noted with resentment that it felt like she'd had more hangovers in the months since she'd met Ethan than in the last few years combined. As she rolled over, however, her annoyance receded at the aroma of sautéed garlic and onions wafting into the bedroom.

She stretched over to the empty side of the bed and wrapped her arms around Ethan's pillow, trying and failing to ignore the pieces of the night before that had already begun to filter in. They'd barely spoken between when their guests had left and they'd gone to bed. There hadn't been a point. Neither of them were in any condition to discuss anything more complicated than who was hogging the duvet. And now she was already second-guessing if it had even been as bad as she remembered. If the worry and embarrassment she'd felt when he'd jumped into that pool, wild-eyed and half clothed, was just magnified through the fog of wine and the comedown of the morning after.

Were they going to fight about it? Did they have to? She'd never fought with Callum—that is, until he'd cheated on her—but she'd realized in retrospect that that was because you had to actually *care* about what the other person did in order to have a problem with it. Arguing was part of being in a relationship, perfectly healthy and normal, or so she'd heard. You needed to drain the poison before the wound could heal.

She heard the door open, followed by Ethan's footsteps, but didn't roll over until she felt his weight on the edge of the bed. He'd pushed the blackout curtains back, and she squinted against the light streaming in from the window. He didn't say anything, just handed her a glass of iced coffee.

Grey took it from him and scooted up until her back was against the headboard. She sipped it, studying him. He had the apprehensive expression of a little boy who'd accidentally broken a window and was waiting to see how badly he would be punished.

"Breakfast should be ready soon. I made, like, a casserole-hash-egg-potato-cheese thing. It might be a mess but hopefully it's edible, at least. Do you want to eat outside, or should I make a tray?"

She cocked her head. "Aren't you hungover?"

"Oh, extremely," he replied cheerfully. She was so taken aback that the only thing she could do was throw her head back and laugh, the anxiety in her chest popping like a balloon. "Yeah, I feel like I'm going to fucking die right now," he continued, trying unsuccessfully to keep a straight face.

"Well, I extra appreciate it, then."

"It's the least I can do." He paused. "After last night."

She took another sip of her coffee, her smile fading. At least he'd brought it up first. "What *happened* last night, Ethan? What was that?"

He looked down into his own mug. "I have no idea." He

glanced back up at her, his brow furrowed. "I know that's not a good answer. I've been trying to put the pieces together all morning. I don't know what I was thinking. I *wasn't* thinking. All I know is that I'm sorry. Last night should've been about you, not my dumb little tantrum."

"It's okay." She wasn't sure if it was okay, even as she said it. Mostly she was just relieved that it didn't seem like they were going to fight after all. He understood that he was in the wrong, he was sorry, he was making her breakfast to apologize, and they could move on. She set her coffee on the bedside table and slid back down until her head was on the pillow again.

"How much time do we have before breakfast is ready? Come back to bed."

He smiled, putting his mug next to hers before crawling onto the bed beside her. "A few minutes. But you better not take advantage of me in my delicate condition."

She grinned as he lay back, lifting his arm so she could rest her head on his chest. "Never."

"I mean it. This is a no-thrust zone."

She closed her eyes, unable to handle the light for another second. "I'm not exactly dying to be thrusted, either. Honestly, just the idea is making me nauseous."

"Ouch."

Her eyes flew open, and she twisted her head up to look at him indignantly. "*You* said you didn't want to have sex with me first!"

"It's not that I don't *want* to. I'm physically incapable right now. There's a difference."

She laughed and closed her eyes again as he leaned down to kiss the top of her head. After a few minutes, he nudged her head up with his shoulder and rolled her onto her side so they were spooning. He mumbled something into the back of her neck.

"What?"

He shifted his head. "Let's go to New York. I want to."

She rolled over so they were facing each other. She needed to make sure she wasn't having some kind of auditory hallucination. "Really? You want to do the screening and everything? What made you change your mind?"

He shrugged. "I don't know. I tried the 'push it all down, pretend it never happened' thing. That's obviously not working out great for me. Maybe I just need to face it."

Grey was silent for a moment, afraid she'd say the wrong thing, make him change his mind. "When's the last time you were there?"

He closed his eyes and shook his head. "It's been years."

She hooked her leg over his hip and pulled him closer, nestling her face into the crook of his neck. He wrapped his arms around her tightly. "Maybe we could go for a week or two, make a real vacation of it. We could even rent a house in Cape May or something. You can show me where you had your first boner or whatever."

He laughed and turned his head to kiss her. The oven timer beeped from the kitchen, faint but insistent. They both groaned as Ethan rolled himself back up to sitting.

"You stay there. We'll do breakfast in bed."

She shook her head, stretching her arms above her head. "No, let's eat outside. If I don't get up now I never will."

IT WAS THE FIRST CRACK IN THE FOUNDATION. SMALL, BUT UN-mistakable.

Grey hadn't said anything to make him worry. She'd seemed almost too eager to forgive him. But as they sat together on the patio, dousing his bland casserole with ketchup and hot sauce, the roiling unease he'd felt since he'd woken up only intensified. She saw him differently now. There was no way she didn't.

He didn't want to go to New York. The idea was still as unappealing as the first time Nora had floated it in his kitchen all those months ago. But he needed to make a gesture, something bigger than a mediocre breakfast, to prove to Grey that last night was just a fluke, that that wasn't who he was anymore—even if he didn't quite believe it. He could be better for her. Be brave. He could try, at least.

Maybe it wouldn't be so bad, though, being there with her. It would be an opportunity to get to know her better, to explore their hometown together, finally take a vacation that hadn't been arranged by Audrey.

Something occurred to him.

"What about your family?"

She looked up at him, fork poised warily in midair. "What?"

"Would you see them? While we're there? You never talk about them."

She shifted uncomfortably. Too late, he realized that there might be something dark lurking behind her reticence. "You don't have to, if you're not—if there's something—"

She shook her head. "No, it's okay. I don't even know why . . . nothing bad happened. We're just . . . not close."

He racked his brain for any information she'd let slide about them over the last few months. "Is it just your mom and your brother?"

She nodded. "Yeah. I never really knew my dad. Actually, that's not totally true. When my show started airing, he tracked down my number somehow and tried to hit me up for money."

"Charming."

"I thought so, too. My mom is remarried now, I don't know

my stepfamily that well, but they seem nice. I think she's happy. My brother lives in San Francisco, working at some app or something. He just got engaged. We see each other every few years, but we don't really have a ton in common. That's pretty much it." She shrugged, but with a feigned nonchalance that indicated there was something she still wasn't telling him. Ethan took a stab in the dark.

"Is it . . . does it have to do with you working when you were a kid, or . . . ?"

She sighed. "Maybe. I don't know. It's complicated."

"Whose idea was it?"

"Mine."

"So what's the problem?"

"I don't know, Ethan," she said, suddenly as irritated as he had ever seen her. "There isn't a problem. It was my choice. Although once it stopped being cute little community theater roles and started paying half the rent on our apartment, it didn't really feel like it was a choice anymore. But I'm still doing it now, so all's well that ends well, right?" She drained her iced coffee, avoiding his eyes.

"You resent her," he said quietly. She shook her head.

"No. Yes. I don't know. In a weird way it feels like I resent her for what *didn't* happen. Like once I got older and started hearing stories from other kids in the industry, what they went through . . . I was really lucky. But if something had happened, there was no one who had my back. I was in a world full of adults with no one to protect me."

She looked down into her empty glass. "I wish . . . I wish she'd felt like my mom for longer. She kind of just feels like some lady I used to live with. Maybe that's horrible to say. But it doesn't seem like she's that interested in being closer, either. Everybody's happy with the way things are." Her voice cracked a little.

He was silent, waiting to see if she would continue. When she spoke again, her tone was light and forced.

"What about you? You have at least one sister, right?" She shook her head. "I can't believe this is the first time we're having this conversation."

"I can, considering how eager we both seem to be having it." That got a laugh out of her. "Four sisters. All older."

"Of *course* you're the baby, it all makes sense now. What about your parents?"

"They're older, too."

"You know what I mean."

"Mom died when I was in high school, right before Sam and I moved out here. My dad is probably still sitting in our living room in Forest Hills, getting hammered and punching holes in the wall."

"What did the wall ever do to him?" she asked in a manner that, now that he knew her better, he recognized as defensive; the kind of filler that meant she was uncomfortable and didn't know what else to say.

He looked down at his mostly untouched casserole. "What did any of us?"

She went pale before reaching across the table and covering his hand with hers. Neither of them said anything for a few moments.

"What about Sam's parents?" Her voice was hesitant.

He jerked his hand back involuntarily, as disoriented as if she'd physically slapped him. "What?"

She pressed on. "Sam's parents. You said you lived with them sometimes. Are they . . . are you still in touch?"

"No." The word was short, staccato, like a gunshot. Her mouth tightened, chastened, and she tried to take another sip from her glass before realizing it was empty.

He reluctantly continued, wanting to assuage her. "I haven't seen them . . . not since the funeral. I couldn't even talk to them. I was such a wreck." He hadn't thought about Sam's parents in years. In his mind, they'd died the day Sam had.

The days following Sam's death had been a blur. It was hard for him to distinguish his own memories from what he'd been told, or from the footage that had played over and over again for what felt like an eternity. In some ways, being escorted out of the funeral in handcuffs had been preferable to facing Sam's parents, seeing the pain and accusation laid bare on their faces. Of course he hadn't been in touch with them since. It was the least he could do. Their son was dead because of him.

Grey pushed back her chair and stood up, the rough scrape of the legs against the pavement bringing him back to the present with a jolt. She moved next to him, placing her hand on his shoulder, and he pushed his chair back, too. She curled herself into his lap and he pulled her to his chest, his racing heart beginning to slow. He leaned his head against hers and closed his eyes.

They sat that way for a long time, still as statues, apart from the breeze brushing a strand of her hair against his cheek. His thumb lightly traced the gap of skin between the bottom of her shirt and the top of her leggings.

He shifted his head until their foreheads touched, then brought his hand up to cup the back of her neck. He had a sudden, overwhelming feeling of déjà vu. The warmth of her skin beneath his hands. Her weight settled in his lap. After everything they'd already been through, he knew better than to take it for granted.

"I'm so fucking in love with you. You know that, right?"

He felt her inhale sharply. She closed her eyes, then opened them. They'd steered clear of that phrase since the night of her birthday—and even then, he'd only danced around it without saying it outright. As he said it now, it felt inadequate to describe the enormity of what he felt for her. But until the English language caught up with him, it was the best he could do.

A slow smile curled at the corners of her mouth.

"I love you, too."

As he drew her face to his, closing the gap, he finally felt the lump of dread in his stomach dissolve like a sugar cube in water. He wasn't going to lose her again. He'd get his shit together. He'd make it work with her.

He had to.

27

THE *DIRTBAGS* SCREENING WAS PART OF A WEEKLONG FESTIVAL honoring the work of Perry McCallister, the director. Grey and Ethan had planned on arriving in Manhattan in time to attend the opening-night party, but their flight was delayed so long that by the time their cab deposited them at their hotel, they were too exhausted to do anything other than strip, shower, and pass out under soft linens and mountains of pillows.

They spent a lazy morning lounging in bed, dozing on and off. When Grey opened her eyes again, the bed was empty. Before she had time to wonder, the door to the room opened and Ethan strode in holding two milky iced coffees and a brown paper bag.

"I've never been more in love with you," she groaned as she ripped open the bag to reveal two greasy, beautiful bacon, egg, and cheese bagels.

Once they felt alive enough to venture outside, they didn't do much more than walk. It was one of those rare, perfect early summer New York days, before the fetid humidity of July and August crept in, sweat plastering clothes to every bodily crevice within seconds of going outside. Today, however, the sun warmed their faces and cool breezes swept their hair into their eyes as they wandered over to the West Village, letting themselves get lost in the serpentine streets.

She'd been skeptical of Ethan's assertion that people generally left him alone in New York, but he was right. Aside from the occasional double take or less-than-sneaky cellphone photo, nobody approached them.

They paused in front of a picturesque townhouse stoop, where a commercial shoot was under way. Though it was still early June, the commercial was set in fall, with fake leaves dusting the steps. Grey and Ethan stood a respectful distance away and watched two sweater-clad models sip from the same Coke bottle with two straws, then give each other a sweet, corn-syrupy peck. They beat a hasty retreat when the female model spotted Ethan, her gasp ruining what was probably a perfectly good take.

They walked farther north, stopping for a late lunch in Koreatown. Ethan's phone buzzed, and he pulled it out to silence it, pausing when he saw the name.

"Do you mind? It's Perry." The two of them had been playing phone tag all day, trying to coordinate a time to get together and catch up outside of the festival.

Grey shook her head. "No, go ahead."

She focused on her hot pot as Ethan muttered into the phone, hanging up promptly.

"Did you figure out the plan?" Grey asked, maneuvering the last bit of her egg yolk onto a clump of rice. Ethan shook his head.

"The only time he's free while we're here is for lunch tomorrow, and that's when we're seeing your mom. Are you going to eat this?" he asked, hovering his chopsticks over the last piece of kimchi in the center of the table. She gestured at him to take it, frowning, and he plucked it onto his plate.

"Oh. I mean, it's okay if you want to go see him instead. I can see my mom alone."

"No, I want to meet her. And I want to be there if you need me."

Grey felt her chest tighten at how casually he was ready to give this up, just so he could be there for her. "It's okay, really. We can find some other time for you to meet her. Trust me, I would bail, too, if I could. But I'll be fine."

"Are you sure?"

"Totally. Call him back now."

After Ethan hung up the phone again, he chased a stray grain of rice around the bottom of his cast iron bowl.

"Do you want to come see Sam's parents with me?" he asked, as nonchalant as if they were already midconversation about that exact topic. Grey blinked, stunned.

"What?"

"I called them. Before we came." He kept his eyes down, like he wouldn't be able to keep going if he registered her shock. "I didn't say anything because I wasn't sure how I would feel once I got here. But I think . . . I want to see them." He smiled ruefully. "I feel bad asking you to come after I just bailed on your mom, but . . ."

"Of course I'll come. Of course," Grey said quickly. "How did . . . how was it? Talking to them?"

"Good. Weird. I don't know. I only talked to his mom. I was dreading it, but . . . she was so happy to hear from me." He paused to collect himself, seemingly surprised at the way his voice cracked with emotion. Grey said nothing, just focused intently on him. "We didn't really talk about anything important, but hearing her voice . . . it was a lot. Brought a lot back."

He got that distant look in his eyes that by now she knew too well. She placed her hand over his. His eyes refocused as he smiled at her, flipping his hand over and squeezing hers.

"I can't wait to meet them."

"WHAT, HE DIDN'T WANT TO MEET ME?"

Five minutes into lunch with her mother, Grey felt like her smile was already cracking at the edges.

"Something came up. He really wanted to be here, I was the one who told him not to."

"I see. So *you* didn't want him to meet me." It was a joke, sort of, though the hard edge in her mother's voice didn't make Grey feel like laughing.

It had been long enough since she'd seen her mother that the experience was slightly uncanny. Their resemblance was undeniable. Her mother had been young when Grey was born; even now, she was barely in her fifties, finally out of the range for the two of them to be confused for sisters. She was smaller than Grey, thin and brittle, with a perpetually harsh expression even at rest. Sometimes looking at her gave Grey the same unpleasant jolt as when she caught a glimpse of herself in the mirror after she'd been thinking something uncharitable.

This wasn't the mother she'd grown up with. When she'd remarried, it was like she'd been reborn into the role of a lifetime: suburban society doyenne. She'd studied hard, gone beyond Method. She tilted her head to give Grey the once-over, her tasteful blond highlights (which looked more expensive than Grey's) shimmering in the sun, her ballerina-pink manicured hands clutching the supple leather strap of her purse. Grey often wondered if her mother's distance was born of resentment toward her and her brother for being living, breathing reminders of the life she'd lived before—except when one of them did something she could brag about at the country club.

Grey craned her neck, desperately trying to locate the hostess. When they'd shown up to the café, it was packed, and she'd forgotten to call and tell them that their reservation was down to two. The frazzled hostess had nodded and darted away, and what had seemed like a simple request turned out to be more complicated than anticipated. She didn't envy the hostess as the line of irritated patrons grew longer behind them.

"Aren't you glad you never had to do that?" her mother asked with a conspiratorial smile once they were seated. Grey bit her tongue to stop herself from reminding her mother that the reason Grey had never needed a side job was because she'd been working since she still had baby teeth.

Instead, she skimmed the menu, trying to stay engaged as her mother filled her in on everything she'd missed at Madison's graduation party several weeks earlier. Apparently, one of Madison's friends had shown up in a nearly identical dress, drawing all the attention away from poor Madison. Grey murmured sympathetically, which was all that was needed from her.

The hostess came over to take their drink orders, apologizing again for the wait. Grey studied her. She looked like she was barely out of her teens, curvaceous and striking, with a platinum pixie cut and a bright slash of lipstick. Grey wondered why she'd moved to New York, what dream she was chasing, whether she would ever catch it. Whether anyone ever did.

"So, where are you staying?" her mother chirped as the hostess scurried away again.

"The Bowery."

Her mother raised her eyebrows. "I assume he's paying?"

Grey went pink. As always, her mother somehow sensed exactly which buttons to press. How could she have known that earlier that morning, after Grey had stepped out of the shower and wrapped herself in a plush towel, she'd looked out at the spectacular view from the bathroom window and felt paralyzed?

She hadn't felt strange about the expensive meals and opulent accommodations she'd experienced when she and Ethan had still been bound by their contract. She'd been able to rationalize them as perks of the job, one in which they were equal partners. But now she was just along for the ride, basking in his benevolence. She knew she should just enjoy it and be grateful, that anyone else would be thrilled to be in her shoes. And she was, mostly. Except for the twisted, anxious part deep inside her that felt like Cinderella two minutes before midnight.

A position her mother could probably relate to, come to think of it.

She rolled her eyes. "Mo-*om*." She was glad Ethan wasn't here to see her this way. The question was always when, not if, she would turn into a brat in her mother's presence.

"Sorry. You're so sensitive sometimes, I never know what's going to set you off."

"I just don't know why you would ask when you clearly already know the answer."

"I didn't know. You don't tell me anything. Everything I know about you two I have to read in the tabloids. How do you think that makes me feel? Do you think I liked having my *dentist* be the one to tell me that my daughter's bare behind was all over the news, and then some?"

There it was. They hadn't talked about Grey's scandal, and a part of her had naïvely hoped they'd never have to.

"Yeah, that must have been really hard for you," she muttered. The sarcasm seemed to fly over her mother's head.

"All I'm asking for is a *crumb* of information every once in a while."

About Ethan, or about me? Grey swallowed the provocation, refusing to let herself revert fully to a sullen teen.

"You're right. Sorry."

"So, where is he, exactly, that's more important than you?"

ETHAN DRUMMED HIS FINGERS ON THE CORNER OF THE TABLE. He'd arrived at the restaurant early, humming with nervous energy. It had been years since he'd seen Perry.

When the studio had declared Ethan too inexperienced to direct *Dirtbags,* insisting instead on bringing in an established director, Ethan had been prepared to hate him. He'd seethed with insecurity the first few days on set. However, Perry had disarmed him immediately with his gruff, no-nonsense approach, coupled with his overwhelming patience and generosity in explaining every decision he was making. Shooting *Dirtbags* had been like Ethan's own personal film school: everything he knew about filmmaking, he had learned on that set.

It had hit him halfway through the plane ride to New York, cruising thirty-five thousand feet above Kansas: Perry should direct *Bitter Pill*. He couldn't believe it hadn't occurred to him sooner. It was perfect. The way to honor Sam would be to return to their roots, recruit the man who had shaped their first screenplay into a classic. He'd immediately pulled out his laptop and forwarded Perry the screenplay.

Ethan had seated himself facing the door, so he saw Perry as soon as he strolled in. He was immediately struck by how young he looked. When Perry had directed *Dirtbags,* he'd seemed a thousand years old to Ethan; now in his early fifties, it seemed like he hadn't aged much since then. Ethan realized with a start that he was now almost the same age that Perry had been then. When Perry spotted him, his face lit up.

"Ethan!" Perry boomed, charging across the restaurant toward him. Part of the reason working with him had felt like film school was that Perry had (what Ethan assumed to be) a professorial vibe: ruddy face, wild strawberry-blond hair, patched elbows. He wrapped Ethan in an enormous bear hug before stepping back and holding him at arm's length, appraising him.

"It's good to see you, old man," Perry said with a grin, the familiar affection in his voice warming Ethan from head to toe as they slid into opposite sides of the booth.

He'd brought Perry to one of his favorite old haunts, a West Village gastropub famous for its decadent burgers. But when he mentioned it as they perused their menus, Perry dropped his eyes and shook his head.

"Can't do red meat these days. Doctor's orders."

He was reluctant to elaborate, but Ethan eventually dragged it out of him: two years ago, after a heart attack followed by a double bypass, Perry had been forced to overhaul his lifestyle. Ethan found it hard to believe that Perry, who'd never met a vice he didn't embrace wholeheartedly, no longer drank, smoked cigarettes, or ate meat. However, he did have to admit that Perry seemed more vital than he'd ever seen him. A brush with mortality would do that to a man. It also explained why someone who famously never watched his own films once the final cut was finished would allow his oeuvre to be so publicly and thoroughly celebrated—let alone agree to be part of it.

"It's fucking bleak, is what it is," Perry said cheerfully, digging into his Caesar salad. "This is it, I've done everything I'll ever do that's worth a damn. I can just wave to the adoring crowd and turn into a pile of dust."

Ethan took a sip of his beer. This was the opening he'd been waiting for.

"Do you have anything lined up next?" he asked casually between bites of a burger that was almost too big to fit his mouth around.

Perry shrugged. "Not sure. One of those streaming sites has been trying to get me to do something or other. Ten years ago I would've told them to go fuck themselves, but I guess that's where everything interesting is happening now, right?"

Ethan nodded vaguely, then cleared his throat. "Did you get a chance to read through what I sent you?"

As soon as he saw the look on Perry's face, he regretted asking. He regretted sending it. He regretted the whole fucking thing.

"I did," Perry replied, unable to meet Ethan's eyes. It didn't seem like he wanted to say more, but the door had already been opened.

"What did you think?" Ethan asked, though he already knew the answer.

Perry sighed and shook his head. "I don't know about this one, Ethan. I don't think it's there yet."

"Well, what does it need?" The desperation in his voice embarrassed him.

"I'm not sure. I'd have to take a closer look at it, but my instinct is it's doomed from the start. I just don't see what benefit there is to remaking it; the original is damn near perfect. It doesn't feel like you've found your own angle yet. You're setting yourself up for failure. What's more, you're selling yourself short. I know you're capable of more than this."

Ethan knew Perry was trying to be kind, but the wad of meat he'd just swallowed felt stuck in his throat. He struggled to reply.

"I know. I know it's not ready. But I really want—I *need* to make this work. For Sam."

He didn't have to say any more. Perry's brow creased with sympathy. Ethan looked away, draining his beer.

When Perry spoke, his voice sounded far away.

"I can't say I wouldn't feel the same way if I were in your shoes. Here's my advice, and you're welcome to ignore it: try to divorce the project from your feelings about Sam. Finishing this won't bring him back. You need to stop wallowing in the past, and figure out what your future looks like." He attempted to spear a crouton with his fork, cracking it in half. "Speaking as someone currently being waterboarded by my own past, it's not pretty."

Ethan felt hot behind his eyes. He'd expected Perry to understand how important this was, how it was the only possible tribute to his and Sam's legacy. If he were to abandon the project, that would be it. He would be fully alone now.

But that wasn't true. He wasn't alone. He had Grey. He suddenly regretted letting her go see her mother without him. He only hoped she was having a better time than he was.

"HI. HELLO?"

A woman approached their table with a wave. Grey was so destabilized by her mother's company that she'd forgotten there were perfectly good reasons for a stranger to approach her. She expected the woman to tell her that Grey's chair was on her purse, or that she'd accidentally dropped something on the way back from the bathroom.

"Sorry?" Grey said, smiling nervously.

"Can I get a picture?" the woman asked with what was probably supposed to be a smile but looked more like a grimace. Her Australian accent was so thick it took a moment for Grey to register what she was saying. *Peeg-cha*. She looked down and saw the woman's phone brandished under her nose.

Grey's smile turned apologetic.

"Sorry, it's not a good time right now. I'm just trying to have lunch with my mom."

The woman's lips slid back down to cover her teeth and she slunk away without another word.

"That was *very* ungrateful of you, Emily," her mother snapped before the woman was even out of earshot. Grey attacked her omelet with renewed vigor and tried to keep her voice low.

"I'm allowed to have boundaries."

"These people are the reason you have a career."

"Wait, I'm confused. Is it them, or is it Ethan? Anyone but me, right?"

"I didn't say that. There you go again, always jumping to the worst conclusion."

Grey closed her eyes. Opened them. This could all go differently. She could put her fork down, unclench her jaw. *I don't want things to be this way between us.* They would sit there for hours, crying and apologizing, reopening all their old wounds before cauterizing them for good.

Or her mother would play dumb. Raise an eyebrow. Shut her down. *I don't know what you mean, Emily.* Make it hurt even more than it did when she didn't try, when it was all still unsaid.

Grey made eye contact with the waitress.

"Could we get the check, please?"

When she got back to the hotel, Ethan was already there, staring out the floor-to-ceiling windows of their penthouse suite, glass of bourbon in hand. He glanced back at her when he heard her open the door, but said nothing.

"How did it go with Perry?" she asked, kicking off her sandals and padding over to him.

"Bad." His voice was hoarse. "How was seeing your mom?"

"Bad." She rested her head on his shoulder.

He offered her the glass. "I'm sorry I wasn't there."

"It's okay. I don't think it would've helped."

She took a sip, even though it was the middle of the afternoon and she hated bourbon. It burned her throat and made her eyes water, but her nerves felt a little less raw. It was hard to remember that not so long ago being this close to him, his scent and his warmth, had made her palms sweat. Now it soothed her like a weighted blanket. She handed the glass back to him and wrapped her arms around his waist.

"Can we stay in tonight?"

He pulled her close and kissed the top of her head.

"Please."

28

ETHAN PACED THE LENGTH OF THEIR SUITE LIKE A TIGER IN AN enclosure. Grey had been gone for hours, getting a late lunch with one of her high school friends. When she returned, the two of them would take a car out to Forest Hills to have dinner with Sam's parents. In the meantime, Ethan had no idea what to do with himself. He'd taken a long, scalding shower, scrubbing his skin until it was red and raw. The minutes ticked by like hours as he wore tracks in the carpet.

Back in L.A., there were a lot of things that reminded him of Sam. But he lived in a different house now, he didn't see any of their mutual friends anymore, and until recently, he barely went out. He'd made his life as small as possible so he'd hurt as little as possible. But even without stepping foot in Queens yet, just being in New York had opened the floodgates. He'd tossed and turned the night before, drifting in and out of dreams filled with fragments of memories so vivid that he woke up gasping.

The first time he'd met Sam had been the summer before sixth grade. Sam had moved in a few blocks away, and Ethan had caught a few glimpses of him as Ethan rode by on his bike while they were unloading the truck. He was short and scrawny, like Ethan; a tiny ball of energy with dark curly hair.

Ethan had been terrified to enter middle school. He was too shy and too pretty for his own good, perpetually trying to slip under the radar to avoid becoming a target. He'd lingered around the edges of a pack of rowdy, unruly boys he had nothing in common with, for no reason other than self-preservation.

Sam had approached Ethan and his friends while they were setting off bottle rockets in the park. The ringleader, Jimmy, had started to push Sam around, taunting him. Ethan had watched this scene play out half a dozen times, and it always ended the same. A skinned knee—maybe a bloody nose—before a tearful retreat. But something incredible had happened: Sam made him laugh. Made all of them laugh. Though Ethan couldn't recall exactly what Sam had said, he'd never forget the looks on everyone's faces, how surprised and disarmed they'd been.

He'd sought Sam out at school, and eventually they stopped hanging out with the other guys at all. They saved up enough money mowing lawns to buy a camcorder, and their afternoons and weekends were occupied with running around the neighborhood shooting their own increasingly elaborate movies.

Ethan loved Sam's house. It was so different from his own. First of all, it was quieter. Sam was an only child, while Ethan had four older sisters who were constantly fighting, crying, stomping, yelling on the phone, slamming doors. When it was quiet in his house, it meant that something was wrong. It meant that something had set his father off and they were all trying to lie low to avoid being singled out as the object of his wrath.

Sam's parents, too, were polar opposites of Ethan's. To Sam's embarrassment, they were still obviously, desperately in love. Sam's mother had been an opera singer, Italian, from Italy, and his father was an art director at an ad agency in the city. Their house was crammed to the brim with books and instruments and mysterious objects that may or may not have been art.

They'd accepted Ethan into their family wholeheartedly, automatically setting out an extra plate at dinner and an extra bowl of cereal in the morning. The first time Ethan had shown up with his shoulder throbbing, nearly wrenched out of its socket, Sam's father had wanted to call the police, but Ethan had begged him not to. It would have only made everything worse. That night, Sam's parents had made up the guest room for him, instead of his usual sleeping bag on the floor of Sam's room. He hadn't gone home for three weeks.

He'd envied so much about Sam: his easy charisma, his creativity, his quick wit. He knew Sam had been jealous of him, too. They'd entered high school the same height, barely five and a half feet tall. The summer before their junior year, Ethan had sprouted up five inches, and then another four before they'd graduated. Sam wasn't unattractive, and he was so damn charming that he'd never had trouble dating, but he'd always joke about how he had to talk women into liking him despite his appearance, not because of it. Once Ethan had grown into his looks, the amount of attention he got from girls just from standing around and scowling had been borderline unsettling.

But even so, Ethan felt like he was always trying to keep up with Sam. When they'd watched their first unpolished VHS "dailies," Ethan had been shocked at how wooden he looked next to Sam. Sam was a natural from the beginning. He'd brought everyone to tears as Tevye in their high school production of *Fiddler on the Roof*; a half-WASP, half-Italian seventeen-year-old flawlessly channeling a middle-aged Jewish peasant. Meanwhile, Ethan had white-knuckled his way through his one song as Perchik, the handsome socialist revolutionary.

When Sam and Ethan were fourteen, Sam's parents had thrown a party, and the two of them had made off with a six-pack without anyone noticing it was missing. They'd sat on it for a week like a pot of gold, waiting for the right moment, before each chugging three warm cans and meeting up with some of their other friends at the park. *This is what it must feel like to be Sam,* he'd realized. He felt lighter, his inhibitions stripped away, making everyone laugh, saying exactly the right things. That is, until his head started to spin and he'd puked in the bushes. But more so than any of the other important relationships in his life—Sam, Nora, and now Grey—it had been love at first sight.

Ethan sat on the edge of the bed, hands pressed against his temples. His breathing was ragged and his head ached. His eyes drifted to the minibar.

He was going to make it through this afternoon. He didn't have a choice.

GREY ARRIVED BACK AT THE HOTEL SWEATY AND OUT OF BREATH. The hours had slipped by before she knew it, and she'd hastily said her goodbyes and dashed out of the restaurant. She fired off a few apologetic texts to Ethan as she dodged cars, running across the street against the light, to no response. By the time she pushed the door of their room open, it was twenty-five minutes after they were supposed to leave.

"Fuck, I'm so sorry," she wheezed, darting into the bathroom to splash water on her face and touch up her makeup. No response. She poked her head out of the doorway.

"Ethan?"

Their suite was empty.

She returned to the bathroom and checked her phone again. Nothing. She swiped it open and called him. A faint buzzing came from the other room, and she dropped her eyelash curler into the sink with a clatter.

When she darted into the bedroom, her stomach plummeted. Ethan's phone was sitting on the nightstand. Her mind raced. Maybe he'd just run out to get something from the bodega and forgotten his phone. As ten minutes passed, then twenty, this seemed less and less likely. It was possible he'd decided to go to Queens without her—but unthinkable that he'd do it without even sending her a text first.

After two excruciating hours, she did the only thing she could think of. She called Nora.

Thankfully, Nora picked up on the third ring.

"Hello?"

"Hey, can you talk?" Grey's voice sounded overly perky.

"Sure. One second." Grey heard her excuse herself, then the muffled sounds of the street. "Is everything okay?"

"Yeah. No. I don't know. I'm really sorry to bother you, I just didn't know who else to call." Grey closed her eyes and took a deep breath. Saying the words out loud would make it real. "It's Ethan. He's gone. He left his phone; I don't know where he is."

Nora was silent for so long that Grey had to check to make sure the call hadn't disconnected. "Hello?"

"How long has it been?"

"I don't know. At least two hours. I came back to the room and he wasn't here."

"And he was supposed to be? You had plans?"

Grey sat down on the edge of the bed and rested her forehead in her other hand.

"Yeah, we were going to go to Queens and see Sam's parents."

Another silence. Then Nora sighed heavily. "Has he done this with you before?"

"No. Never. Do you know where he is? Should I be worried?" Too late for that.

"You shouldn't. But I don't blame you if you are. Trust me, I've been in your place before. There's nothing you can do right now."

Grey took a deep breath. She didn't want to ask. She had a feeling she already knew the answer.

"Where is he?"

"If I had to guess, probably in the back of some shitty bar."

Grey was silent.

"I'm sorry, Grey. I wish I had something better to tell you. But I'm sure he's okay. Or as okay as he ever is. He always comes back eventually." It sounded like Nora was talking about a wayward housecat that'd escaped their yard.

"I just feel really . . . helpless." Grey lay back on the bed, her legs dangling over the side. She covered her eyes with her arm. Nora *tsk*ed sympathetically.

"I knew that coming back to New York might be tough for him. Maybe I shouldn't have pushed. That night at dinner . . ." She trailed off.

The silence hung heavy and significant between them.

"Did you . . . when you were together. Did you ever talk about him trying to get sober? Give him an ultimatum?" Grey's voice was hollow. She felt exhausted.

Nora sighed again. "No. I mean, we fought about it all the time, but I never put my foot down. Maybe I should have. I've always believed that you can't force anyone to change unless they want to. I hoped he would come to it on his own, but maybe I was just enabling him. Things didn't get really bad until after Sam, and by that point I had to do what I could to protect myself, protect the girls. I couldn't sit around and wait for him to get his shit together anymore. But I really wanted things to be different with you two. You're so good together. He seemed . . . better. Like maybe he was ready."

"Yeah." Grey wished the conversation were over. She wanted to crawl into bed and sleep, even though it was barely dinnertime. When she woke up, Ethan would probably be back, and she could pretend everything was normal again. The knotted feeling in the pit of her stomach was no longer about the mystery of Ethan's absence; it was about the conversation that would have to happen upon his return.

"Thank you, Nora. For everything. I'll let you go now."

"Anytime. I mean it."

Though she had been anxious to hang up, once she did, she regretted it. Now there was nothing to focus on but the seemingly endless expanse of time before Ethan showed back up.

Grey thought about texting Kamilah, but she knew what she would say. That if she let this kind of thing slide even once, he would keep pushing it. She would be teaching him how to treat her. This was the moment to tell him to shape up or ship out.

But then, maybe she was being a little dramatic. Was it really such a big deal that he blew off their plans *one* time—the first time ever? She didn't even know for sure where he was. He'd been pushed into coming here. He was overwhelmed. It made sense that he would need to let off steam alone for a while. She was just looking for another excuse to cut and run. No relationship was perfect. There was probably a reasonable explanation for everything.

She twisted open a tiny bottle of wine from the minibar and zoned out in front of the television. At nine, her growling stomach reminded her she hadn't eaten in hours. She ordered a salad from room service and picked at it. At a quarter to two, still wide awake, she heard a loud banging at the door. She leapt off the bed and dashed to open it.

Ethan swayed in the doorway, eyes half closed, mumbling something about forgetting his key. The sight of him was almost pitiful: clothes disheveled and reeking, his skin gray. And yet she instantly forgot her anger, her worry. She felt nothing other than relief so overwhelming her knees went weak.

Tenderly, she helped him undress and eased him into the shower, stripping off her own clothes and stepping in with him. The hot water seemed to revive him somewhat, his eyes now able to focus on her. As she wrapped them both in bathrobes, he tried to say something to her, but it was quiet and garbled. She ignored it and led him to bed.

They lay facing away from each other without touching. Finally, Grey heard him grumble something else.

"Mmmsorry."

Grey shut her eyes tightly. It was easier to pretend she hadn't heard him.

29

ETHAN HAD HAD SOME BAD HANGOVERS IN HIS LIFE, BUT THIS one was an all-timer. He'd blacked out, which he rarely did anymore. At dawn, he'd dragged himself to the toilet to retch, slumping against the side and resting his cheek on the cool porcelain. Maybe he'd drifted back to sleep, or maybe Grey had been there with him in reality, running her fingers through his sweat-soaked hair and placing a cold washcloth on the back of his neck. He was humiliated that she had to see him like this; even more humiliated that she was being so kind to him when he didn't deserve it.

He woke up again in the early afternoon, tangled in the sheets this time, head pounding, mouth dry. Slowly, he turned his head to the left. The bed was empty next to him. He turned it to the right. The nightstand held a glass of water and a notepad. He propped himself up on one elbow and took a few tentative sips of water as he glanced at the pad.

Out to lunch. Be back soon. xo.

The familiar slope of her handwriting sent a fresh wave of

nausea through him. The previous day began to trickle back to him in fragments. An hour before they were supposed to leave to see Sam's parents, he'd panicked. What had started as one drink around the corner to calm his nerves had turned into another, then another. He'd left his phone in the room intentionally, an insurance policy so he'd have to come back before she knew he was gone. That had obviously backfired.

He heard the door of the suite open. Grey's footsteps on the carpet.

"How are you feeling?" Her tone was neutral, her eyes wary. She held a plastic bag at her hip, knotted at the top and fat with plastic take-out containers. "I brought you some food, if you want it."

"Thanks." His voice escaped in a rasp. The smell of grease wafted toward him, making his stomach turn and his mouth fill with saliva. He swallowed, trying not to gag.

Neither of them moved.

She didn't have to say anything. It was obvious. She was done with him.

Finally, she set the bag on the edge of the bed and turned to leave the bedroom.

"Grey. Wait."

She stopped, pivoting on her heel to face him again, chin tilted up expectantly.

"I'm sorry. About yesterday."

Her eyes flicked to the floor.

"I'm sure Sam's parents are wondering what happened."

He flinched. *Sam's parents*. God. He would have to talk to them today, explain everything. Try to ignore the hurt and disappointment in their voices.

"I'm sorry," he repeated dully. "I shouldn't have just disappeared. I should've told you where I was."

"Yeah, you should've." Her tone was flippant, but there was an edge to it. She tucked a strand of hair behind her ear and shifted her weight, her eyes drifting to the window, like she would rather be anywhere else but there. He knew the feeling.

He pulled back a corner of the duvet, then looked up at her. She met his gaze without moving. His heart felt like it stopped. After several interminable seconds, she slipped off her sandals and pulled her sundress over her head before crawling in next to him.

He pulled her body against him, her cheek on his chest, skin still warmed from the sun. Touching her seemed to ease his hangover slightly. Maybe it was the relief of knowing that she couldn't hate him *that* much if she still wanted to be physically close to him.

"Are you ready for tonight?" she murmured, running her fingers over his chest.

Tonight. The screening. He placed his hand over hers and clutched it tightly.

"No," he said truthfully. She nuzzled her face deeper against his torso.

"You're gonna do great."

"Mmmm." He shut his eyes, focusing on the way her deep breathing synced with his, his chest rising with hers in perfect unison.

He had almost fallen asleep again when he felt her stir and sit up, swinging her legs over the side of the bed.

"Where are you going?" he mumbled.

"I can't just lie here all day." He couldn't see her face, but her annoyance was audible.

He sat up, too, his head throbbing more powerfully than ever. She had her back to him, the flawless expanse of her skin bisected by a thin scrap of blue lace.

"You *are* mad."

She raised one shoulder, more of a twitch than a shrug.

"I was last night. Right now . . . I don't know." She inclined her head to look at him. "I don't think this is the right time to talk about any of this. We just need to get through tonight."

His chest tightened. She *was* going to leave him. All she cared about was keeping him calm enough to not embarrass her tonight.

She stood up and plucked her dress off the floor. It hadn't even been down there long enough to wrinkle.

"I'm going to go up to the Natural History Museum. I'll be back by four so we can get ready. Do you need anything? Gatorade? Advil?"

She didn't ask him if he wanted to come. Obviously he was a mess, unfit for anything other than spending the day in bed. He rewound the last twenty-four hours in his mind, torturing himself by retracing every misstep now that it was too late to do anything about it. It would've been emotionally draining to see Sam's parents, sure, but not insurmountable. He would've gotten through it like a twenty-mile run, carried through on endorphins and adrenaline, exhausted but exhilarated at the end. But it had been years since he'd run more than a mile, since he'd been in the market for anything besides a hit of instant gratification.

In that timeline, he and Grey would spend this afternoon wandering the museum—his favorite—together. He'd tell her about how the first time he'd seen the *T. rex* skeleton on a field trip with his first-grade class, he'd had nightmares for a week. How he'd begged his mother to bring him back the following weekend so he could stare down the object of his terror, somehow both more and less thrilling than he'd built it up to be in his mind.

But instead, she was going alone, and he'd lie in bed waiting for her to come back and dump him. Part of him had known this day was coming since the first time he'd seen her in Audrey's office. He'd been deluded to believe that things would be different with her, that *he* would be different. That being with her could some-how heal the ugliest, most fucked-up parts of him.

For a while, it almost seemed like it had.

"No. I'm okay. Thanks."

She hesitated for a moment before moving to his side and kiss-ing his forehead. Not his lips. She picked up her purse and swept out the door without another word.

After she left, he stumbled to the bathroom, tripping over his jeans on the floor. When he picked them up to throw them on the bed, something fell out of the pocket. He bent down to pick it up: a small plastic bag of white powder. His stomach lurched. He hadn't taken anything stronger than an extra-strength Tylenol since Sam's funeral, but apparently last night he'd relapsed without even remembering it.

He considered the baggie. He could throw it out, act like it never happened. Or he could accept it as a sign. The unraveling of everything they'd built over the last few months was already in motion. Fighting the current would only exhaust him. He was going to drown either way.

WHEN GREY HAD LEFT ETHAN THAT MORNING, HE'D LOOKED half dead; now she was shocked at how chipper he seemed. He was nursing a glass of bourbon as they dressed, bombarding her with questions: the gray shirt or the blue? Tie or no tie? Did his glasses make him look smart, or just old? But there was a desperation be-hind the questions that unsettled her. He'd plastered on a hundred-watt smile for her like they were in front of the cameras already. At least it seemed like a good sign that the screening would go smoothly.

Grey dressed simply, in jeans and a silk camisole, both black.

Tonight wasn't about her. She was just here to support him, the woman behind the man. Smiling by his side like everything was fine.

She watched him knock back the rest of his glass, then refill it. As he buttoned and unbuttoned his top button in front of the mirror, she came up behind him and slid her arms around his waist. Though the gesture was meant to comfort him, she felt him tense up. She held on awkwardly for a few more frozen seconds before releasing him, then coming to stand beside him in the mirror. He glanced at her.

"You look good."

"So do you." She reached over to smooth one of his jacket cuffs, then slid her hand up to the back of his neck. "I love you."

He looked down at her and smiled, but it didn't reach his eyes.

"Yeah. Love you, too."

THE SCREENING, AS THEY'D EXPECTED, WAS STANDING ROOM only. The guests of honor were seated upstairs, in a roped-off section with the festival coordinator and the moderator of the Q and A. Grey found it impossible to concentrate on the movie; she was focused only on Ethan. After the first fifteen minutes, he slipped out of his seat. When he returned several minutes later, she could smell the bourbon on his breath, even as he tried to angle his face away.

She lost track of how many times he left his seat—it seemed like he was out of it more than he was in it. She debated saying something to him, but she didn't want to be a scold. He was a grown man, he didn't need her to police him. That would be the beginning of the end for them.

She'd seen *Dirtbags* two or three times, but not in years. Making fun of his bad teen movie together in their hotel room was one thing, but this was on another level. Where *What's Your Deal?* had been glossy and overprocessed, *Dirtbags* was larger than life and achingly raw. It sometimes felt like Perry had left the camera rolling without telling the actors, capturing their most candid moments: the lived-in camaraderie of Ethan and Sam, the spark of chemistry igniting between Ethan and Nora. The experience was uncomfortable enough for Grey that she could only imagine what it was like for Ethan. She felt like sneaking out for a drink herself.

As the credits rolled, Nora, Perry, and Ethan were herded through a side door, making their way to the stage. Grey reached over to squeeze Ethan's hand in a last-minute gesture of support, but he was already out of his seat, walking away from her without a backward glance.

When the applause died down, the moderator, a film critic from *The New Yorker,* introduced the three of them, one by one. Ethan walked onstage last, to rapturous cheers. He squinted against the bright lights, waving vaguely, before taking a seat next to Nora. When the panel started, Grey heard nothing but her heart pounding in her ears.

Ethan seemed alert at first, but it wasn't long before he began to slouch lower in his chair, his head lolling to one side. He answered the moderator's questions about where he and Sam had gotten the idea for the screenplay in short sentences that were only slightly slurred.

The moderator shuffled her cards.

"Now, Perry. Tell us a little bit about how you got involved with this project."

"They wouldn't let me direct it," Ethan interrupted with a hollow laugh. There were a few uncomfortable titters in the audience. Perry glanced at Ethan before clearing his throat.

"Unfortunately, it's not a very interesting story. I got a call from the producers that they had this great screenplay, these two talented young guys, and would I meet with them and see what I thought."

The moderator leaned forward, bangles jingling on her wrists as she moved.

"And what was your first impression?"

"I loved the script, of course. And when I met them—it's funny, I'm not sure if I ever told you this, Ethan. But I had just seen a screening of the restoration of *Purple Noon* the week before, and then this guy walks in the room"—he pointed at Ethan— "looking like the second coming of Alain Delon. It was so uncanny, it felt like fate. I said yes immediately."

"Incredible," the moderator gushed. "And, Nora, this movie was obviously huge for you, both personally and professionally. Your transition from modeling into acting, meeting the man who would eventually become your husband—"

"Ex-husband. Don't forget about ex-husband." Ethan's mouth was so close to his microphone that feedback crackled through the room. The moderator laughed nervously.

"Yes. Well. Could you tell us what that experience was like?"

"The divorce? It was a fucking nightmare. But you all knew that, right?" He grinned at the audience humorlessly.

"I think she meant me," Nora cut in smoothly. Her eyes flicked up to meet Grey's in the balcony, only briefly revealing her unease, before launching into her answer without missing a beat.

The rest of the panel continued in this vein: Ethan was terse and surly when asked a direct question, but was more than willing to interject snide comments into the questions he hadn't been asked. This was an Ethan she'd never seen before, sloppy and cruel; an Ethan whose very existence terrified her. Sweat soaked the armpits of her camisole as she willed each question the moderator asked to be the last.

The moderator grew more and more flustered against Ethan's onslaught. She dropped her cards on the ground, scrambling to put them back in place. She looked down at a card, inhaling deeply as if to ask a question, then hesitated, flipping to the next card.

"Actually, never mind. So tell me, Nora—"

"What was that?" Ethan interjected. The moderator blinked several times, a deer in the headlights.

"Sorry?"

"That card. That question you were about to ask. Please, we're all on the edge of our seats."

The moderator looked offstage for support. "I don't think—"

"No, no, let's hear it." It was clear that Ethan wasn't going to let it go. To her credit, the moderator straightened her posture and regained her composure. She took a deep breath before speaking.

"Now, there's obviously an important person missing here tonight."

"Really? Who?" Grey felt like she was going to vomit. She shut her eyes so she wouldn't have to see Ethan's face, hardened and sarcastic, eyebrows raised cartoonishly high. The moderator pressed on like she hadn't heard anything.

"What is it like being up here together, talking about this movie, without Sam?"

Grey's eyes shot open.

The room was deathly quiet. One person in the audience tried to stifle a cough. Though the question wasn't directed at anyone in particular, neither Perry nor Nora made any attempt to answer, their microphones forgotten and limp in their laps, their attention fixed on Ethan. Ethan was frozen, chin resting on his chest, eyes in shadow. Finally, he brought his microphone to his lips.

"You people are fucking ghouls, you know that?" No one said anything. He rubbed his hand over his face, muttering as if to himself. "What am I even doing here?" He looked out at the audience. "You can all stop gawking now. I hope you had your fucking fun. I hope you got what you wanted."

He slammed the microphone down onto the side table next to him, standing up abruptly. It rolled off and hit the ground with an overamplified *thunk*. He leaned over Nora, who looked stricken, and murmured something in her ear. Her microphone picked up his voice, sending it echoing through the room: *Are you happy now?*

He straightened back up and looked directly at Grey. She had jumped to her feet without realizing it. Their eye contact only lasted for a split second before he stalked offstage. The crowd erupted in confused chatter, as the moderator struggled to maintain order.

Grey grabbed her purse and darted toward the hallway, racing down the back stairs and out the emergency exit onto the street. She spotted Ethan instantly, his broad back moving away from her.

"Ethan!" She barely recognized her own voice, shrill and tight with panic. He slowed for a second, so she knew he heard her, but quickly picked up the pace again. She broke into a full sprint, grateful she'd eschewed high heels for the night as she dodged pedestrians to catch up with him.

He didn't stop and look at her until she'd reached his side and placed a desperate hand on his arm. When she got a good look at his face, contorted and stormy, her heart plunged into her stomach.

"Where are you going?" she panted.

He shook his head, refusing to look at her. "I can't."

"What? You can't what?" People had started to notice them now, to stop and gawk. Out of the corner of her eye she saw phones poised and ready to capture whatever was about to happen. Of fucking course. Even the buffer of anonymity provided by seen-it-all New Yorkers was no match for an impending celebrity meltdown.

She grabbed Ethan's hand and pulled him off the curb, using the line of parked cars as a temporary barrier between them and the gathering crowd. Mercifully, an empty cab drove by, and she flagged it down and hauled him inside.

"Third and Bowery, please," she instructed the driver, stabbing at the obnoxiously loud Taxi TV screen until she finally found the mute button.

She sank back into the seat and turned to look at Ethan. He was already staring at her, his eyes glazed and dull. "This is what you were waiting for, isn't it?"

"What?"

"An excuse to bail. To leave me again. Just like Palm Springs."

Grey's mouth fell open. "Palm Springs? What the fuck are you talking about? What does that have to do with anything?"

It didn't seem like he'd heard her. He leaned his head against the window and closed his eyes, muttering to himself. "I fucked it up. I fucked it all up."

Tears sprang to her eyes. "You just need to get some help. We can fly back to L.A. tonight. I'll call Nora, or Audrey, and we can figure out somewhere for you to go. Will you do that? Please?"

He shook his head violently, pushing himself upright in a lurching, unsteady motion. He spoke forcefully, spit flying. "You can't *fix* me, Grey. Nobody can. This is me. The real me. This is who I am, this is who I've always been."

Grey fought to keep her voice from trembling. "It doesn't have to be. You're in control."

He shut his eyes again, his face a mask of despair. "No. I'm not." The agony in his voice was a blunt object, knocking the wind out of her.

Grey paused to gather her thoughts, trying to keep herself as composed as possible. "I don't believe this is the real you. I've seen the real you. I'm in love with the real you." He didn't move. Didn't even open his eyes. "But it doesn't matter what I think, if *you* don't believe that."

He opened his eyes, his gaze blank. "I wanted to be him, for you. I tried. But . . . I can't. I told you. I warned you. I'm fucking defective."

Grey expected herself to cry, but instead, rage flared inside her, white-hot like a sparkler in her sternum. She threw her head back and dragged her hands over her eyes, groaning in frustration. "Jesus *Christ*. You're almost forty years old, Ethan, take some goddamn responsibility for yourself," she spat, dropping her hands back into her lap with a dull thud.

Ethan seemed taken aback by her lacerating tone, but raised his voice to match hers, practically snarling. "I *do*. You think I don't *know* how fucked up I am? You know how much I fucking hate myself?"

"No. Fuck that. Blaming yourself, feeling sorry for yourself, hating yourself is not the same as accountability. It doesn't help anyone unless you *do* something about it. You need to get it together and step the fuck up." Grey hoisted her knee onto the seat and shifted so she was fully facing him. "People care about you. People *need* you. Your kids need you. *I* need you."

"For your career, you mean."

Grey recoiled. "Is that what you think?"

He shrugged, unable to meet her eyes. Bile rose in her throat. "Just because *you've* forgotten what it's like to have to *work* for anything——" She stopped herself before she said something she'd regret, sinking back into the seat and raising her hands in surrender. "No. No. I'm not doing this with you."

He turned to face her again, the look in his eyes sending a chill down her spine. "I guess that's that, then." They were deep in midtown traffic at this point, and the taxi had slowed to a halt. He groped for the door handle and Grey's eyes widened.

"What are you doing?"

He ignored her. She lunged across the seat and grabbed hold of his arm, bringing her face to his until they were practically nose to nose. His breathing was ragged and unsteady, bloodshot eyes darting back and forth across her face. The man she loved was in there somewhere, but she was running out of chances to reach him. She unclenched her jaw and lowered her voice.

"You think you don't have a choice. You have a choice right now. You can either come back to the hotel with me and we deal with this like adults, or you can get out of the cab and it's over." Her voice was thick with tears by the time she finished, but she successfully kept them from spilling over. He wouldn't walk out on her now. He couldn't. Not if he really loved her. She prayed desperately to any deity that would listen for the taxi to start moving again.

Ethan had turned away from her as she spoke, looking out the window again. When he looked back, it felt like her heart stopped. She wasn't sure when he'd started crying. He hadn't made a sound. Even now, she thought maybe she was imagining it, his expression controlled and impassive to the extent that she could even make it out, cloaked in shadow in the darkened cab. But he turned his head again and a streetlight caught his cheeks, slick and streaming with tears. Her lips parted in a silent gasp. She was speechless.

He leaned forward, grasped her jaw in both hands, and kissed her—salty, brief, harsh. He released her and she gaped at him, dumbfounded, as he opened the door and stepped out into the street without another word. Her body was frozen, her brain in denial, unable to do anything but watch helplessly through the window as he wove his way through the stopped traffic and disappeared into the night.

Back at the hotel, she cried until her eyes swelled shut. She tried to get some sleep, but tossed and turned for hours, floating in and out of tormented dreams, half hallucinating that Ethan had come back, pliant and contrite, pledging his eternal devotion to her and prepared to do whatever it took to turn his life around. But of course every time she opened her eyes, she was still alone in that obnoxiously large bed.

When dawn broke, she booked the first available flight back to L.A. After she finished packing, she picked up a pen and poised it over the hotel notepad, then hesitated. At last, she scrawled: *I'm not the one who ran away.* She immediately tore it off the pad and crumpled it into the trash. Justified or not, it seemed too petty, too melodramatic. She'd already gotten the last word, and it hadn't made her feel any better.

Part of her was still waiting for Ethan to burst in the door at the last minute: ashamed, maudlin, drunker than ever, it didn't matter. At this point, she would have taken any Ethan he had to offer without complaint. Finally, she couldn't linger in the room any longer without missing her flight. In the cab on the way to the airport, she blocked his number so she'd stop checking to see if he'd tried to reach her—and to remove the temptation to reach out to him first.

Numb and exhausted, she flew back to L.A. alone.

Sixteen
Months
Later

30

GREY WAS COVERED IN BLOOD. SHE LAY MOTIONLESS ON A HARD-
wood floor, surrounded by furniture covered in white sheets, her
eyes staring blankly at the ceiling. There were no sounds other
than the whistling wind against the shuttered windows. Although
she was inside, snow began to fall; a few fat flakes at first, then a
deluge blanketing her naked body. As the screen faded to white,
the scene cut to a split-second shot of her laughing, quicker than a
blink, before returning to her placid, lifeless face. Once the screen
was completely white, red words faded in on the screen: *A Film by
Kamilah Ross.*

Grey leaned over and flicked on the light. She settled back
against the couch, and she and Kamilah turned to look at Nora
expectantly.

They were in a luxurious editing suite in a downtown Manhattan postproduction studio. The room was designed to provide
the ultimate in comfort for late-night work sessions, and both
Grey and Kamilah had logged serious hours there over the past

month. But today, they were there at a perfectly reasonable time, screening a rough assembly of *The Empty Chair* for Nora over lunch.

Nora looked down at her pad, then up at them, smiling warmly.

"I hope you know you've done something really special here."

Grey and Kamilah exchanged elated looks. Even their editor, Zelda, tatted-up and intimidating, had a grin on her usually impassive face. Zelda swiveled in her chair and tapped on her keyboard, and the screen went black. Nora continued, flipping through the pages.

"I have a few notes, nothing major. For a first cut, it's in great shape. You three should be very proud of yourselves."

Grey reached over and squeezed Kamilah's hand.

An hour later, she and Nora took the elevator down together. Kamilah had opted to stay with Zelda for the rest of the afternoon to tackle some of the notes. They pushed through the revolving glass doors into the crisp October afternoon.

Grey tilted her face toward the sun and inhaled the sharp air deep into her lungs. She loved New York in the fall. She'd been there for almost two months, hauling her bags into her West Village sublet in the dog days of August, drenched in sweat and daydreaming about weather like today. Kamilah and Andromeda were staying in a spacious one-bedroom down the block from Grey, while Andromeda recorded their new album at Electric Lady Studios.

The two of them paused on the sidewalk.

"Do you have plans before your show tonight? Want to get a cup of coffee or something?" Nora asked.

Grey considered it. She was halfway through her six-week run as Yelena in a sold-out off-Broadway production of a new translation of *Uncle Vanya,* and the combination of the grueling performance schedule and the long days in the edit bay had begun to wear on her. She'd planned to head back to her apartment for a quick nap before her call time, but maybe the coffee would perk her up as much as the nap would have.

"Sure, I know a place around the corner."

Fifteen minutes later, they slid into a secluded corner booth in Grey's favorite coffee shop, clutching steaming lattes in oversized mugs.

"Is there something going on with you and that barista? That heart is awfully elaborate," Nora said teasingly, peering into Grey's mug.

"Who, Karl? No, I just come in here a lot." She glanced up at the barista, catching him staring at her. He looked down and blushed. Nora observed the whole thing, smirking.

"He's cute. Not your type?"

Grey dipped her spoon into her mug, dissolving the intricate steamed-milk heart.

"My type is nonexistent right now." Though her therapist had encouraged her to break her habit of burying herself in her work after setbacks in her personal life, her schedule wasn't exactly conducive to dating at the moment.

After things had imploded with Ethan, Audrey had offered Grey two ways to spin it: either she could set Grey up with an even more attention-grabbing rebound, or they could play up the "strong independent woman" angle. Grey had declined both options. She'd learned her lesson. From now on, to the extent that she had a say in it, her personal life was nobody's business but her own.

Nora furrowed her brow sympathetically. Of all the strange turns Grey's life had taken over the past year and a half, her friendship with Nora was the most unexpected. In those first blurry, excruciating weeks after she'd returned from New York, the two of them had been in constant contact. Nora had been the one to inform Grey that Ethan had gone straight from LAX into rehab, so she wouldn't have to hear it from the tabloids.

The news had sent her into a tailspin. Part of her was relieved that he was finally getting the help he needed. But the bigger, more selfish part was devastated that he didn't seem to care that he'd lost her in the process. He'd looked haggard and miserable in the pictures of him leaving the airport, the ones she'd sought out in a late-night moment of weakness. Those images had rattled her so much that she'd come dangerously close to breaking her vow of no contact, settling for unblocking his number instead. Unsurprisingly, she hadn't heard anything from him. She dreaded the day she'd wake up to see his face splashed all over the internet, blissfully happy with someone decidedly not her on his arm, but so far, she'd been spared. It seemed like after leaving rehab, he'd returned to the same reclusive lifestyle he'd led before they'd met. She tried not to read too much into whatever that might mean.

But through it all, it was Nora who'd taken Grey's late-night crying calls when she could tell Kamilah was tired of hearing about it. Nora who'd invited her on regular lunch dates to get her out of the house. Nora who'd listened without judgment when Grey confessed the true origins of her relationship with Ethan. Nora who'd sat beside her in the back row of the occasional Al-Anon meeting. Against all odds, the untouchably cool red carpet queen of yesteryear, ex-wife of the man who'd broken her heart, had stepped into the role of the big sister she'd never had.

When they'd started preproduction on *The Empty Chair* in earnest, Grey vowed to keep their relationship professional for the duration of the shoot, banning herself from all mention of Ethan—to Nora or otherwise. Nora followed her lead, and they hadn't discussed him since.

Throwing herself into the work had been Grey's salvation.

She'd thought she'd been devastated after her breakup with Callum, but that had been a gentle breeze compared to the category-five hurricane that had raged in her heart in Ethan's absence. It had been easy to cast Callum as the villain, her as the innocent victim. Black-and-white and uncomplicated. But things with Ethan were Gordian knot–level convoluted, solvable only by carving him out of her life cleanly and completely. She'd blamed him at first, but once her head cleared and she'd talked it out with her therapist, she realized that was a trap. Neither of them was at fault, really. The only villain here was human fallibility.

She'd done her best to channel her rage and despair into her performance. It helped that she and Kamilah had spent years tailoring the script to their own strengths, but Vivian—seductive, manipulative, capricious Vivian—was by far the juiciest role of her career. Between the shoot and the play, her love of acting had been revitalized in a way that made the loss of the paper-thin *Golden City* role seem like a blessing in disguise. If she'd signed on, she'd still have another two years of shoots and press tours ahead of her, with no guarantee that her career would be any better off on the other side.

On the opening night of *Uncle Vanya,* she'd practically blacked out from adrenaline. And watching the *Empty Chair* dailies back in the editing room, she barely recognized herself. Nora gave her one glowing compliment after another to that effect as they sipped their lattes, and Grey allowed herself to swell with pride rather than deflecting it.

They chatted about Jeff and Nora's recent trip to visit her family in Thailand, Grey's struggles and victories wrangling Chekhov night after night, and possible festival submissions for *The Empty Chair* once it was completed. Grey drained her latte to dregs and excused herself to use the bathroom. When she returned, the mirth was gone from Nora's face.

"What's up?" Grey asked, easing back into the booth. Nora looked down at her mug, then fixed her with an intense look.

"Has he been in touch with you at all?"

Grey's stomach did a flip, even without Nora mentioning Ethan's name. They hadn't discussed him in months.

"No, why?"

"He's here."

Grey whipped her head toward the door. Nora chuckled, her grave demeanor dissipating.

"Not *here* here. In New York, I mean. I wasn't sure if you knew yet. I think . . . I think he might be here to see you."

Grey felt light-headed. She clutched her empty mug with both hands, her pulse racing in her ears.

"Oh." A thousand questions ran through her mind, but she couldn't manage anything beyond that lone syllable. Just when she thought she was starting to get over him, the mere mention of the shadow of a possibility that he *might* want to see her was enough to knock her sideways, the pain as fresh and raw as the day she'd left him.

"Is that . . . something you would want?" Nora held up her hands as if anticipating Grey's response. "I'm not asking as his messenger, I'm not interested in getting between you two. I'm asking as your friend."

Grey took her time considering it. She ran her finger around the rim of her empty mug.

"I don't know. I mean, yes, of course. Of course I want to see him. The question isn't whether I want to, it's whether I should."

"Why shouldn't you?" Nora's voice was neutral.

"Because I haven't heard a fucking word from him in almost a year and a half?" Grey felt her voice rising with emotion against her will. She took a deep breath and collected herself. "Because I've been working my ass off trying to move on. If I see him . . . I'll be right back where I started. It'll mess with my head too much. It's not worth it."

Nora said nothing, just kept her eyes on Grey's face. Grey turned and stared out the window. When she spoke again, her throat felt tight and irritated.

"You know what the worst part is? I don't think it was even about me. Our relationship. I could've been anyone. He was like . . . like this starving lion, and I was just the first gazelle to wander into his path." Tears welled in her eyes. "I don't know if he ever really loved me. I was just something else to be addicted to. To lose himself in. Postpone the midlife crisis a little longer, or whatever." She blinked rapidly, looking down at the table.

Nora took a deep breath, seeming to mull over Grey's words carefully.

"I know it's tempting to try to diminish what you two had to make it hurt less. But I've gotten to know you both pretty well by now, and—I hope you don't take this the wrong way, but, you're no helpless gazelle."

Grey laughed, a half-choked sob. Nora continued. "Obviously, I don't know the ins and outs of your relationship. But regardless of how it started, it looked pretty goddamn real to me. It's okay to mourn it however feels right for you, whether that means seeing him now or not."

Grey dabbed her napkin at the corners of her eyes. She laughed again, a hysterical gasp bubbling up through her chest. "I guess the fact that I'm getting this worked up when I haven't even heard from him yet is a sign that we still have some unfinished business to work through."

Nora smiled sympathetically, tilting back her mug to catch the last drops of her latte.

"Whatever you decide to do, just remember: don't underestimate yourself. You're very powerful. It's easy to let him steamroll you—by 'you' I mean me, too. Everyone. He's used to the universe bending over backward to give him whatever he wants. But I know part of why he loves you is you've never been afraid to say no to him."

They sat there chatting for a few more minutes before going their separate ways, but all Grey heard echoing in her head was: *that's why he loves you.*

Not *loved*.

Loves.

31

THOUGH GREY WAS GRATEFUL TO NORA FOR GIVING HER THE heads-up that Ethan was in town, now she couldn't walk down the street without doing a double take at every tall, dark-haired man she passed. Her heart leapt every time her phone buzzed. She felt resentment building toward him for putting her in this position, in perpetual anticipation, waiting for the other shoe to drop.

Two nights after her coffee date with Nora, it did.

The production of *Uncle Vanya* was in a small theater in the round, the audience crowding the actors on all sides. Shortly after Grey's first entrance, she spotted him; not in the front row, but two or three rows back. When she met his eyes, it felt like she had been struck by lightning.

He was leaning forward in his seat, arms resting on his knees, staring at her with intense concentration. The dimmed lights blurred his features somewhat, but from the way he drew her focus, the lighting designer might as well have swung the spotlight right to him. She felt naked under his gaze, despite her smothering layers of nineteenth-century clothing, and struggled in vain to regain her composure.

Grey moved through the first two acts in a haze, the lines and blocking thankfully second nature to her by now. When she returned to her dressing room at intermission, he had already texted her. Small mercies.

> Sorry
> didn't know I would be so close
> I didn't want to distract u
> can I see u after
> ?

Whether or not he'd become a whole new man since the last time she'd seen him, his texting style certainly hadn't changed. Her fingers flew over the screen.

> it's okay
> yeah, come to the stage door. i'll put you on the list.

ETHAN TOOK A DEEP BREATH AND RAPPED ON GREY'S DRESSING room door.

"Come in," she called from inside, her voice muffled.

When he pushed the door open, she was facing away from him, still in costume, wiping off her stage makeup. She met his eyes through the mirror and paused.

"Hi."

"Hi."

Neither of them said anything for a beat. She pulled another makeup wipe out of the pack and swiped it across her eyelid.

"You can come all the way in, if you want."

He cleared his throat and shut the door behind him.

"You, um. That was incredible. *You* were."

She smiled a little, looking down at the counter.

"Thanks."

She pulled the pins out of her complicated updo and unwound her hair. It was longer than he remembered, almost reaching her waist. He couldn't decide if it made her look more like a princess from a fairy tale or the jealous enchantress who would lock the princess in a tower. From the way the movement hypnotized him, coupled with the dangerous look in her eyes, he was leaning toward enchantress.

She stood up, keeping her back to him, and swept her curtain of hair forward over her shoulder.

"Can you unbutton me? These costumes are impossible."

His heart hammered in his chest. She turned her head and met his eyes again, challenging this time. He stepped forward and fumbled with the seemingly hundreds of tiny pearl buttons fastening the back of her blouse. Between the familiar scent of sweat on her skin mixed with her shampoo, and the curve of her neck bared inches from his mouth, it was a miracle that he was able to unbutton a single one.

When he was finished, she looked up at him pointedly, and he turned around as she disrobed.

Her whole aura was different than he remembered; her, but not her. Aloof. Icy. Maybe she was still shaking off lingering traces of her character. Maybe she'd changed completely since he'd last seen her. Maybe she just had her guard up around him. He couldn't blame her for that last one.

"Why are you here?"

The question came while his back was still to her. It was easier to talk to her like this, though the image of her naked behind him conjured by the rustling fabric canceled out any comfort it brought him.

"After the reviews you got? I couldn't miss it."

He heard the sound of a zipper, followed by a heavy exhale.

"Don't do this to me, Ethan. If you want to talk, let's talk. But if you just came here to fuck with me, I'm not interested." Her hand was on his shoulder so unexpectedly he almost leapt out of his skin. He turned to face her. She was dressed in jeans and a turtleneck, arms crossed, armored from head to toe.

"I'm not here to fuck with you." He swallowed. "Is there somewhere else we can go?"

"There's a bar around the corner that's usually pretty quiet. Do you want to go get a drink?"

He shifted his weight. "Sure. I just, um. I don't do that anymore. Drink, I mean."

For the first time, he caught a glimpse of the Grey he remembered, as surprise and relief flickered over her face.

"*Oh*. Oh, um. That's great."

"We can still go there, if you want. It doesn't bother me. I just thought you should know."

She glanced to the side, twirling the ends of her hair around her fingers.

"Do you want to come to my place tomorrow? It's my day off, we can have dinner or something. Have a little privacy." She looked up at him again, unexpectedly vulnerable. "Unless you think that's a bad idea."

His chest released.

"No. That sounds perfect. I'll bring dinner. Just tell me where and when."

She gave a brusque nod, then went back to the counter to grab her bag and coat.

"We probably shouldn't walk out together. You want to go first?"

"Sure." He didn't move.

She shrugged on her coat and looked up at him warily. He took a step toward her. Her eyes widened slightly, but she stood her ground. He lowered his head and pressed his lips against her cheek. She couldn't hide her sharp intake of breath. When he pulled away, she looked so flustered that for a split second he was worried he'd lost control and done what he'd wanted to do instead, which was wrap his arm around her waist, bend her back over her dressing room counter, and kiss her so deeply that they'd both forget the past year and a half had ever happened.

But he hadn't. He couldn't. He had to earn it. He took another step back, placing his hand on the doorknob.

"Tomorrow."

Grey's eyelids fluttered.

"Tomorrow," she echoed.

32

GREY LET HERSELF SLEEP LATE THE NEXT MORNING; A HEAVY, dreamless sleep. But as soon as she woke up, she got down to business. Between her days in the editing room and nights at the theater, her generously sized studio apartment had begun to resemble a rat's nest: perfect for curling up and falling asleep, not so much for being able to walk in an uninterrupted straight line.

Kamilah stopped by in the early afternoon, after Grey had finished scrubbing the bathroom.

"You're going to fuck him tonight, aren't you," Kamilah mused, moments after shutting the door behind her.

"I'm not!" Grey protested. "I mean, probably not. I haven't decided yet."

She wiped her hands on her ripped jeans and leaned against the kitchen counter as Kamilah perched on the couch, digging a spoon into a pint of mocha almond fudge coconut milk ice cream.

Though they were only living a five-minute walk away, they barely had a chance to see each other outside of work. Kamilah was even busier than Grey: when she wasn't overseeing *The Empty Chair* edits, she and Andromeda were early in preproduction for an ambitious visual album to accompany Andromeda's new music.

In order to make sure their friendship didn't completely revolve around the movie, they'd started scheduling twice-monthly hangs where they were banned from discussing it. Kamilah coming over to watch Grey clean certainly ranked as one of their more underwhelming ones, but these were extenuating circumstances.

Once they returned to Los Angeles, Kamilah and Andromeda planned to begin house hunting together. "It's so bizarre," Kamilah had said when she'd broken the news to Grey that she'd be officially moving out. "Like, am I an adult now?"

"You just directed an entire movie," Grey had laughed.

"Yeah, but this feels different. This is, like, first-day-of-the-rest-of-my-life shit. Besides, the movie I was prepared for. Andromeda . . ." She shook her head, smiling. "I never saw them coming."

Grey occasionally felt a bittersweet pang for this chapter of their friendship coming to a close, but it was quickly overtaken by excitement for the future of their creative partnership. The process of making *The Empty Chair* had brought them closer than ever, and they'd already started discussing possibilities for their next film together. That is, when the topic wasn't banned.

Kamilah offered the ice cream to Grey, who accepted it, taking a thoughtful bite. "Am I being stupid about this? Should we meet somewhere public? Should I just cancel?"

Kamilah shrugged. "I can't answer that for you." She placed her hand on her chest in mock seriousness, delivering her next sentence melodramatically. "What is *your heart* telling you?"

Grey tried to laugh, but it came out as more of a sigh. "I don't know. When I try to listen to it, all I can hear is the dial-up modem sound. Is that bad?"

"Maybe you need to unplug it and plug it back in again," Kamilah giggled.

"I think I just need to return it. It's obviously defective."

ETHAN ARRIVED PROMPTLY AT SEVEN, LADEN WITH ENOUGH Thai food to cover both her tiny kitchen counter and even tinier table. Their only option was sitting on either end of Grey's couch, overloaded plates balanced on their laps. The arm of the couch dug into Grey's back as she tried to put as much space between them as possible.

"I could never do what you're doing. It's so impressive."

"What? Theater? You never thought about it?"

Ethan shrugged, dipping a skewer of chicken satay into the little plastic tub of peanut sauce.

"Sure. Sam and I talked about doing a run of that Sam Shepard play—you know, the one with the brothers? What's it called?"

"*True West*?" Grey tried to hide her surprise that Ethan mentioned Sam's name so casually, without the gloomy, faraway look that normally accompanied it.

"That's the one. But I backed out at the last minute. Not having that second-take safety net, having to be perfectly on point night after night . . . it's fucking scary." He tore the chicken off the wooden skewer with his teeth and chewed thoughtfully. "I don't think I had the discipline for it then, either. The lifestyle that comes with it, I mean. I would've burned out and stopped showing up after the first week."

"That part has definitely been the hardest," Grey agreed. "I've been living like a nun, without the fun uniform. It feels like all I do is work and sleep."

Ethan shifted a little.

"So. You're not seeing anyone, then?" She could tell how hard he was working to keep his tone casual, and tried unsuccessfully not to let herself be charmed by it.

"No. Are you?"

He shook his head. "Just myself, I guess."

"Well, I've heard that's the greatest love of all." Grey sipped her sparkling water. "How's that been going?"

Ethan readjusted his legs, crossing one ankle over his knee. He looked down at his plate.

"Honestly? It's been the hardest fucking year of my life." He opened his mouth to say something else, then hesitated. He met her eyes with an intensity that sent a thrill up her spine. "I'm so sorry, Grey. You were right. Everything you said that night. Everything I can remember, anyway. I've got a list of regrets a mile long at this point, but getting out of that cab is right at the top."

Her gaze fell to her lap, not wanting him to see it soften. She couldn't let him off the hook that easily. "You could've come back. You knew where to find me. I was at the hotel all night."

He shook his head resignedly. "You saw me that night. I was out of my fucking mind. By the time I sobered up enough to think straight, it was too late. You were gone. And blocking my calls. Which, you know, fair enough."

Grey pushed a piece of shrimp across her plate with her fork. Another memory from that night nagged at her. "Did you really think . . . that I was just with you for my career? Still, after every-thing?"

Ethan cringed. "I said that?"

She nodded, and he exhaled loudly.

"Jesus. I'm sorry. It's what I was afraid of, sure, but you never did anything to make me feel that way. It was just my insecurity talking."

She looked up from her plate, meeting his eyes again.

"I wasn't going to leave. You know that, right? If you'd wanted to get help . . . I would've supported you. I wanted to."

He ran his fingers through his hair, his face contemplative and serious. "That wouldn't have been fair to you. That was the whole thing. I thought being in love with you would solve all my problems, and when it didn't, it felt like everything was hopeless. I think a part of me even blamed you, which is so fucked, I know. If we'd stayed together, we never would have made it. I was too far gone, I couldn't handle the pressure. I'd keep disappointing you, you'd keep resenting me. I don't think I could've gotten sober with that hanging over my head. I had to get it together on my own."

Grey was silent for a long moment. She turned his words over in her mind like they were shells on the beach, contemplating whether to bring them home with her or toss them back into the ocean.

"If you've been sober for this long, why didn't you try to contact me sooner? Why now? Why . . . like this?"

He stacked a few of the empty plastic containers on top of each other on the table to make room for his plate. He stretched his legs, looping his arm over the side of the couch, his bare foot inches from her knee.

"As soon as I got to rehab, all I wanted to do was call you. You were all I could think about. But you're not really supposed to reach out and try to fix your broken relationships while you're there. And once I got out, it felt like it would be worse if I tried to come back into your life before I was sure I was . . . stable. Turns out it takes more than three months in rehab to untangle forty years of bullshit. Not that I'm done yet. I don't know if I ever will be. But . . . I'm trying. I'm getting closer." He rubbed his hand over his jaw. "I couldn't figure out the right way to do it, the right time, and then I saw you were doing that play . . . it felt like a sign. I'm sorry, I shouldn't have ambushed you like that. But I was scared if I told you I was coming you'd tell me to go fuck myself. I just . . . needed to see you. Even if you refused to talk to me after."

Grey stacked her plate on top of his. Her head spun as she tried to process everything.

"So is this . . . what do they call it? Making amends?"

He shook his head. "Not officially, although I do owe you one. I wasn't ready the first time around. Apparently once you finish all twelve steps you just keep doing them over and over forever, did you know that?"

"I had no idea."

He smiled cheekily, the earnestness lifting from his expression. "My therapist gives me homework, too. Sometimes it feels like I'm going to college after all. Majoring in not being a self-loathing alcoholic piece of shit." He held up his hands. "Wait, sorry, I'm not supposed to call myself a piece of shit anymore. I was 'doing my best with the pain that I had.'" He delivered that last part in a wry, singsong tone.

She grinned back, unable to help herself. "Sounds like a lot of work."

"It is. But it's not so bad. Beats the alternative."

She allowed her gaze to linger on his face. Take all of him in. He really did seem different. Even the best versions of Ethan were never free of a hovering cloud, ready to unleash a storm at a moment's notice. But for the first time since she'd known him, that cloud was absent. It was subtle, something she never would have noticed if she weren't so attuned to his moods, even now. He seemed lighter. Calmer. Fully present.

"You really haven't had a drink in a year and a half?"

"Almost. Sixteen months, to be exact. It's been . . . yeah. I wish I could say every day gets easier. But I have more good days than bad now. And even the bad ones aren't as bad as . . . well, you know."

"I'm really proud of you," she said softly. He ducked his head and smiled, color rising to his cheeks. She realized she'd never seen him blush before. It was so damn charming she thought her heart would explode.

"Thanks." He looked back up at her. "Did Nora tell you we just redid the custody agreement? I have the girls half the time now."

Grey tried to ignore the way her heart leapt. If Nora had agreed to that, he really must be doing better—not just parroting what he thought she wanted to hear in a hollow attempt to win her forgiveness. "No, that's great. We, um. We don't really talk about you."

He nodded slowly. "That's probably for the best."

"Yeah."

She noticed his glass was empty, and held her hand out to him. He passed it to her and she went to the fridge to refill them both. With her back to him, she felt a surge of courage.

"Can I ask you something? Unrelated." She finished off one glass bottle of mineral water and cracked open another one.

"Sure. Trying to get through the last of those love questions?"

"What? Oh. Ha. No, I'm freestyling this one." She brought the glasses back to the couch and handed him his. When she sat back down, she sat closer this time, her knee firmly pressed against his outstretched leg. She leaned her other elbow on the back of the couch and rested her head on her fist.

"Why did you sign the contract in the first place? I don't believe that you couldn't have made your comeback without me. But it didn't even seem like you wanted to. You barely showed any interest in work the whole time we were together. What made you say yes?"

Ethan took a long sip of his sparkling water, then stared into the glass like it held the answer.

"Well, two things, really. I showed up because Audrey basically begged me to. I guess it was her form of an intervention. I almost didn't make it at all."

"Oh, I remember."

"My plan was to eat my free lunch, make a little small talk, and get the hell out of there." His lips curved into that half smile that was as familiar to her as her own. "But you kind of ruined everything. Once I met you, that wasn't an option anymore."

Grey's stomach fluttered. "So what sealed the deal? Was it when I told you to fuck off and die?"

He laughed, a real laugh from deep in his chest. "What can I say? You know how to make a first impression." His face turned pensive again. "It's hard to describe. I don't even really understand it now. I've never felt anything like it. It was just this . . . pull. I felt it the first time I saw you. And it just kept getting stronger the more I got to know you."

"Are you sure you weren't just horny?"

He laughed again. "That was definitely part of it. There was something else, though. Something like . . . recognition, maybe? Like I knew you already. But at the same time, like I'd never run out of things to learn."

Grey bit her lip, forcing herself to ask her next question before she lost her nerve. "Do you still feel it?"

His eyes swept over her face. "Don't you?"

Her breath caught in her throat. Slowly, he set his water glass on the table, without taking his eyes off her. She slid her legs out from under her and scooted toward him as gracefully as scooting allowed, until she was draped across his lap. She was tempted to nestle against his shoulder, but sat upright instead, as he ran his hand up her denim-clad shin, then up her thigh, and back down again.

Something inside her released, something she hadn't even been aware was tensed.

His gaze drifted to her lips. As he leaned in, she placed a hand on his chest.

"Wait." She shut her eyes for a second, trying to gather her thoughts. "Is this . . . what is this?"

He chuckled. "I thought it was obvious."

"Spell it out for me. I'm not feeling so smart right now."

He took both her hands in his, kissing the back of her left hand, then her right. Staring deep into her eyes, he intoned:

"Emily Grey Brooks. I am madly, desperately in love with you. I haven't stopped thinking about you since the day we met. If you would do me the honor of giving me another chance, I swear I will spend the rest of my life proving that I am capable of being the man you deserve."

She'd be lying if she said she hadn't pictured this moment hundreds of times over the past year and a half. Maybe thousands. But she'd been so focused on what he would say, the different ways he'd beg and plead and grovel his way back into her life, that she'd never stopped to think about how she would respond. Whether she could look into the eyes of the man she'd allowed to hurt her more deeply than anyone ever had, and agree to give him the power to do it again. Whether she could trust that he wouldn't.

When they were together, his need for her had been so powerful that it was almost like a living thing. But there was an ugly side to it, a side that overwhelmed her, smothered her, left her helpless and flailing in his absence. But she'd learned to live without him again. She didn't need him anymore. And tonight, there was no familiar edge of wild-eyed desperation to his plea. He didn't need her anymore, either.

But they still wanted each other. They would still choose each other over anyone else on earth.

And in a way, that was even better.

Grey couldn't help it: she melted. She struggled to stifle her grin as she rolled her eyes. "I need to stop dating actors. You're all so fucking *dramatic*."

Before he could respond, she knotted her hand in his shirt and pulled his face to hers. They both exhaled softly, a communal sigh of relief. They kissed like they had all the time in the world. Smoothing over their old fears, their doubts, their recriminations with their lips and tongues and hands like a skilled massage therapist working the kinks out of a gnarled back.

Too soon, he pulled away again.

"I almost forgot. I have something for you."

She gave a little whine of protest as he slipped out from under her and went to his jacket. He pulled out a rolled-up sheaf of paper from the inner pocket and handed it to her, sitting back on the couch next to her. She looked down at it, confused. Unfurling the pages, she read the title: *Bitter Pill*.

"You finished it?"

His eyes lit up.

"I rewrote it. For you."

She flipped through the pages, then looked up at him. "I don't understand."

"You'll star. I'll direct." His eyes flicked to her face nervously. "What do you think?"

She leaned in and kissed him softly.

"Ethan, I—I don't know what to say. Thank you. I know how much this means to you. I can't wait to read it." Her trepidation must have shown in her expression, because his face fell.

" 'But . . .' "

"*But . . .*" She hesitated. "I'm not saying no. But I'm not sure if this is right. I don't know if I want to be retrofitted into something that was about you and Sam. I would love to work with you. But I want to be your partner, not your muse."

She searched his face, waiting for him to retreat, to get upset. To take back everything he'd said and storm out the door. But she couldn't lie about her feelings just to coddle his. She'd never minced words with him before, but her honesty felt even riskier now than when she'd told him off that very first day in Audrey's office.

He slowly took the script out of her hands, his head dipping low. But when he looked at her again, there was only warmth in his expression. Her heart soared in relief.

"Okay," he said simply.

"Okay?"

He shrugged. "Makes sense to me." He ran his thumb across the edges of the pages. "It's just a script. Just paper. It doesn't have to mean anything more than that."

Grey exhaled, then laughed under her breath.

"What?"

She gently took the script out of his hand and placed it on the ground before sliding her leg over his hips and straddling him. "Remind me to send a thank-you note to your therapist."

He laughed, low and husky.

"I guess I deserve that." He settled his hands at her waist. "He would've loved you, you know. Sam."

Her breath caught in her throat. "I wish I could have met him."

"Me, too. You have a similar sense of humor. You're so quick. You both . . . you make me want to be better. To be able to keep up with you."

She took a moment to let the weight of the compliment settle over her, her lips curving slightly. She lifted her head and looked into his eyes.

"You know it's going to take time, right?"

He leaned back, resting his hands on her hips. "For what?"

"For me to trust you again." She paused. "If I'm being totally honest . . . I don't think I ever trusted you. Not fully. There was always a part of me holding back."

He nodded slowly. "I get that. I felt it. But you weren't wrong. I wasn't exactly acting like someone who deserved your trust."

"Maybe. It wasn't just you, though. It's . . . it's a problem I have. I'm working on it. But I don't want our relationship to be like that this time."

She brushed away a lock of hair that had fallen into his eyes, resting her hand on the side of his face. "This shouldn't be about repairing what was broken. It should be about creating something new. Something beautiful. Together."

He brought her hand to his lips and kissed her palm.

"I like the sound of that."

She felt giddy, almost light-headed. She had to fight to get her next words out as he brought his mouth back to hers, stealing her breath away with deep, drugging kisses. "Okay. Good. Because I—*mmph*—love you, too, so fucking much. Did—*mmph*—I already say that? I feel like I forgot—*mmph*—to say that."

He laughed, pulling away just enough to press his forehead to hers. "It may have slipped your mind."

They didn't do much talking after that. They spent the rest of the evening getting reacquainted, with and without words, their bodies moving in perfect harmony, casting off the shadows of the past, luxuriating in the promise of their future.

Epilogue

THEIR LIPS ARE SEALED

Within the first six months of their relationship, Grey Brooks and Ethan Atkins navigated leaked photos, public tantrums, break-ups, and makeups—but more than three years later, the formerly scandal-prone couple has turned downright boring. In a rare joint interview, Atkins and Brooks spill on sobriety, their upcoming first project together, and becoming one big, happy family.

BY SUGAR CLARKE

It's 9 A.M., and Ethan Atkins and Grey Brooks are fighting. Make no mistake: this is no lover's quarrel. Their weapons of choice aren't passive-aggressive barbs about long-brewing resentments, but a flurry of fists, feet, and elbows. Despite the size difference between them, they're well matched, Brooks's agility compensating for Atkins's power.

Finally, a well-placed sweep of her leg has Atkins on his back, utterly at her mercy. Brooks plants her bare foot on his chest and crows with victory—that is, until Atkins brushes his fingers under her arch, leading her to yelp with outrage before collapsing on top of him in a giggling heap.

We're at the Santa Monica training facility where Brooks has been spending six hours a day, five days a week for the past few months, getting in fighting shape for her role as Roxie, a member of an all-female team of vigilantes in the upcoming action movie *Sirens*. Atkins, planted on the sidelines for moral support, had given in to the goading of Brooks's trainer, Malcolm Davis, to test her skills in an impromptu sparring match.

"Not fair," Brooks grumbles, disentangling herself from Atkins and leaping upright. "No tickling in the dojo!" But she's smiling as she reaches down to help Atkins to his feet. He pulls her against his chest for a split-second squeeze before letting go. Over the course of my time with them, there's no shortage of this kind of gesture: quick kisses, hands held beneath tables, inside jokes communicated by nothing more than a glance. The secret language of two people unequivocally delighted by each other.

Over a long lunch at a nearby café, I do my best to unravel the thorny beginnings of their current domestic bliss. They're both evasive when pressed on details of how they met, other than that they were introduced by a mutual friend whom they seem reticent to identify.

"I was fascinated by her from the very beginning," Atkins recalls over a burger and side salad. He's eschewed the fries out of deference to Brooks, who's eating her own protein-packed, nutritionist-approved meal out of a plastic container. (When I express my sympathy for her slightly sad-looking lunch, she just grins and offers an impressive bicep for me to feel.)

Atkins continues. "She made me realize how much work I had to do on myself before I was ready to be with her. With anyone, really."

It's clear he's referring to his well-documented struggle with addiction over the past two decades. As Brooks glows with pride beside him, Atkins confirms that he's just celebrated three years of sobriety. He resists the impulse to blame his substance use on the demands of the spotlight: "It's something that's followed me around my whole life, even before I was famous. At the end of the day, it's an internal battle. Yes, there's more pressure with what I do, but it didn't make me an alcoholic."

"But it sure can make it worse," Brooks adds.

They should know. The early months of their relationship were a supernova of drama: first, steamy paparazzi photos of a romantic Palm Springs getaway were splashed all over the tabloids. Then, a visibly intoxicated Atkins stormed offstage during a panel discussion of *Dirtbags,* his breakout film. After that, the two weren't seen together again for over a year. That is, until Atkins was spotted in New York City, slipping through the stage door after a performance of *Uncle Vanya* that just so happened to star Brooks. The rest, as they say, is history.

These days, the couple is bicoastal, splitting their time between Atkins's home in Pacific Palisades, and Brooks's newly purchased West Village townhouse. They both have roots in New York; Atkins was raised in Queens, while Brooks grew up just outside the city. And despite their rocky, publicity-filled start, over the last few years they've mostly stayed out of the press.

Unless, of course, they have something to promote.

It's been nine years since Atkins last appeared on-screen, in the drama *Saint Paul*—his fourth and final collaboration with Sam Tanner, who passed away in a car accident shortly after the film's release. But in two weeks, his mysterious new film *One Night Only,* cowritten with and costarring Brooks, will open in limited release. I was granted access to an early screening, under the condition that I not reveal any details. Without giving too much away, all I can say is it's an enthralling, tightly scripted two-hander, featuring raw and galvanizing performances from both of them. Audiences who have missed seeing Atkins in action will not be disappointed, and his real-life chemistry with Brooks is even more scorching on-screen.

Though Atkins has done more than his fair share of directing, he surprisingly handed over the reins on *One Night Only* to Dee Lockhart—an alumnus of the Tanner Emerging Artists Program, Atkins's recently launched initiative that provides grants and mentorship to up-and-coming filmmakers who lack resources and industry connections.

When I ask if they ever discussed having Atkins direct the film, they both shake their heads.

"She'd never listen to me," Atkins says drily. Brooks laughs.

"I just wasn't interested in that dynamic," she explains, draining her water glass. "I wanted us to be on as equal footing as possible, especially since it was our first time working together."

I ask Atkins about the status of *Bitter Pill,* the last project he and Tanner had been working on before Tanner's death, which has languished in development hell ever since. Will it ever see the light of day? He shakes his head.

"I needed to let it go. It had turned into something bigger than a movie for me. Something it could never live up to. But what I've been doing now, with the [Tanner Emerging Artists] program—when Sam and I first moved out here, we were clueless. So much of our early success was plain dumb luck, meeting the right people at the right time. But for every story like ours, there are hundreds who never got those opportunities, who were just as deserving. Doing what I can now to even the playing field, help talented people get their foot in the door . . . that feels like the right thing. To, uh, remember him. Honor him. Whatever you want to call it. Trying to pay it forward, nurture the next generation, instead of fighting to keep the past alive."

Brooks, in contrast, has kept busy. Last year, after arthouse thriller *The Empty Chair* sparked a Sundance bidding war, Brooks, along with director, cowriter, and costar Kamilah Ross, had a strong showing at the Independent Spirit Awards, taking home Best Director for Ross and Best Supporting Female for Brooks. The studios took notice, tapping Ross to direct *Sirens* in her major-studio directorial debut, and hiring the two of them to doctor the script, as well as star.

In what may seem surprising to newcomers to the Atkins-Brooks extended universe, Atkins's ex-wife, Nora Lind, recently signed on for a supporting role in *Sirens* alongside Ross and Brooks. (Rounding out the cast are newcomer Simone Haley and Brooks's former *Poison Paradise* costar Mia Pereira.) Considering the coverage of their ugly, extended divorce, this should be a sore spot, but this isn't even Brooks and Lind's first time working together: *The Empty Chair* was brought to the screen by Lind's production company, First Dibs.

But how does Atkins *really* feel about his girlfriend working so closely with his ex-wife?

"He likes it a little too much," Brooks says, rolling her eyes in good-natured annoyance. "He keeps calling it *Ethan's Angels*."

Indeed, the photos that surfaced several months ago of Atkins and Brooks on vacation in Cape May, New Jersey, with Lind, Lind's husband (cameraman Jeff Hernandez), and Atkins and Lind's two daughters, seem to indicate that the harmonious blended family routine isn't just an act.

In Cape May, the six of them were photographed with an older couple that eagle-eyed fans immediately identified as Tanner's parents. When I bring it up to Atkins, he smiles enigmatically and changes the subject. Brooks slips her hand into his, and they exchange an intimate glance. In that moment, it's clear that no matter how many secrets are dug up about them and plastered on the front page, there's something perfect and private between them that no one will ever be able to touch.

That united front only becomes more impenetrable when I try to prod into the future of their union beyond their professional collaboration—if marriage and children of their own are in the cards.

"I think we've both learned the value of taking things one day at a time. Also the value of keeping our personal lives personal, as much as we're allowed to." Atkins glances at Brooks, his glib tone revealing a glimpse of something more sincere underneath. "But I'm not going anywhere. Are you?"

Brooks sips her drink and shrugs. "Wasn't planning on it." She leans back in her seat and grins playfully at him. "Unless I get a better offer."

Acknowledgments

I'd like to say that becoming a published novelist was a lifelong dream, but that would imply that it was something I considered within the realm of possibility. I want to express my bottomless gratitude to the following people for making this impossible dream come true:

My amazing agents, Jessica Mileo and Claire Friedman. None of this would've happened without you. Thank you for your enthusiasm, your tireless support, and your fierce advocacy for me and my work.

My brilliant editor, Shauna Summers, whose astute guidance helped me shape this book into the best possible version of itself. Thank you for your patience, your insight, and for seeing the potential in Grey and Ethan—and in me.

The incredible team at Ballantine: editorial assistant Mae Martinez, publicist Melissa Sanford, marketing manager Taylor Noel, production manager Erin Korenko, production editor Andy Lefkowitz, as well as Kara Welsh, Jennifer Hershey, Kara Cesare, Bridget Kearney, and Kim Hovey. Thank you to designer Elena Giavaldi and illustrator Mercedes deBellard for the gorgeous cover.

My friends who read and gave notes on this book in its earliest incarnations—Victoria Edel, Tim Kov, and Grace Critchfield. Your thoughtful feedback made it exponentially better, and your enthusiasm for it gave me the courage to seriously pursue something more with it.

My parents, for three decades of unconditional encouragement of all my assorted creative endeavors—no matter how misguided. I think I finally figured out the right one! Please don't ask me why every page of your copies has been blacked out except for this one, it was probably a printing error or something.

My sister, Isabel, for being my best friend, for always understanding exactly where I'm coming from, and for making me laugh more than anyone.

Hannah Milligan, for promptly answering all my deranged texts about various L.A. details, no matter the hour.

My friends and extended family, whom I love for many reasons, not least for putting up with me talking about nothing else for [redacted] months.

The Wholigans, my comrades in the pop culture trenches, who constantly inspire me with their ability to engage with the circus of celebrity gossip through a hilarious, smart, and nuanced lens. Crunch crunch.

The publishing friends I've made so far on this journey: even though I didn't know you when I wrote the book, it turns out that writing it is only the first step of this bizarre, thrilling, exhausting ride. Thank you for your support, for your empathy, for sharing your amazing words with me.

And finally, Walker. Even bookending this whole thing with my gratitude to you doesn't feel like enough. Thank you for giving me the love and support to flourish into the version of myself who was capable of accomplishing something like this. I truly couldn't have done it without you.

About the Author

AVA WILDER is a professional video editor with a degree in media studies and cultural criticism. She currently lives in Oklahoma City with her fiancé and their toothless cat.